SINISTER SUMMER

A WICKS HOLLOW BOOK

COLLEEN GLEASON

AVID PRESS

© 2018 Colleen Gleason, Inc.

A radically different version of this book was previously published under the title *The Cards of Life and Death*.

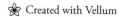 Created with Vellum

AN IMPORTANT NOTE FROM THE AUTHOR

Sinister Summer was previously published under the title *The Cards of Life and Death*. The book has been significantly revised and rewritten to make it part of the Wicks Hollow series.

If you've read *The Cards of Life and Death*, I hope you find this updated, revised, and (I think) improved edition even more enjoyable.

Thank you for giving it a read!

— Colleen Gleason
February 2018

PROLOGUE

Wicks Hollow, Michigan

HE CREPT SILENTLY into the house, aided by the light of the full moon. It streamed though the windows like a beacon, casting everything with a film of blue-gray.

There wasn't a sound but the distant lapping of water against the lakeshore and the barest rustle of breeze through the trees.

Such a remote area.

So convenient.

He smiled to himself as he passed through the kitchen. Only hours before, the old lady had pressed tea and cookies and a delicious chicken salad sandwich upon him at that very table.

She'd been delighted to see him—and he'd actually enjoyed their visit quite a bit. Genevieve Fickler was an interesting and amusing old woman, if not a little batty. She actually believed she could tell the future by looking at a deck of Tarot cards. Absurd, but entertaining nonetheless.

He'd humored her, of course. He knew how to charm a

lady. Old ones, young ones—any of them. Especially when he needed something from them.

It was too bad things had to go this way, but a man had to do what a man had to do. Especially when things got…difficult. His jaw tightened with determination and his fingers curled into their palms. Soon, his troubles would all be over.

A complacent smile on his face, he continued silently down the hall. When he caught sight of a shadow slinking from beneath a table, he crouched to greet the cat in case it had the tendency to yowl at night-time visitors.

He'd made friends with it and its companion earlier, and tonight he'd come prepared with tuna sandwiches in order to distract them.

He could afford for nothing to go wrong, for this was his one and only chance to set things in motion.

No sooner had he pulled the sandwich from its plastic wrap than the second feline appeared, also interested in the delicious smell.

He left them there, delicately eating their treat, and slipped into the old woman's bedroom.

Her soft snores told him she was dead to the world (he grinned silently at this appropriate metaphor). Not only was she deeply asleep, but her face was upright, and her arms safely beneath the blankets.

It was almost as if she were trying to make it easy for him.

He hesitated only for a moment, then moved quickly and with efficiency—snatching up an extra pillow next to her on the bed and jamming it over her face.

Genevieve jolted beneath the onslaught, but he was kneeling over the blankets, pinning her in place as he pressed the goosedown pillow onto her nose and mouth…holding it, holding it…pressing harder, harder, *harder*.

Come on, come on, he thought silently, as the round old

biddy struggled and jolted beneath him like a fish out of water.

Then suddenly, at last, she was still.

Breathing heavily, he held the pillow over her face a few more minutes just to be sure.

Then he slid off the bed, checked her pulse (none), replaced the pillow, and stood back to look down at her.

"Thanks in advance, Genevieve."

His smile was cold and pleased as he strode from the room.

He paused only to scoop up the remains of the tuna sandwich bribes and dab the floor where they'd been with a damp paper towel. Then he walked out of the house without a second glance.

Though his hands were shaking a trifle, he was still smiling as he strode down the dark, shadowy drive.

Mission accomplished.

ONE

Chicago

DIANA IVERSON JUGGLED A LARGE COFFEE, her laptop case, and her smartphone—all the while scrolling through a parade of emails—as she breezed through the doorway of the large glass and chrome appointed suite that housed McNillan, Busher, Percy, and Stone. Her employer was one of the premier corporate law firms in Chicago, and she one of their rising stars in environmental law.

It was nearly six o'clock on Friday, and she was finishing an eighty-hour week—but Diana was exhilarated. She'd just settled one of the biggest litigation cases in her career, and been handed another—the one that could help her make partner. Not only partner, but the youngest female partner in the history of the firm, and only the third woman ever whose name would appear on the letterhead.

"I can't believe you're still here, Mickey," Diana said as she barreled around the corner in the depths of the nearly-empty suite to find her legal assistant typing busily at her desk. "It's after six-thirty on a Friday."

Mickey, who wore a conservative navy shift and *not*-conservative garnet-colored, golden-tipped spiky hair, looked up. She had a shrewd, knowing look on her face. "So what happened with Gallatine today?"

"You won't believe this: they *settled*." Diana couldn't hold back a grin as she did a little pirouette without spilling a drop of coffee. "The Gallatine case is *over!*"

"I knew you'd get them to settle."

She looked at Mickey, who now had a smug look on her face. "How did you know I'd get them to settle? *No one* thought they'd settle—even McNillan. The two sides were oceans apart, and had their heels dug in up to the ankle."

Her assistant settled back in the chair and crossed her arms over her middle. "Because you did that thing you do—right before you left."

Diana felt her body go to ice, then a rush of warmth rise in her face. Her heart thudded hard. "What do you mean 'that thing' I do?"

"You know."

"No, I don't know what you mean." Diana tried to keep her voice calm, but inside, her nerves were jangling more than when she had to face Judge Bentley at the state appeals court.

Mickey sighed, still looking at her. "I don't know what it is, but you know—you go in your office, turn off the lights, and sit in your chair for a while. Usually when things look bad —like we're going to lose, or there's no end in sight. Then you come out and you know what to do—and it *always* works."

Diana knew her fair skin was probably displaying red blotches in her cheeks, but there was nothing she could do about that. "I'm just sitting there thinking."

"Right. Just thinking." Mickey lifted her brows. "Sometimes you come out with an entire brief written in less than an hour. And, it's perfect—"

"Well, sometimes things just come to me," Diana said and, desperate to change the subject, went on with a rush, "But the reason I'm late isn't because of Gallatine."

"I had a feeling," Mickey said, looking at her smugly again. "You walk away with a solid victory like that, and they're not going to let you rest on your laurels. I'm guessing... the AutoXTech case."

Her legal assistant obviously saw and heard and *knew* a lot.

"Yes. McNillan gave it to me. Lead litigator." Diana was both trepidatious and energized by the trust the founding partner had placed in her.

AutoXTech, a tier-two auto supplier based in Michigan, was one of the firm's most important clients—their billing topped six million dollars a year.

This was going to be a big case with lots of publicity. There'd already been articles in the press, and The Sierra Club and Greenpeace were watching closely.

"Awesome. I think." Mickey gave a half smile.

They both knew it was going to be mountains of work to prepare for the case in which AutoXTech was being sued by real estate developer LavertPiper over a piece of property the auto supplier had sold them. AXT had counter-sued in order to litigate on their side.

"Mansoni—AutoXTech's CEO—told me today that his company is absolutely not going to back down or settle, because if they do, it'll just open the door to more litigation in the future. In fact, they intend to make an example out of LavertPiper."

"And it's not like LP didn't do their due diligence before buying a piece of land that held an old factory—everyone knows, thirty years ago, environmental laws weren't what they are now. It's a prime piece of land, right on Lake Michigan."

"That's right...oh, *crap*. I've got to call my Aunt Jean

again. She called me on Monday—here's the message—and I tried her back Wednesday, but she didn't answer. She must have been in bed already." Diana had been thumbing through an old stack of phone messages she'd tossed into her inbox. "Or maybe she was out on a hot date. I guess there's this college professor who lives nearby—sounds like they might have something going on. She won't come right out and admit it—she can be cagey like that." She looked at the old message, quelling a pang of guilt. "I'll try her again when I get home tonight."

It had been too long since she'd seen Aunt Jean. They talked every couple of weeks or so, but it had been over a year since they'd actually been in the same city—and that was only because Aunt Jean had come down to Chicago to see *Hamilton*.

"She's the aunt that lives in Michigan? In that cute little town everyone from Chicago goes to for vacation?"

"Right, Wicks Hollow," Diana said. "Trendy town, not far from Lake Michigan. I haven't been there in…well, more than a decade."

The guilt came back, along with a brisk wave of memories—of the big clapboard house, the bright, sunny kitchen, the walks in the woods, the smell of the lake on a summer day. The reminiscences assaulted her, and made her feel sad and yet hopeful at the same time. Those had been wonderful summers. And it had been too many years since she'd visited.

Maybe this summer. McNillan *had* told her to take some time off…

Yes. *I'll make sure I get there this summer.*

"I should have tried her back again yesterday, but I've been—"

"So busy. Tell me about it," Mickey said. "So what are you

going to do tonight, now that you have this new assignment under your belt?"

"Well, I'm supposed to take some time off before I start on AXT, but I—"

"But you what? Diana, when's the last time you actually had fun? Relaxed? Slept past seven?"

"Try six," Diana muttered.

Mickey rolled her eyes. "Had sex—I mean good, long, *gourmet* sex? Spent the whole weekend with Jonathan, rolling around in those 600-count Egyptian sheets you splurged on—"

Diana was laughing by now, shaking her head. "Jonathan's been in Vegas for a conference since Wednesday, and he won't be back till Sunday night. I *was* thinking of settling down at home on the sofa. With my feet up and a bottle of cabernet and—"

"And your laptop. And your email." Mickey shook her head. "Live a little, girlfriend. This is a big deal—the biggest. You won a huge case, and you're taking on another that's going to be front-page news. And Mr. McNillan's right—you need to take some time off. At least the night. Or—maybe even the *whole weekend*." She made a mocking shocked face as Diana laughed.

"I don't know…I really should start looking over Mansoni's notes—"

"Why don't you grab a flight to Vegas and meet up with Jonathan?" Mickey said—which surprised Diana, since she wasn't exactly a big fan of Diana's fiancé. "Take a breather this weekend. Play a little blackjack or something fun. Go see Thunder from Down Under—that's the male dance show, though they don't strip all the way down. *Unfortunately*," she added in an undertone.

"Jonathan doesn't gamble," Diana replied, still laughing.

She could only imagine what her serious fiancé would be doing: sitting in his hotel room, working on the speech he was giving to a group of cardiologists at their annual convention. "But...I suppose I could bring my files with me—wait, what's this?"

Her heart gave an odd thud when she saw the top message from today's calls, left in a separate stack by her administrative assistant. "Joe Longbow. From Wicks Hollow. Chief of police..."

Her hands felt clammy and her head light. Why would the chief of police from Wicks Hollow be calling her? She automatically thumbed through the rest of the stack of messages as she tried to assimilate the information into her already overloaded brain...and then she saw a second message from Captain Longbow from later today.

Oh no.

No.

The phone rang, its low, tasteful bleep breaking into her thoughts. Mickey looked down at the phone, then at Diana. "Caller ID says it's from Michigan. It's probably him again."

Diana took the phone, a sudden surge of trepidation replacing the nostalgia.

But even as she had the thought, a sharp pain streaked across her temple and settled in a dull, harsh thud behind her left eye. Great. A migraine now too...

"Diana Iverson," she said into the phone.

"Ms. Iverson," said a man in a very slow, comfortable drawl. "This is Captain Joseph Longbow from the Police Department in Wicks Hollow in Michigan. Are you related to Genevieve Fickler?"

"Genevieve? Yes, she's my aunt. My aunt Jean," Diana replied, her mouth going dry.

But she already knew what he was going to say.

Three weeks later
Wicks Hollow

It had been more than ten years, but Aunt Jean's cozy, weather-beaten home looked exactly the same as Diana remembered it—and exactly the same as it had looked when she visited as a young girl in the summers.

A white clapboard farmhouse with peaks and sharp pitched gables, it sprawled like a comfortable chair in a small, grassy clearing surrounded by forest.

Shutters, curlicue trim, and doors painted in dark gray gave it a stately, calm look. A covered, wrap-around porch stained the same sedate charcoal hugged two sides—and as if to combat the monochrome of the house, a colorful array of perennials burst and bloomed in slender gardens embracing the house: azaleas, early roses, honeysuckle, snowballs, spirea, and hydrangea. She'd missed the lilacs, but the bushes flanking the garage looked healthy and bore the remnants of their early blooms.

Pines, birch, and maples ringed the clearing, sprawling into a full-fledged woods, and on the west side was a small incline that led down to Wicks Lake. Diana could see a hint of blue sparkle through the trees, and best of all, she could *smell* it through her open windows.

She parked her car on the patch of gravel in front of the detached garage, and Diana turned off the ignition. She blinked rapidly as her eyes clouded with tears.

"Oh, Aunt Jean."

When she climbed out of the car and closed the door, its slam the only sound other than the quiet lap of waves in the distance. The air smelled clean and fresh, and of freshwater lake tinged with pine and roses.

It was all so familiar and comforting—except this time, there would be no Aunt Jean rushing out onto the porch to greet her. No shrieks of delight, or soft, cushy hugs.

And now, oddly, strangely, the house belonged to Diana.

She left her luggage in the car for now and only brought her briefcase as she climbed up the steps to unlock the door. Once inside, she leaned against the door and closed her eyes, breathing in the aromas of age and summer, dust, lavender, and the faint scent of cat litter.

She'd had so many happy summers here as a young girl, staying with her eccentric, intelligent, and interesting great-aunt.

"I should have called you back sooner, Aunt Jean. I should have come for a visit—I know I kept promising," Diana said aloud. "I'm so sorry, Aunt Jean, I hope you'll forgive m—"

Thud!

The noise had her spinning like a nervous schoolgirl. It came from down the hall, and the timing made it seem like a very emphatic reaction to her confession—as if Aunt Jean's spirit was there, listening in irritated agreement...

Ha. Diana laughed, but it sounded nervous to her ears.

"A ghost? As *if*," she said aloud. "*Ha.*"

Thunk.

Thud.

Crash!

This time she actually did gasp as she spun in the direction of the noise. Diana shoved a hand into her briefcase, searching for the can of Mace as her heart galloped in her chest.

For a moment, she almost wished she *did* believe in ghosts—but she certainly didn't.

Since she didn't, that meant someone else was here.

Even so, Diana wasn't about to run off without confronting whoever it was. Maybe someone had been squatting here for the last few weeks since Aunt Jean died. The big house had been empty, for nearly a month, though one of Captain Longbow's teenagers had come over daily to see to the cats. And the house itself was well outside the town, tucked away in the woods on the north end of Wicks Lake.

She gripped the Mace and crept down the hallway, hardly noticing the sunbeams shining through in random shafts, spotlighting the glitter of dust motes. The noise sounded like it had come from Aunt Jean's library.

For the first time, she mildly regretted declining the offer from her aunt's attorney, who'd volunteered to show her around her newly inherited property now that probate had, shockingly, been quickly and efficiently completed. But Diana wanted to be alone the first time she came to the house again, especially after everything else she'd been through in the last three weeks…

It seemed like months since that Friday when she'd settled the Gallatine case and been assigned as lead on the new one, then received the call from Captain Joe Longbow with the bad news about Aunt Jean.

That night, in a blur of emotion—guilt, grief, exhaustion—Diana had flown on a whim to Vegas. She'd needed Jonathan. She'd needed to unload, to relax, to try and find a way out of the grief and guilt that swamped her.

And now she needed more space: from people, from work, from questions and demands.

And, most of all, she needed space from Jonathan.

The door to Aunt Jean's library had spilled open in a narrow vee, revealing a small slice of sunshine from somewhere inside. Everything else was quiet and still. She stopped to listen, keeping her breathing slow and steady. Then, angling the Mace's spray nozzle in a defensive position, Diana peeked around the door into the library.

There was no sign of anyone in the room. The windows were closed, the curtains had been pulled back in preparation for her arrival today, and nothing seemed to be disturbed—

Then she saw it. On the floor: the mahogany box, a swath of black silk, and a tumble of brightly-illustrated cards.

Aunt Jean's Tarot deck.

It looked as if it had been knocked off the table—the small, walnut piecrust table that had been next to her aunt's favorite rocking chair, both tucked in the corner near the window, for years. The rocking chair had been replaced with a large, upholstered armchair the last time she was here, but the table was still the same, with what appeared to be the same potted African violet holding court.

Strangely enough, the plant was completely undisturbed.

It could have been one of the cats making the noise, knocking over the box…But Diana hadn't seen either of them come out of the den, and they were nowhere in sight now.

And the cards…there they were, strewn on the floor as if someone had thrown them there in anger or frustration.

Her breath and heartbeat hitched. Diana forgot about the Mace and the possibility of an intruder as she crouched. The cards might not mean anything to her, Diana—but to her aunt they'd been a source of comfort and guidance. This Tarot deck had been more personal to Genevieve Fickler than any of her other possessions except her wedding ring. Thus, even for pragmatic Diana there was something sad and horrible about seeing those cards lying on the floor. It was like a violation of her aunt's privacy or some deep part of herself.

Like another death.

As Diana crouched next to the pile, she noticed all the

cards had landed face down except for one. She plucked up that single card first instead of gathering up the entire lot.

The Fool.

Its artistic rendering was exquisite, with a bold red and blue design. She examined the card, with its depiction of a carefree man with out-flung arms as he danced down a slight incline. The Fool looked like he hadn't a care in the world. He was handsome and smiling—which was more than Diana could say for herself. That probably explained the recent return of her migraines, which had come back with a vengeance after years of relative quiet.

Maybe the next few days here in Wicks Hollow would help her relax a bit. At least with the spotty cell phone access here on the northeast end of the lake, thanks to the thick pines and rolling hills surrounding it, and no wifi in the house (yet), she'd be slightly less obsessed with connecting back to her office—something Mickey had been delighted to hear.

"You need a break, Di," she'd told her. For the hundredth time. "Even Mr. McNillan insisted. He said to take a month."

"That's only because he wants me sharp and ready for AXT," Diana said ruefully.

"And that's a bad thing? Look, you need some space, girlfriend. *Lots* of space."

The problem was, Mickey was right. Diana definitely needed some space. Particularly between her and her fiancé.

Her former fiancé.

Her *maybe* former fiancé.

Diana's heart squeezed and her stomach pitched whenever she thought of breaking things off permanently with Jonathan. She could already hear her mother's wounded, weary voice: *I knew you'd never be able to keep a man like Jonathan Wertinger.*

She closed her eyes and took a deep breath, pushing her mother and her criticisms away. *I am a rising star litigator. I'm going to make partner at thirty-five. I've got a successful, handsome fiancé who loves me.*

Her stomach ground tightly.

He does *love me.*

As if she'd brought him to mind, her cell phone rang—Jonathan's picture flashing onto the screen.

She hesitated, then, both hating herself and feeling relieved that he'd called, she answered. "Hello Jonathan."

"How are you, Diana?" he said in his soft, empathetic voice. "How are things up there? I really miss you."

"I've only been gone six hours, Jonathan. We've seen each other far less during a regular work week." Then she gave herself a mental shake. *I need to forgive him and forget. It's the mature thing to do. We all make mistakes.*

She walked out of the den, back down the hall toward the kitchen. She needed water and to take medication for the brewing migraine before it got away from her.

"I know. But the fact that you're not here in Chicago makes it feel more…distant. I guess because it is." He gave a little chuckle that sounded strained—which was only right, she reminded herself.

He'd been the one who strayed; *he* was the one who'd put the chink in their relationship.

If only she *hadn't* flown out to surprise him in Vegas after winning the Gallatine case and getting the news about Aunt Jean.

But then she might never have known. She drew in a deep breath and tried to calm her churning stomach. If she could face down Judge Stern (more than appropriately named) and argue a difficult point with eloquence and brevity, she could handle the man she loved.

"How are you?" Diana pulled the refrigerator door open. She found a six-pack of beer—Aunt Jean drank beer?—a bag of prewashed carrots, a half gallon of milk long past its expiration date, and three-quarters of a stick of butter. *Guess it's going to be Trib's or the Lakeshore Grille for dinner tonight.*

She realized Jonathan had paused in a stream of complaints about the other partners in his practice and seemed to be waiting for a response from her. Normally, she followed his explanations closely, asking thoughtful questions to prove she was listening, but all she could think about this time was whether *She* was one of the new partners.

She. *Valerie* Somebody.

Doctor Valerie Somebody: the young, sexy, bodacious cardiologist who'd been sharing a hotel room with Diana's fiancé at the Venetian in Las Vegas.

Her fingers tightened on the phone as she swallowed a ball of nausea and blocked that image as quickly as it came. But the dull pain of her migraine thudded deeper and more insistently in her temples. "Sorry, Jonathan, what were you saying? The line's a little fuzzy up here."

"I asked if you wanted me to bring anything when I come up this weekend."

Diana frowned. She'd been trying to think of a good way to dissuade him from coming, but so far nothing had presented itself. She could just tell him not to come, but that, she knew, would cause more drama and pleading—something she simply didn't have the energy to deal with now. Especially since, at the moment, her head felt as if a low, harsh bell was tolling inside it.

"Well?" he asked, a tinge of impatience in his voice.

"I really can't think of anything I need right now," she replied—then forced herself to joke, "other than a cell tower in the yard here, but I don't think even you can make that happen."

He chuckled at her compliment, her lapse in attention

obviously forgiven. "Well, then, that's it. My flight gets in Friday night—can I text you the details? How far of a drive is it up there to your aunt's?"

"Yes. I'll pick you up at the airport in Grand Rapids. Wicks Hollow is a little more than an hour from the airport." She briefly closed her eyes when a telltale flicker of white light skittered across her vision. This migraine was coming on fast.

Just then, a knock sounded on the front door—the old, heavy brass knocker thunked twice, then paused, then twice again.

"Jean," a masculine voice called as Diana heard the door open. "Jean, it's me!"

The door *open?*

"Jonathan, I've got to run. Someone's at the door."

Who on earth thought they could just open the door?

"Jean?" The door closed and footsteps thudded across the wood floor as the man called out again.

And walk in?

Diana, annoyed and a little nervous, disconnected the call before Jonathan could reply, and started for the foyer.

"What was so important you wanted to talk to me about? Anyway, I'm also here to pick up the beer you owe—" The man stopped as Diana swung around the corner from the kitchen. "Oh! I'm sorry, I just stopped in to see Jean—er, Genevieve."

"Excuse me, but who are you?" A pang of apprehension at the sight of a tall, unshaven and very unkempt young man standing in her foyer made her voice high and tight.

And, oh crap. She'd left her Mace in the den.

Diana came halfway across the high-ceilinged foyer and folded her arms beneath her breasts. Obviously the guy knew her aunt—or, at least, she *hoped* he knew her aunt. So he probably wasn't a squatter.

"I'm Ethan Murphy, a friend of Genevieve's. Who are you?" his voice was polite, but the dark gaze that examined her was thorough enough that she *felt* it.

He was young and fit, probably late-twenties, and looked like a hipster gone mountain man. He had a wild-looking beard and mustache that needed trimming, long sideburns, and a dark ponytail that rode low upon his neck. Other than that, he didn't look like a vagabond, for he was dressed in clean, neat clothing: jeans, a t-shirt, and a denim jacket that appeared to be in good shape. His casual leather shoes looked expensive.

By now, Diana wasn't nervous—mostly irritated, and a little confused. Maybe he did the lawns or was a delivery courier.

But still—he'd just walked in without even knocking.

"I'm Diana Iverson, Mrs. Fickler's niece," she told him coolly.

"*You're* Diana?" To her surprise, he smiled, and the crinkles that fanned from the corners of his eyes required her to adjust her estimate of his age upward a notch. Closer to thirty. "I'm so glad to meet you. She's spoken often of you. So you were finally able to make it up here for a visit? I'll bet she's thrilled." He took a step toward her, then hesitated when she didn't respond with her own smile.

"Mr.—uh—" Her head was *pounding*, and she could hardly think.

"Actually, it's Doctor—Murphy. Ethan Murphy," he said as if surprised that she didn't know his name. Now his eyes became wary, perhaps even suspicious.

He didn't look like any doctor she knew, unless he'd just come back from a stint with the Peace Corps or Doctors Without Borders, where, clearly, they had no access to razors or scissors. Though…hmmm…the name rang a faint bell…

"Dr. Murphy, I'm not sure what you're doing, barging into my aunt's house like this—"

"I'm sorry if I startled you. She'd been trying to get ahold of me, but I was out of the country."

She put a mental checkmark in the Doctors Without Borders column.

"And I also stopped in to get the beer she owes me. It's probably in the fridge." The smile returned and she noticed a deep crease on the left side of his face that ended at the unruly beard. "We had a little bet, and she lost."

Diana frowned as headache pain radiated in a sudden shaft above her left ear and nausea rolled in her belly. The flashes of light were becoming stronger, nearly blinding her as they skittered across her vision. It was coming on far too quickly, and the migraine would soon be unbearable. She needed him out of the house as quickly as possible.

"Dr. Murphy, I don't know when you spoke to my aunt last—"

"Like I said, she tried to contact me—it was a few weeks ago—"

"—but I have some bad news for you," she continued to speak over his congenial explanation while trying to ignore the agony that was beginning to seep toward the front of her temples. "I buried her about two weeks ago. She's dead."

"*What?*" Shock replaced confidence and charm.

"My great-aunt passed away three weeks ago Wednesday night," she told him. "Heart failure—in her sleep. They didn't find her till Friday morning." Nausea settled in her stomach like an immovable boulder and she swallowed hard, blinking against the string of lights that hovered at the edge of her vision.

Please go away before I lose it and vomit right here.

"My God." Murphy skimmed his hand over the hair

pulled smoothly back into its tail. "I had no idea—I'm sorry." He stepped toward her then seemed to think better of it. "What happened? She was fine when I talked to her. She sounded *fine*." His eyes were a sharp, hard beer-bottle brown as they looked closely at her. Almost as if he didn't believe her.

The migraine was becoming more insistent and she had to resist the urge to push her fingertips into the sides of her forehead to keep from sobbing. "She died in her sleep, Dr. Murphy, and the funeral was the Monday following. Two weeks ago. Now, if you'll excuse me, I really have quite a bit to do."

"Of course." His voice was clipped and Diana felt the weight of his intent stare as he persisted. "Uh…are you all right?"

"Yes. I'm fine. I just didn't expect visitors at this time." She forced herself to say the words as politely and calmly as possible. "Especially ones who let themselves in." A large black spot leapt before her eyes and she blinked rapidly, and in vain, to make it disappear. She gagged and managed to hold back the nausea.

"Right. Sorry about that." But he sounded less apologetic than offended. "I apologize for barging in on you like this." Murphy backed toward the door while he continued to study her with a frown. "Your aunt was a good friend of mine. If there's anything I can do to help you out, please let me know."

"I'll do that," she said, purposely neglecting to ask how to contact him. "Thank you for stopping by."

She barely closed the door behind her unwanted visitor when a moan escaped from the back of her throat. Fighting the black spots and flashes of light that accompanied the debilitating pain, Diana hurried to find the bag where she'd left her medication.

Moments later, she was curled up on Aunt Jean's bed, hands fisted over her closed eyes, fighting the agony.

Ethan strolled down the lane from Genevieve Fickler's house and cut across the Hornbergers' yard to his own, two houses down a twisting, narrow tire-track lane that ended at his small log cabin.

How could Jean be *gone*?

Just…all of a sudden *dead*?

He was devastated.

Strangely enough, despite an almost fifty-year difference in their ages, the elderly woman had become one of his closest friends here in Wicks Hollow. She was funny and interesting, and passionate about everything from legalizing marijuana to protecting the environment to playing Scrabble and reading Tarot cards. She'd been at Woodstock, and hadn't left any part of her hippie days behind except, as she put it, the bra-burning and the LSD.

Ethan was even more disturbed that he'd missed the funeral—and no one had thought to contact him. What the hell was up with that? Joe Longbow should have known he'd want to know.

But he *had* been out of the country. And he'd arrived here too late last night to go into town, where he surely would have gotten the news.

And what was up with the cold brush-off given him by Jean's niece? Not that he should be surprised. He'd heard enough about Jean's beloved Diana over the last couple years to make his own assessment—the woman was a self-centered, career-focused ballbuster who had no time for family or anyone but herself.

Her bitchiness was annoying and maybe not all that surprising, but what was far worse was that Jean was *gone*.

Aw, dammit. I'm going to miss the hell out of you, Jean.

To his surprise, a wayward tear stung one eye as he yanked open the door to his cabin. Cady bounded across the room to meet him, leaving a telltale imprint on the couch from which she was supposedly banned.

"Hey, girl." Ethan knelt to ruffle her thick fur, pulling the black lab's face close to his. "Jean's dead. Can you believe it? I sure can't. I'm going to have words with Joe Cap about him not telling me. He could have at least texted me while I was gone." A big pink tongue slathered his face, carefully avoiding his bristly beard, as Ethan sank to the floor and brooded.

The last thing he'd heard from Jean was a voice mail on his office phone—she'd left it the day after he'd departed for his month-long trip. She asked him to call her as soon as he could; she had something to talk to him about. She must have forgotten when he was leaving the country.

And now he'd never know what she wanted to tell him.

He brooded and simmered and grieved, surprised at the depths of his emotions.

Some time later, when the sun had dipped behind the fringe of trees spearing up from the edge of the lake, Ethan hoisted himself to his feet. His face was damp from Cady's attentions as well as a narrow rivulet of tears that had settled in his thick beard.

I really could go for a beer just now.

He peered into the refrigerator, but the six-pack of B-Cubed IPA he'd gone to collect was still sitting in Jean's fridge—at least, as far as he knew.

At least Diana Iverson didn't seem like a beer-drinker. She was probably someone who only sipped fifty-dollar bottles of

French Bordeaux—which, he admitted, were stellar. But there was nothing like an ice-cold beer at the lake house.

Ethan closed the fridge door with more force than necessary, sorrow welling inside him again.

In her sleep, the niece had said. Jean had died in her sleep.

He shook his head, pulling out a frozen pizza. Jean hadn't ever mentioned her niece was beautiful—just that she was very smart, a little repressed, and a crazy workaholic. Mainly, she was screwed up because of her mother, who had been married to Jean's brother, who was now dead.

Jean had *not* liked the mother.

Diana Iverson *was* lovely—in a classic way. With her elegant nose, oval face, dark blue eyes, and thick dark hair that curled in short, sexy waves, she put him in mind of Jackie Kennedy. Maybe because of the prim dress she'd been wearing. She looked like she'd just come from a board meeting.

Apparently, she was an environmental lawyer back in Chicago, and was obviously used to working long hours for massive fees in prim suits and sensible heels.

"Don't know why anyone would be wearing a dress here in Wicks Hollow. Did she drive all the way from Chicago in it? And those heels too?" He only knew that sort of thing—driving in heels and a suit—was a consideration for women because his sister Fiona had lectured him about it once when he was in a hurry, and she wanted to change clothes for the drive to Wicks Hollow.

She made him wait, of course.

Cady flopped in a heap on the floor and groaned.

"So sorry if I'm boring you." Ethan grinned down at his best friend and lifted the lid from a glass jar on the counter that held dog biscuits. Instantly, Cady scrambled back to her feet, her soft ebony ears perked in anticipation. He lightly tossed his pet a treat and replaced the jar.

Diana Iverson, he thought again, with a short laugh that turned bitter. He'd been delighted that the niece had finally come to visit—until he'd learned why. The too-busy, ass-kissing lawyer who couldn't bother to visit her great-aunt in years had finally made the five-hour trip—just in time to collect her substantial inheritance. The beautiful farmhouse on Wicks Lake was worth a *lot* of money.

And then there was the way she'd looked at him when he'd told her his title was doctor—like he was some sort of furry, crawly bug. As if she wanted to smash him with her pointed-toe heel.

Just then, he caught sight of himself in the mirrored microwave door—spotless, thanks to his cleaning lady—and grimaced.

Oh. Well, that might explain a little of her reaction.

He'd forgotten about that god-awful beard and that he hadn't trimmed anything in weeks. Ethan cheerfully admitted he looked like a mountain man. He'd kept the scraggly look during the academic year because it did the trick to keep the young things away from him on campus. And of course he hadn't wanted to spend time shaving while he was in Macchu Picchu. But now he understood—maybe a little—why Diana Iverson had been so wary, and so intent upon getting rid of him.

Fiona had been giving him shit about the beard too, for months. "You look like a derelict," his sister told him the last time they video-chatted. "And since the hipster look is in, I'm not sure the beard's doing anything to keep the young girls—or guys," she added with a grin, "let's be inclusive—from being interested in your oh-so-hot self. You're the epitome of a sexy college prof: tall, lanky, with long hair and a beard and *fascinating* stories. Not to mention being semi-famous on top of it."

"It's a real trial being me, Fifi," he'd replied modestly. "But I manage. Did you say *semi*-famous? I'd say I'm way past the semi- and into the fully famous."

She rolled her eyes. "Whatever. I'll see you in a few weeks for Maxine Took's birthday bash, and I hope like hell you're clean-shaven before then."

The timer beeped that his pizza was ready, and Ethan returned to the moment.

He and Fiona—she, who'd been described as airy-fairy more than once—could hardly be any different. At least on the surface.

He was a popular and respected anthropology professor at the University of Chicago as well as a bestselling author who'd done the talk show circuit two years ago, and Fiona was…well the best way to describe his sister was that she enjoyed life and lived for the moment. Her myriad of employers over the years always loved her, but could rarely keep her for more than a year at a time. Fiona was as free-spirited as a sprite.

Ethan settled in a heavy cedar lounge chair on his screened porch that overlooked Wicks Lake—a long, narrow lake that wound down along the eastern side of the county like an arm. Beyond the trees, to the southwest, he could see the last of the sunset sinking over Lake Michigan, which was less than four miles away.

Ah. Summer in Michigan. Couldn't ask for any better place. He wished he could live here year around, even with the winter weather. Not that Chicago was any better when it came to lake effect snow.

Though the sky held only a pinkish-red glow near the horizon and the trees speared up into the graying darkness, there was still plenty to see. Lights winked along both lake shorelines in homes that were inhabited year-round. The tops of tall pines swayed with a faint breeze, brushing against each other high in the sky. A bold streak of pink in the western sky echoed the fading sunlight. There were the sounds of whippoorwills and crickets, the rustling of various wildlife in the forest that surrounded the lake, and, occasionally, the hoot of a lonely owl, the call of a loon.

It was peaceful.

Ethan looked through the trees along the lake and picked out Jean's home. One faint light shone through a window in the old clapboard structure. Sadness washed over him.

Abruptly, he decided he wasn't hungry for cardboard food and flipped a piece of pizza to Cady, thinking, still, about Diana Iverson.

Diana dragged herself awake into darkness, blind fear crushing lungs that dug deep for air. Struggling to push the weight of terror from her chest, she grappled with the tentacle-like sheets and pulled herself upright in the bed.

Moonlight streamed into the room as she sat there, gasping, shaking, trying to push away the remnants of the black nightmare that twined around her, engulfing her with its heaviness. She saw the pale oval of her face reflected in the mirror on Aunt Jean's bureau drawer and shrank from the vision made by the dark holes of her eyes and the stark terror on her face.

She'd never had a dream so completely consuming, so mind-numbingly frightening—yet she didn't know what it was about. There had been only blackness descending upon her, smothering her, pressing her down…down…*down*, into some dark, horrifying state.

Diana dragged her shaking limbs out of bed, glad she'd never had such an experience while sleeping next to Jonathan.

Looking warily at the tussled bedclothes, she decided she didn't trust herself to go back to sleep without falling into the dark pit again.

She'd curl up on the settee in the den and sleep there. Maybe the cats—of whom she hadn't yet caught a glimpse and she wondered if they really were even there—would deign to join her.

She could use the comfort.

TWO

THE NEXT MORNING, Diana awoke to sunshine. It glared from a crack between the den's heavy velvet curtains and the windowpane, making a crooked line over the floor. She sat up and blinked a few times to clear her vision. Yesterday's migraine was gone, as was the terrible dream. She felt relatively well rested, though a bit hollow.

She caught sight of the digital clock on the desk—an anomaly in the lacy, Victorian room—and started. Nine o'clock? Could that be right?

Diana rolled quickly off the velvet-upholstered settee, her feet landing on the rug with a profound thump. She couldn't remember the last time she'd slept past seven. Even on the one vacation they'd taken, she and Jonathan rose early to golf.

As she started out of the library, her attention fell on the silk-nested mahogany box. It was still sitting on the floor with the cards in a haphazard pile next to Aunt Jean's chair. For one absurd moment, the thought struck her: had that been the reason for her wrenching dream?

No. Why on earth would it have? She began to gather up the cards, arranging them in the box on top of the Fool.

But suddenly a flash of memory—a dream?—snapped into her mind. The vision was so abrupt and so vivid she sank back onto the chair.

He—the Fool—was alive in the image that presented itself, cavorting and mingling with obscure images of Aunt Jean and Jonathan, as well as a dark-haired man she didn't recognize. Papers fluttered about, along with wide-eyed cats and all sorts of strange, shadowy images.

It was weird—almost as if she were dreaming, right here in the middle of wakefulness.

The Fool is the Number Zero, and is the beginning of the Major Arcana, she heard Aunt Jean say. As clearly as if she were standing next to her. *He is also as we are at the beginning of any journey—gay, innocent, inexperienced, artless, and open-minded.*

Diana squeezed her eyes closed hard. The vision snapped and the voice disappeared. She realized she was clutching the arm of the chair and breathing heavily. Her body felt clammy and strange.

What the hell was that?

When she finally opened her eyes, she found herself the object of four green feline ones.

"Well," she managed to say when she caught her breath. "There you are, you naughty kitties."

The two black and white cats—for some obscure reason named Motto (the skinny one) and Arty (the fat one)—stared at her unblinkingly. Accusation burned strong in their twin expressions, as if to say, "Took you long enough to get here."

"I'm sure you were just fine having the run of the house," she told them firmly. "Though maybe a little lonely, without Aunt Jean. And, yes, it's been a while since I've been here. I'm sorry. I *really* am," she added, looking up at the ceiling as if Aunt Jean was listening—which of course she wasn't. "I promise I'll pick up some catnip for you when I go into town to make up for whatever abuse you might have suffered. After all, you must be missing Aunt Jean." Her voice softened with compassion, and she reached out to give each of them a brief stroke on the head.

Then she stooped once more to gather up the Tarot cards. They were oversized and awkward for her to straighten into a neat stack. She had just wrapped the cards in the black silk and placed them in the box when she noticed Motto sitting on the floor near the dark green, floor length curtains. The cat's paw was placed on one of the Tarot cards, as if holding it in place.

Or drawing Diana's attention to it.

Now how had that card gotten way over there?

Motto deigned to allow Diana to remove it from beneath her paw, then stalked away as if bored with the whole process.

The card was titled *The High Priestess*. A Roman numeral two identified it as the second numeric card of the Major Arcana.

The High Priestess was crowned and seated on a throne behind which were pomegranates and palms. She held a scroll in the lap of her blue gown, and seemed to be tucking it under her cloak. On the left of the throne was a black column labeled **B**, and on the right was a second column—white—labeled **J**. A crescent sat on the floor in the trailing pool of her gown.

Diana studied the card for a long moment as she became aware of a strange sense of unease. She couldn't help but wonder what the High Priestess signified to one who believed in the Tarot.

Not that she bought into any of that metaphysical stuff, but Aunt Jean and her friends Maxine and Iva certainly had.

With a sudden *tsk* of irritation, she returned the card to its place in the stack and replaced it once again in the smooth wrapping of black silk and mellow mahogany. She set the box of cards on the back in its place on the piecrust table and, after an (ignored) invitation to the cats to join her, Diana headed to the grocery store.

An hour later, Diana stumbled back into the house, arms hooked through plastic bags filled with groceries and hands filled with mail from the post office. She dumped the whole pile on the kitchen counter with a sigh of relief and went back out to make another trip.

As soon as she walked back in, Motto and Arty decided it was the perfect time to make an appearance—directly underfoot, of course—and she nearly landed on her face trying to avoid Arty's bottlebrush tail.

By the time she dropped the bags onto the counter, the cats had disappeared again. No surprise.

Against her better judgment (after all, when did cats actually do what you wanted them to?), she called for them, singing the silly song to the Munchkins from *The Wizard of Oz* in a gay falsetto: "Come out, come out, wherever you are."

Of course they didn't come. Even when she opened a package of catnip and wafted its aroma around near the floor, neither deigned to show a whisker.

Diana shrugged and turned back to the bags of groceries sprawled on the counter. It was then that she noticed the note.

Note?

Diana snatched it up, eyebrows furrowing. *"Just dropped by to pick up a book I loaned Jean, and my beer,"* the bold, black letters read. *"Hope you don't mind I let myself in. Sorry to have missed you—since we're neighbors, maybe we'll run into each other on the lake. Call me if I can be of any help. Ethan Murphy."*

A little shiver raced down her back. He'd been in the house *again*. But her twinge of discomfort was abruptly replaced by a wave of irritation. *Hope you don't mind I let myself in?!?!*

Of course she minded.

People didn't just let themselves into other peoples' houses. Not where she came from, anyway. They might do it in Wicks Hollow, but she wasn't a resident of the town and wouldn't be here long enough to get to know the residents that well.

And what if he'd still been there when she got home and was singing and talking in that silly voice to the cats? Her cheeks burned at the very thought. *That's just like you, Diana —making a fool out of yourself*, came her mother's voice as if in a memory.

She shoved it away, suddenly angry with herself for allowing her mother to intrude so often in the last few days—even though she hadn't talked to her for over three months, and even then it had been just a brief call to wish her a happy birthday.

It was as if Melanie had planted herself and her caustic voice firmly in Diana's mind all of a sudden—after months of silence. She hadn't even come to Aunt Jean's funeral—though, Diana realized, it was probably better that she hadn't. The two women never liked each other, and once Diana's father had died, they had no reason to interact. And having Melanie at the funeral would have been just another stress for her to deal with.

But what was more important than the imagined criticisms of her mother was the fact that a strange man had let himself into Diana's house twice in the last two days.

How good of friends *had* Dr. Murphy been with Aunt Jean? Was he exaggerating now that the elderly woman was dead? Maybe they'd hardly been friends at all, and he was just—

She crumpled up his note and flung it into the trash can, then picked up her cell phone to search for a number. But the data connection was being wonky, and the browser didn't connect, so, fuming, she yanked open the drawer beneath the behemoth of a black telephone—*wired,* and attached to the wall!—and found a very skinny local telephone book. Laundromats, liquor stores, *locksmiths.*

"I'll fix *Doctor* Ethan Murphy," she muttered as she dialed the number.

After she arranged for a locksmith to come and change all the locks later that afternoon, Diana strolled through the house just to make sure he hadn't disturbed anything.

The library, furnished as it was with heavy, dark antiques and bookshelves groaning with hundreds of volumes, didn't appear to have been disturbed. The mahogany Tarot card box sat in its place next to the African violet on the piecrust table. She noticed some thick white cat fur on Aunt Jean's chair and paused to brush it off.

Diana moved on down the hall to the office. A heavy oak desk dominated one wall, and stacks of magazines, papers, and books littered its top. She flipped on the light and glanced at the papers on the desk. Even if Murphy had rummaged through the contents of the room, she doubted she'd be able to tell.

Aunt Jean's bedroom—the only one on the first floor—was next. The sense of *something* Diana had felt earlier still hung in the air here, as though a fine fog hovered. This room also seemed undisturbed, but she was distracted from a thorough search when she heard her cell phone ring from where she'd left it on the kitchen counter.

The ringtone was Mickey's, and so she hurried to take the call. Just as they were finishing their conversation—a brief update on the literal *boxes* of evidence her assistant was marking and categorizing for AXT vs. LavertPiper—Diana heard a thunk from the library.

Those cats. She disconnected the call, finished her notes on the laptop, and went to see what they'd done.

The mahogany box was off the piecrust table, and the cards were in a tumble on the floor again. Neither feline was anywhere in sight, of course. Probably skulking in the corner after making the disturbance.

For the third time, Diana crouched to gather up the worn, oft-handled cards. As she did so, she considered putting the box away somewhere safe from the clumsy paws of Motto and Arty. But it didn't seem right, when it had sat on that piecrust table for decades.

Although, she supposed, when she sold the house that would change anyway.

Once more, she wrapped the cards in their black silk, settled them in the box, and replaced it next to the African violet, which, she noticed, needed watering and dead-heading. Diana started back out of the room when she caught the glimpse of a slender white tail behind Aunt Jean's chair.

"There you are," she scolded lightly, recognizing Arty's fatter shape. The cat moved, sauntering off without a care in the world as cats were wont to do, and Diana realized Arty had been sitting on top of one of the Tarot cards.

She bent to pick it up and her heart gave a little skip when she saw that it was *The High Priestess*.

Again?

Diana glanced at Arty's rear end as it disappeared casually around the corner, slender tail held high and twitching at the very top like an irritated snake.

"Hmm," she said aloud, looking at the card. Was there something about this particular one that attracted the cats?

She examined it, but found it no more smooth or worn than any of the others. It didn't smell different or feel different.

Random. A strange, random coincidence, Diana told herself.

But when she left the den this time, she took the box of cards with her and put them on the kitchen counter.

Ethan twisted off the cap of a B-Cubed IPA, courtesy of Baxter's Beatnik Brewing from here in good old Wicks Hollow.

"To Genevieve." He toasted her memory, her ghost, her presence—whatever it was that seemed to hover around him. The full-bodied beer slid down his throat, cool and smooth, and the tangy, hoppy flavor settled on the back of his tongue. "Thank you, Jean!"

He'd felt strange, entering her house now that she was dead, but he thought it was appropriate to toast her memory with the beer she'd bought him—and had always enjoyed herself. She always said the addition of B-Cubed to Wicks Hollow was the best thing that happened to the small town since she'd moved there, and Ethan didn't have any argument with that.

Not only was Baxter James a great guy who did freelance writing for several local newspapers while he was getting his beer business going, but he was also a friend of Ethan's. Which meant Ethan—and their other friend Declan Zyler—got to taste-test new brews. Not a hardship in the least.

Most of the time, anyway. There had been that one Bax had tried when he blended honey and coffee in a stout. That hadn't gone over well with anyone.

Ethan sipped again, mulling. Jean had always told him he

could come and go as he pleased. And since he insisted on taking care of her yard work when he was in Michigan during the summer—which she repaid by baking for him, allowing him to interview her as much as he liked, and the occasional Scrabble game—he was over there quite a bit. Now, he supposed, that would change.

Ethan had knocked on both the front and back doors for a good five minutes before retrieving the key hidden beneath the bluebird house. He thought he'd seen someone moving around inside the house, even though there was no car in the drive or the garage, but he must have been mistaken. After calling and knocking, he finally went in, Cady on his heels.

"Ms. Iverson," he'd called, stopping in the foyer and listening for her response. Silence. He hurried down the hall to the kitchen, feeling like an intruder—which, of course, he was—and opened the refrigerator door to retrieve his six-pack.

About that time, Cady began barking wildly. He heard her running around up and down the hall, and he went to investigate—and to make sure she didn't knock anything over in her exuberance. On his way, Ethan glanced outside and didn't see any evidence of a rabbit, squirrel, chipmunk, or bird—the usual suspects in a Cady bark-a-thon. The cats were nowhere in sight.

But...he thought he'd seen someone at the window. Could Diana Iverson be so determined to avoid him that she'd sneaked out the back door?

That was an unsettling thought.

A small thump had him hurrying down the hall to Jean's library, where Cady was currently barking. By the time he got there to investigate whether she'd knocked anything over (she hadn't), the black lab was rushing past him back to the kitchen.

But there in the library, his attention landed on the

mahogany box in its place on the piecrust table. Jean's cards. A twinge of melancholy prompted him to remove the lid and open the silk wrappings. He wondered what Diana Iverson was doing with them—if anything.

Diana doesn't believe in anything unless it's in black and white and been proven beyond a shadow of a doubt. And even then, if she sees it in black and white, she's gotta question it and question it. That's mostly thanks to her mother—who pushed her and criticized her, and never let up on—well, there's no use in me going on about Melanie. A good lawyer she is, Diana, but she's missing a whole layer of the world, Ethan—thanks to that so-and-so of a mother of hers. Never let her enjoy life.

He pushed away a flicker of sympathy for Diana Iverson, and opened the black silk wrapping to reveal the diamond-shaped blue, red, and black pattern of the back of the deck. He closed his eyes, settled his thoughts, and shuffled for a moment. Then he opened his mind and picked up the top card. Flipping it over, he saw *The Lovers.*

Ethan knew what it implied—and not necessarily the obvious. Relationships, sexuality, yes, of course, but the card also could mean the joining of any two entities—whether it be people, ideas or thoughts.

If she were there, Jean would tell him to mull on the card for the day, to open his mind and let the image dig into his unconscious, unlocking answers to questions in his life. She said that the cards unleashed her psychic abilities by opening doors in the back of her mind.

The thing most people didn't understand was that Genevieve Fickler never claimed the cards helped her to tell the future. Never once had she done that—and that was why Ethan respected her and the innate sensibilities and intuition she'd clearly possessed. Jean was a believer in using tools like the Tarot for guidance, direction, affirmation, and clarity—as a way to open blockages in one's mind.

Not to foresee the future.

Never that.

"Everything's already locked away in your mind—in your subconscious and in the metaphysical that we can all tap into. You just need to open up the channels," she'd say—telling him something he already believed and understood. "And the cards help to do that by giving you something to focus on."

He stared down at *The Lovers*.

He'd known Jean for three years—since he bought the cabin here in Wicks Hollow—and they'd spent a lot of time talking about the metaphysical, and how certain, consistent beliefs about it were present in every culture, everywhere—and had been for millennia.

Ethan, who'd grown up with a mother and a sister who both read palms and tapped into everything from *feng shui* to chakra balancing, didn't find Jean's interests the least bit unsettling. Not that he'd sit around and chat about those things with guys like Declan or Baxter, but there was a time and a place for everything.

Cady began barking again from the kitchen, jolting Ethan from his thoughts. *What is with her?*

He wondered again whether Diana had slipped out the back door to avoid him. The possibility compelled him to make tracks ASAP. If he wasn't wanted here, he wasn't wanted.

Guiltily, he replaced the card, wrapping the deck and slipping the cover back onto the box. Then he found paper and a pen and scrawled a note to Diana, planning to leave it on the kitchen counter where she'd see it right away.

He was heading to the kitchen to soothe Cady, but as he glanced down the hall he saw the door open to the bedroom that belonged to Jean. Ethan went to it and stopped in the doorway, looking around the room.

The bed was made—smooth as glass—and a half dozen lacy, Victorian pillows had been organized in a neat, symmetrical pile at its head. But the rag-rug that covered the wooden floor had a corner flipped up as if someone had left in haste—strange that it was the only thing out of place in the room.

And it didn't seem like something the uptight Diana Iverson would overlook.

Something prickled over the back of his neck.

Had he interrupted someone inside?

Ethan stilled and listened. No, he didn't sense the presence of anyone else nearby. And Cady had stopped barking.

Maybe he should take a look around outside. Just in case. After all, apparently the place had been empty for a few weeks. Someone might have decided to move in.

He didn't like that thought, and though he dismissed it as foolish, Ethan did take a quick walk around the house's perimeter. The whole time, he was uncomfortably prepared to encounter Diana, as it was probably she who'd left to avoid him.

He didn't notice anything that bothered him, so, in an effort to make certain he didn't run into the ice-cold attorney, he left with his beer.

And even now, as he relaxed at home in his leather armchair with a cold one in hand, Ethan felt an unpleasant tightening in his middle. Whether someone had been there or whether Diana was purposely staying away from him, he didn't know.

But either way, he didn't like it.

THREE

DIANA HAD another debilitating migraine that forced her to go to bed at seven o'clock that evening, snuggling under the quilt in Aunt Jean's bed before the sun had even set.

Some time later, she woke, sweating and shaking, trying to throw off the heavy blackness of another horrific nightmare. She couldn't breathe, and she felt as if a great weight had settled on her chest, pressing and pressing down into her...

Confused, exhausted, and terrified, she stumbled down the hall into the library and dove onto the sofa, where a short time later she was able to find a more peaceful rest.

When she finally peeled her eyes open to bright sunlight, it was nearly ten o'clock—but today, she wasn't surprised that she'd overslept. Time and place seemed different here in Wicks Hollow. And aside from that, Diana realized with clinical detachment that she was surely suffering from a bit of depression, thanks to Jonathan's betrayal and Aunt Jean's death.

When Diana entered her aunt's bedroom to select her clothing after an invigorating shower, trepidation skittered up her spine.

There was something about this room that made her feel as

if the nightmares lingered, heavy and dark and hot, even in the broad daylight. She hadn't spent a full night in the room since she'd arrived.

Yes, Aunt Jean had died in here, but there was nothing more natural than an elderly lady easing into death while in repose. After all, Aunt Jean had been over seventy. Practical Diana had no qualms about such a natural occurrence.

She tightened the scratchy, threadbare towel from Aunt Jean's aged collection tighter around her chest and told herself firmly she was being ridiculous. Still, she hesitated before stepping into the room, as if afraid the nightmares might come back even in broad morning light—but upon seeing Motto, the smaller cat with a fat, bottle brush tail, sprawled in the middle of the bed, she forgot her disquiet.

"Hi kitty," she crooned, moving carefully toward the beady-green-eyed feline. The cat had burrowed right into the center of the maelstrom of sheets and was busily licking the inside of her back leg until the interruption of a mere human caused her to pause.

Diana was surprised but pleased when she was able to get close enough to scoop Motto into her arms. She nuzzled the thick white fur of the feline's head. "I'm so glad you decided to come out of hiding, sweet-thing," she said. "Now if only Arty would be as brave."

The annoyance plain on her face—most likely due to Diana's undignified tone—Motto struggled out of her captor's arms and plopped lightly to the floor. Tail swishing in a last gesture of disdain, the cat ducked her head and disappeared under the bed.

"Well, fine, then. See if I bring you anymore catnip toys," Diana told her. But the cat's presence and warm, furry body had done something to alleviate her strange discomfort with the bedroom.

And just at that moment, it struck her that Jonathan was arriving tomorrow and they would be, presumably, sharing the bed in here.

She bit her lip and pushed the thought away. "I really should grow a pair and tell him not to come," she said aloud.

But Diana was honest enough with herself to know the reason why she hadn't: she wasn't quite ready to end things with him.

She didn't want to be alone again, and it was so difficult to meet people and have a social life with her demanding job. She wasn't good with people anyway; she knew she often came across as stiff and reserved. But Jonathan didn't mind, and he was the most interesting and accomplished man she'd ever dated

I knew you'd never be able to keep a man like Jonathan Wertinger. If you'd just—

Diana closed her eyes against the memory of her mother's voice and blocked it away. "I have to go to the FedEx drop box," she said out loud, like a mantra to stop the thoughts. "I have to get there before noon so they're on the early truck."

The locksmith had come the day before, and now that all the locks were changed, Diana felt much more secure about leaving the house. Not that there was much of value actually here in Wicks Hollow. Most of Aunt Jean's considerable wealth was in securities and a few real estate investments, due to her husband's successful business—and was not at all evident in her manner of living, Diana thought with a wry smile at the memory of the threadbare bath towels and off-brand strawberry shampoo.

There's not much here of any value except a few antiques—unless someone wants a deck of old Tarot cards.

At the thought, queasiness started in her stomach and she took another sip of the tea she'd made.

It was cold and it was...*tea*.

Diana mentally added another stop at the market to her list of things to do. How could she have forgotten to buy coffee yesterday?

The only brew available in Aunt Jean's house was her choice of herbal tea: peppermint, chamomile, and blends of rose hips, lemon verbena, all of the mints, and comfrey. The lack of options for caffeine was alarming.

Oh crap...she'd need to buy a coffee maker too.

Curiously, Diana had also found a box of dog biscuits when foraging for a source of caffeine, and wondered if the cats liked canine treats. But when she offered, neither of them bothered to even show and turn up their pink noses at the cookies, and so she left to go on her errands.

The quaint town of Wicks Hollow was cocooned in the center of a handful of rolling hills—none of them large enough to be considered even the smallest of mountains, but nonetheless, they had the effect of protecting and containing the village like a large hand cupping the village in its palm. During most of the year, the town's population was barely two thousand. But when the tourist season came—beginning with Memorial Day and ending with Labor Day, and then at the end of September into October for the Fall Color Tours—its population swelled to five thousand or more.

Many of the houses were considered historic "painted ladies"—built at the turn of last century with all the curlicues and garrets and towers characteristic of the Victorian era. They were painted bright colors: sky blue, rose, tangerine, Kelly green, and many different shades of violet and purple. They had small, neatly manicured yards, sprawling, mature trees, and some even boasted iron-spiked fences along the front.

Some were mansion-sized, and others were single-family residences or cottages, and others were stately farmhouses.

Three blocks of Elizabeth Street were lined on both sides with the most charming of homes. That was known as B&B Row, where each house was a small inn or bed and breakfast. A few even had glimpses of Lake Michigan, only two miles to the west, from their upper floors.

The downtown, business and tourist district was just as manicured and inviting. It boasted two main streets—optimistically named Faith Avenue and Pamela Boulevard after the daughters of the town's founder, George Wicks—that intersected in the middle of the tourist district. Despite their lofty names, neither were anything close to an avenue or a boulevard, but were barely wide enough for two cars to pass if there were vehicles parked on one side. However, huge, overflowing flower pots and Victorian style streetlamps decorated the walkways, and the broad sidewalks themselves provided plenty of room for the tourists that filled the streets.

For two blocks in each of the four directions from the town's center, shops, restaurants, cafes, and other businesses sprang up. Every one was a brick-fronted building of various heights, widths, and brick choice. Diana eyed all of them, including the Balanced Chakra Yoga Studio, a vintage clothing shop, and the trendy, urban-looking Trib's, which Diana had been told was the best restaurant in the county.

The post office and visitors' center, which moonlighted as the town hall, were near the central intersection. But beyond the main tourist area, yet still within walking distance, were the three blocks of B&B Row.

To the south and east of the town, a bank of thickly wooded hills rose like a natural, protective wall. Through the trees, she caught a glimpse of some of the peaks and towers of more Victorian mansions—including the empty Shenstone House, which sat on the highest hill and was reputed to be haunted.

Upon leaving the post office, Diana decided her first—very first—order of business now that she'd dropped her packages at the FedEx box was to locate some caffeine.

The sign for Orbra's Tea House caught her attention and since it was closest, she thought she'd stop there. Tea and coffee went together, didn't they—except in Aunt Jean's house. She smiled affectionately, then felt a sharp stab of grief. She'd never see her quirky aunt again.

A lovely antique tea service of highly polished silver was arranged in the front window of Orbra's, and Diana remembered that the eponymous owner had been one of Aunt Jean's Tuesday Ladies, as their social group was called.

It wasn't Tuesday, but why not? She opened the door and walked in. Instead of the expected pink cabbage flower and melting roses Victorian decor, dripping with lace and knick-knacks, the style was much more restrained but no less tea-shop-appropriate.

There was a minimal amount of lace in the form of several antique table runners, but the color scheme was cornflower blue and a paler sky-like hue, as well as white and sunny yellow. Lemon-colored Gerbera daisies and tiny vases of violets studded the tables, each of which were set with mismatched but somehow coordinated plates of white, all shades of blue, and lavender.

She'd barely stepped over the threshold when a voice boomed. "Why, it's Jean's Diana!"

Orbra van Hest, whose build was the tall, large-boned and sturdy one of her Dutch heritage, moved with surprising efficiency for someone who was nearly seventy. "Well, come on in, there, Diana. We've been waiting to see you! Why don't you sit yourself here with Cherry—she's taking up one of my best tables anyway. Always likes to sit in the one by the window. Once tourist season is in full swing; she'll be relegated to the back corner there. Besides, the others ought to be along any minute now, so your timing couldn't have been better. They'll all want to see you."

During this speech, Diana found herself being hustled over to a large round table near one of the front windows. It had a generous vase of short-stemmed sunflowers in the center, and a cluster of more petite vessels with daisies and violets. The small plates were white with tiny blue and purple flowers and gilt around the edges.

"It's nice to see you again, Diana," said the slender, toned woman sitting there with a pot of tea. She was a very fit midsixties and had short, cropped hair of a soft platinum shade. The fact that she wore workout clothes helped Diana to place her immediately. "We met briefly at Jean's funeral."

"Yes, of course. Cherry Wilder is it? You own the yoga studio," Diana said. All she wanted was a cup of coffee…she didn't really have time to socialize. But, nevertheless, she took a seat.

Cherry smiled. "I do. For forty years now, in fact. Any time you want to come by for a class, you'd be welcome. First one is on me. We've got mats and blocks and anything you might need." As Orbra stood there, arms crossed like a sentinel, she glanced up at her. "And don't complain about me taking your best table," she said with a wave. "You know Maxine will insist on it the minute she blows in." She turned back to Diana. "The old bat—don't worry, I call her that to her face—likes to sit here so she can see everything going on in the town."

"And tell everyone else what to do," Orbra added. Cherry laughed and lifted her tea to sip.

"Right." Diana was just about to ask for some coffee when the front door opened and two more elderly women came in.

One held a smooth, gnarled cane in her equally smooth,

gnarled hand. She had skin the color and texture of polished walnut and iron-gray hair arranged in a sort of styleless mop that tried to curl and could possibly have been a wig. She possessed sharp, dark eyes, and wore orthopedic shoes that looked like they belonged to Frankenstein's monster.

The other had improbably paprika-red hair curled and sprayed into a helmet-like arrangement in the shape of a mushroom cloud: cropped close at the neck and sides, but teased and poofy on the top and around the crown. Her fingernails were such a bright pink they drew the attention immediately, and she wore lipstick to match.

The redhead, who appeared to be of Hispanic heritage, carried a large tote bag over her shoulder, and Diana saw the reason why: one of the cutest dogs she'd ever seen was poking its face out from inside. He was about the size of a Chihuahua, but he had huge, butterfly-shaped ears and a white face with black and brown splotches on it.

Both of the women looked as if they were pushing eighty. They were squabbling over something about a bingo and blanks, but the moment they saw Diana, the one with the cane crowed with delight (or alarm; it wasn't immediately clear which) and clomped speedily from the door to the table.

"Well, it's about time you decided to show your face, missy. Didn't leave no way for any of us to contact you after the funeral, and I was getting damned tired of waiting for you to come back. Don't you have no respect for your elders?"

Diana had met her once—and that was all she needed for the old woman to be indelibly printed on her memory. It wasn't the cane she wielded like a weapon or a steam engine that made her unforgettable; though that was just as much a part of Maxine Took as her sharp, all-seeing eyes and her curled, arthritic fingers.

"Good morning, Mrs. Took," Diana said as the elderly

woman maneuvered the chairs around the table. She used her cane along with surprisingly strong hands and facile hip movements to shove and shift the seats—requiring Cherry and Diana to move as well—until she positioned herself in the chair with the best view of the window, the shop, *and* Diana herself.

"It ain't *Mrs.* nothing," she growled, banging her cane on the floor to emphasize. She was a little out of breath from her exertions, but no lower in volume. "Never was. Woulda been either *Doctor* or *Ms.* Took—but you just call me Maxine. Ain't no reason to put on airs. And this here is Juanita. Not Mrs. Alecita. Just Juanita. And don't put your fingers near her bag or Bruce Banner will take them off."

For someone who'd just complained about lack of respect for elders, Maxine seemed strangely informal about her form of address. But her diatribe reminded Diana that the elderly black woman had been a chemical engineer with a math PhD back in the Sixties. In her mind, that gave Maxine the right to be as much of a cranky old bat as she wanted.

Diana smiled. "Very well, then, Maxine. Nice to see you again, Juanita." She remembered that Juanita had owned a chain of ten Mexican restaurants in Michigan and Indiana before selling them off in late 2000. "That is the sweetest looking dog I've ever seen." Then she seized the moment and looked up at Orbra. "I really need a cup of coffee. Could you—"

She stopped speaking when she realized all four of them were looking at her as if she'd just asked for their heads on a platter.

"This is a tea shop, dear." Juanita, who had been granted the chair on the other side of Diana, spoke kindly. "There's no coffee here." She said "coffee" the same way one might say "steak" in a vegan cafe.

"Right. I...know that. I just thought..." Diana drew in a deep breath and looked up at Orbra. "What do you recommend? I need some caffeine. Lots of caffeine. Is there a tea equivalent to espresso?"

"Contrary to popular belief, and what do they call 'em—urban fantasies?" Maxine looked at Cherry.

"Urban legends, I think you mean," replied the yoga instructor.

"Right. That's it. Anyhow, contrary to urban legend—"

"What Maxine's trying to say it, there's no one type of tea with more or less caffeine. But if you want caffeine, I recommend a yerba maté or one of the needle tip teas," Orbra told Diana in a slightly offended voice. "I can brew either one extra strong if you like. But we don't have any of that fluffy milk here or those fake milks that come from nuts—what is it, Cherry? Hazelnu—no, it's cashew, isn't it?"

"Or almond or coconut," said her friend, eyeing Diana over the rim of her teacup with a laughing glint in her gaze.

"Right. Just plain old tea," Orbra finished. "Five pages of it listed in the menu," she added, as if to belie her previous comment.

"Right. I'm sure a yerba...maté, is it? That would be lovely." Diana didn't see any other choice in the matter, and aside from that, she had a feeling Maxine Took wouldn't allow her to take her leave any time soon. The old bat (to take a descriptor from Cherry) had a determined gleam in her eyes—and she'd angled her cane in such a way that Diana would have to clamber over it in order to leave her chair.

"All right, then, Diana, dear—would you like the Sri Lankan yerba or the the Chinese? Loose or bagged? A pot—or just a cup?" The way Orbra said the last seemed as if she were throwing down a gauntlet.

"Er...just a cup," she replied bravely. "Loose tea is fine. And whichever is your favorite."

"I want some of your cinnamon scones, Orbry," said Maxine before Diana had finished ordering. "And I'll have that vanilla oolong—and mind you, don't brew it at one-seventy-five. I want it cooked right. Two-oh-eight, and not a degree different."

Orbra lifted her nose and gave her friend a steely look. "I know how to brew tea, Maxine. Black tea," she said to Diana —for clearly, she was lacking in her tea education, "is always brewed with water near the boil. Not so for other teas, you know."

"That's right. A scalded white tea is a waste of leaves," said Juanita as she tenderly adjusted the large leather purse on her lap. Diana could see the tops of Bruce Banner's ears poking out from inside the top. "And white tea is expensive. I'll have one of Maxine's scones—oh, you won't eat them *all*," she said over her companion's snarl. "And a whole-grain blueberry muffin. Have to watch my carbs, you know," she said.

Diana was torn between amusement and mild frustration over the interplay between the ladies—mainly because she couldn't see herself being able to make a break for it anytime in the near future.

So much for having a day to do nothing...

Although it was a rather good thing she didn't *have* anything pressing that needed to get done.

Orbra was just bustling off to get their orders together when the bell jangled over the shop door once more.

The woman who stepped in was a petite, matronly sort—soft, pleasingly plump, neatly put together but not fussy—in her late sixties. She had white cotton candy hair in an easy style and wore understated makeup. As she drew closer, Diana smelled the classic scent of White Shoulders wafting gently from her.

"What happened? Your alarm not go off?" Maxine demanded of the new arrival. "You're *late*, Iva."

"More likely she was getting some morning delight from her new man," Cherry murmured with a grin.

"Now, Cherry," said the woman as she took the last empty seat, which was next to the yoga instructor, "how do you know I'm not saving myself for marriage?" Her bright blue eyes twinkled with humor—but her round apple cheeks were flushed with pleasure that conflicted with her statement.

Everyone burst out laughing except for Diana as Iva Bergstrom reached over to pat her hand. "How nice to see you again, Diana! How are you getting along up in that big old house? Any sign of ghosts?"

"Ghosts?" Though she'd felt a little jolt at the question, Diana replied calmly. "What do you mean?"

"Well, you know Jean, she always enjoyed a good party—never liked to leave early. Always had to be the last one. And life's got to be the best party, ever, right?" Iva leaned forward with a bright smile, her eyes twinkling merrily. "I'm sure Jean didn't want to leave this party early, so if anyone was going to come back to haunt a house, it would be her."

"I'm not—"

"Besides, this is Wicks Hollow! Don't you know this town abounds with ghosts and hauntings and curses and the like?" Iva said. Diana wasn't certain whether the sparkle in her eyes was due to repressed laughter or honest enthusiasm.

"I never heard that," she said, trying to be polite.

"Iva's right," Maxine interjected, snatching control of the conversation. "It's like in that Taffy show—where they had that Hell's Mountain and attracted all those demons and vampires and things. Though we ain't got no demons—just a few ghosts. And a curse, too."

Diana blinked, confused and more than a little concerned over Maxine's lucidity.

Cherry, laughing silently, brushed tears from her eyes. "How many times do we have to tell you, Maxine—it's *Buffy*," she said. "Not Taffy. And it was a Hell*mouth*." She disintegrated into laughter again and ended with a little snort. "Taffy the Vampire Slayer."

Maxine waved her off with hook-like fingers and leaned in to Diana. "Taffy, Buffy—they all sound like something fluffy to me. It don't matter. But mark me—there've been ghosts like to hang around in Wicks Hollow since my granddad Abraham Bell Took settled here. Something about the area I think. What do they call 'em? Ley lines?"

"Shhhh! Not so loud. We don't want the tourists to hear," Cherry said.

"There ain't any tourists *yet*," Maxine retorted, looking around as if to be certain. "But by next week, we'll be overrun."

Orbra arrived just at that moment, rolling a tea cart laden with their drinks, and Diana was thankful the conversation was overtaken by Maxine giving orders about where pots and cups and plates should go, and why the scones were so small today ("They're the same size as always," Orbra snapped), and *where was the clotted cream?*

Mercifully, just as things settled down, Diana's cell phone rang. "Oh dear, it's my office," she said, standing quickly as she answered the call. "Hold on, Mick." Then she turned to the group. "I'd forgotten the time, I've been enjoying myself so much, but I do have to take this call." It wasn't a complete lie —the five Tuesday Ladies (she didn't know why they were called that) were interesting and rather amusing.

She tossed a ten dollar bill onto the table and was just about to make her escape when Iva said, "You'll be there Tuesday evening, right?"

"Tuesday?"

"It's my eightieth birthday," Maxine announced, cinnamon scone crumbs flying. "Big party at Trib's house on the lake. He's closing the restaurant for the evening. Does it every year. *Everyone* comes."

"Oh, I—"

"Of course you'll be there. Everyone wants to get to know you better, Diana," Iva said kindly. "Now that you're taking over Jean's place. It'll be fun—and Maxine's birthday is like a town holiday for us here in Wicks Hollow before the tourists get too thick. Besides, Hollis will be there—and I'm trying to convince him to bring his grandson Gideon. He's very handsome, and he's a lawyer too, just like you. You can meet him—Hollis, I mean—then." Her cheeks pinked again, and she went on. "He has a business associate who knows you or worked with you, I think. And we all miss Jean so much…it would be really wonderful for you to come."

"Well, all right," Diana replied, remembering she still had Mickey on the phone. "It does sound like fun."

"Of course it's fun. It's my *birthday*." Maxine glowered at her, then dove into a second scone. "Seven o'clock. There'll be cake. And food. And *presents*. Don't be late."

"Right. I'll…find out where Trib lives," Diana said as she made her escape from the tea shop…still without her dose of caffeine. "Thank you for saving me," she said into the phone as the door closed behind her.

"What was that all about?" Mickey asked.

Diana told her as she walked briskly down Pamela Boulevard.

"Ghosts? In Wicks Hollow? Well, that shouldn't bother you any."

"What is that supposed to mean?"

"Well, you know—with that *thing* you do, I suppose you're probably connected to all sorts of—"

"Mickey, I don't know what you're talking about. There's nothing—I don't know, *supernatural* about me thinking about a case and coming up with a logical, effective approach." Diana's insides felt tight and desperate. It wasn't like she had any sort of *magic* or anything. She just…got the ideas. They just sort of dropped into her head.

Magically.

No, it wasn't magic.

And, well, yes, sometimes they were pretty specific. And oftentimes crazy. But they did work. Always.

"Whatever you say," her assistant replied airily. "Anyway, I've got a few things to go over with you."

A few minutes later, after working through the list Mickey had, Diana said, "Everything else okay there?"

"We're fine. With the depositions not scheduled until late August, there's no reason for you to rush back," Mickey told her—obviously reading her mind. "Didn't you say McNillan told you to take a month?"

"That seems so long—"

"You deserve it. Enjoy your time with Jonathan over the weekend."

Diana gave a mental wince. She hadn't told Mickey what happened in Vegas. She hadn't actually told anyone about it. Except her mother, which had been a mistake of *major* proportion.

Diana's brows knit. She'd almost forgotten Jonathan was arriving tomorrow. Out of sight, out of mind?

"Thanks. All right then—I'll talk to you tomorrow."

Just as she disconnected, Diana saw her Nirvana: a small cafe called Hot Toddy, whose painted sign proclaimed the availability of lattes, cappuccinos, and espressos. The building had the look of a cottage, with hot pink shutters and matching trim that unexpectedly went beautifully with its mint green siding.

Inside, there was a huge framed movie poster from *Victor/Victoria*, and several stills from the same film—most of Julie Andrews and Robert Preston. They all seemed to be signed by Preston.

Diana ordered a double macchiato to go from the short, wiry man behind the counter. Inhaling the boost of caffeine with relief, she meandered down the street, taking in the many changes in town over the last five years.

She passed Gilda's Goodies, a vintage clothing store that had Diana coveting a beaded handbag and matching wrap displayed in the window. They looked like couture from the Fifties, and she had a weakness for the classic styles of Jackie O and Grace Kelly—which was why she'd adored and actually made time to watch *Mad Men*.

Beyond Gilda's was a small structure set back from the sidewalk with a tiny, shaded courtyard that held two small iron tables with matching chairs. The building had a narrow doorway, and it was open to let in the early summer air. *New & Used Books*, its sign read. Before Diana knew it, her feet had propelled her through the cozy courtyard, up the single step, and into a musty bookshop.

An oscillating fan blew in the direction of the shop's proprietor, who sat at a table laden with books and was surrounded by even more stacks and shelves of tomes upon tomes. She was in her late fifties, and had a colorful silk wrap tied around what appeared to be a bald head. She wore cheaters of neon lavender that complemented her purple and lemon head covering and sunny yellow sundress.

She looked up, frowning slightly at Diana's large paper cup, and said, "Hello—oh, you're Jean's niece, aren't you? I'm Pam. We met briefly at the funeral. She used to come in here all the time." Her wispy voice dropped a little, then she went on brusquely, "Let me know if I can help you find anything. The shelves go all the way into the back and up those stairs there. New books are up front here—including the latest T.J. Mack thriller and the professor's book. Those are signed, of course."

"Thank you." Diana walked past her, careful not to jostle a particularly tall stack of books.

Unsure what she was looking for—it had been forever since she'd had time to read for pleasure, and T.J. Mack's Sargent Blue thrillers had caught her eye more than once—she pressed on through a rabbit's warren of stacks and shelves toward the back of the shop. On the way, she noted the faded, curling handwritten labels: *Fiction, Mystery, Science Fiction & Fantasy, Romance, History, Business, Biography, Religion,* and, finally, a more recent tag that read *New Age*.

Catching a glimpse of some of the books, which had titles like *Find the Angels in Your Life,* and *Shamanic Journeying for Everyone*, Diana smiled to herself. Aunt Jean and Iva both would have a field day in this section. *Runes*, read another one, *Palmistry Made Easy*, and *The Tarot Explained* were lined up along with them.

Before she thought too hard about it, Diana reached for the last title. Setting her covered to-go cup down on a half-empty shelf, she flipped through the yellowed pages of the book. They were brittle and stained with what looked like coffee, and several of the corners were torn off. She paused at a chapter entitled "The Major (or Greater) Arcana."

She turned the fragile pages and read the list of card names, aware that her pulse rate had sped up.

Why did she feel so odd—a little expectant, a little light-headed, a little *nervous*? Even her palms felt damp.

The Fool, Number Zero.

The Magician, Number One.

The High Priestess, Number Two.

That one caught her eye, and she kept reading: *The High Priestess is*—

"I didn't peg you for a New-Ager," drawled a male voice from behind her.

Diana whirled and fumbled the book to the floor. "You startled me."

"I can see that," he replied with a lifted brow. "Sorry—I didn't realize you were so engrossed."

Despite her shock, Diana noted his height (tall), his amber-brown eyes (twinkling with humor), and his face (chiseled and objectively quite handsome). The moisture evaporated from her mouth and sprang to her palms.

Engrossed? She hadn't really been…had she?

He bent to retrieve the book. "Hmm…*The Tarot Explained*." He straightened and offered it back to her. "Your aunt would be astonished."

Diana didn't take the book. Instead, she stared at him. She didn't remember meeting him, but he was acting as if they had. Maybe at the funeral…

But then all at once, his voice and easy smile connected sharply with her memory. "Oh, it's *you*," she said, finally recognizing Ethan Murphy. She couldn't help that her tone came out less than warmly.

But what else would he expect, having walked into her house uninvited *twice*? And then him sneaking up on her…

She hadn't immediately recognized the man because he

was now clean-shaven and had cut his hair. Though the shearing added a couple years to her estimate of his age—he was definitely mid-thirties—it did wonders for his looks. It made his eyes look bigger and darker. His lips, which had settled into a sort of smirk, were no longer hidden by a thrush of facial hair. Nor was his square, chiseled jaw.

Suddenly, Diana felt awkward in the presence of this imposing, wildly attractive stranger—a man who'd been in her house twice. Somehow now, especially in this small, crowded space, he seemed more intimidating, with more presence and —and something. Irritated with herself for slipping back into the shy, tongue-tied ways of her youth, she picked up her coffee as a way to break the moment.

"Oh, right. I forgot you haven't seen me shorn." Murphy's hand smoothed over his clean jaw line, then dropped to sling loosely on his hip. He continued to lean against the shelf, holding the book, looking down at her as if he was trying to figure her out. That made Diana feel even more awkward. "I really didn't mean to startle you," he added.

"Forget it," she told him coolly. "I was just—deep in thought."

He glanced down at the book. "From everything your aunt has told me, I didn't think you were all that interested in the Tarot."

A hint of accusation in his voice caused her to bristle—and to wonder again just how well *had* he known Aunt Jean?

"Although I can't imagine why my aunt would have discussed me with you, I admit you're right. I certainly don't believe in that sort of foolishness."

"Okay," he shrugged. "Would you like me to put this back, or were you going to buy it?"

"No," she said sharply, too quickly. "No, thanks." She softened her tone, ignoring the familiar migraine throb that was just beginning to tom-tom at the back of her temples.

Not again. Not here. Not in front of him—again.

"No," she repeated. "I wasn't going to buy it. As I told you, I haven't any use for a book about Tarot."

"I'll just put it away, then." Ethan turned, sliding the book onto the shelf in an approximation of where it had been. "Hmm. Palmistry. My sister might like this," he mused, pulling out a book two slots away.

Not that Fiona needed a book to tell her how to read palms, Ethan thought with a grin. She was quite gifted in that regard, just like their mother.

He glanced at Diana Iverson and noticed her face had gone bone white and tight. She was obviously in some sort of pain.

"Are you feeling all right?" he asked, shoving the palmistry book back onto the shelf.

"Yes." Her lie was so obvious he nearly scoffed.

"Are you sure?"

To his surprise, she looked up at him for the first time with truly honest eyes. Misery and pain had dulled their rich sapphire to a foggy gray-blue. Her face was like marble: dead white and cold. "No, actually, I'm not. I've been getting these debilitating migraines...and sometimes the onset is very sudden."

"Sit down." He took her arm and directed her into a well-worn armchair. It was shocking how quickly she'd gone from her cool, stand-offish self to appearing ready to collapse, or be violently ill. Or both. "What do you need?"

"A glass of water," she said in a thready voice, eyes closed. "I have medication in my handbag."

Ethan hurried to the front of the shop where Pam sat going through her books. "I need a glass of water for Jean's niece—she's got to take some medicine. She's ill." He slipped past her nod, into the private bathroom, and filled a small cup with water.

When he returned to Diana, she was reclining in a corner of the armchair, eyes closed. Her features were even more ashen and sharp. He pressed the water into her hand. She half sat up, palming the pills into her mouth then drinking greedily.

"Thanks. I'll be better in a few minutes." She sank back into the chair and closed her eyes again.

Feeling helpless as well as reluctantly intrigued, he stood next to her, looking down at her lidded eyes fringed with thick dark lashes. The tension began to melt from her face, and a bit of color returned. Her mouth relaxed, and the tightness around the bridge of her nose and jaw eased. As he looked at her elegant features framed by soft, dark curls, Ethan was surprised by a jolt of very real, unavoidable attraction.

After a few more minutes, her eyelids fluttered and she opened them fully. "I'm sorry," she said in a soft sort of groan, "that one came on shockingly fast. They've been doing that lately." Now she looked both sleepy and bewildered, but as he offered her his hand, the glaze cleared from her eyes.

"I'll drive you home," he told her.

Ethan didn't expect her to acquiesce, but she surprised him. "Would you? I don't think I should drive right now."

He assisted her to her feet, but when he tried to support her by holding her arm, she slid out of his grasp and walked toward the front of the bookstore.

As they stepped out into the beautiful June sunshine, Diana drew in a deep, cleansing breath. He couldn't help but appreciate the way her breasts lifted as she did so, outlined by the blood red blouse she wore—of clinging silk and far too fancy for Wicks Hollow, but very eye-catching nonetheless.

"I'm feeling better already," she said, and he averted his eyes just as she smiled up at him.

"I'll drive you home anyway." He held out his hand for the key fob. "Where are you parked?"

He thought a flicker of relief flitted across her face. She jerked her head to the right. "In front of Trib's. But what about you? How will you get back?"

He started across the street, forcing her to follow him. "I can walk home from your house and pick up my car later. We're practically next door—only the Hornbergers between us, and they're set ever further back from the lake than you are. I'll show you my driveway."

When they reached Jean's large clapboard house, Diana was out of the car before he'd turned off the engine as if to ensure he wouldn't attempt to open her door or help her out —reinforcing his initial impression of her as prickly and stiff.

She started up the porch steps—he noticed they could use a new coat of paint— then turned toward him. "I'll need the keys, please."

He dropped them into her palm and watched as she turned to fit one into the lock. She stopped, shook her head, and looked down at the keys, sifting through them one by one. "Oh…*crap*," she said in a low voice.

"What's wrong?"

She heaved a sigh then looked up at him, sheepishness poorly hidden in her features. "I forgot to take the house keys when I left. I haven't added them to my car key ring yet. I guess I'm locked out."

"I can fix that," Ethan explained easily. "Genevieve always kept an extra beneath the bluebird house." He started off the porch toward the detached garage.

"Dr. Murphy," she called as he disappeared behind the building. "Uh…it won't work."

"What do you mean, it won't work? It's right here." He came back around, holding a key for her to see.

"I—uh—" She looked embarrassed, her fair cheeks suddenly rosy.

Ethan came back on the porch and brushed in front of her to fit the key in the lock. Then he halted, noticing how shiny and new the doorknob and the deadbolt above it was. He didn't even have to try the key to know it wouldn't fit.

Understanding dawned and he stepped back as she said, "I changed the locks."

"I see that." He looked out off the porch, suddenly furious and mortified at the same time. "I'm sorry if I imposed on you in any way. If you *like*," he flashed a stony glance at her, and was gratified to see an even darker flush rush over her face, "I'll open a window and help you get back in. Then I'll just be on my way."

Diana felt miserably ashamed as Murphy stalked off the porch, striding purposefully around the corner of the house toward the kitchen. She followed slowly, wondering why she cared that she'd offended him, and wishing the heat in her cheeks would dissolve.

She'd never been confident or comfortable around men—especially ones as devastatingly handsome as this one. Though she'd worked hard to get past the insecurities, her mother's sly, sharp criticisms always seemed to lodge in the back of her mind. Of course, when she argued trials or took depositions, that was different. Then, she was wholly prepared—she knew precisely what to say, and how and when. But around men in a casual situation…not so much.

That was why she'd been so swept off her feet by the handsome and successful Jonathan. He'd been the one to pursue her —and when she would have discouraged him, or allowed her cool reserve to keep him at arms' length, he was persistent and charming, wooing her until she got caught up in the wonderful romance.

And now…well, what had she expected? That someone like Jonathan would be content with her?

The ugly thought made her feel nauseated again and she ruthlessly closed her mind to it as she hurried after Murphy.

As she came around the back of the house, she found him struggling with one of the basement windows. It's painted shut," he grunted, trying to lever it open with a stout stick. "I think I can get it open without breaking it."

"Dr. Murphy, I'm really sorry—"

"Just call me Ethan," he said over his shoulder, voice tinged with annoyance. "And don't worry about it."

Diana had just stepped closer when he succeeded in forcing the window open. He tossed the stick aside, kicking the windowpane so that it opened wider. "I'll climb in, come around, and unlock the door."

"You really don't have to—"

Her voice trailed off as he ignored her and somehow maneuvered his tall, lanky body through the small space. His shirt rode up a little as he did so, exposing a toned, golden torso that looked as warm and smooth as whiskey. She heard a dull thud (*that didn't sound good*) as Ethan landed on the floor inside, and, biting her lip in consternation, Diana turned to go meet him at the kitchen door.

When he came out, brushing the dust off his jeans, Ethan was brusque but polite. "Well, there you go. Now, don't forget to add the new key to your keychain." With a smile barely touching his lips, he started to walk off the back porch.

"Ethan, wait." She didn't know what to say, and why she felt she needed to repair the awkwardness between them. Perhaps out of respect for her aunt's memory she should at least properly thank the man who obviously knew her well enough to know where the house key was hidden.

Suspicions as to why an attractive young man would befriend an old, odd lady like Aunt Jean suddenly blossomed in her mind and her thoughts turned considering. Just what had he gained from the friendship?

Or *expected* to gain?

Aunt Jean was, after all, very wealthy.

Ethan paused and turned back. His eyes were unreadable, shadowed, as he stood half in sun, and half in shade.

"Why don't you come in for a minute?" She needed to find out more about him. "I'd like to make this…up to you. Without your help, I'd still be trying to find a way in."

"What about your headache?"

"I'm fine now. The medicine kicked in on the drive home. Come on in, won't you?"

He hesitated for a moment, then, giving a more genuine, but still restrained smile, he acquiesced.

In the big, bright kitchen, Diana bustled about, realizing she was trying to keep busy while she decided how to eliminate the awkwardness between them. She should have just let him leave. It wasn't as if she was going to see him more than once or twice ever again. But, yet, the awkward situation with the key bothered her, and she felt she needed to make it up somehow.

"I'm going to have a bite to eat—will you let me make you some lunch? Please?"

Ethan leaned against the counter near the old-fashioned black phone, propping a hip against it and folding tanned arms over his chest. Very nice, muscular arms, tanned more darkly than his torso, she couldn't help but notice.

And she swallowed hard.

The lines in his face relaxed a little more. "I could eat.

Hell, I can *always* eat. Thanks." He smiled at her as though to indicate all was forgiven.

A little sizzle zipped through her belly. He was damned attractive with all that dark hair and that charming smile. And those muscular arms and tight square shoulders, outlined by the soft gray tee he wore.

He was probably used to easily getting his way around women. She wondered what he had charmed—or tried to charm—from Aunt Jean.

Guilt washed over her. She of all people should not cast stones. She hadn't made the time to visit Wicks Hollow for over ten years. Somehow the months had just slipped away, and she hadn't even returned Aunt Jean's phone calls in a timely manner. And now…

She pushed the uncomfortable thoughts away. "Iced tea?"

"Yes. Thanks."

Diana poured two tall glasses of iced tea and garnished them with lemon wedges, then started to put something together to eat. Just as she was pulling cheese and grapes from the refrigerator, the land line phone rang. She turned from her task, arms laden with food, in time to see Ethan reach for the black phone next to him. He stopped suddenly, snatching his hand back as if burned.

"That's okay, go ahead," she said, and unloaded the food onto the counter, her cheeks warming again.

He caught it on the next ring. "Genevieve Fickler's," he said in a smooth voice that felt like velvet over her skin. Then, after a pause, he said, "She's right here."

She took the proffered phone. "Diana Iverson," she said, expecting Aunt Jean's lawyer or some local business or even a telemarketer.

She was startled to hear Jonathan's voice—irritated and rushed. "Who was that?"

Taken by surprise, Diana hesitated, then replied coolly, "A friend of Aunt Jean's. Are you still getting in tonight?"

"I tried your cell, but you didn't pick up." His voice was still tight and fast. "Diana, who is that man? Is that why you aren't answering your cell?"

Diana felt a spark of annoyance, followed by a shameful bit of thrill that Jonathan might be worried about *her* fidelity, about whether he could trust her.

He *did* love her, and he wanted things to work out—just as she did.

"Jonathan," she said in a firm voice, wholly aware of Ethan standing there listening without appearing to listen. "I told you—the cell phone service up here isn't very good."

"Are you sure?" he insisted. As if a switch flipped, his voice had changed into that mellow, empathetic tone he normally used. She used to love hearing his low, deep voice on the phone when they first started seeing each other. "I can't wait to see you. But that's why I'm calling—to let you know I've gotten tied up with an emergency surgery. I had to change my flight and I won't get in until tomorrow. Eleven a.m."

A sudden, ugly feeling lodged in her belly. He wasn't flying in tonight, but tomorrow morning instead?

Why?

So he could spend the night with Valerie the Wonder Slut?

"All right," she forced herself to say lightly. She realized her fingers were a little unsteady as she unwrapped a chunk of Gouda. "Are you still on United?"

"Yes, of course. You know I always fly United out of O'Hare. Flight 439. I'll text it to you."

"I'd better write it down in case the text doesn't come through." Diana turned to get paper out of the drawer near Ethan and became flustered when she noticed he had opened the mahogany Tarot card box—which she'd left on the counter.

And that he stood between her and the drawer.

She hesitated, then reached past Ethan. It seemed he waited a little too long to step back so her arm brushed across his warm, solid midriff when she pulled open the drawer. And he took the box of Tarot cards with him when he moved.

Irritated that she'd been forced to touch him—the skin on her arm still prickled—and distracted by the mahogany box in Ethan's hands, Diana had to ask Jonathan to repeat his flight number and arrival time twice more before she got it written correctly.

"Okay, then," she said hurriedly, watching as her guest pulled a chair from the kitchen table then sank into it. The mahogany box in his hand was like a magnet to her attention. "I'll see you tomorrow morning."

"All right darling," Jonathan replied. "Diana, remember: I love you. I only love you."

"Mm, love you, too," she managed to reply, acutely aware of her guest—and also strangely obligated to respond to Jonathan in kind.

But of course she still loved him—she was just hurt and shocked by his actions, and it was going to take some time for her to feel comfortable again.

Diana hung up the phone with some relief and turned back just as Ethan pulled the deck of cards from its black silk swaddling. She couldn't turn her eyes away.

"Husband?" he asked casually, seemingly unaware of her attention on the cards.

"No," she told him, and further explanation stuck stubbornly in her throat. "What are you doing?"

Ethan looked up at her, innocence written all over his face. "These are Jean's cards, aren't they? I just wanted to see them again. You're not supposed to use anyone else's deck, but I guess they belong to you now." His face sobered and she felt a fresh stab of pain for the loss of her aunt. "You don't have any use for them, do you?"

"No." Diana turned defiantly away, ignoring a jab of nausea in her stomach.

Why did it bother her so much that he was touching them? "The cats seem to like them," she said forced herself to say casually.

"Oh?"

"They've knocked over the box at least three times since I've been here. It was on the table in the den—where she used to keep it."

"Is that so?" He sounded a little skeptical. "I wonder how they did that. Did they knock over the African violet as well?"

She ignored the question—for it was one that had remained unasked, and thus unanswered, in her own mind—and focused on washing grapes and strawberries, then cutting thick slices of dark whole grain bread. She wanted to ask Ethan questions about his relationship with Aunt Jean, but her thoughts scattered when she realized he was shuffling the cards.

He seemed absorbed and thoughtful. Just as he finished shuffling, one slipped out of the deck and flipped to the floor under the table. Diana made an involuntary noise.

Ethan looked up, still holding the rest of the deck. "Something wrong?"

"No." She shook her head as if to clear the cobwebs, trying to still the churning in her belly.

It wouldn't be The High Priestess that fell out, she told herself. That would be crazy.

And why had the thought even crossed her mind?

"You dropped one," she said.

"Right." Still looking at her, he reached down blindly to pick it up.

When he straightened, she could no more have kept herself from asking than from taking another breath. But she tried to make her question sound casual. "What is it?"

Ethan glanced at the card, then up at her. "Death," he told her solemnly. "It's the Death card."

Diana felt the tension drain from her body. She almost smiled. "I see. Would you like some Dijon mustard with your bread and cheese?"

He looked at her, cocking his head to one side as if unsure what to make of her. "Lots of people would be freaked out if the Death card turned up," he said, still watching her.

Diana shrugged. "It doesn't bother me—I don't believe in that stuff."

"Thanks," he said as she placed the food in front of him: fresh bread, a green salad, fruit, and a few slices of cheese. "This looks much better than the peanut butter and jelly sandwich I would have made." He set down the card he'd been holding, resting it face-up.

The High Priestess.

Diana fumbled her plate as she put it down, clattering it onto the table.

Ethan looked at her, pinning her with sharp eyes.

"I thought you said it was the Death card." She sank onto a chair. *Don't be ridiculous.*

"I was just joking." His gaze was still focused on her. "Diana, why don't you tell me what's going on here."

"That—*card*," her voice came out angry, "*only* that card, keeps showing up. Randomly. Two—no, this is the third time now—three times in a *row*. It's too weird!"

He sat down in a chair across from her, linking his powerful hands loosely together and studying her carefully.

Nevertheless, he didn't seem to be looking at her as if she needed to be admitted somewhere with padded walls.

"That is definitely weird. And interesting. Tell me more about what happened."

She reluctantly told him about how she'd picked up the spilled deck three times, and how two of the times, one of the cats had been sitting there with their paw on *The High Priestess*. "It's as if they wanted me to see it. I know that sounds strange, but—"

Ethan shrugged. "I've heard much stranger things come out of your aunt's mouth—and Iva Bergstrom's too—and discussed with great seriousness. So, ah...do you know anything about The High Priestess?"

Diana shook her head.

"I'll get Jean's book. Sit there, I know where she keeps it. I'll be right back." He started to go, then to her shock, he stopped to brush her cheek with a forefinger. She was too confused to jerk away from the unexpected gesture. "There's nothing to be upset about, Diana. You just need to figure out what the message is."

And with that cryptic statement, he snagged a piece of cheese and left the room. *Message?*

Don't be absurd.

No longer hungry, Diana stared at the card. It looked the same, but this time she noticed more details: the woman—the priestess—seemed to be pushing a scroll under her cloak, as if to hide it. She sat in front of a backdrop of pomegranates and palm trees.

Ethan returned with an old, tattered book—one that was in similar condition to the one at the bookshop—and he had already marked a page with a forefinger.

With a brief smile, he took his seat, opened the book, and began to read: "'The High Priestess, Number Two. She is meant to represent the Guardian of the Unconsciousness. Her throne rests between our conscious mind and the innermost thoughts and knowledge of our *un*conscious mind.'"

Ethan looked up at Diana. "Well, that's a pretty clear message, if you ask me. She's telling you to look beyond the obvious—to allow your intuition and inner voice to guide you. Let your imagination and dreams abound, open your mind to the unknown, seek that which is concealed."

The nausea that had been lingering in the pit of her stomach lessened. "I don't believe in this kind of stuff," she repeated, shaking her head. "It's a bunch of bunk. *You* don't believe it, do you? That a deck of cards can tell the future?"

"No, no, I don't believe that..." He leaned forward, his eyes serious and his face sober. "But I know that there are people in this world who have abilities beyond our understanding...and I know that our unconscious minds have capabilities of which we've hardly scratched the surface. Your aunt was one of those people. And, to be blunt, she believed you are too—and that you've been stifling it. Repressing it."

"What a load of *crap*." Diana stood and folded her arms across her chest as if to hold in her fiercely pounding heart. "You're talking nonsense. I know Aunt Jean thought she had some crazy powers, and she liked to tell people's fortunes using Tarot cards, but you're talking about her as if you took her seriously. That's ridiculous!"

Ethan remained seated, tenting his fingers together, staring at them as if trying to decide what to say. "Your aunt had ESP—actually, to be more specific, she had precognitive capabilities. It's a fact, Diana. She had a gift." He looked up at her as if to gauge her reaction. "I know. I worked with her."

"What do you mean, you worked with her?" Diana shot back, ignoring the odd, sinking sensation that was tumbling in her middle. *Who is this guy?*

"As an offshoot of my profession, I have a specific interest in the supernatural and metaphysical—and I've—"

"Supernatural? You mean you're a *ghost hunter*?" Diana couldn't hold back an incredulous laugh. Then she sobered sharply. "Wait. What do you mean you *worked* with Aunt Jean?"

Wait. Could he be the "professor" friend Aunt Jean had mentioned? No wonder Diana had had the impression there was something going on between Aunt Jean and the professor—she just hadn't realized he was thirty years her junior.

And then like the dawn, it all became clear to her why this "Doctor" Ethan Murphy should have befriended an old, *wealthy* woman like Genevieve Fickler.

And why he should be here now, with her, Diana.

Fury lanced through her, replacing the shattering reality of their conversation, and she turned on him. "*That's* what you were after, then, wasn't it? Trying to fleece an old, gullible, *loaded* woman like my aunt by letting her believe she was psychic! Or that *you* were. What were you doing—talking to Uncle Tracer's so-called spirit for her?"

That made more sense. It was the oldest con in the books.

He blanched as she pulled to her feet and stood nearly nose-to-nose with him. She channeled all of her suppressed emotions into the accusations. "How much did you get from her? How much did you con her into giving you for your *work?*" Despite her passionate words, she used the same firm, cool persona she engaged when cross-examining a witness—and forgot that he was a dangerous and attractive man.

Even when his face darkened with an anger that matched her own, Diana did not back down. He rose, too, forcing her to step back from his chair, eyes flashing. "How dare you accuse me—"

"No," she shot back, folding her arms across her middle,

"how dare *you* come into this house uninvited—twice!—and how dare you pretend to be a great friend of my aunt's when I suspect all you really were after is money. What was your plan now that she's dead? To con her mousy, timid little niece into giving you more? By wooing and flirting and pretending to care?" That, she realized, was the worst of it—her old insecurities bubbling to the surface.

Ethan's lips were drawn together so tightly they nearly disappeared and the tic of a muscle wavered slowly, deliberately in his jaw. "You are a grand fool, Ms. Iverson. You certainly don't deserve the pride and affection your aunt had for you—not to mention the money. Good day."

He spun and walked heavily, angrily out of the house.

FOUR

ETHAN'S FURY with Diana Iverson was still simmering a day later, Saturday evening, when he drove to a place on the eastern side of town for dinner. He replayed their conversation over and over—wondering what it was that had caused Diana to go so quickly from confused and bewildered to a harpy, firing unfounded accusations at him. He'd never been so insulted in his life.

Tamping back a renewed sense of irritation, he pushed open the door of The Lakeside Grille and ambled across its worn, warped hardwood floor. The place was more popular with the locals than the tourists, mainly because it was a few miles outside of town and only about a half-step up from a dive...that is, until you tried the food.

The food, as Ethan often told the owners, was a national treasure. And as far as the residents of Wicks Hollow were concerned, the tourists could eat their fill at Trib's and the other small cafes that were in the downtown area and leave the Grille to them.

"What can I get for you tonight, Ethan, honey?" asked the

proprietress, Mirabella, as he took a seat at the thickly-shellacked bar.

"How about a tall B-Cubed? What's in now—the Wicks Hollow Wheat?"

She nodded in affirmation as he settled into his seat as she bustled over to two levers that dispensed the stingy choice of draft beers—a B-Cubed (whatever brew was current) or Budweiser. "I like that new shade of red on your hair, Bella," he called down to her. "You look like Flo from that old TV show *Alice*."

"Why thank you, honey," she patted the bouffant hairdo that sparkled like a ruby even in the dim light. The amount of hairspray she used to hold each swirl and curl in place was approximately as thick as the shellac on her bar. "Reggie likes it too—even better than that Dusty Gold color I was wearing a few months back."

She placed a tall glass of beer in front of him. "You eatin' here tonight, too, honey? Reggie made a good soup today—chicken barley—and we got a special with broiled whitefish and rice. There's always a hamburg or a basket of fresh-caught smelt, nice and crispy—and I got some potato salad and co'slaw if you want that too."

He sipped his beer and it went down very nicely. Bax was getting pretty good at his craft brewing. "How about a Reuben, with some coleslaw on the side," he suggested. "And a cup of that soup."

There was a holler from the back room and Bella rolled her eyes, making her penciled brows jump. "That Reggie. I wonder what he needs now. I'll be right back with your soup."

Despite the peremptory yell, Mirabella took her time making her way back into the kitchen. Her lime green dress splashed with daisies and thick white lapels hugged Rubenesque curves and the generous bottom that Reggie Bloom had fallen in love with twenty years ago...or so she'd boasted to Ethan many times.

Twenty years. That was a long time to be working and living with one person. Two decades of commitment, ups and downs, and so on.

His amusement faded. Any lingering desire for a long-term relationship had been destroyed at about the same time he signed his name to the divorce papers.

It was pretty much not gonna happen again—trusting a woman more than just casually dating—now that he'd been well and thoroughly screwed by his ex-wife Jenny. Not to mention Lexie, one of his female students who'd wanted to get in his pants badly enough to lie about it. Oh, and Colin—a friend and colleague who, as it turned out, had been boinking Jenny for more than a year before Ethan found out.

Nope. He was done with all of that.

The whole clusterfrack had been hell—and along with his guy friends, Genevieve Fickler was the one who'd listened to Ethan blather about it over more than a few six-packs. An unlikely pair they'd made, the two of them—along with Cady—sitting on the porch, talking for hours. Sometimes coherently, sometimes, he thought with a wry smile, not so coherently. But always heart-to-heart. Jean Fickler had been one smart, compassionate, *classy* lady—and he'd been half-serious when he told her he'd give up his moratorium on women for her if she would have had him.

Using one long forefinger, Ethan systematically wiped the condensation off his glass, his lips flattening. He'd come to the conclusion that, at the core, ninety-nine percent of women were either conniving, sneaky witches like Jenny and Lexie, or cold, haughty ones like Diana Iverson—and he figured he was safest staying far away from any of them. Except for a no-strings attached night once in a while. And even then, he'd had a moratorium on that for well over two years now.

He just hadn't been interested. In anyone.

A burst of raucous laughter caught his attention as a group of five women came through the door. They ranged in age from sixty to eighty, and he knew every one of them—as did most of the town regulars—for they were known as the Tuesday Ladies. And, *en masse*, they were a fearsome thing to behold...though slightly less so, now that they were missing one of their members.

Sad once more, he slid off his stool, beer in hand, intending to pay his regards before his meal came and was interrupted by the inevitable demands to join them.

"Ethan! There you are. Where have you been?" Juanita Alecita plumped heavily into her seat—a daring move for a woman whose generous size threatened the stability of the chair—as her perfectly manicured nails fluttered with indignation. For once, she didn't have her little dog with her. "We expected you back weeks ago."

"You missed the funeral," growled Maxine Took, who was turning eighty next week but still possessed eagle eyes and super-bionic hearing. "Have a seat, young man." She pointed a dark, arthritic finger to an empty chair next to her. "And tell us how you're doin'. You must be missin' Jean."

"I'd have been at the funeral if I'd known about it," Ethan said soberly, doing as directed and taking a seat. He cast a helpless look over at Mirabella, who was already bringing his soup and table settings to him. Obviously, he wasn't going anywhere anytime soon. "I was in Peru, and didn't hear about anything till I got back here just this past Wednesday night."

Iva Bergstrom reached over and patted his hand with her soft one. "It was quite a shock to all of us. She seemed so healthy and vibrant. We miss her something awful."

"She went in her sleep," said Orbra in that matter-of-fact way she had. Though she was a tall, sturdy Dutch woman and loomed over her companions—along with most other people—she had a practical manner that was neither too soft nor too overbearing. "That'd be the way I want to go, truth be told."

They all murmured agreement, which gave Ethan a moment to scarf down some of the most excellent soup. Then Mirabella came over to deliver his sandwich and take their orders—which became a web of arguments, alterations, and demands. Mostly from Maxine Took.

"You coming on Tuesday?" she demanded as soon as Mirabella made her escape.

"Wouldn't miss it for the world," Ethan replied. Because if he didn't attend her annual birthday party, she'd never let him live it down. And even though he was only able to live in Wicks Hollow for less than six months out of the year, that was six months of hell he didn't want to experience.

"Good." She smacked her lips in satisfaction, then spun her attention back to Iva. "Is that man of yours coming too?"

"Man?" Ethan lifted his brows and looked at Iva, who was blushing prettily. "I don't know anything about this."

Cherry Wilder, who owned the yoga studio and reminded him of a slightly older but still very hot Sharon Stone, spoke up. "She met him a few months ago—when was it? In April? And, come to think of it, I haven't seen Iva at a hatha class since. I think she's trying out all the yoga asanas at home. With Hollis. Aren't you, Iva?"

"A lady never kisses and tells," Iva replied, fluttering her eyelashes.

"You once were snow white," teased Cherry. "And then you drifted."

"Now that sounds more like you. A *long* time ago," retorted her friend primly.

"If the shoe fits," Cherry agreed, laughing, and the others joined her.

"Oh, look! It's Diana!" Maxine lumbered to her feet, cane clattering and table jolting.

But Ethan, who'd been facing the door, had already seen her come in.

Damn it. Why wasn't she and her companion—a handsome, well-dressed man with thinning hair and presumably the Jonathan she'd been on the phone with the other day—at Trib's? That place seemed much more their style.

In fact, Ethan was honest enough to acknowledge he'd chosen the Grille tonight because he *assumed* they'd be at the trendiest restaurant in town. Not at this off-the-beaten-path place.

Good thing he'd eaten most of his meal before the couple showed up and put off his appetite.

Maxine waved her arm vigorously, its loose skin flapping with the effort. "Diana! Over here!"

Because he was watching, Ethan saw the range of reaction as it swept her expression: surprise, exasperation, then reluctance. But she spoke to her companion, and they both came over wearing warm, genuine smiles. He gave her credit for that.

"Meet the Tuesday Ladies," she said, sweeping her arm to encompass the group around the table. "All friends of my Aunt Jean. Cherry, Iva, Juanita, Orbra and Maxine. Ladies, this is my—this is Jonathan Wertinger."

"The Tuesday Ladies?" asked Wertinger as he greeted each one in turn with a charming smile and a personal comment. "I'm sure there's a story about that."

Ethan, not being a member of the ladies club, had heretofore been ignored. And thus the flurry of introductions and greetings, interspersed with demands and directions from Maxine, had allowed him the luxury of observing unnoticed.

As he took in Diana's figure with an impersonal gaze, Ethan decided—oh so objectively—that dark purple was a great color for her. The rich fabric next to her creamy skin made it look almost luminescent, while pushing the color of her thick, curling hair closer to black, and her blue eyes nearly to violet. The not too-tight cut of the dress didn't hurt either, he thought, allowing his attention to wander idly over her curves while she was involved in greeting the ladies. Her slender arms were toned and unadorned except for a wide silver bangle at a narrow wrist. And best of all, Diana's long neck was slender and elegant, bared by the short tousle of inky hair—making her exposed nape look like the perfect spot to place a kiss.

When Ethan finished his leisurely perusal and turned his gaze to her companion, his eyes locked with those of Diana's boyfriend.

Oops. He smiled as if he didn't see the chill in the man's eyes and offered a hand from his relaxed seat in the chair. "I'm Ethan Murphy—obviously not a member of the Tuesday Ladies. Glad to meet you."

"Doctor Jonathan Wertinger," the man replied coolly, shaking his hand with a firm grip. Because Ethan hadn't bothered to stand and remained lounging in his chair, the man was required to step closer to him.

Wertinger had sharp, intelligent eyes and enough bravado to eye his imagined rival with frosty interest. Ethan could have silently signaled that he had no designs—*definitely not*—on his girlfriend, but since he didn't like the man on sight, he decided it would be far more entertaining to let him wonder.

Ethan lifted his beer, sipping as he smiled to himself. That was exactly the type of thing his sister Fiona would do: delicately, gently stir the pot. Just for the hell of it.

Maybe they weren't so different after all.

Because of this, Ethan was warmer and more charming than he felt when he stood to greet her. "Hello, Diana. You look nice tonight."

"Ethan," she said in a studiously neutral voice. "Thank you. Did you meet Jonathan?"

Tension radiated from her, and he sensed it wasn't directed at him—which was a mild surprise, considering the harsh words they'd exchanged yesterday. Curious, and suddenly even more relaxed, Ethan snagged a chair from the table next to them and brought it over next to his. "I did meet your Dr. Wertinger. Here's a chair—aren't you going to join us?"

As he'd intended, Maxine took up the idea and began to shove chairs and tables around with surprising strength to make room for the two of them, leaving Ethan to watch in amusement as Diana realized she'd completely lost control of the situation.

She noticed and cut him an Arctic stare, then she angled away in a blatant dismissal of Ethan and returned her attention to the ladies.

As Diana sat, Ethan was unwillingly captivated as she absently tucked her hair behind an ear, revealing a large pearl stud earring. The tip of her tamed curl peeked out from beneath the earlobe, just brushing the pearl. Even in the dim light of the restaurant, the luminescence of the jewel and the shiny embrace of her hair struck him as a combination of classic beauty and elegance. The rest of it, rising in soft waves from her forehead and brushing her bare nape, was tousled and full—messy, a little wild, and very sensual. All he could think was: sex hair.

That souring thought had him glancing at Wertinger, then Maxine's accusatory shriek snagged his attention.

"You aren't going to sell Genevieve's house are you?"

"I haven't decided what I'm going to do with the house yet. I have a lot of paperwork to go through before I can make a final decision anyway." Diana smoothed the skirt of her aubergine-colored shift, relieved when she felt the weight of Ethan's gaze move away.

She was incredulous that he would just sit there, as calmly and innocently as if nothing had transpired between them and she hadn't uncovered his ulterior motives. Didn't the man have any sense of shame?

Before Maxine, Iva, or any of the others could comment on her vague response, Jonathan came to her rescue. "It's only been a few weeks since Genevieve passed," he said in his calm, even voice. "I'm certain Diana will make the right decision once she's had the chance to think things over."

Diana smiled gratefully at him, but when Jonathan leaned closer to her so his shoulder pushed companionably against hers, she suddenly and inexplicably felt claustrophobic. As she shifted slightly away from her fiancé, she felt Ethan's attention return to her—an amused smile twitching his mouth. It seemed as though he was enjoying some joke at her expense, and she couldn't help but bristle at his arrogant, patronizing look.

If she weren't so tactful—and fully aware of the ramifications of slander—she'd bring the whole subject up again, right here, about his questionable relationship with Aunt Jean. Then she'd see if he still looked so benevolent and charming.

And who could know, perhaps he'd been working on one of the other old ladies. Why else would he be having dinner with a group of them on a Saturday night?

At that moment, Ethan stood, taking Maxine Took's hand

in his. "It's always a pleasure to see you ladies. Thank you for a wonderful evening."

He bid each of the others farewell, and when he finally turned that smile and those warm, crinkling eyes toward Diana, for a moment she, too, was almost disarmed by them.

"It was nice to see you again," she told him, ignoring the fact that his grip was firm and warm and made her uncomfortably aware of the heat of his touch.

"Enjoy your evening," he said.

Diana expected to feel more relaxed after he left, but she wasn't. Instead, she focused on getting through the meal without being cross-examined by Aunt Jean's friends. That was impossible, but at least she was able to turn the conversation back around more often than not.

"I'll see you Tuesday night," Maxine said when Diana and Jonathan finally rose to leave.

"Tuesday?" Jonathan asked as they left the Grille. "What's Tuesday?"

"Maxine's birthday party. It's a big deal here—"

"I thought you'd be back in Chicago by then. In fact, I expected you'd go back with me tomorrow."

She looked across the roof of her car at him as she opened the door. "I don't know why you thought that, Jonathan."

He frowned, then climbed in. She'd insisted on driving, and being denied that bit of control had put him in an irritated mood from the beginning.

With a start, Diana realized she didn't care in the least, and the fact almost made her smile.

"How long *are* you planning to stay here?" he asked as she pulled out of the parking lot. "Surely you can't be away from work that long anyway. Won't McNillan have a problem with that?"

"McNillan told me to take some time before the AXT case

gets going. So I am." Diana purposely declined to answer his first question—partly because she didn't know the answer.

Jonathan murmured something under his breath, then he reached over and touched her arm. "Diana, I—er—made some plans for tonight. For us."

"Plans?"

He smiled a little bashfully. "I booked us a room at that fancy boutique hotel south of town—The Worthington Inn."

"Tonight? Why? What's wrong with Aunt Jean's house?" She braked at the stop sign and turned to look at him.

"Nothing. I just thought it would be nice to stay somewhere fancy, where we would be treated like guests. There's a claw-footed hot tub in the room, and they promised breakfast in bed, and—" He sighed. "All right, I'll be honest. I also thought it would be a little strange staying in the house where she died. That's all. She did die there, right? Didn't you tell me that?"

"She did. And I haven't found it strange at all," Diana said.

But that was a cold, hard lie.

For, early this morning, she'd awakened from another terrible nightmare. She remembered how difficult it had been to battle herself awake this time, to claw her way out of the dream where heavy darkness suffocated her.

A sob jerked from deep inside her chest as she'd struggled to bring herself back from the nightmare. Her hair was plastered to cheeks damp with sweat, her skin clammy with fear, and her breath catching and rasping in the dead silence.

Though the dream ebbed at last, the fear, the visions, and the sense of terror did not. And at last, as she stared into the darkest part of the night, Diana finally realized what the awful sensation she'd been dreaming about was: the heavy, claustrophobic sense of being smothered, of heavy softness pressing down, over and into her nose and mouth as her arms and legs fought helplessly, unable to pull it away, unable to free herself from the dull, hot staleness of stunted air.

But what had stayed with her—all day—was the instant before she fully shook herself from the nightmare's grip. A remnant of the dream had crystallized in her mind with clarity so perfect, so sudden and perfect, it was as though she was looking at a film before her eyes.

Only it had been in her head, not on any screen anywhere.

It was Aunt Jean on the screen.

No, *she* was Jean—she, Diana, *was* Jean: struggling against a heavy force that pressed against her face, filled her nostrils, silenced her gaping, gasping mouth…then she slowed, weakened, succumbing to the inevitable end…then sagged into stillness. Darkness. Death.

When she realized this in those early, dark hours of the morning, Diana's whole world stopped. Her mind and body had gone deathly, silently still.

Even the murmur of her heart, the shallowness of her breathing, the trembling of her nerves paused, and an incredible certainty flooded her. She knew.

She knew.

"Diana? Are you going to drive or are we going to sit here all night?" Jonathan's voice jolted her back to the moment. She shoved away the dark memories and the horrifying realization that had somehow settled in her mind.

"Sorry. I thought I saw—I thought that was a deer over there," she replied.

"Well, you've been sitting here for long enough for the deer to cross—if there even was one. Let's go. I'm tired. It's been a long week."

It was the memory of the ugly dream that quashed the last bit of her reluctance to drive them to the Worthington Inn. She did not want to be sleeping next to Jonathan and be awakened by that sort of horrible nightmare—and have to explain to him.

She was still trying to fully comprehend it herself.

"I wasn't completely honest with you," Jonathan said once they were alone in the small, elegant suite he'd booked for them. It was beautifully decorated with gleaming antiques—glossy mahogany and maple furnishings, including a huge four-poster bed swathed in vintage lace. A large silver bucket held a chilling bottle of champagne next to a massive vase spilling with fresh flowers and two glass flutes, ready for the bubbly.

Jonathan's serious tone pulled Diana from her private thoughts, making her insides squish nervously. "What do you mean? Honest about what?" Was he about to confess more indiscretions?

"About why I wanted to stay here tonight." He had an almost bashful look on his face, which made her even more nervous.

"Well, tell me," she said, her apprehension making her tone sharp.

Jonathan looked at her with a wounded expression, then smoothed it into a smile. "I wanted tonight to be special, because...I thought it was time we made it official. Time that you had a ring."

That was when she noticed the dark blue velvet box he held.

"Jonathan," she said, both horrified and shocked. "I—I'm not sure..."

"Diana, you know I love you." He opened the box to reveal a glittering diamond sitting proudly in its tall, platinum setting. "You're the only woman I love and want."

"What about Valerie?" She couldn't stop herself. Though the ring was gorgeous—Jonathan did have impeccable taste—

she couldn't bring herself to touch the square cut diamond. She felt almost repelled by it.

"Dammit," he said, his voice tight. "When are you going to stop bringing that up? It's over, it's done, it's—"

"It's been less than a month," she said calmly. "I saw you together. That's not the sort of thing that one forgets easily."

He seemed to need a moment to decide how to react, and when he spoke again, his voice was quiet and soft. "Let's not talk about that tonight. Let's not fight…I haven't seen you all week."

Taking her hand, he tugged her to him. "I've missed you, darling," he murmured into her hair. "So much."

Diana slid her arms around his waist and dropped her head onto his shoulder, willing herself to stay in the moment, to *be* with him. To let it go.

But she couldn't relax, she couldn't give in to the affection and emotion she'd once had.

She felt nothing. Absolutely nothing.

Bitter tears filled her eyes and she blinked them back, furious once again with him for breaking her trust, and with herself for this empty, bland feeling toward him.

And grief over the loss.

He dropped a kiss into her hair, then tilted his head back to kiss her on the mouth. Closed lips, warm and dry, the kiss was a formality, a prelude to what would follow—or what he clearly hoped would follow.

Diana had never been a particularly eager lover. Sex could be messy, and she worried about how she looked naked, along with a variety of other things—but now she felt a complete absence of interest. She felt nothing. Not even aversion.

Just…nothing.

"Why don't you come to bed now," he suggested in her

ear, his mouth slipping to kiss a tender spot on her neck. "I'd like to see you wearing the ring...and nothing else."

Diana wanted to *want* to go with him. She wanted things to be all right. She didn't want this blank feeling rising between them, this sense of loss and confusion and grief.

"I..." She pulled away, looking down at the boxed ring he'd set on the table. "Not tonight, Jonathan."

"What do you mean, not tonight?" He sounded shocked and irritated. "I just asked you to marry me, Diana! There's *champagne*. And I came all the way up here to see you. I have to go back tomorrow."

"I'm still trying to deal with what happened. You have to understand it's not as simple as giving me a diamond ring and that means everything's over with and forgotten. Plus, I'm still grieving for Aunt Jean. You're going to have to give me some time."

He was looking at her with shocked eyes. "I see," he said after a moment. "All right. All right, I guess I must have just... rushed things a little. Just...come to bed. We can just sleep. I want to be near you."

Diana nodded. She'd give him that, at least.

And maybe, just maybe, in the morning she'd wake up next to him and things would be better.

Sunday mornings were lazy ones at the Murphy household. Ethan finally rolled out of bed—to Cady's immense relief—at ten o'clock, and staggered sleepily to the door to let the prancing dog out to do her business.

He stood in the doorway, arms folded over his bare chest and enjoyed the feel of the morning breeze over his naked body. Yawning, he stretched one arm straight into the air, and let it drop to scratch his head, then to his rump, then to adjust his balls. It was heaven living in a place where you could walk in your back yard naked.

Cady finished her business and decided she wanted to play, and Ethan, now fully awake, stepped off the porch onto the lawn. His yard was a half-acre of clipped velvety grass, studded with a few trees and surrounded by sky-scraping pines and heavy woods—and was less comfortable in the evenings than the morning because of the flies and mosquitoes. Wicks Lake glittered blue just down a small incline, between pines and maples and cottonwoods.

"Come on, Cady, let's go swimming." He grabbed a pair of shorts that hung over a chair on the deck.

At the suggestion, the lab dropped the stick with which she'd been dancing about, and tore down the incline, splashing gleefully into the water. Though he didn't strictly need them, Ethan pulled on the shorts, then followed Cady down a cedar chip path. He knew better than to hesitate when he got to the bottom, so he dove off his dock into the lake.

He surfaced, whooping from the shock, and whipped his hair back. Cady paddled up next to him, thumping against him with her paws (and occasionally, with a nail), then headed back toward the shore where she could chase a goose. Ethan swam out from the tree-lined, shady shore and turned to look back.

His gaze went to the white clapboard house and its detached garage just a half-mile down from his. Jean's house sat on a bigger hill than his cabin's, and had a larger yard cleared of trees. Ethan could even see Diana's pale gold Lexus sitting in the drive, presumably because Jean's car was still in the garage.

He floated on his back, narrowing his eyes against the sun. He tried to stop the mental image—but there it was: the ice-queen and her cardiologist, messing up those lacy pillows and embroidered sheets on that high Victorian bed.

Disgust roiled inside him once again—anger for Genevieve, and annoyance with himself. Although Diana's accusations had infuriated him at the time, he'd since come to realize that he didn't give a rat's behind what she thought about him...

And he actually felt more than a bit smug, knowing that she thought the worst of him while he *knew* the worst of her.

Ethan allowed himself to sink under the lake's surface, then rise back up and let the water plaster his hair back. Cady was paddling back out to him, her nose just above the water, whuffling and snuffling. "Wanna go back?" he asked, then did a shallow dive, resurfacing several feet away.

They stumbled to shore at the same time, Cady shaking herself from head to tail as Ethan tossed his hair back and wiped the water from his eyes. They hurried back to the house, refreshed and hungry.

Just as they stepped onto the screened-in porch, Ethan heard his cell phone ringing from inside. He snagged a towel slung over a chair, pointed a finger at a dripping Cady and ordered, "Park it." He looked at his phone and saw that Joe Longbow was calling. "Yo."

"Hey, buddy, get your lazy ass outta bed and let's go catch us some walleye," said Joe. "It's practically noon."

"Hey, man, I've been up and swimming already."

"Great. Well, I hope you didn't scare away all the fish. Bax and I—and that new guy, Declan—'ll be over in fifteen with the worms, brews, and sandwiches if you supply the boat and the poles." Joe Longbow's voice had such a drawl to it that even when he was furious, the end of the sentence didn't catch up to the beginning until the next day.

"Sure sounds better than what I had planned—which was

mulching around the trees. Make sure you bring one of Mirabella's corned beef sandwiches for me. A big thick one. With lots of dressing." Ethan hung up the phone, feeling pretty content.

Sure, the walleye or pike didn't bite much at noon, but fishing was just an excuse to sit in the boat and relax with a couple of buddies, and jump in the lake when it got too hot.

True to his word—for he drove faster than he spoke—Joe Cap, as he was commonly called, pealed down the gravel drive in his shiny, nick-free, black F10 pickup minutes later. Baxter James, creator of Baxter's Beatnik Brews, sat in the front seat, holding onto the granny handle. In the hop seat behind was another guy Ethan didn't know.

Baxter was a little older than Ethan—mid-thirties—and hit at just under six feet tall. He kept his afro shaved almost to the scalp but allowed his precisely-shaped, trimmed-daily goatee and mustache to grow a little longer. He was a freelance journalist and wrote for several local papers, including the *Grand Rapids Press*, while trying to build his microbrew business on the side. So far, he'd been successful juggling both; but as Baxter often bemoaned, he'd like to have a woman in the mix to juggle too.

The third guy was a well-built man about their age as well. He had dark auburn hair and broad shoulders. His short sleeves displayed muscles that would probably make the ladies swoon and had Ethan automatically flexing his own.

"Declan Zyler," said the newcomer, offering his hand to Ethan. "Appreciate you letting me come along today."

"Dec just moved here. He's got a daughter at the high school and he's going to be doing the single-dad thing."

"Well, I wish you the best with that," Ethan said with a grin as they shook hands. "A teenage daughter sounds…fun."

Declan laughed and nodded. "Yeah. Talk about making my way blindly."

"That looks like it hurt," Ethan commented when he noticed a burn on the guy's forearm.

"Hazard of the trade," he replied. "I'm a blacksmith. Do a lot of restoration and repair."

"He just finished some work for Trib," Joe Cap said, walking over with a handful of rods and a large tackle box in the other hand.

"Hey, be careful with those." Ethan was distracted as Baxter hefted out a large cooler that clinked with beer bottles and ice. "We don't want any casualties."

"Only empty bottles," replied Joe Cap. Almost fifty, happily married with three kids—and going gray to prove it, as he was often heard to say—Joe was an easy-going guy unless something threatened the peace or safety of Wicks Hollow. Then, as the town's police chief, he drew on his experience as a Marine in the first Iraq war and handily took care of business.

Taking the tackle box and three fishing poles, along with a net and a six-pack, Ethan looked at the older guy. "So you're not on today, Joe Cap? Or is that all just for Bax and Declan and me?" He gestured to the beer. "*Might* be enough for the three of us." He grinned.

"Naw," said Joe, adjusting his Tigers ball cap. "We had enough excitement down the station the last month, with Bella and Reggie's till bein' broken into, and Jean Fickler bein' found, and a fender-bender down over on 69 with some drunk tourists, that I decided to give myself the day off. Helga's on today."

The four men trudged down the incline with their supplies, with Cady tramping through the brush in a zigzag toward the lake.

"Yeah," Ethan said as he tossed the tackle box into a leaky

dinghy that was only useful for fishing. His bright blue canoe sat upside down on its stand near the shore. "That's too bad about Jean. I didn't hear about it till I got back here." He took and loaded the beer crate from Baxter, then a big-ass cooler with their lunch from Declan.

"I didn't know if you'd get the message—where were you?" Joe said as he checked that the fishing pole lines were hooked tight. "The armpit of Brazil or something? I figured it'd cost too much to call your cell when you're out in the jungle."

"Peru," Ethan told his friend. "Macchu Picchu. It was pretty rustic there."

"You seen her niece here in town?" Joe pulled off the ball cap, scratched his head, then yanked the hat back down. "She's pretty hot, and now she's loaded, too."

Ethan stepped into the softly rocking boat. "Maybe hot looking, but she can freeze your balls with a look. Besides, I don't think Penny would take too kindly to hearing her husband call another woman hot."

Joe actually looked a bit frightened at the thought, then his face shifted into a grin that matched his drawl as he settled in the prow of the boat. "Naw, Ethan, I'm not looking for me—I'm looking for you—and Baxter and Declan, here, too. Though Bax here's been sniffing around that Emily Delton for a couple years now, huh? How's it going, there, Bax?"

"I keep hoping she'll invite me to come up for a massage at the spa, but hasn't happened yet," replied the brewmaster with a mock wounded smile. Emily Delton owned a fancy-schmancy spa and salon on the edge of Wicks Hollow. Fiona raved about something they did there called an aromatherapy mud wrap, which to Ethan sounded sticky and stinky.

"Doesn't Emily have a teenager, too, Dec? Don't know why you'd want to get involved with someone who's got one of those, Baxter." Cap spoke from experience, as he and Penny had seventeen-year-old twins and a fourteen-year-old. "But what about you, Murph? How long's it been since you and Jenny split up? Two years? You've had that—what'd ya call it?—moratorium thing going on for long enough. You got t'be mighty lonely in that big old cabin."

"Don't be an ass, Cap. My cabin's not that big, and yes, I'm still staying far away from any females. Especially that ice-queen Diana Iverson. Cady and I are just fine all by ourselves." Without waiting for Baxter to sit, Ethan shoved the boat away from the dock with enough force to set it rocking. "Besides, she's got a boyfriend."

"Geez, be careful there, Murph." Baxter glanced at him from under the brim of his sun-bleached cowboy hat as he sat down just before he tipped over the side. "Did you say she's an ice-queen? What happened? She seemed nice when I met her."

"I thought so too," Joe Cap drawled from his safer position at the front of the boat. "Quiet, and a little fancy, but nice enough."

Ethan chose a pole and unlatched the hook from its moor through one of the rings. Digging into a Styrofoam carton of rich black soil, he pulled out a squirming worm and wove it onto the hook. Then, setting it down, he gave the oars two powerful strokes, shooting them out toward the middle of the lake. "You meet her at the funeral?"

"Yeah—you know, I was the one found Jean, and it didn't seem right not to go." Joe baited his own hook as he added as hastily as he ever did, "Not that I wouldn't've not gone anyway, yannow. She was a real nice lady, and Penny liked her a lot."

"You said you don't like the niece—but you weren't at the funeral," said Baxter, popping the top of one of his beers. The bottles were unlabeled, which meant they were a "mystery brew"—still in the testing phase. "When'd you meet her,

Murph? Here. Try one of these—I'm doing an amber this month. Gonna call it Red Hart—hart like a deer, you know, not the one here." He thumped his chest unnecessarily.

Ethan took the bottle and set it between his feet so he could row. "I didn't even know Jean died till I showed up at her house the other night. I surprised the hell out of the niece 'cause she didn't take too kindly to me walking in like I always do." Ethan folded the oars back into the boat and looked out over the sparkling lake as they slowed to a mere drift. The clapboard house glinted like a white beacon in the noon sun and he looked away.

"I'll bet she didn't. Coming from a big city like Chicago, as she does," Baxter said, giving him a side-eye. "She probably was a little taken aback by a strange man walking into her house."

Ethan frowned at his buddy as Joe Cap grunted in something like agreement and Declan gave a bark of laughter. *Well, hell.* He hadn't *known* Jean wasn't there, and that Diana was, for chrissake.

The blacksmith dumped the anchor into the water with a minor splash and, with a quick flick of his wrist, sent a long, smooth cast over the lake. The fishing line glinted like a cobweb in the sunlight, then settled over and into the depths of blue.

"So you found Jean, huh?" Ethan's line soared in a different direction, and was followed by Bax's expert cast, then Joe's...and all was peaceful. The waves lapped gently against the side of the dingy. "How'd that happen?"

"Yeah. She didn't show for a doctor appointment on that Friday, and Gallagher got worried and called the station. I went down and got into the house and found her. Poor old woman—die alone like that. Looked like she'd been dead a while. At least a day."

"She died in her sleep is what Diana told me."

"Yep, so it appeared."

"At least she didn't go through any pain," Declan mused.

"Nope. Hope not." Joe's attention was not fixed on the fishing line he owned. Nor his beer, Ethan noticed. His lips were pursed like he was gnawing on something.

"Everything all right, there, Cap?"

"Mm." He thought about it for a moment, staring out at the lake. "She had a heart problem—documented in her medical records. There was no sign of struggle, of forced entry, of robbery...but something don't seem right about it. It's been bothering me...but I dunno what it is." He sighed, then abruptly jerked to attention when one of the silvery lines shivered. "Bax, hell, wake up—you got one!"

The other man jolted and grabbed his arching pole before it went overside. Ethan sipped his beer—the Red Hart was pretty good; much better than the raspberry stout he'd sampled last time Baxter tried to get fancy—and watched as his buddy began to manipulate the reel: in and out, in and out...pull 'em in...slowly let it out...all in a natural rhythm that echoed the lapping of waves against the boat.

Something about Jean's death didn't sit right with Joe Cap...which could explain why Ethan himself had felt so unsettled. Had something more sinister happened to Jean that night?

Was that why those Tarot cards had been teasing Diana so much? He didn't believe it was a coincidence that the same card had shown up three times. Not at all. The problem was getting Miss Facts and Logic to believe it.

Hell, he thought as the tip of his pole began to bounce, if anyone were to bring a message from the grave, it would be Genevieve Fickler.

The wind rushed through the Lexus's moon roof, tossing Diana's hair with the same abandon as her mind zipped through her thoughts. She was cruising at a speedy seventy miles per hour along Interstate 69 after dropping Jonathan off to catch his late afternoon flight.

As she maneuvered the car around smooth curves and up and down slight inclines, Diana considered the other question that had been brooding in her mind since her dream yesterday: *Was* it possible? Had Aunt Jean been smothered in her own bed?

And could it have been Ethan Murphy who'd done it?

Keeping her lawyer hat on, and refusing to allow her dislike of the man—or her reluctant attraction to him—to color her thoughts, Diana considered the situation.

First of all, she was basing this on a dream. A mere dream.

But, yes, a terrifyingly real one. One that she'd had every night since she arrived in Aunt Jean's house, even though she hadn't immediately recognized it for what it was. And yesterday morning, she'd awakened with a certainty that even she couldn't shake, using her logical, science-based mind.

If it were true, if Aunt Jean had been smothered —*murdered*—who could have done it? And why?

Ethan had known Jean well. Well enough to walk into her house uninvited. He obviously hadn't known she was dead until Diana told him…but, then…if he *had* killed her and he knew she was dead, he would have walked into the house intending for Diana to *think* he had that kind of freedom. And playing dumb—as a sort of alibi?

He said he'd been out of the country, but of course that might not be true. She wondered how she could find out for sure.

Yet he knew where the house key was hidden—so obviously Aunt Jean had trusted him. Tapping her finger against the steering wheel, Diana frowned. Poor Aunt Jean…so gullible and trusting to be taken in by a pretty face.

But now that she was dead, Ethan Murphy's source of money would also be gone, for Diana knew he hadn't been named in the will. She and the local animal shelter run by Melvin Horner were the only beneficiaries. So what motive was there for someone to kill Aunt Jean if they weren't going to inherit any of her money?

Ethan had been friendly to Diana—but not overly so, as if he were trying to inveigle his way into her good graces in order to keep the flow of money going.

She grimaced. If he had meant to cozy up to her, he'd definitely blundered that part of it, for it seemed he only knew how to rub her the wrong way.

He didn't appear to have a very favorable opinion of her either, based on his seething words before he left Aunt Jean's the other night: *You're a fool. You don't deserve a bit of the pride and affection your aunt had for you.*

But, then again…she'd caught him studying her at the Grille last night. She wouldn't lie to herself—that steady, avid gaze had caused her fingers to become clumsy and her heart to pump just a little faster.

Even now, her heart fumbled a beat at the memory. That had been a dangerous look, coming from a dangerous man.

So caught up was she in her train of thought that she almost missed the road leading to the north end of Wicks Lake. Slowing the car, she made the turn and forced her thoughts onto a different track. As she navigated along the paved two-lane road, Diana looked to her right and was just able to see glimpses of the dark blue of the sinuous lake. The sun was low in the sky, and dropping nearly as quickly as she was driving. Soon, she wouldn't be able to see the water at all through the darkness.

The forest was so dense along the lake that the houses were completely private—you couldn't see the lights of a neighbor's though the trees at night unless you were on the lake. Diana didn't mind the isolation, but as she turned onto the dirt lane that led to the house, she realized just how far away from civilization she was.

Ethan Murphy lived on the lake too, for he'd shown her how, when the dirt road made a triple fork near the lake, she turned right and he turned left to go slightly more south. Nevertheless, there was no more than a mile as the crow flew between their houses.

Somehow, the thought that Ethan Murphy lived so nearby both relieved and disturbed her.

The Lexus's headlights cut beams through sudden, enveloping darkness as the car bumped down the road through the forest. The intermittent winks of fireflies broke the solid black, and twice she saw reflections of the eyes of some critter crouched by the side of the road. Of necessity, she drove slowly—between the potholes, the curves of the road, and the possible intrusion of deer, she had no choice but to do so. Bugs collected, thick and angry, in the lights, and as a result splashed onto the windshield like raindrops. *So much for late-night swimming*, Diana mused, shuddering at the thought of moths, mosquitoes, and deer flies swarming around her.

It was nearly pitch-black by now, and Diana was thankful that she'd left a porch light on, as well as two lights in the house. For, as she got closer, she began to feel inexplicably unsettled. Even nervous.

When she came to the fork in the lane, she tossed a glance toward the darkness where Ethan's house would be and was surprised and, to be honest, relieved to see the faint glimmer of light through the forest. He was closer than she'd realized.

But that strange, prickling feeling of foreboding still disturbed her as she turned onto the tire-track lane that led to Aunt Jean's house. If she kept the house—which she wasn't certain she would—she'd get this driveway paved. Or something.

But she wasn't going to keep the house.

She didn't think.

Driving here required her full attention, as tree limbs brushed into the car's path and the ruts were enough to jounce the vehicle like a rough boat ride, even when it crept along at five miles per hour. How did Aunt Jean do this in the winter? She must have a four-wheel drive in the garage. Diana smelled a skunk from somewhere in the darkness—someone or something had gotten sprayed, and *whew!*—it was nearby.

The rank, musky scent was still strong in the air when she pulled up a slight incline into the clearing. The sedate clapboard house, with its three gables and large wrap-around porch and detached garage, sat in the center of an open area surrounded by trees.

In darkness.

Diana pulled the car up next to the pitch-black house and stared, her heart lodged in her throat. She *knew* she'd left the lights on—on the porch, and in the front hall and kitchen. She turned off the ignition and sat in the car for a moment, unease kneading her stomach.

Why was she so creeped out?

Steeling herself, telling her odd nervousness to go away, she slowly opened the car door. Perhaps she'd meant to turn on the lights, and had forgotten. But, no, she distinctly remembered going into the kitchen to turn on the over-the-sink light just before she walked out to take Jonathan to the airport.

Maybe the power had gone out. Though she wasn't sure if that would be a relief or not.

Diana grasped the door handle and pulled the latch to open it, stepping into the night air. There hadn't been a storm, but out here in the middle of nowhere, there could be other reasons for a power outage.

But Ethan Murphy's lights had been on.

He probably had a generator.

The darkness of the forest hovered at the far edges of the open yard, and she glanced up to see the glittering display of stars. The Milky Way and a quarter-moon lit the clearing nearly as well as a porch light would, bolstering her flagging courage. She muddled through her key ring and located the key to the front door, then grabbed her handbag and stepped lightly up the porch steps.

It was a bit of a struggle to fit the key into the lock, shadowed as it was, and she realized later she could have used her cell phone light. Once the key slid into place, she had to rotate it one way, then the other, and back again before the knob would turn.

Finally, the door caved open into the dark house and Diana stepped in gingerly, her heart still doing odd things in her chest. She felt along the wall for a nearby light switch, and just as she was about to flick it on, she caught a movement out of the corner of her eye.

Whirling, she gasped at the sight of the tall, murky silhouette, which froze. Then it was a flurry of movement, rushing toward her. A powerful shove sent her slamming full-force into the wall, the impact knocking all of the breath from her body. Diana slid to the floor, bracing for another blow as she blindly grasped for something to use as a weapon. But the intruder dashed past her—out the open door, stomping across the wooden porch and thudding down the steps.

Shaking, Diana managed to struggle to her feet in time to rush to the door and see a figure dashing into the woods.

Into the woods toward Ethan Murphy's house.

FIVE

FIERCE ANGER SWEPT OVER DIANA, and all of her fear slid away. *Oh no you don't!*

Without a second thought, she picked up the keys, turned on the foyer light, and slammed out the front door. Not even bothering to lock it behind her, she ran down the steps, gripping the key chain, her lips tight and her eyebrows puckered so firmly that her head ached even more than from hitting the wall.

This was going to stop.

She yanked the car door shut behind her to punctuate her fury and determination, and cranked the key so far that the engine ground for a split-second before it caught. The tires spewed gravel from the drive into the air, raining onto the porch as she turned the Lexus around and started down the bumpy, winding lane.

Driving much faster than she had on her arrival, Diana had little care for the scrapes and nicks her beloved gold car would get from the tree branches. She rammed her head on the ceiling when she took one of the potholes too quickly.

But she didn't care. She was shaking with anger now,

instead of fear. But even as furious as she was, she remembered to feel around inside her purse for the can of Mace.

Although she had never been to Ethan Murphy's home, she knew where it was and turned down the curving drive that could only lead to his doorstep. When her car rounded a sharp corner to face a closed garage entrance, she slammed on the brakes and turned off the ignition, leaving the keys in the car, and jumped out.

Blind fury drove her as she stalked around the side of the house, the can of pepper spray at the ready, into the small clearing...and stopped short.

Three men had turned to gape at her. They stood near a smoking grill. A floodlight illuminating the yard clearly indicated that they were in the midst of preparing to eat. The luscious scent of grilled steak permeated her anger, as did the casual demeanor of the men and the fact that none of them were breathing heavily from a dead-heat run. Nor were they dressed in black.

"Well, now, Ethan, you didn't tell me we were gonna have company for supper," drawled one of them in a voice she vaguely recognized. "Who's that?"

Wishing the earth would open up and swallow her, Diana forced herself to start forward nonchalantly, crossing her arms over her chest to obscure the pepper spray.

When she stepped into the illumination, she heard Ethan's soft exclamation. "Well, well. Diana Iverson, what are you doing here?" He eyed her warily.

Not the most welcoming of greetings, she thought, trying not to dwell on how incredibly stupid she felt. "I—uh..."

Words failed her, and stuck even further in her throat when she actually looked at him. Her gaze became trapped, fixed on a shirtless, muscled, lightly-haired torso that belonged to someone who clearly worked out a lot more than Jonathan did. Diana swallowed, jerking her attention away so that it bounced down over his swim trunks, to legs that matched his abdomen in physical hotness, and finally up to a stony, set face.

"Is there something I can help you with?" His voice was calm, but even in the faulty light from a garage light, irritation glinted his eyes. "Unless you normally go speeding up someone's driveway like the hounds of hell were after you, on your way to a neighborly visit."

The man didn't have to like her, but he didn't have to be so rude either, Diana thought desperately—conveniently dismissing her own previous rudeness.

Hoping for assistance, she glanced at Ethan's companions for the first time, and, with a flood of relief, recognized one of them. The other man, about Ethan's age, with a lanky build and dark skin, wore a cowboy hat. He also looked familiar—but it was the older one, the police chief, who grabbed and held Diana's attention.

"Captain Longbow, I'm so glad you're here!"

He stood, unfolding a solid body topped by a worn baseball cap. Ink-black hair streaked with gray stuck out from around the hat in endearing little curls, giving the fiftyish man a boyish look. "Is ever' thing all right?"

Suddenly, the impact of what she'd experienced rushed over her and, as her surge of angry adrenaline dissipated, weakness and shock flooded her body. What a stupid thing to do, she thought numbly. She'd chased after someone who'd broken into her house and assaulted her.

It was probably a good thing she hadn't actually found the intruder. Even with her pepper spray.

Ethan must have seen something change in her demeanor, for he snagged a lawn chair and swung it to a place right in front of her. "Sit down, Diana. Do you want something to drink? Then you can tell us what's wrong," he added, glancing at Longbow.

"Yes, yes." But then she began to babble—something she knew she was doing, that she hated herself for, but she couldn't help it under the circumstances—and poured out the whole story of what happened.

Ethan thrust a cold bottle into her hand and she took a gulp of beer—then had to swallow the awful stuff because she wasn't going to stoop to spitting it out. She hated beer.

Diana handed the bottle back to him and finished her explanation, "So after I stood up, I got in the car and—"

Ethan wasn't slow. He knew exactly why she'd clamped her mouth shut. The woman had done it again—thought the worst of him—and nearly accused him to his face of breaking into her house. Attempting to hide his growing pissed-offness, he brought the beer bottle to his own lips, and, as he sipped, realized that her full, sexy mouth had just covered the very same opening. And it was warm. And a little moist.

Christ. What the hell was wrong with him?

He thought he heard a soft, teasing chuckle from Baxter, who was standing next to him, but Ethan didn't give him the satisfaction of acknowledging it.

Instead, he drank again, watching Diana from beneath lowered lids while Joe Cap slid into police officer mode and began to question her.

Man, she'd come roaring up the drive like a maniac. Lucky she hadn't hit anything on the way or spun into a tree. She wouldn't have surprised them like that if Cady hadn't gotten herself sprayed by a skunk—a regular happening in the summer that they were both used to, which was why he kept a stock of large cans of tomato juice. The black lab was currently locked away in the laundry room while the remnants of the juice bath did its work.

Ethan shook himself out of his mad. What the hell was wrong with him? The poor woman had come home to find an intruder in her house, had been pushed around by him—it could have been *much* worse—and all Ethan could think about was his own pride...and zero in on those full, sexy lips touching to his beer bottle.

"Are you hurt?"

His sudden question had her turning to him, her dark blue eyes large. They displayed more vulnerability than he'd yet to see, and something twisted deep inside him. *Not good, Murphy.*

"Nothing more than a bang on the temple and a bruise on the hip. Thanks for asking," she added—as, maybe, an olive branch. Then, turning back to Cap, she said, "So I'll need to file a report tomorrow?"

"Yep. Come down to the office and Helga or I will help you. Got any idea why someone might have wanted in the house? Was anything disturbed?"

Diana shook her head. "I didn't stick around long enough to see. I had the crazy idea that I might be able to—uh—catch the guy."

Ethan snorted. He folded his arms over his bare chest. "*That* was a smart thing to do."

Temper flared in her face, bringing a sparkle back to her eyes and a slight flush to her cheeks. "I had *this*." She shoved a can into his face, just under his nose. It trembled slightly. "Want me to try it out?"

He blinked, looking down at the spray nozzle that was aimed right at his mouth. At least her finger wasn't on the trigger. "I guess you were prepared."

And then, just because he couldn't resist and because she really did need to be taken down a notch, and maybe also because he sort of needed to get close to her like he needed to draw another breath, he moved—fluid and sharp.

Suddenly the can was in his hands, and she was slamming into his bare chest, one arm folded back behind her.

The instant she connected with his body, heat shot through him so strongly that he nearly released her as quickly as he'd grabbed her. Thanks to his post-divorce moratorium, he hadn't had female curves plastered against him for more than two years.

Diana's eyes flared wide and her lips parted in a startled gasp. Her breasts rose with quick, shallow breaths, pressing against his chest, and one knee had somehow got cocked into his thigh. He could smell a floral, feminine scent from her hair, and felt the fragility of the narrow wrist he'd captured behind her back. For a moment, it was just the two of them caught in an awkward, intimate pose. Then with a short laugh to cover his surprise, he released her.

"Chasing after him—that was a foolish thing to do," he said, handing her back the can of pepper spray and absolutely *not* looking at Baxter James, who'd snorted again in a poor attempt to hide his laughter.

Still, Ethan's hormones were doing leaps and dives as Diana snatched back the spray can, turning away with pruny lips.

"All right then," Cap spoke up. "Now that we've got that settled...how about I see you home, Miss Iverson. I'll check things out and make sure nothing else's upset."

Ethan didn't even consider offering to go along, for the frigid look Diana was giving him was almost making his balls shrivel.

He didn't want to go anyway.

He wanted to put Diana Iverson and her issues out of his mind.

Aunt Jean's house loomed dark and forbidding in the center of the clearing, with only the single light spilling out the front door. But returning in the company of a police officer did wonders for her perspective.

Captain Longbow led the way inside, and she followed, dogging his footsteps silently as he went from room to room, thoroughly checking them. He even looked in the garage. Nothing seemed out of place at first glance, and when they returned to the kitchen, Diana felt even more comfortable knowing that there was no one in the house.

"You've got sturdy locks and there's no easy entry," he commented in his snail's pace drawl. "Looks like he forced his way in through that back window. You'll want to get that fixed, get a safety lock on it and the rest of them. Doubt he'd come back tonight. You caught him in the act, he knows you're home…and since he didn't—er—attack you, violence is not his intent. I'll send Helga down here a coupla times the rest of the night, though, so don't worry if you see headlights. And I'll let the sheriff know about the break-in as well. But are you sure you want to stay here by yourself?"

"I'll be fine. Tomorrow I'll come down and file a report, and get the locks changed again, but—"

"Again?"

She felt the slight flush of embarrassment creep over her face. "I just had them changed a few days ago."

"Has the house been broken into before?"

She might as well tell him, for the record. Just because she had been wrong about Ethan tonight didn't mean he was innocent of everything else. "Ethan Murphy was in here the other day when I was in town. It was the second time he let himself in."

The dawn crept over his face. "Ahh. So that's why..." He blinked, and she actually saw the change in his face as he altered the route of his words. "How do you know that?"

"He left a...note." As she said it, she felt even more foolish. Who would leave a note advertising a break-in?

The expression on his face echoed these thoughts, but manners obviously won out. Longbow just looked at her very seriously and said, "Now, Miss Iverson, I know you're new to these parts, but Ethan Murphy is the last person you'd ever have to worry about in that way."

She shot him a disbelieving look. "You're right, I am new to these parts. But I don't trust him as far as I can throw him. You may all be part of the good-old-boys' club, and if I hadn't seen him hanging out so casually tonight with my own two eyes, I would still suspect he was the one who was here this evening. He was taking advantage of my aunt, and her eccentric beliefs, and when I find the proof, I'm going to nail him."

Longbow made a strange noise that sounded like a choking laugh, but when she turned to look at him, his face was deadpan. "Right, miss. Well, I sure hope for the professor's sake you don't take too long to...uh...nail him."

Having the suspicion he was laughing at her, Diana drew her lips together. "The professor?"

"Yeah, that's Murphy. He's a bigwig down to U of C in the anthropology department—though when he's up here, he's just a regular guy who likes to fish and drink beer. Nasty divorce a coupla years ago, and—"

"The University of Chicago?" she repeated, frowning, and a tiny snake of uncertainty zapped her. Then, she regrouped. If that's what he was telling people, including Genevieve, that was easy enough to check on. She'd do that first thing in the morning, before going down to the police station.

"Well, thank you very much, Captain Longbow. I'm sorry

if I interrupted your dinner, but I do appreciate your checking things out down here. I'll take a look around to see if I can tell whether anything's missing."

"No prob, miss." He touched his fingers to the brim of his cap. "Gotta get home anyway. Wife's probably chewed a hole through her lip, wondering where I am."

It was nearly midnight by the time he left and Diana closed—and locked—the door behind him. By all rights, she should be a bundle of nerves, alone in this house where she had surprised an intruder only hours before.

But she wasn't. It was odd…it was as though she *knew*. As she looked around the foyer, she somehow knew things were safe here in the house.

She'd felt nervous during the drive back tonight—for no apparent reason. As she'd drawn closer to home, she'd sensed something was wrong…even though she didn't know what it was, nor had she had anything specific or logical to point to.

As she thought about all of this, pain began to throb at her temples, and Diana heard Ethan's voice in her mind, remembering what he'd said to her the other day.

The High Priestess is telling you to look beyond the obvious— to allow your intuition and inner voice to guide you. Let your imagination and dreams abound, open your mind to the unknown, seek that which is concealed.

Intuition and inner voice.

Well, that was *exactly* what she was doing right now, wasn't it—listening to her intuition and inner voice. Diana felt a little nauseated and weak-kneed at the thought. Her head hurt.

This stuff isn't real. I'm just grasping at straws.

He was just giving me a line—the same lines he gave Aunt Jean. He's obviously very good at it.

"This is *crazy*," she said aloud, fervently, angrily. She fisted her hands at her sides and glared around the room. "This is *nonsense*. I'm making things up, and hearing things, and believing dreams are real, and There's No. Such. Thing. As. Ghos—"

Crash! Thud-thunk!

She jumped and spun around, looking down the hall toward the den. Her heart lodged in her throat, and she forced it back down. Silence reigned except for the thudding of her heartbeat in her ears.

"Stupid cats," she muttered out loud, hoping to convince herself that's all it had been. Yet, her voice was shaky. And she didn't march down to the den to confront them...or to confirm the accusation.

And when she caught sight of something from the corner of her eye, she whirled once more...to find both Motto and Arty standing halfway up the stairs that led to the second floor. They stared down at her with wide green eyes, upright tails flicking like animated question marks as if to call her out on the false accusation.

"Fine. So it wasn't you. This time." Diana was proud that her voice came out strong and smooth this time.

Then she looked down the hall toward the library. Something had fallen over. Something had caused that noise.

The house was empty—she knew it because she and Joe Cap had looked everywhere inside and locked all the doors and windows. He'd even boarded up the one the intruder had broken into. They'd checked the cellar, too, and the garage.

No one could possibly be there.

No one could have made that sound.

Jean's not haunting you, is she?

Iva Bergstrom's silly comment wafted into Diana's mind and she thrust it away with an emphatic "*No.*"

With that, she gave the pair of cats a glare then marched

down the hallway to the den. She'd see what made that noise, and then she'd know exactly what had happened. Maybe the intruder had tipped something off-balance during his (it had definitely been a he) snooping, and gravity had finally won out.

That was the most likely explanation, and the one she held on to as she flipped on the light in the den.

Her eyes went immediately, automatically, to the piecrust table where the mahogany box sat, pretty as you please, next to the undisturbed African violet.

Diana released the breath she hadn't realized she was holding, and moved further into the room, looking for whatever had fallen and made the noise.

She saw it then: a trail of books in a tumble on the floor. They looked as if someone had come along and swept them from the shelves—and indeed, that was consistent with the sound: an initial crash, then the thudding of several books dumping to the ground.

A little chill prickled over the back of her neck. The books definitely *hadn't* been on the ground when she and Joe Cap came through a while ago.

And there didn't seem to be any way they could have spontaneously fallen—

She shook her head, stopping her thoughts in their tracks. Whatever the cause, the books were on the floor. They'd made a sound that had startled her, but she knew she was alone in the house except for Motto and Arty, and there was no harm done except to jumpstart her pulse.

Diana bent to pick up the books, and as she did so, she noticed the titles.

Murder on the Orient Express.
Murders in the Rue Morgue.
Murder at Hazelmoor.

Murder on Lexington Avenue.
Murder of the Century.

She paused, feeling slightly nauseated again and the renewed tom-tom at her temples. Surely it had to be a coincidence that all the titles of the books that had fallen… randomly…from the shelf began with the word "murder."

But even Diana, logical and pragmatic as she was, couldn't quite convince herself of that. Particularly as, when she began to replace the books, she realized they all couldn't have come from the same shelf as might have happened if something (like a cat) had caused them to tumble.

Going by author, size, and subject matter and looking at the way the rest of the books were organized, it was obvious the placement of these volumes was not from the same shelf. And some of them fit in so tightly between the titles next to them that all should have fallen—or none at all. And the ones left there were still in place, tucked back on the shelf.

Their titles became a chant in her mind: *Murder. Murder, murder, murder. Murder.*

She'd dreamed of murder. Of being smothered until she breathed no more.

Diana sank onto Aunt Jean's desk chair and stared silently at the shelves. She didn't know what to do. What to think. She didn't want to believe any of this, yet what else could she do?

A movement from the corner of her eye had her jumping again, then calming when she saw it was only Motto who'd padded into the room. Weren't felines supposed to be sensitive to the supernatural? If so, why wasn't the cat reacting?

"I don't understand any of this! What is going—"

Brrrring!

The jarring ring of the old, monstrous telephone from the kitchen startled her.

Diana scrambled to her feet, heart pounding wildly, vision

disoriented—as if she'd just awakened from a deep sleep. Strangely frantic to stop the shrill, discordant sound that made her nerves jangle, she bumped the desk's sharp corner painfully and jolted the piecrust table as she left the room.

No one called after midnight unless it was something bad. She was practically running for the phone, rubbing her thigh where she'd hit the desk.

Brrrring!

"Hello."

Silence.

"Hello?" she said again, more firmly. "Hello?"

"Diana?"

"Jonathan! What—what are you doing, calling so late?"

"I'm home from the airport. I couldn't stop thinking about you…especially when I got back here. My condo is just so empty. And lonely. And it feels emptier, knowing you won't be here for a while."

She'd brought her breathing under control and sank onto a stool by the kitchen counter, still rubbing her leg. She'd have a bruise for sure. "I'm glad you're back safely," she said, careful to keep her voice steady.

"What's wrong? You sound tense."

"The way this landline rings is so shrill and loud, it startled me. You know—in the middle of the night."

"I'm sorry. I tried your cell, but the call didn't go through again. I just wanted to talk to you."

"Well, it's late and I was getting ready to go to sleep. I'll call you in a day or two, all right?"

"Diana," he said quickly, as if to keep her from disconnecting. "Will you wear the ring?"

She looked down automatically at her bare hand. "Maybe."

"Maybe?"

"Probably."

"Thank you."

She stared at her ringless finger, wondering why she'd lied—but then immediately knew the answer. Less drama. Less stress. Less arguing.

Whatever happened to being a strong woman?

I'll be strong tomorrow, she told herself. *Tonight, I'm going to be...less strong.*

"Good night, Jonathan," she said, putting power into her words at least. "I'll talk to you soon."

She stared through the kitchen window into the darkness for a while after she hung up the phone. The moonlight filtered over the lake like a swath of sparkling diamonds. It seemed so calm and peaceful. She heard the hoot of an owl in the distance, and for some reason it made her feel more calm. The *eau de skunk* had dissipated some time ago and barely lingered in the air. Now the scent of summer, and lake, and pine filtered to her nose.

She was tired. She wanted to sleep.

But she was a little nervous about doing so. Not because she feared someone would break into the house again—Captain Longbow had been right; if the intruder had wanted to hurt her, he'd have done more than push her into the doorframe.

No, she was nervous about trying to sleep here. The last time she'd done so—Friday night—had been the worst of the dreams. She didn't want to live through that again, even knowing it was a dream, because...

Maybe it wasn't just a dream.

Murder.

The five books tumbled onto the floor couldn't have been an accident.

But who or how or why?

Her head was throbbing again.

"I'm going to bed," she said aloud. "And I'm *not* going to dream tonight. I understand the dream, all right? I just don't know...I don't know what to do with it."

Diana turned off all the lights in the kitchen except for the one over the sink, checked the cats' water dish (though they'd tried to convince her otherwise, they only got fed in the morning), and started down the hall to Aunt Jean's bedroom.

The light was still on in the library, so she went in there to turn it off.

And there was the mahogany box of cards: upended from the piecrust table she'd bumped as she went by. They'd tumbled onto the chair next to the table.

"At least I know how it happened this time," she said aloud. "My own clumsiness."

She began to pick them up swiftly, wrapping the worn pieces of card-stock in their blanket of black silk, then slipping the bundle into the box. She put the lid back on, set the box in its place on the table, then went over to the desk to turn off the green-shaded lamp.

And gasped.

There, sitting on the desk, pretty as you please, were two Tarot cards, side by side.

"No *way*," she breathed, turning in a slow circle as she looked around the room. Her body broke out in a cold sweat. "No *way*. There is absolutely *no way*—"

Suddenly Diana felt the air stir and swirl and chill...and at the same time, she smelled something spicy and musky. The distinct scent of sandalwood. Aunt Jean used to burn sandalwood incense all the time, and used a perfume made from the oil. She claimed it was a holdover from her Woodstock days.

Even as the tip of Diana's nose went cold from the chill, a

strong sense of comfort swept over her—as if someone put an arm around her shoulders

"Aunt Jean...?" she whispered, feeling like a fool for talking to a dead woman. Yet there was no other explanation for it.

Unless she was going crazy.

Or was overtired and stressed...

Diana was facing the doorway of the den when she saw Arty—the fat black and white cat with the skinny tail—standing in the hall. He was looking into the room, his eyes wide and still—as if focused on something behind Diana. The fine hairs on the back of her neck prickled when the cat tensed and reared back a little, as if gathering itself up to attack.

The waft of musky sandalwood buffeted more strongly, and the air shifted enough to brush a wisp of hair against her cheek. She saw small, short puffs of cold breath coming from her nose and mouth. Her fingers were icicles.

Diana didn't move. She tried not to breathe, tried not to make a sound.

Then, all at once, it was gone.

The cat relaxed.

The air stopped.

The perfume disintegrated.

The cold air warmed.

Panting with shock and disbelief, a little lightheaded, Diana turned around to face the desk again. The cards were still there. Still sitting as if someone had laid them side by side for her.

If that *had* been Aunt Jean—oh, God, how could she even form such a thought?—she meant Diana no harm. That knowledge, that confidence, was all that kept her from bolting out of the house and driving away.

This is crazy.

Whatever was going on, it seemed someone—Aunt Jean—wanted her to know something.

Murder.

Her knees trembled, but Diana made herself walk over to look at the cards that had been placed on the desk.

She had a moment of relief that neither of them were *Death*—nor were either *The High Priestess*.

They were cards she must have seen at some point in her life, but didn't remember anything about what they were supposed to mean.

Wheel of Fortune, one was labeled. The other had no title, but bore the Roman numeral two at the top.

Wheel of Fortune was labeled with the Roman numeral ten, indicating that it was the tenth card of the Major Arcana. The Wheel itself hung suspended in what appeared to be the heavens, for it was surrounded by clouds and all types of creatures. Each creature seemed to be reading a book.

Diana looked more closely at the picture of the Wheel. There were two concentric circles drawn on it, and lines cut the two innermost circles into six pie-shaped pieces. Symbols that she thought might be those of astrological signs ringed the outermost portion of the Wheel.

She turned her attention to the second card. A blindfolded figure sat on a beach, holding two swords crossed over his or her chest. The swords were long, creating a v-shape and bisecting the drawing at the horizon line between water and sky.

Two of Swords, she thought. A very simple image. Yes, it was a picture with little detail, but the impression it gave her was a powerful one. The person on the beach, blind to anyone approaching, held the swords in such a way so as to ward off any encroachment upon the ocean with those two sturdy weapons.

Wheel of Fortune.
Two of Swords.
She left the cards on the desk when she went to bed.
And for the first time since arriving in Wicks Hollow, she didn't dream.

Diana woke the next morning to the sound of a motor rumbling very near the bedroom window. It came closer, then backed away; closer, then away. It sounded like someone was mowing the lawn.

But, despite the unexpected awakening, she'd *slept*. Without dreaming.

She sat up in bed, and her gaze went automatically to the digital clock. Eight o'clock. A little early for lawn service, wasn't it? She spewed out a long breath and closed her eyes.

A week ago, she'd have been up and at work already for an hour at this time.

But she wasn't at work. She was on vacation. One that it was becoming clearer and clearer she needed.

Ghosts. *Crazy.*

She shook her head. She wasn't going to think about that just yet.

So she turned her exasperation toward whoever was mowing the lawn. Diana's heels made little annoyed thumps as she strode down the hall to the front door. As she passed by the den, she glanced at the desk. The two Tarot cards were still sitting there, just as she had left them, looking innocent and unimportant.

Ugh.

By now, she'd reached the front door. She whipped the

chain lock open and snapped the deadbolt back, then turned the knob and pulled the door open.

Though she wore nothing but a modest nightshirt and no shoes, Diana walked out onto the porch and followed it around the back, where the sound of the mower was louder.

As she came around the corner, she stopped. Her breath caught, and she just stared for a moment.

All right, it was almost worth it being woken up to see this. Nice choice for lawn service, Auntie Jean.

From behind, all Diana could see was a tanned, broad-shouldered back, well-toned with muscle and glazed with a light sheen of sweat. It narrowed to a slim-hipped waist, covered with a loose pair of shorts that looked like hacked off sweatpants. Regardless of the fact that they were loose, they covered a very pleasing, well-defined rear end. His legs were long, lean, and muscled from thigh to calf.

Wow. Maybe I won't lodge a complaint after all.

He turned a corner then, facing her, and Diana wasn't really surprised that it was Ethan Murphy. After all, she'd been up close and personal with that very fine chest last night.

It was just a lot different seeing it in the full light of day. Her mouth had gone embarrassingly dry.

Ethan looked up and gave an obvious start at seeing her. His face settled into a remote expression as he released the mower, and it puttered into silence. "Good morning." He slung his hands at his hips, walking toward her with a hint of defiance.

"Good morning. What are you doing?" As she came closer, she felt him take in her lightly clad figure. She tried to be inconspicuous as she tugged the hem of her nightshirt down, stretching it to mid-thigh, and wondering why she cared.

Shorts and a tank top are more revealing than my nightshirt.

But my hair must look like a disaster. Nevertheless, she managed to keep herself from fussing with it.

"Mowing the lawn," Ethan replied, giving himself a leisurely look at her from head to toe. It had taken her long enough to wake up. He'd been working for over an hour, trimming and clipping, trying to get as much done as possible before the day got too hot.

It hadn't strictly been time for him to see to the yard work, but considering what had happened last night, he figured he should have an excuse to check on things over here. Joe Cap had called him after he left the house last night to assure him all was secure and calm, and Ethan trusted him.

But that didn't mean he didn't wonder and worry a little bit. And it didn't mean he hadn't taken a walk over after midnight, when Bax left, just to make sure everything seemed all right.

He'd seen Diana in the kitchen, outlined by the glow of light. She was staring out the window; he could tell from her expression it wasn't because she saw him, but because she was thinking.

Nevertheless, he made certain he stuck deep in the shadows so she *didn't* see him—the last thing he needed was her to be accusing him of spying on her (which he was, sort of) or coming back to break in. Again.

Now, when she pulled the nightshirt down in a vain attempt at modesty, it did nothing but tighten over her chest. Moratorium or no, he wasn't about to deny himself the pleasure of looking at the pretty apple-sized breasts with outlined nipples.

"Did I wake you?"

She seemed to struggle with how to respond: irritation or frustration or gratitude—he could almost see the emotions march over her face, one after the other. Ethan grinned to himself, realizing he was still in a mood to stir things up. When she poked at things like that, Fiona would say the imp had gotten hold of her—and it seemed that Ethan was possessed by his own contrary imp as well. Must be a Murphy trait.

"As a matter of fact, you did wake me." Diana must have realized that drawing the edge of the t-shirt down did nothing to preserve her modesty because she let go of the hem. The shirt boinged up, giving him a better view of her smooth white thighs.

"I'm sorry," he told her with some sincerity. After all, he was doing this for Genevieve—in her memory. And because he'd been raised to do the right thing.

Diana was a woman living alone in a remote house. Someone had broken in—at least once, and, Ethan suspected, possibly more than that. He'd been certain he saw someone in the window that day he'd come over for his beer—and he'd mentioned it to Joe Cap last night when they talked later.

Regardless of his reason for being here, he didn't have to like the woman. Though it sure as hell wasn't a hardship to look at her, dressed as she was, all rumpled and heavy-lidded from sleep. His fingers itched to touch those thick, full curls that tumbled in a riot about her head, leaving her long, slender neck bare.

"I thought you'd be an early riser," he added, but with more sincerity this time. "But to answer your question, I'm upholding my end of the bargain your aunt and I have had for years—and I'll do so until you can make other arrangements for having the yard work done."

"Bargain?"

"Yeah. She never would accept any payment from me for all the time I spent working with her, so we had an agreement that I would take care of her lawn work in the summer, and make sure the plowing was done in the winter."

"Work you did with her? You wanted to pay *her*?" The consternation on her face would have been more gratifying if he hadn't seen the wheels turning in her mind—considering whether she should believe him or not. *She really does think I'm a shyster.*

Despite the anger rising in him, he kept his voice even and well modulated. "Yes, I compensated her—or tried to, anyway—for the time she gave me over the last two years. Because, you see, Diana, regardless of what your lawyerly, ambulance-chasing brain might think, I don't need money. I'm tenured at U of C and have other sources of income. Go ahead—check me out. It'll be easy enough." He flashed her an arrogant smile, one that was sugarcoated with niceness, but had the underlying steel of his outrage at her accusations. "Start with the U of C website—under *Staff.* Picture and all—although they haven't updated it since I shaved."

"I certainly will check it out." Her voice was frosty, although he saw the waver of uncertainty in her eyes.

He wondered if she'd apologize when she found out how wrong she'd been. Unlikely, he thought, taking in the cool facade of her beautiful but stony face and defiant stance. Why would someone like her bother to eat crow?

Diana took a step backward, obviously trying to find a way to excuse herself politely. "Well I do appreciate your taking the time to come over here and do this. I have to run into town in a little while to file my report with Captain Longbow, so I may be gone when you get finished. But—uh—could I get you something to drink before I go?"

Although he'd have liked to continue teasing her, Ethan decided against it. Perhaps it was time to call a truce—for Jean's sake, at least. "I don't mind doing the yard work because

I know you probably have your hands full and I don't teach classes during the summer, so I have the time. I probably won't be much more than another hour—I have to finish mowing, then run the mulcher over it."

"All right. Thank you. If you'd like to stop in for something cold to drink before you leave, that would be fine. Just holler when you come in if I'm still here."

He felt one eyebrow lift. She was inviting him to just walk in the house?

"Thanks. That'd be great. I'll take you up on it." *And now, you rumpled sleepyhead, you'd better get in the house and get some clothes on before I forget I don't like you.*

But the problem was, he was beginning to wish he did.

As it turned out, Diana didn't make it into town before Ethan finished the lawn, because Mickey called and there was a long list of things to review.

Diana was still on the phone with her when she heard Ethan's "helloooo!" reverberate through the house.

"Who's that?" her sharp-eared legal assistant asked.

"One of the neighbors. He just finished mowing the lawn," Diana explained. "In the kitchen," she called to him.

"Is he a young neighbor or an old neighbor?" Mickey asked with a sly tone in her voice.

"Young," Diana whispered as she heard Ethan walking down the hall. "Take off your shoes, please," she called to him.

"How young?" Mickey demanded. "Please tell me he's legal."

"Already did," Ethan said as he came into the kitchen.

He'd put on a t-shirt, but he must have taken a swim, for the cotton clung to his shoulders and the front of his chest, and his hair dripped onto its shoulders. She noticed bare, tanned biceps rounding smoothly from under the cuffs of the sleeves. Somehow, the shirt made him look even less decent than when he was bare-chested outside.

Diana realized Mickey was talking to her. "I'm sorry, what did you say? The phone lines are kind of staticky up here."

Ethan tossed her a grin. "I've never had any trouble with my phone," he told her, turning one of the chairs around and straddling it backwards. The teasing look in his eyes held a second layer of some other emotion.

Heat.

"I'll bet they are," Mickey said in a tone that surely had a smirk attached to it. "Anyway, I just got another batch of documents from AXT. We've got bankers' boxes lined up all over your office—good thing you aren't here. You wouldn't be able to find your desk."

"What sort of documents are in this batch?"

"Ugh. Everything and nothing important. Mostly paperwork from the '20s and '30s, when it was the Woodstock Tool and Die shop, but there are some other files that look like they're later. I don't know whether they're important or relevant, but Fran, Aziz, and I are poring through them."

"Thanks. Let me know if you find anything important or strange. I'll be back a week from today."

As Diana hung up the phone, she found Ethan watching her with warm, interested eyes. When she caught his gaze, he blinked and the heat disappeared—replaced by easy friendliness. He'd propped his chin on hands that rested on the back of the chair.

Diana's stomach was filled with hot butterflies—and not just because of the way he was looking at her. Owning up to her mistakes and shortcomings was something she would not neglect.

"I owe you an apology, Ethan," she said, meeting his gaze. "More than one, as a matter of fact."

The warm surprise that rushed over his features was a bit of a balm to her raw emotions. "I take it you did some research on the U of C website," he said.

She certainly had—and what she learned made her completely mortified.

How could Diana have not realized that Ethan Murphy was Ethan Murphy, PhD, author of *The Welcome Blue Light: Stories of Death and Moving to the Other Side*.

The book, which described the experiences of hospice workers, nurses, first responders, and others who'd witnessed death and near-death experiences, had been a popular topic of conversation and in the media last year. It had been on the *New York Times* bestseller list for weeks, and the author—sitting right at her kitchen table—had even been on *Late Night With Colbert* and NPR to promote the book. There was even talk of a television special to be aired on the National Geographic channel.

Thus, he definitely was, as Captain Longbow said, a bigwig in cultural anthropology at U of C.

And he definitely didn't need Aunt Jean's money.

Diana continued, for he deserved every bit of her humbleness. "I jumped to conclusions and made assumptions about you—and acted on them. I hope you'll be able to forgive me." She drew in a deep breath and continued to look him in the eye. "Quite truly, it's very unlike me. I usually require much more solid evidence before making judgments. I don't know what I was thinking. I was completely out of line in my behavior and suspicions of you."

He blinked, and appeared to be pleasantly stunned. "Thank you for apologizing. I have to admit, I didn't think you would—and especially with such grace." He smiled the most genuine smile she'd seen since the first time they'd met. "Apology accepted."

Diana drew back, a little offended at his bluntness, and yet chastised at the same time. "I don't have any issue with admitting when I'm wrong. And if everyone else did, there'd be a lot less strife in the world."

Nodding in agreement, he took the tall glass of iced tea that she handed him. "Very true." As their fingers brushed, he commented, "As your aunt used to say, 'Diana has to see it in black and white before she believes anything.'"

She stared at him, an uneasy feeling rising inside. "Aunt Jean used to talk about me?"

"All the time." A chill tinged his words and that smile faded. "She missed you. She talked about you as though you were her daughter instead of her great-niece."

Shame and deep sadness crested over her, and she had to blink back a sudden welling of tears. With an impatient hand, she brushed them away, hoping he didn't notice.

"I feel so guilty about it. It's been more than ten years since I've been here, and though she came to Chicago several times and we talked regularly on the phone...well, that doesn't really make up for me not coming up to visit. I always intended to, but then another case would come along, and I'd get busy, and then the months and years went by...There's no excuse. I should have made the time." Her eyes were still wet. "I wish I had. She called me the week before she died. I called her back, but didn't get her...and I didn't have the chance to try again before I found out...." Diana wasn't ready to put her suspicion of murder into words. "I'll live with that guilt forever."

Ethan looked at her contemplatively, and for the first time, that faint hint of accusation in his eyes was gone. Instead, she thought she saw sympathy and understanding there. "Then I owe you an apology as well," he said. "For thinking that you ignored your aunt, and only came back into her life for the money."

Diana opened her mouth to say something sharp, then closed it. "All right. I can see that," she conceded. "A little. We were actually quite close, even if I didn't physically get to see her very often."

He smiled, a little sadness warming his eyes, and settled back in his chair. "I really enjoyed your aunt. She was like a mother figure as well as a good friend of mine, as odd as that might seem considering our age difference. Besides being an inspiration for my next book, she helped me through a very rough time."

Diana nodded and sipped from her iced tea, realizing she was more relaxed around Ethan than she'd been so far. "Aunt Jean as a mother figure?" She gave a little laugh. "Much as I loved her, I never really thought about her in that way. More of an eccentric, interesting character with a warm heart, tons of common sense, and *lots* of color."

He looked at her for a moment, then said, "I got the impression your mother and Jean didn't get along very well."

She gave a short laugh. "Not at all. They were very… different. Jean was my father's sister, and once he died, my mother saw no reason to keep in touch with her. She's very— well, my mother likes things to be neat and perfect, and she has always had very high expectations. Of—of me, I mean. Aunt Jean was…more laid back, I guess you'd say."

"Well, I love my mother, but *she's* more of an eccentric, interesting relative to me," Ethan said dryly. He seemed to realize the topic of Melanie was not a good one on which to dwell. "My mother—she insists we call her Claudia instead of the more accepted title—is a modern day flower child. My sister and I were raised in a commune in Western Pennsylvania abounding with free love, marijuana plots, a nude beach, and lots of other earthy things. *The Whole Earth Catalog* was our bible.

"Now Claudia lives off the grid down in Costa Rica with her partner—a man at the moment, though that could change. She was with a woman for two years when I was in my twenties." He gave a wry smile. "She makes hemp baskets to sell on Etsy and draws henna designs on the tourists. She makes a pretty good living doing so, believe it or not. So next to Genevieve Fickler, I think of my mother as the eccentric."

"You were raised by a flower child in a commune with free love?"

"Yes, indeed—free love." His voice had dropped to a low rumble as he caught her gaze…and held it. "And nude beaches." He lifted his brows in a sort of silent, teasing challenge.

Suddenly self-conscious and unaccountably warm, she stood abruptly and walked over to refill their glasses. Surely he wasn't flirting with her.

"What sort of rough time was it?" she asked, hoping to turn the conversation to something less intense. At least for her. "That you went through. If you don't mind saying."

He stilled, then began to move his glass in small circles on the counter. "My wife and I split up a little more than two years ago. Just as I was finishing *Blue Light*."

"Oh, Ethan. I'm sorry to hear that. Really sorry."

"She was sleeping with one of my friends—but somehow the divorce was *my* fault." Bitterness flattened his tone.

"Because she was sleeping with one of your friends?" Diana repeated, allowing full irony into her voice. "That sounds logical." Now she regretted bringing it up, for it clearly bothered him. And aside from that, it was a situation too close to home for her comfort.

"Yeah. Well, as it turned out, Jenny figured she'd get out of our marriage since I was screwing around with one of my students, even though *she'd* been sleeping with my friend for months. Maybe even before we got married. I don't know for certain. So it was my fault. Except that I wasn't screwing around with Lexie, even though Lexie, a student and one of my teaching assistants—are you following this?—made everyone *think* that's what was going on."

"Nice," Diana said.

"Yeah, my life was like a soap opera around that time." He grimaced. "And that was even before my book took off. I suppose I could be grateful for that—the success of the book came after the divorce."

Diana nodded with sympathy. "Thankful for small favors. How did she set you up? Lexie, I mean."

"Oh, she was very smart, and I walked into it like a complete idiot. Lexie had been trying to get my attention for awhile, taking every class she could—as either student or TA—stopping by at the end of every office hour session so she could walk with me to wherever I was going next. She made sure we were seen together. A *lot*. By everyone. It was the perception, you see. Like I said, she was smart.

"Anyway, I wasn't having any of it—not only was I married for Christ's sake, but she was a student—*and* ten years younger than me, and I wasn't into that.

"So she got desperate, I guess, and one night, she locked her keys in her car outside a place she knew I'd be. She got me to give her a ride home—with witnesses, of course—and then when we got there, she tried her best to get me to come in." He looked up sharply at Diana, as if expecting her to accuse. "I didn't. Not even to see her safely inside. I didn't even step onto the porch."

She was staring, listening in disbelief. "That does sound

like a soap opera. I take it your wife heard about it and didn't believe you when you told her what happened."

He shrugged, his mouth a hard, flat line. "It wasn't only my wife who heard about it—it was the whole damn anthro department and half the campus. You know what they say about a woman scorned—and Lexie considered herself scorned.

"She made a lot of noise, and a lot of trouble otherwise because of the way she'd set things up by always being seen with me. She didn't actually come right out and accuse me of anything—fortunately—but she'd set the stage well enough that people made their own inferences. And of course, she didn't deny anything. It was a very difficult time, and instead of defending and supporting me, like you'd expect a partner to do, Jenny used it as an excuse to end the marriage."

"Jenny sounds like a real winner."

"Yeah. I really know how to pick 'em. Friends, wives, teaching assistants." He gave another one of those wry smiles, but she recognized hurt lingering in his golden-brown gaze. He lifted his glass to take a long drink. "So, when I walked by the den just now, I noticed you had some of those Tarot cards out on the desk."

Nothing like changing the subject, turning the spotlight back on her.

"I knocked the box on the floor last night," Diana replied casually—which was technically true; she was a lawyer, after all, and knew how to split words like hairs—but her insides tightened and the ease she'd felt with him dissipated.

Ethan cocked an eyebrow, letting her know he didn't quite believe her. It arched like a dark, inverted vee, the point edging into his hair. "And two cards ended up on the desk, nice and neat?" He gave a little laugh, adjusting his position on the chair.

"Well, yes," she replied. That was also, technically, true. But her cheeks heated again and she realized she was biting her lip in consternation.

He looked at her with an exasperation. "You aren't going to give even a little, are you?"

"I have no idea what you're talking about," she said firmly. "The cards are nothing to me."

He shook his head, folding his arms across his chest. His biceps shifted smoothly, round and sleek. "Diana, everyone has instincts and gut feelings. It's evident in every culture, all over the world, all through the ages. Believe me—I've been studying various cultures for decades. I've seen both evidentiary and experiential proof that there's more to the world than meets the eye.

"Some people have honed those innate intuitive skills to become even more than just a sixth sense. If you have such an ability, it's a gift. And if you want to talk about what's been going on with those cards you dropped on the floor, I'll listen."

"There's nothing going on with them." She felt the force of the denial like a Biblical Peter, and pushed it away. "I just had a few odd coincidences and it unsettled me a little."

Even as she said it, Diana felt the air shift a little. Like a nudge. The faint scent of sandalwood wafted to her nose. She felt her insides clench, and held her breath. *No. Not now. Not with him here...*

Ethan didn't seem to notice. "You aren't ready to believe me, or to talk about it. That's okay," he held up his hand to fend off her intended fiery retort. "Just think about it, Diana, think about it *rationally*—the way you always do. A card—The High Priestess—that has shown up randomly *three* times signifies that one should look beyond the obvious and listen to your inner voice. Isn't that a bit hard to swallow as mere coincidence?"

He unstraddled the chair and stood, looming down over her as she tried to ignore the scent of roses in the air and the light breeze that was *not* coming from the window behind him. It was getting colder in the room, and behind Ethan, in the hallway, Motto stood frozen, staring up at something behind Diana. *Crap.* The cat's tail swished angrily and she looked ready to hiss.

"Like I said—when you're ready to talk, Diana, I'll be happy to listen. Until then, I guess I'd better get going. You must have a lot to do."

"I appreciate the work you did in the yard." What else could she say besides, *Go. Now. Before something happens…*

"No problem." He gave her one last easy smile that, in spite of everything, sent a long, slow curling through her stomach. Then he ambled to the front door.

"By the way," he said, leaning his head against the doorjamb and giving her a calm look, "I don't study ghosts. Just people."

SIX

WHEN DIANA HAD ASKED for directions to Maxine Took's eightieth birthday party, Cherry Wilder insisted on picking her up so they could ride together.

"That way you can have a glass of wine or two and not worry about driving back home in the dark," she said. "And it's not very intuitive to find, Trib's house. It's kind of tucked away."

When they arrived at the party shortly after seven, Diana realized she was a little nervous—and she didn't understand why. She wasn't a big socializer, but neither was she shy and retiring. You simply couldn't be shy and retiring or unable to skillfully manage small talk if you wanted to make partner at a firm like McNillan, et al.

But she didn't have a chance to dwell on her inexplicable nerves, for Maxine spotted her and Cherry as soon as they came into view.

"You're *late*," she said, jabbing her cane toward them from across the broad stone terrace, narrowly missing a slender redhead in long, flowing skirts with wild, curling hair. "Party started at seven, you know."

Diana took one look at the guest of honor and the large, throne-like chair on which she sat and choked on a giggle. Cherry elbowed her and muttered, "If you laugh, she'll *never* let you get over it. She might even skewer you."

"Happy birthday, Maxine," Diana said instead, controlling herself, and brought the gift bag forward as if she were making an offering to a queen. The woman was, after all, wearing an actual tiara over her iron-gray hair—which had been tamed into a cloud of tight curls for the evening. She also wore a flowing, sequined gold evening gown that, thankfully, had a high neckline and wasn't a tight fit. It actually suited her quite well, despite being overly formal for the occasion. "You look lovely tonight. Very festive."

"Nice words, but you're still *late*," the old woman grumbled again, but she seemed taken by the bag Diana offered. "Lots of sparkles on that one," she said, sniffing a little—but she reached for it with greedy fingers. "Lemme see it."

Diana had taken a chance, selecting the fanciest, most glittery and lacy gift bag—which had cost almost as much as what was inside—and added sparkling tissue paper. Apparently, she'd made the right decision, for Maxine spent a good amount of time admiring it—although she complained about the sequins and crystals and tulle flowers adorning it ("don't know what's wrong with plain old brown paper wrapping anymore").

Once she finished examining it, Maxine relinquished the bag to Diana with the command, "It goes on the table over there. I'll look inside later."

Thus dismissed, Diana made her escape and edged over to the table laden with gifts.

The party was outside on Trib's three-tier stone terrace staggered into the side of a hill. It overlooked the lake and was surrounded by a colorful, well-tended landscaping of blooming trees, sprawling bushes, flowering plants, fountains, and arbors. The view from the terrace—and the relatively small house attached to it—was magnificent, and the entire outdoor space looked as if it belonged in a photoshoot for some architectural or celebrity magazine.

Lanterns of yellow and white hung near each set of broad, stone steps that led from one level of the patio to the next, sofas and chairs were arranged in conversation groupings (surely he didn't have all of this leather furniture out here all the time?), strings of lights wove and dangled like fairies through the trees, bushes, and along the edges of the patio. Flowers—in the sprawling gardens as well as in vases and pots—added color and scent to the scene. A large fire pit enclosed by an ornate wrought iron enclosure was situated on the highest level, but as it was still warm and the sun hadn't lowered too far, the logs hadn't yet been lit.

And the food…it smelled sensational, and seemed to be everywhere on little tapas tables. Diana saw chicken satay, tiny crab cakes, macarons of every pastel color, and a tower of fresh fruit just in her vicinity.

"There you are! Finally!" Trib descended upon Diana the moment she'd placed Maxine's gift on the table. "Jean's lovely niece! I hardly had the chance to speak to you at the funeral; it was just so awful and sudden, and of course I had to see to the food. Only the best for our fabulous Genevieve. But here you are. You look smashing! As cool and summery as a tall glass of ice wine."

"It's very nice to see you again," she replied as Trib crushed her to his designer shirt of lemon silk, and she inhaled the expensive, spicy scent of his cologne. He wore a lavender and purple paisley bow tie and creamy tailored trousers of sharply creased linen—without a wrinkle in sight.

The restauranteur and chef was in his forties with close-cropped white hair and a neat black-to-gray goatee. "You have a lovely home, and a wonderful place for a party," she told him after he kissed her enthusiastically on both cheeks.

"Thank you, my darling Diana. If only I had someone to share all of it with," he said with a dramatic flap of his hand.

"Oh, pish," Cherry said from behind them. "You'd be—what was the word you used—*smothered* if you had to share your perfect space with anyone for more than a weekend."

Smothered. Diana's belly dropped sharply at the word, and the ugly thought of Aunt Jean's death. And, unfortunately, the reminder made her think of Ethan Murphy—which she'd been doing far too often since their amiable chat in the kitchen yesterday.

Far too often, especially for a maybe-engaged woman.

Come to think of it…she hadn't given Jonathan or his ring a single thought since the phone call Sunday night. And the blue velvet box remained unopened and ignored in the depths of her suitcase.

Diana looked around and saw Ethan. He was standing two levels down on the lowest terrace, talking to the tall, gorgeous redhead who'd nearly been stabbed by Maxine's cane a moment ago. The woman's long hair billowed sensuously around her face and shoulders, and her magenta and violet maxi dress—which somehow did not clash with her hair but instead looked fabulous—fluttered at her ankles. The two of them appeared very intent in their conversation, and as Diana watched, the woman leaned forward to slide a hand over Ethan's cheek in an intimate fashion.

Diana's belly tightened, and she tore her attention from them, furious with herself that the sight bothered her so much. She was still technically in a relationship, and even if she hadn't been, Ethan Murphy was *not* anyone she'd be interested in.

He was too eccentric. Too different.

Too…male.

Besides that, he was practically a celebrity. He'd never be interested in Diana.

"Here you are my lovely," Trib said, shoving a tall slender *glass* flute (using glass vessels on a stone patio for a party was surely tempting fate) at her, and bringing Diana back to the moment. "One of my specialty champagne cocktails. Now, come with me. There are *tons* of people who have been absolutely *clamoring* to meet Jean's niece!"

"Now, Fifi," Ethan said as his sister patted his cheek a little harder than necessary, then ended with a sharp pinch. "*Ow.* You know how I feel about your little hobby."

"Hobby?" Fiona retorted, then tried to snatch his hand. "You try saying that to Claudia—calling our family tradition, and how she made a living when you were born, a *hobby*—and see if you live past the lecture. She'd skin you alive. Come on, let me see it. I want to see if anything's changed."

Long practiced at avoiding her grabby fingers, he tucked his hands behind his back, barely managing not to spill his beer in the process. "No. You are not reading my palm again. Especially here, where everyone can see. Why don't you go take a look at Maxine's? Tell us how much longer we're going to have to avoid being thwacked by that lethal cane."

"Ethan!" Fiona gasped, laughing as she pushed the curling hair from her face and tried to glower up at him. "That's terrible."

He was laughing too. "I know. You know I don't mean it."

"It's a good thing I do—and that no one else heard you."

"Not that anyone else here has ever wondered when The Cane was going to be put to rest."

She looked up at him, sobering. "It's nice to see you laughing again." She searched his face with her eyes—the same amber-brown ones he had, with the same thick lashes and black flecks in the iris. "How are you?"

"I'm fine," he said. "Just sad about Jean."

"I wish I'd met her."

"You would have loved her. You and another one of her friends—Iva Bergstrom; you haven't met her either—and Jean? The three of you would have had a lot to talk about."

"Well, sadly, that ship's sailed." Fiona looked around, pushing her hair back again. He wondered why she never wore a clip or pinned it up; she was always having to brush it out of her face.

"Yeah. I was…" Ethan's voice trailed off when he saw Diana Iverson standing at the top of the terrace.

She looked cool and elegant in a slim, ice-white dress that ended well above her knees, left her arms bare, and showed off her curves without being too obvious. Her short velvet hair was full and tousled, kissing the nape of her neck—but not out of control like the wild mess with which Fiona contended. A wide bracelet glittered at one slender wrist, and the pale pink lipstick she wore was a subtle, sexy slash of color that drew the attention to her lush mouth even from a distance.

"Who is that?" Fiona asked, poking him in the side.

"*Ow.* That's the second time you've bruised me tonight."

"Well, pay attention when I'm talking to you," she snarked back. "She's gorgeous, but even from here I can tell she looks *really* uptight. Who is she?"

Everyone seemed uptight to Fiona—but in this case, Ethan couldn't disagree. "That's Jean's niece. Diana."

"*Really.* Are you—"

"No. She's got someone."

Fiona frowned. "Well, that bites. I haven't seen you look at anyone like that for years."

"Christ, Fi, you haven't seen me hardly at all since you moved to Grand Rapids. How do you know how I look at women?" Ethan wasn't sure why he was so irritated, but he supposed that was part of the deal when it came to sisters. Especially bossy ones who liked to try and manage his life, when their own lives were pretty topsy-turvy.

"My, my," she replied, looking at him with an expression that made his hair want to stand on end. It was the way she looked when she was planning to make like a witch and stir the pot. "Aren't we touchy tonight. Maybe I should just go on over there and introduce myself to this Diana."

"Do *not* try and read her palm," he said from between clenched teeth, but Fiona had already laughed gaily and spun away.

He thought about going after her, but as he turned, he nearly ran into Melvin Horner, Wicks Hollow's veterinarian.

"Ethan, nice to see you again." Horner was drinking a thin, colorless beer that was definitely not one of Baxter's. In fact, Ethan was surprised Trib even allowed the likes of a Budweiser on his property. Maybe the vet had sneaked it in.

"How's that black lab of yours?" Horner was a short, stout man of sixty-something with a bristling mustache and a shock of straight white hair. Ethan thought that if Albert Einstein had been caught in the rain and his famous bushy hair gone flat, he'd have looked just like Doc Horner.

"Cady's just fine—swimming in the lake, chasing her tennis balls every day, barking at the squirrels and chipmunks. You know, the usual." He smiled at Juanita Alecita, who was making a beeline across the terrace toward the two of them as quickly as her bulk allowed.

"How are you tonight, Mrs. Alecita?" he said as she approached. It was as close as he could get to giving the warning "Incoming!" for Doc Horner—in case the man wanted to make an escape.

"Just fine, Ethan, just fine. What a lovely sunset it's going to be. Good evening, Mel," said Juanita, fluttering her soft, pink-tipped fingers at him. "You look very handsome tonight."

Ethan considered the options of playing buffer for Horner —who looked as trapped as Cady did when she was dragged into the vet's office—or trying to waylay Fiona before she said something regrettable to Diana.

The latter, more selfish option won out, and he slipped away as Juanita moved in on her prey. The last thing Ethan heard was her asking about some malady affecting Bruce Banner.

Ethan had taken two steps when Baxter caught him, and they got talking about the sad start to the Tigers' baseball season, which led to a discussion about the upcoming college football schedule. Then Joe Cap and his wife Penny joined them, and Ethan sincerely wanted to hear all about their children—who were teens at the high school and kept an eye on his cabin when he was in Chicago. They were what most people called "good kids."

"I got Helga driving up to Jean's house and check things out a few times tonight," Joe Cap said in an undertone to Ethan. "Thanks for the suggestion."

"That's good." Ethan looked around at the crowded terrace. "With everyone in town here at the party—and everyone in the county knowing about it—I figured whoever's been poking around there might take the opportunity to get back to whatever they're up to. I don't want Diana coming home to a surprise again."

"It was a good thought, and Helga's already been over

there twice since seven—it's a slow night with most of Wicks Hollow here at Trib's." Cap grinned and reached up as if to adjust his nonexistent ball cap—then dropped his hand. "Penny wouldn't let me wear my hat to the party. Don't know why it matters, but it sure is good at keeping the bugs away."

"There's Emily Delton," Baxter said, his eyes going to the blond with a nice rack and shapely legs displayed by tall, impractical heels. "She's talking to Declan again," he muttered. "He's a nice guy, but damn—I saw her first. Three years ago," he added dryly.

"Well, their daughters are friends. They're both fifteen you know," Penny said with a knowing a smile. "I'm sure they're just catching up on kid-stuff." Everyone in town seemed to want to set up Baxter James and Emily—except Emily, a recent divorcee who seemed oblivious to the brewmaster's interest and, obviously, fascinated by the newcomer blacksmith.

"And besides—if I'm reading his body language right—and of course I am—he's not really into her, Bax. But she's trying. Oh, and there's Diana Iverson—over there, talking to Fiona," Penny went on. "She's very nice-looking too, though I think she was at the Lakeshore Grille last week with a man. But who knows. And of course Fiona—she brought that big blond guy with her. Are they dating, Ethan?"

"I'm...I have no idea." Ethan wasn't really listening. Nice-looking was not the way he would have put it when it came to Diana Iverson. Sleek, cool, elegant...just itching for a man to mess up all that perfection when he got his hands all over her.

Whoa.

Ethan tore his attention from the ice-queen attorney before someone noticed him gawking. Like Maxine Took. He shuddered at what would happen if she did.

"I'm going to go get some food," he said. "Those short rib tacos smell like heaven."

He slipped off before anyone could ask him to bring something back for them, suddenly terrified by what could be going on in the conversation between Diana and his sister.

Fiona and her impish personality made him very nervous.

SEVEN

"I DON'T LIVE in Wicks Hollow," the gorgeous redhead was saying. "I just come down for a visit once in a while, so this is actually the first time I've been to Trib's house. It's pretty spectacular, isn't it?"

Diana was trying to be polite, but she couldn't understand why this sultry gypsy had literally zeroed in on her, threading her way across the terrace like she was on a mission, then trapped her in conversation in a walled corner of the patio. She could, however, understand why Ethan would be attracted to someone like her—having been raised by a hippie and who'd written a bestselling book on, basically, the afterlife. The sultry, flowy woman seemed like a perfect match for him.

"I hardly know anyone here myself," Diana told her.

"I'm Fiona, by the way." The other woman smiled, and her eyes danced with mischief.

"Diana Iverson. I haven't been to this house before either." Part of her wanted to interrogate—tactfully, of course—the woman to find out what her relationship was to Ethan, and the other part of her wanted to make an escape and talk to someone else who hadn't just been in an intent, intimate conversation with him. "It's a lovely home, though."

"Oh, what a gorgeous bracelet! Do you mind?" Fiona didn't wait for an answer and took Diana's hand, pulling it close to admire the sparkling metal cuff.

"Fiona," said a sharp voice behind them.

Diana looked up to see Ethan standing there with an alarmed look in his eyes. His jaw was smooth from a recent shave, and his dark hair ruffled a little in the breeze. She noticed it had a few chestnut-red streaks in it now; probably from all his work in the sun. That thought had her attention wandering to the rest of him, which she'd seen all smooth and sweaty yesterday morning.

But this evening he was fully dressed—in a casual button-down shirt of fine black fabric woven with subtle white thread, and a hemmed and creased pair of shorts. His arms and legs were bare—a tanned and muscular reminder of the rest of him.

"I was just admiring Diana's bracelet," Fiona told him with a very innocent expression, turning Diana's wrist around as if to demonstrate.

"Sure you were," he replied. "I thought you weren't supposed to do that without permission."

Diana felt as if she were missing something important in their exchange, but the desire to escape what was clearly a comfortable and intimate relationship won out over curiosity. "It was a pleasure to meet you, Fiona. I'll just—"

"Oh, don't run off," the redhead replied with a feline smile as she continued to hold Diana's hand. "It's time for me to leave, and I wouldn't want my poor brother here to be left unattended. Maxine Took might swoop in with her Cane of Death and monopolize him."

Brother. Diana kept her expression clear, but a little well of something pleasant bubbled up inside her. And now that she knew it, she could see the resemblance: they had the same eyes, and same thick, curling hair—although Fiona's was fiery red. But just as clearly, she was an apple that hadn't fallen far from their mother's tree.

"You're leaving already?" Ethan asked Fiona in a suspicious voice. "It's only eight o'clock. Maxine will have a fit."

"I promised Carl I'd have him back in Grand Rapids before nine-thirty, and if I don't get started now, I won't be able to extricate him from Trib in time," his sister replied, looking across the terrace.

Diana followed her gaze and saw a large blond man with classically handsome features in deep conversation with Trib.

"I think they're discussing Hepplewhites or early Louis the Fourteenths or something like that. Besides, I already told Maxine about our timeline, and the queen granted me permission to leave early." Fiona grinned up at her brother from under a mass of curls. "You just have to know how to handle her."

"What did you do—tell her she'll live to be a hundred?"

Fiona merely smiled, then turned her attention back to Diana, releasing her hand at last. "Hope I'll see you again soon."

"It was a pleasure to meet you," Diana replied, still feeling a little lost in the undercurrents between the Murphy siblings. Then, in a whirl of skirts and coppery curls, Fiona was off on her three-inch platform sandals, and Diana and Ethan were alone.

"I'm sorry about that," he said, watching after his sister with exasperated affection.

"Sorry about what?"

He shook his head, then turned back to Diana. "Never mind. Fiona is just…Fiona. Are you having a good time?"

"It's a lovely party," she replied, then took a sip of her second champagne cocktail. She concurred with the general opinion: Trib was a genius with everything from food to ambience to cocktails. "And the weather is perfect. Do they really do a bash like this for Maxine every year?"

"I don't know how well you know Maxine Took, but could you imagine what would happen if they *didn't* throw a bash like this for her every year?"

Diana laughed. "You have a point there." Then she sobered self-consciously when she saw the look he gave her. Smoldering.

"You should do that more often," he said, holding her gaze with his. "Laugh. Smile."

Her cheeks went hot and Diana tore her eyes away. "I suppose we all should. Laugh more."

"Ethan! There you are."

Diana was heartily relieved by the interruption, and they turned to see Iva Bergstrom making her way toward them. She was dressed in a silky, robin's egg shell set off by a chunky necklace of silver and blue beads. A white sweater tossed over her shoulders matched her white capris and practical, low-heeled sandals—which revealed pale coral nail polish. Iva's fluffy hair was neat as a pin, and her round cheeks flushed with pleasure.

She was accompanied by a handsome, distinguished looking man about her age—though he was much taller than the petite woman, and dressed in well-cut, expensive clothing that seemed a little formal for a summer patio party. He was the only other man besides Trib who was wearing a tie, and he also had on a sport coat.

"I was hoping you'd still be here," Iva said as she and her companion approached. "We just arrived. Was that your sister leaving just now, Ethan? With the curly red hair? I'd so wanted to meet her. Anyway, Ethan—and Diana, you too. I wanted *you* to meet Hollis. Hollis Nath, this is Ethan Murphy, the author of *The Calm Blue Light*. And this is Diana Iverson. Hollis and I met just a few months ago."

"Back in April—I was in the area with some business contacts for a golf outing," said Hollis as he shook hands with Ethan and Diana. "A group of us ended up at Trib's for dinner one night, and the Tuesday Ladies were there. Best decision I ever made, walking into Trib's for pizza," he said, smiling down at Iva as he patted her hand. "That's how I met the woman who changed me."

Iva's cheeks flushed more pink, but she had the same stars in her eyes that he did. "Now, Hollis, don't be silly. You were always who you are, you just hadn't met the right woman yet."

He laughed heartily. "You're telling me. Three wives, and none of them stuck more than five years," he said to Ethan and Diana. "Well, I'll tell you, this one's going to stick." He lifted Iva's hand to noisily kiss the back of it.

"Now, Hollis," his companion replied with a demure flutter of eyelashes. "We've only known each other for two months. Let's not rush into any grand pronouncements."

"At our age, we don't have time not to rush," he said. "We aren't getting any younger." Then he turned his attention to Ethan. "I haven't read your book, young man, but Iva has been talking of little else. I'm not much into all of that—what do you call it, sweetheart?"

"*You* and Gideon—that's his grandson, and just as much a stick in the mud—call it woo-woo stuff," Iva said with an affectionate roll of her eyes. "I call it metaphysical interests."

"Yes," Hollis said, still smiling. "Whatever—it's a little out of my wheelhouse," he said.

"Well then you and Diana would get along quite well," Ethan said to the older man, glancing at her with a teasing smile. "She's a left-brained litigator and deals with facts and evidence—and avoids even a hint of hearsay like the plague."

"A litigator are you?" Hollis Nath looked at her with interest, then back to Iva. "Is this the young lady your friend was talking about, back in April?"

"That's right, darling. This is Jean Fickler's niece—she works for one of those large law firms down in Chicago." Iva looked at Diana. "Hollis and his grandson Gideon are partners in a very reputable firm in Grand Rapids, but they deal with wills and trusts and estate planning and all of that sort of business."

Nath spoke to Diana, "That's right—I remember now; your aunt was bragging about you and some of the large cases you'd litigated. Is it McNillan or Purdy that you're with? Forgive me, but I can't remember what she said."

"I'm with McNillan," she replied, a little abashed that her aunt had been going on about her to a group of strangers.

"Jean had a long conversation with that other gentleman —who was it, Hollis? The bald man with the Abe Vigoda eyebrows? Turned out your Uncle Tracer had done some work for his company, Diana, way back when it was called something else, and the Abe Vigoda man and Jean were going on about how it was such a small world that they should meet up in little old Wicks Hollow." She looked up at her companion with those same starry eyes. "I thought maybe it might be the beginning of a special friendship for Jean, just like you and I, Hollis...but now she's gone." Iva sighed, and sadness limned her eyes.

"And that," said he quietly, "is exactly why, at our age, there's no time to waste, sweetheart."

Iva was gazing up at him, and Hollis down at her—and suddenly Diana felt as if she and Ethan, and everyone else at the party, had disappeared from the scene—and that the older couple were, for all they noticed or cared, completely alone.

For some reason, that realization made her both hopeful and sad. Deeply sad.

The sun was low and the sky had become a dark, rich blue. Trib lit the logs in the wrought iron-enclosed fire pit and brought out a sea of citronella candles. Maxine had opened all of her gifts, and the loud voices of the party had begun to wind down—mainly because the guest of honor had left.

"I turn into a pumpkin at ten o'clock," Maxine was fond of saying.

"A pumpkin? How about a witch?" Baxter had muttered to Ethan.

"No, that's her *until* ten o'clock," he replied, and they clinked beer glasses, sharing the joke.

Despite missing Jean, Ethan had enjoyed the evening immensely, chatting with everyone from Maxine herself, to Mirabella and Reggie, to Cherry and Trib, to Orbra and her husband, and more. He and Bax and Declan Zyler had spent a good fifteen minutes discussing the prospects for the two big college football rivalries in the state, and who was going to end up Big Ten Champ.

Now he lingered on the lower terrace still talking to Baxter and Declan while he tried to keep from watching Diana. She sat nearby on one of the sofas, deep in conversation with Emily Delton as a half-empty champagne flute dangled from her fingers.

"I'm going to see if Emily needs a ride home," Baxter said, casting a glance at Declan. When his perceived rival didn't seem to care, Bax tossed down the last glug of his beer, smoothed his very close-cropped hair, and squared his shoulders.

"I've got to get going myself," said the blacksmith as Baxter walked off. "Still not used to this single-dad stuff, and I like to be home by eleven. Even though she's fifteen, that just doesn't seem old enough for Steph to be home alone after dark." Declan gave a pained smile and Ethan nodded.

"I don't have children, but I've got a dog. Sometimes it feels almost like the same thing. But most of the time—not so much."

They laughed companionably and Declan clapped him on the shoulder in a casual manner. "Let me know when you want me to take a look at your upper deck railing. Sounds like it wouldn't be too big of a job—I can probably squeeze it in between two restorations I'm working on in Grand Rapids." He paused before he started off. "And good luck, man."

When Ethan looked at him in confusion, Declan jerked a thumb toward Diana and grinned. "Like I said, good luck."

"Right." Feeling a little exposed, Ethan shook his new friend's hand in farewell, then ambled toward the sofa where Diana and Emily Delton were sitting.

As he approached, he heard the two women talking about a blowout and a gloss treatment.

Hmm. Cars? Maybe. But only because it was Emily, who owned the spa and salon outside of town, he guessed their conversation probably referred to something mysteriously feminine.

As Baxter took a seat next to Emily, who half-turned on the sofa toward him with a smile (that was encouraging), Ethan touched the back of the couch behind Diana.

She craned her head around. "Oh, Ethan," she said, rising immediately, "I was just thinking about you."

He looked down into her eyes, his heart stuttering a little. "Were you?"

He didn't intend for his voice to rumble so low and be filled with such meaningful interest—but there it was, helped along by the several beers he'd had over the evening and the fact that *he'd* been thinking about *her* all night.

And her response—eyes widening in surprise and a little confusion—was just fine with him. There was something about Diana Iverson that made him want to set her off balance whenever possible. Shake up that stiff lawyerly attitude and give her something to think about other than that damned cardiologist.

Stir the pot. Hmph. Maybe he was more like Fiona than he wanted to admit.

"Want to give me the details?" he asked, resisting the desire to step closer. He could smell her perfume though—a soft and feminine essence that delivered a little punch to the gut. Her scent mingling with the woodsmoke from the fire pit and the silver moonlight filtering over the dark curls of her hair made an irresistible combination. And her bare neck...it was so long and smooth and creamy and inviting...

"I was just..." It seemed he'd succeeded in tipping her out of that prim reserve, for she seemed unable to collect her thoughts. "I meant to tell you that I picked up a copy of your book at Pam's book shop, and I'm looking forward to reading it."

"Then I'm looking forward to hearing what you think—you being someone who's not all that receptive to elements of the metaphysical or supernatural."

She looked away, and for a moment he thought she was about to respond to his delicate prod. Maybe even with a little fire—which he realized he would enjoy. But instead, she said, "I'd better find Cherry. I'm sure she's ready to leave."

And that was when Ethan was, thankfully, able to disrupt her even more. "Cherry's already gone. She has a six a.m. yoga class, and she drove Maxine back too. I told Cherry I'd take you home—since it's on my way." Kind of.

"Oh." Her pretty mouth formed a circle that was glossy, soft, and inviting rather than tight and pruny. "Well, that's nice of you. Thank you."

"I'm ready to leave when you are."

She looked around. "Shouldn't we help clean up?"

"I asked Trib, but he's got his crew from the restaurant here. They'll all sit around and drink the rest of the champagne and beer, eat the leftover food, and have it all cleaned up by around three in the morning. It's sort of a tradition."

"Well, then, yes—I'm ready to go. It's nearly eleven."

She said goodbye to Trib, then started to walk up the terrace steps to the house and, presumably, to the driveway.

"Diana? This way." Ethan gestured down toward the lake with his thumb. "I came by boat."

"Oh," she said again, looking down at her pristine white dress and silvery, high heeled sandals. She didn't sound happy.

"Don't worry. I promise you won't end up in the lake," he said, then gestured to the set of stairs that led down to Trib's dock.

She looked as if she wanted to argue, then, with a shrug, began to descend the stairs.

"A canoe?" she said, stopping short when she saw his vessel tied up at the dock.

"It's cleaner than my fishing boat," he said with a chuckle. "I'll put my jacket over the seat, though, to make sure your dress doesn't get dirty." He did so, then turned back to her. "Let me help you in—it's a little tippy."

Once he got Diana in the front of the canoe, facing the

stern, Ethan climbed in the back. "Good night," he called, waving up to Trib as he pushed away from the dock.

"Good night." Their host's voice carried easily across the widening expanse of water as they drifted out into the silent, black lake. Even the wave-runners and motorboats had gone in for the night.

For a moment, there was only the fading sound of the last of the guests, then the soft plop of the paddle into the water and a quiet dripping as Ethan changed sides with the oar. The light from the shore grew fainter, leaving only the moon and stars and the disappearing sun to light the darkness.

Tall trees made a dark, forbidding fringe along the shoreline, and there were occasional splashes of light from houses or docks. But most of the illumination came from the quickly darkening western horizon. A streak of bright red glazed the sky where the sun had just dropped behind the forest, and then it, too, faded.

A loon called out, sending a shiver of familiarity down Ethan's spine, and its cry was joined by a whippoorwill and chirping crickets: the comforting, familiar sounds of Michigan in the summer.

The canoe moved silently through the water, the oar cutting into its blackness with clean, smooth strokes. After a while, Ethan drew the paddle from the water and rested it across his thighs, letting the canoe drift. He was in no hurry to get home.

Diana's silhouette only hinted at her features in the dim light, but he could picture the wide, full curve of her mouth with no trouble at all. The moonlight gleamed over her ivory skin and iced her hair with a blue tint. She sat on the canoe bench, facing him with her knees to one side, and feet tucked modestly under her seat as women did when wearing short skirts. She had taken off her sandals, though, and the silver shoes gleamed on the dark floor. He could see the soft ripples the breeze made, playing with her thick, sexy hair.

Ethan drew in a long, slow breath and admitted it: he hadn't felt this depth of attraction for a woman since…well, forever. Maybe even *ever*. No matter how much he didn't *want* to be attracted to the stiff, repressed attorney, he was.

And, sadly, the knowledge that Diana was involved with another man was the only thing that kept him from making a move, female moratorium or no.

"This is so peaceful," she said after a moment.

She didn't ask him why he'd stopped paddling, nor did she seem to mind that they simply drifted—odd for a woman so hesitant about taking the canoe in the first place. Not that he minded in the least. She was a lot more approachable now that she'd mellowed out a bit. Since they'd had that talk yesterday in her kitchen. He had to admit he really admired the sincere admission of her mistake and her gracious apology.

"Did you enjoy yourself tonight?" he asked.

Diana's smile gleamed in the darkness. She turned so that the wind caught her full in the face, allowing the breeze to lift and toss her thick hair. "Yes. More than I thought I would. The people of Wicks Hollow are an interesting bunch."

"With Maxine topping the list of interesting characters," he added, and she laughed.

"Yes, but it's obvious that, despite her caustic ways, she's got a heart of gold."

"And a spine of steel. Impossible to get that woman to do anything she doesn't want to."

"That's the way it should be—when you get to be eighty years old. Aunt Jean was that way too. She didn't care what anyone thought of her. She was just who she was."

"I think that's part of the blessing of age," he said, thinking of his mother. "And a lesson we can take from our elders."

"Spoken like a true cultural anthropologist," she said dryly, and he laughed.

Silence reigned between them for a moment. Again, there was only the cry of the loon and the occasional plop of the oar sliding into the water as he adjusted their path. He would have been lulled by the peacefulness if he weren't so damned *aware* of her.

At last he spoke. "Have you looked up the meaning of those two cards you have lying out in the den?"

Diana's shoulders drew up and he saw her stiffen across the boat. "Of course not. I told you, I don't pay any attention to those things."

"Would you like to know what they mean?"

She didn't respond; just stared up at the heavens.

Way to ruin the mood, Murphy. He continued to paddle, debating with himself whether to remain silent or to share what he knew.

The latter won out—as it most often did. He was, after all, at the heart, a teacher.

"The Wheel of Fortune often indicates a turning point in one's life," he spoke quietly. "It suggests that one is experiencing a change—such as in a relationship or career—or becoming aware of a larger picture...or even learning one's true role or purpose in life."

When Diana didn't speak, he continued, trying to keep his tone conversational. "The interesting thing is that the Two of Swords is an opposing card—it's very odd that you should pull those two up together."

"I didn't pull them." Her body language indicated some sort of struggle, as her shoulders rounded and her hands fisted in her lap.

"The Two of Swords alludes to someone being at a stalemate, or having blocked emotions and denying one's true feelings. It can even mean someone is avoiding the truth."

He adjusted the boat's drift once more, and to his dismay, saw Jean's white clapboard house looming far too close. A single light burned in one of the windows.

"What were you thinking about when you drew those cards, Diana?"

She bent forward, resting her head in her hands. "I didn't draw them, Ethan." Her voice was muffled. "I think Aunt Jean did."

"What did you say?" He stared at her, questioning his own hearing as much as her words.

She looked up from her hands, eyes wide with shock and despair, glistening in the faulty light. "I don't know." Her voice trailed off into a pained moan. "I don't know what to think, Ethan."

Was she crying?

Oh, Christ.

He set the oar aside and stood carefully, one foot on each side of the gunwale. Holding the sides of the canoe to steady the vessel, he took careful, crablike steps until he was able to crouch in front of her.

Any other words he may have uttered froze in his throat as he became wholly, startlingly aware of her—her nearness, her scent, the soft brush of her knees against his legs. Ethan tentatively touched her head, his fingers sinking into the depths of her hair and sliding down the back of her skull. "I'm sorry. I pushed too hard."

She raised her face, inches from him, and he could see that, yes, tears glittered in her eyes. He was shocked that the cool facade had been stripped from her face, and naked emotion—fear, pain, confusion—shone in her moonlit features.

"Migraine," she managed to say, agony lacing her voice. "So sudden...I think I may be going to...get sick."

His hormones pulled back, replaced by instant concern. "Do you have meds in your purse? Can you take them without water?"

She shook her head, huddling back into her lap. "No." Her voice was muffled with pain. "At home."

Ethan turned quickly, gingerly, and hurried back to the end of the canoe as the boat rocked with his haste. But he was careful—the last thing she needed was to get dumped in the lake.

He picked up the paddle and began to make clean, strong strokes. The boat surged through the water and moments later, he was helping her out of the tipsy canoe at Jean's dock.

Through a haze of pain, Diana made her feet move in the proper direction. She stumbled over a sharp rock and gasped in pain—she'd left her shoes in the boat. Before she could protest, Ethan swept her up, gathering her against his chest. As his strong arms encircled her, she allowed her head to drop onto the front of his shoulder.

It was so nice to just...let go.

His steps were sure and smooth, and she closed her eyes, trying to relax against the pain, while being very aware of the strong arms around her, and the heat of his granite-like chest seeping through his shirt.

The bob and sway, the easy ebb and flow that jolted her against him as he made his way up the path was surprisingly comforting. Her cheek rested on the taut, warm material of his shirt, and when she drew in a deep breath, she caught his scent —that deep, masculine essence that seemed comforting and invigorating all at once.

His stride changed as they neared the top of the incline.

"Almost there." His voice was quiet and steady in her ear, despite his exertions.

"Thank you." Her mouth almost brushed the warmth of his neck, and she turned slightly away, aware that beneath her misery was a strong flare of attraction toward him.

"I'm going to have to set you down," he said, stepping onto the porch. "Do you know where your keys are?" His voice was more gentle than she'd ever heard it, and he set her carefully, as if she were made of the most fragile glass, on the porch swing.

He got both of them into the house efficiently, and settled her in Aunt Jean's chair in the library. "I'll get you something to take those pills with."

When he returned, she gulped two capsules and the water, and allowed Ethan to take the glass from her limp fingers. Resting her head back against the chair, she closed her eyes as she heard him turn on the lamp with a soft click. "Thank you."

Without speaking, Ethan pulled up a chair next to her. There was silence for a long while, and if he hadn't been sitting next to her, Diana would have thought he'd left. When the pain eased and she opened her eyes, she found him watching her from his seat.

"Better now?"

Diana nodded, suddenly very aware of his nearness and the blatant heat in his eyes. She shifted in her seat to shake off the intense awareness, her heart thumping crazily, and looked away from him—anywhere but at those steady, deep brown eyes fringed by thick, curling lashes.

By some misfortune, her gaze landed on the two Tarot cards that remained in their places on the desk, and Ethan's attention followed hers.

Nevertheless, he said nothing until a few moments passed, and then it wasn't what she'd expected.

"How often do you have migraines like this?"

"Hardly ever anymore," she replied. "But I've been having them much more frequently in the last week. And they've been more intense, coming on more quickly than I can ever remember. Maybe there's something in the air up here."

Ethan gave her a significant look. "I was thinking the same thing."

But Diana was already violently rejecting the idea—whatever it was. "I'm under a lot of stress," she explained. "With work, and…other stuff."

"Diana. At the risk of infuriating you, I'd like to suggest something." He grinned crookedly, but his eyes became wary.

"Infuriating me?"

"Is it possible the migraines could be the result of an inability, or an unwillingness, to allow parts of your unconscious to surface to your conscious mind?" His gaze searched hers as he continued, "Because you're suppressing something from your consciousness?"

She gaped at him, ready to argue, but just then, a shrill *brrrringg!* cut the silence. She looked down the hall toward the kitchen, where she could see the phone sitting like an ugly black toad.

It was either Jonathan calling…or it wasn't. But it was nearly midnight. Who else would be calling here?

"Answer it. Please?"

Ethan gave her a measured look, but he rose to do as she asked. She watched him pick up the phone and realized she'd curled her fingers in to fists.

"Hello," he said. There was a pause, then, "Yes, she's here. Who's calling?"

Diana was already out of the chair. She didn't need Ethan

to convey any message, for Jonathan's irate tones were audible. Her insides were a jumble, for she knew she'd just crossed a chasm, making a leap from which she and Jonathan might never recover.

And for some reason, it didn't bother her.

She held out her hand for the receiver. "Hi Jonathan."

"Who is that?" he demanded. "I've been calling you all night, and you haven't answered your cell phone either. What's a man doing at your house this late?"

"Definitely not the same thing Valerie the Voracious Vixen was doing in your hotel room in Las Vegas," she said, much more calmly than she felt.

"*Diana*," he gasped, his shock reverberating over the wire. "When are you going to let that go? I told you, I made a mistake. Is this—is this some sort of revenge play? So you can get even with me?" He heaved a deep, wounded sigh. "I guess I can understand it, Diana-baby. And if that's what it takes for you to get over this, then I guess I have no choice."

She avoided looking at Ethan as she replied, "Think what you like, Jonathan." Then she lapsed into silence—a powerful place to be. Waiting for him to speak.

"Diana," he said again, a little more strongly this time. "When are you coming home? I miss you," he added, his voice softening. "I don't know how you think we can work this out with you gone like this."

"I don't think I'll be here for more than another week or two."

"Another *week*? Or *two*?" His voice rose. Then, as if realizing his mistake, he softened his voice yet again. "I miss you, Diana. I *love* you. Come home soon to me. Please?"

"Good night, Jonathan," she said, and reached across Ethan to hang up the phone. Only after the receiver settled into place did she look at him.

"Valerie the Voracious Vixen?" A smile played around the corners of his mouth.

Diana couldn't contain a little smile of her own. "That's one of the more polite things I've called her." She bit her lip and then, suddenly feeling utterly awkward, began to play with the twisty phone cord. "Thank you. For—for everything tonight."

Ethan stood, still watching her. She could fairly feel the curiosity and unspoken questions rolling off him, and appreciated it when he only said, "I guess I'll be heading home now."

But he made no move to do so.

Diana's palms felt damp and something alive seemed to be squiggling around in her stomach, not at all unpleasantly. In fact, the feeling was warm and expectant, and exciting.

The cool air of summer night wafted in through the open window, bringing the scent of lake and a distant bonfire. But it was him she was most aware of—the crisp, masculine scent in which she'd buried her face only a short time ago, the warmth of his presence, the solidness of his strength.

Diana's heart began to thump harder as she looked up at him, and it was all she could do to keep from backing away. His eyes were dark, glittering with sudden heat as he assessed her.

"Have a good night, Ethan," she said, her pulse rate suddenly skyrocketing. "Thank you again."

"Don't you think we ought to make this mutually beneficial?" he asked, his voice low and tinged with irony. His gaze seemed to pin her there, against the counter in the kitchen. Even though he still had not moved to leave.

"What do you mean?"

"I mean, if you're going to use me as a deterrent to your boyfriend, or a pawn in your game of revenge, I think it's only right," he said, reaching for her smoothly but unequivocally, "that I actually earn the reputation." He closed his hands around her elbows, tugging her so close that her bare feet bumped his shoes. "Don't you, Diana?"

She couldn't move, even when she saw that his attention had fixed on her mouth—the mouth that she knew was parted slightly, moist from the tip of her nervous tongue...and waiting in anticipation for his to close over it.

"I..." Her heart was ramming hard and loud in her chest, and a flush of heat surged up through her body.

"That's what I thought," he murmured, his face moving closer, filling her vision as he captured her mouth with his.

His move was soft and sensual, coaxing her to relax against him as his lips covered hers. He caressed her mouth lightly at first, teasing her, playing with the taste and texture of her lips as his fingers tightened at her waist.

Diana settled her hands against him, against his broad chest, feeling the warmth and firm shift of muscle beneath. That lively squiggling in her belly turned to heat and pleasure, rolling through her, spiraling down to her core.

Oh God. She lost her brains right then, lost every bit of common sense and control as she turned her face up to take more of his kiss, to absorb him. He gave a soft sigh at her surrender, and their lips and tongues tangled in a sleek, sensual dance. His hair felt soft and thick around her fingers, his shoulders spanned wide and muscular beneath her palm.

When he moved from her mouth, trailing his lips to the curve of her jaw to whisper her name near her ear, Diana realized she was sagging weakly, her body plastered to him, the edge of the counter pressing into her spine. It was that sharp bite from the formica that brought her back to herself. She pulled away, panting a little, and definitely muddle-headed.

Ethan was watching her with those hot amber eyes, his chest rising and falling, his lips full and damp from *her*. She pressed a hand to her own swollen mouth and stared up at him.

"Well, then," he murmured in a low, rough voice. "That was a good start." He started to reach for her again, but she slipped away.

"Do you feel better now?" she asked, forcing a little bite into her voice.

"Not precisely." He was still looking at her with dark intensity, and her stomach gave a surge and flip at the heat in his brown eyes. "But if that's what's going to happen when you use me to get back at your boyfriend, I'm not going to complain."

"I didn't—I wasn't …." Her voice trailed off. "Hell. Yes I was. I'm sorry."

"Don't be sorry—for that," he murmured. His eyes slid over her, as sure and heavy as if he touched her with his hands. "I'm not."

"Ethan," she said, struggling to keep her composure. "I didn't mean—I mean, this doesn't *mean* anything. Jonathan is still—" She crossed her arms over her middle as a shield against him. "Everything was innocent until…you…" Her voice trailed off. Her lips were still throbbing, and there were other areas of her body that were hot and damp and pulsing as well. "I think you'd better go."

He gave her one last steady look, then a curt nod. "All right. Good night, Diana."

EIGHT

THE NEXT EVENING, Diana was in the kitchen making pasta for dinner. She'd spent most of the day working—responding to emails, reviewing documents from the office, and beginning to schedule depositions for the AXT case.

As she tossed her serving of bucatini with garlic and oil, she realized she kept glancing at the ugly black phone, half expecting its shrill ring.

Of course Ethan hadn't called. She hadn't expected him to. Because he wouldn't.

He'd just come over and walk right into the house, she thought with a sudden smile.

She touched her lips, remembering that long, hot kiss. No, he didn't have any reason to come here. Not while she was still tied up with Jonathan. And even if she wasn't.

It was only a kiss. One, simple, *hot*, crazy kiss.

But the quivers in her belly made her think maybe it hadn't been so simple.

Jonathan hadn't called since Ethan answered the phone late last night, and she wasn't certain how she felt about that.

She wasn't certain how she felt about anything regarding

Jonathan anymore. In fact, she was rather enjoying her life without him in it. She hadn't missed him at all.

He was, she'd realized, a lot of work.

Not only that, but she was beginning to feel very much at home in this restful lake house. Far more than she ever thought she would, coming from an exciting, rewarding, high-speed job in the big city. Despite the odd things that had been happening, she was actually enjoying the opportunity to relax and be carefree.

The thought struck her: *The Fool.*

It was the first card she'd seen from the Tarot deck. And hadn't her first thought upon seeing it been that she couldn't remember the last time she'd felt as carefree as the Fool seemed?

A shiver ran across the back of her shoulders and the hair on the nape of her neck prickled. She placed her dinner on the table and contemplated the absurd, ludicrous, impossible thought that the card—which had fallen randomly from the deck—had a pointed meaning in her life.

Besides…soon she'd be back at McNillan—in another two weeks at the absolute latest—and she'd have to decide what to do about the house. Did she really want to have to maintain and manage the property from Chicago?

But if she sold it, she'd feel a little like she was betraying Aunt Jean.

Don't sell the house, she thought suddenly. *It would make a nice retreat. It's not that far from Chicago—only a few hours, and it would be nice to have a place to take the kids—*

Whoa. What? She tried to stop the thought, but it roared in from nowhere and would not be ignored—instead, settling in her mind like a stubborn anchor.

Two children, she thought, her mind galloping off—maybe three. And suddenly, a picture—as clear and tangible as a photograph—flashed into her mind: two small dark-haired boys and a toddling little girl chasing a big, dark dog, and Diana herself laughing at them, joining the chase over an expanse of green grass—

A big dog? She didn't even *like* dogs.

And she was afraid of the big ones.

But the image in her mind had been so *real*.

"Don't be silly," she said aloud, looking at Motto—who sat waiting hopefully for more food to appear in her dish. Diana gave a sharp shake of her head, then poured a healthy glass of the Pinot Gris she'd pulled from the fridge. "It was just a random thought."

But as she sat at the table and settled in to eat, Diana thought about The High Priestess. She looked at Motto again. "How did you manage to pick out that card more than once, anyway?"

The cat swished its tail and gave a guttural meow that sounded annoyed.

The High Priestess. *Look beyond the obvious. Open your mind.*

That was what Ethan had said about the card.

And that card, Diana reminded herself as the queer feeling rumbling in her stomach became more insistent, had turned up three times.

Or *been* turned up.

Here, in the full light of day, she could no longer deny it. Something or some*one* had made those cards turn up. It couldn't be a coincidence. It wasn't random.

Even her logical, science-based mind had to acknowledge that.

She bit her lip and looked around as if to see a ghostly presence hovering nearby, as if her unspoken thoughts had summoned it.

I can't believe I'm actually thinking this.

Diana took a gulp of wine so large she didn't even enjoy it, then she set the glass down. Her heart was beating hard and her palms were damp.

She closed her eyes, gripped the edge of the table, and said aloud: "Aunt Jean…if you're really there…give me a sign."

Ethan tossed the tennis ball straight into the air so high that it sang through the topmost branches of a pine, then caught it when it came whistling back down. He threw the neon yellow ball up again, flickering a glance at an at-attention Cady, who was frozen, poised to take off after it should he pitch it horizontally.

"Ready?" he asked, excitement lighting his voice. The lab's ears perked up and her eyes brightened even more, riveted on the ball. Ethan wound up and fired the ball over the lab's head, toward the lake.

Cady was after it like a shot, thrashing through the forest down, and probably into, the water. Ethan stood, hands on his hips, watching her black tail spiral down the incline. It was just brushing up against evening, and this was the first time he'd really been outside all day. He'd been working on thoughts for his new book, ignoring Cady's pitiful, hopeful eyes, from ten a.m. until now—which was, he glanced at his phone to check—almost seven.

Ethan looked up at the towering pines enclosing the clearing that was his yard. Then he found himself looking northwest, toward Jean's house. Something kindled in his belly.

Hot damn. What a kiss.

And damned if he hadn't tossed and turned more than a

little over it last night. Diana had taken advantage of Ethan—manipulated his presence—to get back at her cardiologist for cheating on her. That much had been clear from her side of the conversation.

It *had* been easier for him to get to the phone—she was still recovering from her migraine. She still looked frail and fragile.

It had been logical for him to answer the call.

Still, he knew she'd deliberately made the decision for him to do so. She was not the type of person to do anything impulsively.

Clearly there were issues between her and Wertinger, and while part of Ethan would relish it if Diana dumped the pinhead's ass, at the same time he didn't want to play any part in the reason.

But Ethan's tolerance for infidelity was nonexistent after his experience with Jenny and Lexie, and clearly Wertinger had already crossed that line. So, in his mind, the guy deserved what he got.

In the end, after weighing out everything, Ethan figured he hadn't been totally gypped in the bargain. He might have been taken advantage of, but he'd also taken some of that advantage back.

The problem was, one kiss hadn't been nearly enough. Now that he'd tested things out, he definitely wanted more.

Cady came crashing up the slope, dripping wet, ball clutched in the back of her jaws. She pranced proudly in front of Ethan, circled him four times, squatted to pee, then paused to shake the water from her short fur. Then she dropped the ball at his feet.

Ethan picked up the ball, this time using a baseball bat to thwack it into the woods toward the general vicinity of Diana's house, and wondered what the chances were of it making the mile to her yard so he had to chase it down.

And then, just as if he'd conjured her up, the sleek gold Lexus came around the corner of his drive.

Surprised and delighted, Ethan nevertheless managed to keep a carefully polite, easy look on his face as he ambled over to greet her.

"You took the drive a little slower this time," he teased as he approached her window. "I didn't hear you coming."

"Ethan," she said, leaping out of the car without turning it off. "I—" She glanced over, gasped, and practically fell back into the car, slamming the door shut as Cady barreled up to them, barking like a maniac.

Ethan took one look at her wide eyes and pale face and realized that though she was afraid of the dog, something else had also upset her.

"Cady, *down*." His voice was low and firm, and the black lab dropped to the ground as if she'd been shot.

Good girl, he thought proudly, and bent to give her the kudos she deserved. That was one of the most important commands for a dog to learn to heed—especially one that lived near deer, skunks, and other wildlife.

Nevertheless, as he petted Cady, Ethan looked up into Diana's car window. "Something's wrong. Something happened."

She nodded vehemently, and her face was still pale. But he didn't think it was only because of Cady. "It's all right. She won't hurt you. You can get out of the car," he told Diana.

"I—Ethan, can you come back to my house? Now? Please?"

The taut urgency in her voice put to bed any possibility that she wanted him back at her place so she could tear off his clothes and take advantage of him (damn). So he replied,

"Sure. Just let me put Cady—this is Cady, by the way—inside."

His heart broke when he saw the crestfallen expression in the lab's eyes—not only was this interrupting their playtime, for which she'd waited patiently all day, but she didn't even get to meet or greet the new person? And now she had to go inside while he left? And she hadn't even done anything *wrong!*

"Aw, damn it, Cady, I'm sorry," he told her as she followed him inside, tail and head drooping. "I promise I'll make it up to you."

And he did—rummaging in the fridge to find half a hamburger he had left over from a few days ago. "Here you go, good girl. Hope this takes some of the sting out of this. I promise you'll get to meet her next time," he said, giving her a last pat on the head. "I'll make sure there is a next time, and, trust me, you'll like the way she smells."

Because he knew Diana was waiting, and that something had upset her, he didn't linger. Nothing like being caught between two females, he thought grimly. But at least with Cady, he knew exactly where he stood—and dogs were far more forgiving than their human counterparts.

"Did someone break in again?" he asked as soon as he closed the door to the car. "Joe Cap had one of his officers drive by every hour or so last night, but she might have missed something."

Diana glanced at him as she navigated the drive. She seemed calmer but her fingers were white knuckled on the steering wheel. "He did? That was nice of him."

"We figured with everyone being at the party, whoever tried before might be tempted to try again, knowing the house would be empty." Ethan shrugged. "I guess if Helga—that's her name, Officer Helga van Hest; she's Orbra's granddaughter, you know—had seen anything, she would have let you know. And if you'd noticed anything you'd have done so before now."

"No, I didn't hear anything from the police. But something did happen. I wanted to show you."

Mystified, he settled back in his seat for the two more minutes it took to get to Jean's house.

She took him to the back door, by the kitchen. "I was getting ready to eat dinner—"

"Whatever it was, it smells amazing," he said as she put her hand on the door to open it, and realized he was starving.

She cast a mildly exasperated glance at him, then continued. "And I don't know why—I *really* am not sure why I did this—it's just not like me to—well, anyway, I…was annoyed with everything. About the Tarot cards, and—and some other stuff. And I just kind of called out to Aunt Jean…"

By now Ethan was staring at her as she fumbled through her explanation in a very uncharacteristic manner. "You called out to your dead aunt?" he repeated carefully.

"I told her if she was really there, could she give me a sign," she finished grimly.

Ethan's pulse had kicked up and he looked at her hand, which was still closed over the doorknob. "I take it she did."

"See for yourself." She shoved the door open.

NINE

WHOA.

Ethan stepped over the kitchen threshold and took in the scene.

Diana's uneaten dinner, neatly arranged with a wine glass, napkin, and flatware, sat undisturbed on the table.

But the rest of the place was pretty much a disaster—and he didn't think it was from her cooking. Broken plates. Tumbled pots and pans. A half-open drawer with tongs, spatulas, and other utensils spilling out. The narrow rag rug that had been in front of the stove ever since Ethan had met Jean was now *hanging* from the open door of the pantry.

"Fortunately, she didn't go for the knives," Diana said in a surprisingly calm voice.

"Or your dinner," Ethan said, matching her tone.

Because what else could he do? He couldn't laugh...not quite yet.

"Right." She still stood on the threshold. "It was like a cyclone, Ethan. I was sitting there, and all of a sudden..." She shrugged, at a loss for words, and just flapped her hands around.

Diana's face was pale and her eyes wide, but to his surprise, she didn't seem frightened. She seemed...subdued. And strangely accepting. It never occurred to him not to believe her account; not only did he have a wide open mind for the metaphysical and supernatural, but there was no other explanation.

"I'll help you clean up," he said. "And then we can talk. But I am kind of hungry," he added wistfully, looking at the untouched plate of pasta.

Diana gave a short laugh. "It won't take me long to make you a plate, too."

"Thank God," he said with his own desperate chuckle. "Because that smells amazing. In fact, why don't you cook and I'll clean up."

It didn't take all that long for him to put the mess to rights. Aunt Jean hadn't gone for total destruction; she'd just wanted to make her point.

"Wine?" Diana asked as Ethan swept up the last bit of broken china.

"I think a big glass would be in order," he told her.

"I'll say." She gave him exactly what he asked for: a very generous pour of the straw-colored vintage she'd had open.

And by the time he swallowed his first sip, she was tossing two portions of oily, garlic-scented pasta in large, shallow bowls. His mouth watered as she grated cheese over each one, then sprinkled each mound with shredded basil and red pepper flakes.

"I didn't eat lunch or dinner," he confessed as they sat down. "I'm really glad you asked Jean to give you a sign."

Diana chuckled, and he felt another clutch in his gut. She was laughing more in his presence now, and he hadn't exaggerated—she was breathtaking when she relaxed and smiled.

Was she also more relaxed now that she had irrefutable, black and white proof of what she'd tried to resist? Ethan had a strong suspicion that was the case, though he thought better of saying it.

But when, after two small bites of pasta and a large gulp of wine, Diana finally spoke, her words stopped him cold.

"Aunt Jean was murdered."

He had a mouthful of the hollow, spaghetti-like bucatini, otherwise he might have responded—though he didn't know what he would have said.

Diana went on. "It's a long story, but after today—after this," she said, sweeping the vicinity of the kitchen with her hand, "I kind of have to believe it."

She took a sip of wine, then continued. "I've been having nightmares ever since I got here. Every night, when I slept in Aunt Jean's bed, I would wake up from these horrible dreams. It took me until Saturday morning, after the worst of them all, before I realized I was dreaming about being smothered."

She looked at him from under her lashes, and he recognized the mixture of shyness and determination in her eyes. This was difficult for her—the entire situation was, but also—and perhaps even more so—the verbalization of what she'd experienced and her obvious change of belief. Thus, he didn't interrupt. He did nothing but nod encouragingly and keep his expression steady. He didn't want to spook her—so to speak.

"I was not only dreaming of being smothered, but I was dreaming that *I* was Aunt Jean *being* smothered. At first I just thought it was related to sleeping in the bed where she'd died, but…it seemed like more than that. And then I was kind of speaking out loud—to the cats," she added quickly, bringing a quick smile to his face, "about how I didn't believe in stuff like that, or ghosts or…whatever." She hunched a little, looking up as if expecting another cyclonic sign from Jean.

"And I heard this loud noise from the library—this was Sunday night, after Captain Longbow checked out the house and left after I was broken into—and so I knew I was alone. I thought it was the cats, but they were upstairs. So..." She drew in a deep breath, exhaled, sipped her wine, then continued.

"I went into the den. And there were five books on the floor. They had to have just fallen—or been tossed—because they weren't there when Captain Longbow and I looked through the house. And the title of each one of them began with the word 'murder.'" She twirled bucatini around her fork, then slipped it in her mouth.

"Well," said Ethan after a long moment. "I would say Jean was giving you a pretty clear message." He started to take another bite of the most excellent meal, then paused. "Last night, in the boat...did you say what I thought you said? That *Jean* had picked those Tarot cards?"

She was staring at him with such soft, warm, emotion-filled eyes that his pulse skittered more wildly than Cady's nails on wood floors.

"You believe me."

It took him a moment to steady his voice so he could speak. "Of course I believe you, Diana. If anyone had the ability to come back and haunt someone so they could find her murderer, it would be Genevieve Fickler."

She laughed, and tears began to sparkle in her eyes. He understood they were tears of relief and release rather than mirth, and that made him fall even harder for her. Right then.

Boom. He was cooked.

"Tell me about the cards Jean picked for you," he said in an effort to distract himself from the wild mess he was in.

"When I was putting away the, uh, murder books, the phone rang in the kitchen and I ran out of the den to answer it. I knocked into the piecrust table, and the Tarot card box fell off. That had happened before," she said, then bit her lip as she collected her thoughts, "and that's yet another thing I have to tell you—how The High Priestess kept turning up. Anyway, when I came back from answering the phone—this was still Sunday night, I picked up the spilled cards and put them away. And then I saw the two cards—the ones you noticed: the Wheel of Fortune and the Two of Swords. They were just sitting on Aunt Jean's desk. Like someone had put them there."

"Apparently someone had."

She nodded, looking at him with that same soft, deep gaze—like a trusting child. And coming from a strong, pragmatic woman like Diana Iverson, that sort of open, vulnerable expression shook a guy to the core.

"So…now what?" she said. "I believe—no, I guess I *know* Aunt Jean was murdered. There's no way Captain Longbow—or any authority figure—is going to believe me when I tell them I know she was smothered because of a few dreams and strange incidents. They'll cart me off to a mental hospital."

Ethan suddenly felt a little wary. "But maybe the author of the bestselling book on near-death experiences could help give you some credibility?"

Diana's eyes flared, and the soft look vanished. Her face smoothed into creamy marble. She became, he imagined, the pragmatic, practical, assertive litigator.

"No," she said coolly. "It's more like, maybe someone who supposedly cared for my aunt might be willing to help find out who killed her."

Ethan cursed himself. Well, he'd stepped into that one, and he had no one to blame but himself for ruining the momentary connection between them.

"Right. That makes far more sense. So I guess we should talk motive," he said, in an effort to get past the awkward moment. "The common ones for murder: love, revenge, hatred, and the most obvious—at least in Jean's case—money. Who benefits from her death?"

"I do." Diana's voice was still flat and hard.

"Obviously. But just as obviously, you didn't smother her."

She lifted a brow and gave him a measured look. "I'm glad you realize that."

"But who else benefits from her death—monetarily or otherwise?"

"Well, I inherited most everything. The house here on the lake—"

"Which in itself is worth a nice chunk of change. A couple acres on Wicks Lake, five miles from Lake Michigan, in the middle of tourism central? Yes, you're talking a million—maybe closer to two—right here."

Diana nodded; she was well aware of the value of the property. But she also knew that was only a piece of her inheritance. The question was, what did anyone else know? She no longer suspected Ethan Murphy of anything underhanded, but that didn't mean she was going to tell him everything. She settled for saying, "Aunt Jean had some other investments worth quite a bit. Those came to me as well, except for a nice annuity that goes to the Wicks Hollow Veterinary Clinic and Animal Shelter."

"I can't imagine Melvin Horner creeping into this house and doing away with Jean," Ethan said. He'd finished his dinner and was looking longingly at what was left on Diana's plate—which was more than half her meal.

Having a ghost destroy your kitchen could put a real damper on your appetite, Diana discovered. But apparently not so for Ethan. She pushed her plate across the table to him. "Eat up. We don't want you to expire from lack of food."

He didn't hesitate, and dumped the rest of her pasta into

his bowl, mixing it in the dredges of olive oil and peppers left over from his. The man certainly enjoyed his food.

"What about other family members? Didn't Jean have anyone else who might be angry you inherited and they didn't?"

Diana shook her head. "She and Uncle Trace didn't have any children—he was fifteen years older than she was. And my father, who was Aunt Jean's brother, died fifteen years ago. They didn't have any other siblings. So I can't think of any other family that might have expected to inherit."

They both lapsed into silence.

"What other possible reason could there be to kill her?" she said after another sip of wine.

"Have you thought about—well—asking her?" Ethan said, gesturing with a fork rolled thick with bucatini. "I mean, she seems to be pretty well-versed in from-the-afterlife communication."

Diana's lips twitched. She was sure *reams* of students at U of C had wild crushes on him. And why couldn't she seem to stay irritated with him? "I suppose I could try that. Did you hear Ethan, Aunt Jean? We need a hint or a clue about who killed you and why."

They both waited, still and silent. But nothing happened.

"Maybe she used up her quota of comm skills for the day," he said, pushing back from the table. He stood, collecting the two bowls and sets of flatware, and brought them over to the sink. The dishes clattered quietly as he scraped then washed them with the efficiency of a man used to the task. He slipped the pasta bowls into slots on Aunt Jean's dish drainer to dry.

"I wish I had a way to talk to her—oh. *Wait.*" Diana stilled, feeling a certain buzz in her belly. The same sort of buzz she often got—and tried to ignore—when she was working on a case. She stood to gather up the wine bottle and their glasses. "Aunt Jean called me three times the week before she died. That was really unusual."

"You don't know why she wanted to talk to you?"

Diana appreciated that he kept any hint of judgment or accusation from his voice. "No, but she did leave a voice mail on my cell phone. It didn't sound urgent or I would have called her back right away. But she was obviously determined to talk to me. I'll have to check whether I still have the voicemail. Maybe she said something that will help."

"Jean called me as well, but she just missed me. I'd left for Peru the day before, and I didn't get the message till I got back. She wanted me to call her right away."

They looked at each other. "All right. Maybe there was something going on neither of us knew about that had something to do with—with her death," Diana said. "Or maybe the calls had nothing to do with anything but her wanting to talk to us."

"Don't forget, Diana, that someone's broken into the house at least twice. Possibly more."

"Twice?" She paused, standing next to him by the sink.

"Right." He sucked in a breath through his teeth and shoved a hand into his hair. "I didn't tell you about that—well, for reasons which will become obvious. The day I came over here and left the note...well, when I got here I thought I saw someone at the window—even though I didn't see a car in the drive. So I knocked and knocked, and no one answered."

"So you let yourself in." As he'd done, Diana made certain she kept her tone from being confrontational or accusatory.

"Right. But I was certain I'd seen someone, and I thought it might have been you not wanting to answer the door." He gave her a weak smile. "But when we were inside, Cady went nuts—barking and running around. At the time, I thought she'd seen a squirrel through the window—that usually sets her off—but maybe she saw something else."

"Someone sneaking away." It wasn't difficult for her to finish his thought process. She set the glasses on the counter. "Out the back or the cellar door."

He shrugged. "At the time I thought it might have been you, just trying to avoid me. But now, I'm wondering if it could have been someone else."

Diana's face heated and she bit her lip, feeling awkward again. "I wouldn't have been sneaking around trying to avoid you," she told him. "I would have just told you to leave if I didn't want to see you."

She looked up and their eyes met. To her relief, she saw humor in his. "Yes, I got that," he said dryly. "But I am certainly glad we're past that point."

"Oh, I'll still tell you to leave if I don't want you here," she said, pursing her lips to fight back a grin.

Now he gave her a full-blown smile that made her belly do a soft, pleasant roll. "Or if you want me to stay."

His voice was hardly more than a murmur, and it had the same effect on her as if he'd touched her with one of those wide, powerful hands. He was certainly standing close enough to her to do so, there in a corner of the kitchen.

Diana swallowed through a dry throat and dredged up the courage to address a related topic. "That reminds me—I want to apologize again about last night. I didn't intend to make you feel manipulated, or used, Ethan. It was irresponsible and—"

"No sweat. It was easier for me to answer the phone. It was innocent," he said, looking down at her. "Until I made it otherwise." His voice dropped so low it seemed to slide along her skin. He held her eyes for a moment. "So maybe I ought to be the one apologizing."

Diana almost couldn't breathe. He didn't look the least bit sorry, and, to tell the truth, she didn't feel sorry either.

"Apology accepted," she said, her own voice unexpectedly husky. "No big deal."

She started to move past him, but he stood firm, forcing her to wait or to press against him to get by. He looked down at her, his brown eyes warm and steady.

"I think you should know that I find you incredibly sexy and intelligent—and terribly prickly."

It was the last part of his speech that saved her from sliding into the web of heat he was spinning. "Prickly?"

"*Terribly* prickly," he replied with a devastating smile. "Which, for some strange reason, I find interesting, challenging, and attractive."

Then, to her surprise and relief, he stepped back. His expression flattened. "And I'm way out of line, saying those things to you. My turn to apologize. Again." He shook his head, giving her a wry smile. "We seem to be spending an awful lot of time apologizing to each other."

"Right." Diana's pulse had returned to something normal, and the heat simmering beneath her skin had cooled. "So, back to the matter at hand…"

Ethan leaned back against the counter, arms folded over his middle. He appeared more remote and reserved than she'd ever seen him. "I say we sleep on it. See if anything else comes to mind. Tomorrow, if you're willing, I'll go with you and we can talk to Joe Cap. He might not be as difficult to convince as you think. Besides…I owe Cady the rest of her play time."

"Right. Of course." She nodded, feeling somehow let down by the veil of tension that had dropped between them. "Yes, I think it would be best to at least tell Captain Longbow of my suspicions. To get it on record."

They agreed that Ethan would pick her up in the morning.

"Thank you again," she said as he opened the kitchen door. "For everything."

He paused, his hand curling around the screen door. "I'm here for whatever you need, Diana. I loved Jean too." Their eyes met and she felt that pleasant jolt in her heart...and then he was gone, striding off into the woods toward his cabin.

It was after nine o'clock and just getting dark. The night was peaceful and calm and warm. The smell of the lake wafted along a light breeze, and the loons and frogs made a quiet chorus in the background.

As Diana closed and locked the door behind Ethan, she felt a stirring of something she hadn't in a long while.

Contentment.

"Thanks for meeting with us, Joe," said Ethan as he and Diana entered the police chief's office.

It was a compact room furnished with a metal desk and wheeled office chair—both of which looked as if they'd been there since the sixties—two large metal filing cabinets, and a small round table with three chairs skirting it. On the round table was a sad looking kalanchoe that could still be saved, and on Longbow's desk were photographs of three children and his wife—the latter whom Diana had seen at Maxine's party but hadn't actually met. The cramped office smelled of the coffee that left cup stains on the large desk blotter and lemon-scented disinfectant cleaner.

"Not a problem," drawled the captain in his easy voice. "You all have a seat there. Helga will likely be here in a minute...oh, here she is."

Diana hadn't met Officer van Hest, who, along with Longbow, made up two-thirds of the trio of law enforcement personnel for Wicks Hollow, and she rose to shake the hand of the young woman who stepped in.

Like her chief, Helga van Hest wore a dark blue and gray uniform—but hers was pressed and creased and starched into crisp submission, while the captain's was, though not shabby, appeared more comfortable and worn. Helga van Hest's badge and brass name tag were polished enough to mirror one's reflection, and her thick strawberry blond hair was tucked back into a no-nonsense chignon. She was tall—probably six feet—and sturdy, with intelligent hazel eyes, a splash of freckles over her fair skin, and a stubborn set to her chin. Her only obvious nod to femininity were her short, neat, French manicured fingernails.

Helga's handshake was firm and businesslike, and Diana sensed that this was the type of woman she would like and respect upon getting to know her.

"All right, there, Ethan. What's on your mind?" Longbow said.

"I think—and Diana does too—that there was something strange about Jean Fickler's death. It's difficult to put a finger on, but between the break-ins and some other things that have been happening, we believe it bears looking into."

"Other things?"

Ethan shifted in his seat, glancing at Diana. They'd agreed to let him start the discussion with Longbow because he knew the police chief better. "This is where things get a little murky."

"Is it?"

"Yes." Ethan drew in a breath, seeming to consider how to approach it, but in the end it was Diana was the one who took the plunge: "I believe the house is haunted. By my aunt Jean. I think it's because she was murdered."

As soon as the words came out of her mouth, Diana

regretted them: their bluntness, the specificity, and most of all, the fact that they made her—a rising star litigating attorney, a professional, a *sane* and pragmatic woman—sound like a lunatic.

Joe Longbow lifted a brow, raised his #1 Dad white coffee mug, sipped, then set the cup back down. "Well," he said after he swallowed, "this *is* Wicks Hollow."

"And she was Jean Fickler," Helga said from where she sat, legs crossed primly, feet tucked under her chair, spine rod-straight.

Diana looked from one to the other, then at Ethan—who seemed just as startled by the cops' reaction. "What do you mean?" she said warily.

Helga and Longbow exchanged glances. "Let's just say," said the female officer, "that we get a lot of strange calls here in Wicks Hollow. Unusual reports. Strange…happenings." She shrugged. "Can't discount anything, as far as I'm concerned. And," she said, zeroing in on Diana, "from what I know about you, you're not the sort of person to make up ghost stories."

"Definitely not."

"In fact, you probably abhor the fact that you had to come in here and actually admit it. Aloud."

Diana almost smiled. Yes, she could definitely get to like this woman. "Precisely."

"Besides all of that" —Helga continued to control the conversation, which Longbow seemed perfectly content to allow— "I'm fairly certain I witnessed a bit of spectral activity myself Tuesday night."

"Yep. So you said." Longbow sat back in his chair, which squeaked as it tilted away from the desk. "You wanta tell them what you saw?"

"I made a few rounds up to Jean's house on Tuesday night when everyone else was at Maxine's party." Helga didn't sound the least bit disappointed to have missed the big event. "Just to make sure there was no monkey business going on. On my second trip, I wanted to eat my lunch, so I sat on the front porch instead of in that stuffy patrol car. Cap, you've got to authorize a stipend for a detailing on that vehicle," she said. "It still smells like moldy maple syrup and skunk. Don't ask," she added, looking at Ethan and Diana with a shake of her head.

"All right." Ethan rubbed his forehead, wearing an expression that exemplified exactly how Diana was feeling.

"I'll get around to the auth," Longbow sighed. "Tell the story, Helga."

"I was sitting on the porch—such a peaceful view—eating cold pizza when I saw a light flicker on inside. I knew there was no one on the property—hadn't I just been there thirty minutes ago, and was back again? No tire tracks, no vehicle, no evidence anyone was there. Butch was sitting there with me—"

"Butch is Helga's dog," Ethan told Diana. "He and Cady are good friends."

"Right. And Butch didn't twitch an ear—which he'd've done if someone was around. But there it was—a light had come on in one of the windows. Then, another light came on in a different room. Then upstairs. Then they all blinked three times—one, two, three—together. Then they went out. And that was it." Helga spread her hands. "I can't think of any other explanation than spectral activity."

"All right." Though Diana could have come up with at least a few explanations, it would be counterproductive to her goal. "So the purpose of our meeting with you," she said smoothly, looking at Longbow, "is to suggest that the break-in at the house is related to my aunt's death, and to request an investigation into said death. Including an autopsy. Do you have any hesitations or concerns about doing so?"

"Can't say I do."

Diana blinked. That was it? That had been remarkably simple.

Ethan seemed less surprised at the captain's easy acquiescence. "When we were fishing the other day, Cap, you said something about Jean Fickler's death not sitting quite right with you."

"That's right." Longbow looked at Diana. "I remember thinking that when I found your aunt's body, there was something odd about it. She was in her bed, and had died probably of heart failure in her sleep. There were no signs of forced entry, no signs of struggle, no robbery. Nothing. But..." He faded into silence. Of course with Longbow and the way he talked, Diana couldn't be sure he wasn't just pausing between words.

"But what?" she asked, trying not to sound too eager.

"Well, the bed was just too neat. I wondered later how anyone could have slept without even wrinkling the sheets. But that was nothing to pin my hat on, you know."

"And no reason to do an autopsy." Ethan mused. "An elderly woman with a documented heart condition dies in her sleep, and no one thinks twice about it."

"Yep." Longbow scratched his head, then flattened the ruffled hair into a smooth sheen. "Shoulda gone with my gut. There were some faint bruises on one wrist, but they coulda been there awhile. Doc checked her over too, and said it was a heart attack. Coulda assumed too much there. He is getting up there in years."

"Smothered. She was smothered," Diana said quietly.

"What makes you think that?" asked Helga. "Specifically."

Diana felt the weight of her scrutiny, but plowed on. "I dreamt it. I dreamed I was her, being smothered, in her own bed."

Still looking at her, Helga nodded slowly. "All right."

"Only way to find out for sure is to order an autopsy. And don't be expecting it to happen fast like it does on TV," Longbow warned. "Especially not here in Wicks Hollow. We're chump change compared to Grand Rapids and Kalamazoo. It'll take a month or more, I suspect."

"I know some people," Diana said. "I might be able to pull some strings, make it happen more quickly. After all, we are talking about probable murder."

Murder.

Aunt Jean was murdered.

Though she still had to wait for proof, Diana no longer had any doubt.

Longbow nodded. "I'll—naw, Helga, you're better at paperwork than I am. Helga'll get the paperwork together for you."

"Thank God for small favors—you're finally learning," Helga told him, then she turned to Diana. "If he tries to do it, we'll end up with a printer exploding, or the computer spontaneously combusting, or some other horror—and then I'll end up wasting half a day trying to fix it. I swear, if anyone knows about hauntings and spectral energy, it's me—because the captain here can't walk by the damned copy room without messing everything up. He must have hated technology in a past life. Give me an hour to get that release together, all right, Ms. Iverson?"

"We can grab lunch," Ethan said before Diana could respond. "Thanks, Cap. Appreciate everything."

"Sure. Now I've got to get over and check out what's going on at the Wicks Farm Clubhouse. Morrie Devine called and said someone let a slew of raccoons into the spa room." He shoved on a wide-curly-brimmed cowboy hat decorated with the Wicks Hollow police insignia in front. "More likely, the coons found their way in all on their own."

"Or a ghost let them in," Helga said with a grin. "After all, this is Wicks Hollow."

Ethan and Diana went to Trib's for lunch and were seated at a table next to the removable glass wall. Because it was a gorgeous June day, the wall had been folded out of sight, leaving the restaurant wide open to the street side. A warm breeze tinged with the scent of Lake Michigan and summer flowers wafted over them, and the sounds of conversation from passersby and crying gulls filled the air.

The tables were nearly full for lunch, but it was Thursday and in the middle of June—which was the beginning of high season. It would be like this, or worse, through the end of August, and still relatively busy during the latter part of September into early October for the fall color season.

Ethan didn't mind at all, for the busyness kept Trib too distracted for the amiable restaurateur to spend much time chatting with them. Normally, he wouldn't mind—Trib was a nice guy and, fortunately, he understood the importance of a good selection of beers on tap—but Ethan didn't want to be interrupted. He had things to talk about with Diana...and he wanted to enjoy her company.

"That went far better than I expected," Diana said as she set down her menu.

Before Ethan could reply, the waitress came over to take their order. Once she left, he said, "We haven't given much thought to *why* someone broke into Jean's house."

"He—it was definitely a man. Or a tall, solid woman, I suppose," Diana replied, tucking a curl behind her ear. Today she was wearing a pair of square ebony earrings that matched a chunky bracelet. She'd dressed professionally for their meeting with Joe Cap: in a business suit of black with wide cobalt blue trim and high-heeled shoes that showed off her legs.

"My guess is that he—let's stick with the male pronoun for now—was looking for something," she concluded.

"I agree. You haven't noticed anything missing?"

"Nothing obvious. It looked like the papers and drawers at Aunt Jean's desk could have been messed with, but I can't be certain, for the desk was always pretty disorganized. I haven't even begun to look through her office and papers, so I hadn't touched anything." She played with her fork as she mused. "Aunt Jean's jewelry box seemed undisturbed, and the few good pieces she had are still there—I have a list from her lawyer. A strand of pearls and a sapphire ring, plus a gold brooch with small diamonds. Not all that much to attract a thief."

"Someone got into the house twice—let's just go with the assumption I was right that when you were in town that day, someone was in the house—"

"Besides you," she said, giving him an arch look.

"Besides me. I'm guessing he hasn't found what he was looking for yet, because he was still there when you got home. You surprised him, probably, when your headlights lit up the driveway."

"That's a reasonable assumption."

"So if we can figure out what he was looking for, we might be able to come up with the who and the why."

"We?" Diana asked delicately as their beverages arrived. Her lips, glossed with that subtle iced pink, curved in a wry smile. "Are you suggesting we play homicide detective, Dr. Murphy?"

The way she said his name—title and all—with that smirk

and the teasing lilt to her voice took him by surprise and demonstrated yet another facet of the woman he'd once thought of as an ice queen. She was almost—*almost*—flirting with him.

"Well, now that you mention it…" He smiled back with a burst of heat, and had the satisfaction of seeing the response flicker in her eyes: she definitely wasn't immune to him.

But she wasn't *available* to him.

Not while she still thought she loved Wertinger. His good mood soured.

Their meals arrived just then, and Ethan was grateful for the disruption. If things were different—if she were unencumbered—he might feel differently. Even though it was clear Wertinger had cheated on her, that didn't mean she would—or should—respond in quid pro quo.

And he wouldn't respect Diana if she did, even if it was with him—the single kiss he'd coaxed from her notwithstanding. He took full responsibility for tempting her into that. But anything else—on either of their parts—would constitute the adulterous behavior he despised. He didn't wish that sort of pain and anguish on anyone. Even Jonathan Wertinger, who appeared to genuinely love Diana.

By the time Ethan came out of his web of thoughts, he noticed that his companion had also fallen silent. And she was picking at her food—a large, appetizing salad with every color of the rainbow in vegetation, along with a side of house made crackers and a small pot of herb-flecked cheese to smear on them.

"Is something wrong?" he asked.

She didn't look at him right away, but toyed with her salad for a moment. Then she lifted her face and he saw pain and dismay there.

"It's just really hitting me—just now—that someone *killed*

my aunt. Someone actually hated her enough, or wanted something badly enough, to *take her life*, Ethan. To kill a defenseless old woman in her bed." Diana's voice roughened and she shook her head. "Who would do something like that?"

"A coward."

She nodded soberly. "Yes. A coward. Ethan, I've never experienced anything like this before—someone I loved being subjected to real violence. In this case, murder."

"It's ugly," he agreed quietly, and quelled the urge to reach over and touch her busy fingers. Probably not a good idea. "It's the ugliest thing possible. It's better that we know what happened, though, so the killer can be brought to justice, than to have gone on without a clue."

"Yes." She smiled faintly and turned back to her food.

He kept an eye on her as he worked through his meal—a salad with grilled salmon in a grainy, spicy-sweet mustard sauce like nothing he'd ever had before. He wanted to lick the plate. But his enjoyment was tempered by her grief, and his own anguish over the reality of Jean's death.

Diana was staring into space again when the waitress returned. The only part of her that seemed to have life was her dark hair: the breeze played with it, toying with a curl here, tossing a wisp into her face there. She jolted back to the moment when the waitress took her plate, and Ethan got caught staring at her.

"You have such beautiful hair," he said with a quick smile.

She clapped a hand to her head, pushing the tousled mass flat, and looked at him as if he were crazy. "It's always so out of control and messy. My mother used to say—well, never mind what she used to say. Suffice to say, I always think of it as my worst feature," she added with a wry laugh. "But thanks for saying that."

"It's definitely not your worst feature," he said. "I think it's one of your best features."

"Well, thank you. You might not feel the same way if you had to contend with such a wild mop," she said with a little laugh.

"Do you want to know what your worst feature really is?" Ethan said before he could think better of it.

Diana went still, and he could see even her breathing stop. "What?" Her whole demeanor changed: walls went up, eyes went flat, body went stiff.

Wow. Hit a soft spot there. But he wasn't going to let it go.

"As far as I'm concerned," Ethan told her, "your worst feature is Jonathan Wertinger."

TEN

DIANA AND ETHAN were walking back to the police station so she could sign the release papers when Maxine Took and her cane erupted from inside Orbra's Tea House. She swung the heavy wooden stick down in front of them like the barrier at a railroad crossing, narrowly missing the couple who were walking in front of them.

"What's this I hear about Jean being murdered?" the old lady demanded, heedless of tourists along the sidewalk who might be taken aback by the talk of murder in sweet Wicks Hollow. "Now you come right in here and tell us all about it. Both of you."

"Sounds like you already know," Ethan muttered, but he did as she demanded.

"How on earth could she hear about it already?" Diana said in an undertone as she reluctantly stepped inside the tea shop.

"I don't know, and I don't want to know," he replied. "It's uncanny—she *always* knows. Everything. It's like she's got a crystal ball or something. Hi Orbra," he said, then leaned in to give the tall woman a kiss on her powdered cheek. "We just came from Trib's but didn't have dessert because we were saving ourselves for your scones. The frosted ones."

Diana noticed that Maxine's chair—the same one she'd sat in before, at the front table—was on its side, as if the woman had bolted from it with enough force to knock it over. The old termagant had probably seen them coming down the street.

Iva and Juanita (along with Bruce Banner, peeking up from inside his tote-bag) were sitting at the table as well with the remnants of tea, English biscuits, muffins, and quiche crusts around them. There was a deluxe Scrabble board in the center with a game in play.

"Sit there," Maxine said, pointing at two empty seats. "Cherry's got one of them vine-yessa classes on right now, so her chair's empty. *Don't bump the board*," she screeched before Diana even got close to the table. "I got a bingo I'm ready to play when we're done here, and I don't want Juanita getting any ideas about calling the game off because the tiles got knocked around." She gave her friend a steely look.

"You're the only one who does that," Juanita replied primly. Today, her fingernails were lavender and she wore a maxi dress of the exact same color. They both clashed wildly with her candy-apple red poof of hair.

"I never—"

"*Ay-yi-yi*, Maxine—you do it when you think I'm not looking. She can't stand it that I've got a 1500 ranking and she's only got a 1485," Juanita told them with a satisfied smile.

"Lies. All of them. *Lies.*" Maxine looked at Diana and Ethan as if challenging them to side with Juanita. "Now tell us about they're digging up Jean. To find out if she was murdered?"

"I told you she was going to haunt that house," Iva said wisely. She held a delicate white cup filled with steaming tea, eyes fastened expectantly on Diana. "Didn't expect it to be because she was murdered, but that's a better reason than just not wanting to leave the party and going on to the afterlife. Not that she was murdered, you understand—but the reason she's hanging around. To settle the score, to right the wrong, to bring justice to bear."

Diana looked at Ethan, who shrugged as if to say, Just go with it.

"Did you want some tea, honey?" asked Orbra. There was a bit of a challenge to her tone, and Diana figured she was remembering her faux pas from last time.

"I would love some tea," she said, infusing enthusiasm in her voice. "Do you have something you recommend? What about a chai?" That was close to coffee, wasn't it?

Orbra seemed content with that response. "With or without milk? You add your own sweetener."

"With milk," Ethan said in a stage whisper. "It's good that way."

Diana nodded. "All right. With milk. Skim."

"Two-percent," corrected the proprietress. "Skim's hardly any better than adding water or that almond milk Cherry makes me put in hers."

"Right, two-percent."

By the time the orders were figured out—of course Maxine had demands to renew, and Ethan, who seemed to have two hollow legs, ordered an entire spread of scones, biscuits, tiny sandwiches, and fruit—Diana had had the opportunity to consider the situation.

What exactly should she tell the ladies about Aunt Jean's death? Clearly the idea of a ghost didn't faze them, but how much detail did they need to have—and how little would Maxine allow her to get away with giving?

As it turned out, Diana didn't have to decide, because Maxine and her cohorts seemed to know about everything already—from the plan to order an exhumation and autopsy, to Helga's experience with the blinking lights on the night of the party, to the fact that the house had been broken into at least once. Probably twice.

Once Maxine had finished badgering Diana with all of her knowledge, Iva was able to get a word in. "Who do you think would do such a thing to Jean?" Her voice and expression were uncharacteristically sober, and astonishingly, Maxine's demeanor changed to match hers as well.

"Whoever it was deserves to be hung by his balls," the older woman said in a flat, business-like tone—so different from her usual strident, ear-splitting one. "Hurting Jean like that. If I could, I'd put a curse on—"

"Now don't be saying things like that, Maxine," Orbra said loudly, looking nervously at a table of customers nearby. She set down a rosebud teapot in front of Diana, and another one with yellow daisies in front of Ethan, then followed with pitchers of milk and dishes of brown sugar lumps. "There's enough gossip about you being a witch as it is," she hissed at Maxine.

"Gossip?" Juanita said, slapping her hand against her bag so the little dog jolted. "It's not gossip if it's true." She giggled merrily, and Orbra rolled her eyes.

When she looked over and saw Diana's expression, the Dutch woman immediately moved to soothe. "It's a standing joke; don't look so serious about it, Diana. The only type of witch Maxine is is the kind that grumbles and grouses about everything."

"Believe me, if Maxine *was* a witch, she'd never allow me to beat her in Scrabble," Juanita said archly.

"You only win because you—"

"I've been saying a rosary every day for Jean, but now I'm

going to say two. I'm thinking of asking St. Anthony for intervention," Juanita announced.

"St. Anthony?" Ethan asked, looking up from the crumbly orange lavender scone he was devouring. A tiny flake of the glaze from it was caught at the corner of his mouth, and Diana was very glad she caught herself before she reached over to brush it away.

"Anthony's the patron saint when you want help to find something," Juanita told him, fiddling with the Crucifix she wore on a chain around her neck. "You say 'Tony, Tony, look around, there's something lost that can't be found.' We want to find Jean's murderer, don't we?"

"I'll say we do." Maxine seemed to like that idea. "St. Anthony, hmm? All right. Maybe you Catholics got something we Baptists don't." She nodded. "I'll get working on that. Tony, Tony," she muttered. "Look around…"

"Ladies," Ethan said suddenly. "If someone—er—did away with Jean, and has been breaking into the house, they probably would have been seen here in town at some point. Have you noticed any strangers—"

"Dearest Ethan, we get strangers in Wicks Hollow all the time," Iva said, patting his hand.

"Overrun by them from June to September," Maxine grumbled. "Used to like summer, after school got out, but now it's people every where you look. Always underfoot, and—"

"But my aunt died in late May," said Diana, seizing the conversation before Maxine was off to the races. "So you might have noticed a stranger then, before all the tourists come. And maybe you saw the same person in the last week or two also, since I got here…and the break-ins started."

All at once it occurred to her that her arrival seemed to have sparked the break-ins. She looked at Ethan and from his expression realized he'd just come to the same conclusion. Diana found this silent meeting of the minds both comforting and surprising. But the fact that she might have been the catalyst for the person sneaking in and out of Jean's house was worrisome.

Why now? Why her?

Or was the timing just a coincidence?

"We get small business conferences and golf outings in April and May before Memorial Day," Iva was saying. "That's how I met Hollis, you know. But those are groups, and they're usually planned and scheduled far in advance, so it seems like someone who killed Jean wouldn't be in a group like that."

"I never forget a face," Maxine announced, snatching the last paper-thin cucumber sandwich from Ethan's plate.

"Well, then, did you see him, Miss Know-It-All?" challenged Juanita. "What did he look like, hmm?"

Diana's head spun as the discussion devolved into an argument and competition between the ladies about who knew what and saw what and who had the best memory and the keenest hearing and sharpest eyesight. She looked over at Ethan and saw that he was barely holding onto his laughter, agreeing to everything with a poker-faced nod as he buried his face in a tea cup.

He was really quite amazing—so patient and endearing with the old ladies, despite their nonstop bickering. And even though he was amused, it was an affectionate amusement—not a condescending one. He was so—

Diana's insides stilled and froze, and then she felt heat rush up her throat. She had no business thinking of him in that way.

None.

"I need to get over to the police station to sign those papers," she said, standing abruptly.

Ethan followed suit, and they were able to extricate themselves with a minimum of fuss—mainly because Maxine and Juanita had gone off on a tangent debating who had been wearing glasses longer, with Iva playing referee.

"Whew," Diana said when they got out onto the street. "That was...exhausting."

"But they're so damned cute," Ethan said with a grin. "All of them. Each so different, each as stubborn as the next, and all such good friends. You can't tell it, being an outsider, but they're really a little lost without Jean."

"Lost? With Maxine in charge?" Diana scoffed with a laugh. "I can't imagine that."

He laughed too. "Well, Jean had a way of defusing the bickering by completely changing the subject and grabbing their attention. Everyone loved her." His voice got a little rough, and she looked up at him to see that he was looking determinedly ahead as if to hide any emotion in his eyes.

Her heart softened even more, and she ruthlessly told it to stop. Ethan Murphy did not equal anyone of interest to Diana Iverson. End of story.

She had a partner.

But at the thought of Jonathan, she realized instead of feeling happy or warm, she felt tense and stressed and unhappy.

"So," she said, focusing her attention back on the comfort of facts and logic. "The break-ins, as far as we know, started once I arrived in Wicks Hollow. That's probably significant."

"There were no signs of anyone having tried to get in before, right?"

"That's right. Not that there were any signs of someone getting in now—both times you or I saw the culprit. But the house was undisturbed—and, frankly, if someone had broken in during the three weeks or so that it was empty, he would have had plenty of time to find whatever he was looking for."

"Yet he keeps coming back. Which means he hasn't found what he's looking for."

"But what? All of a sudden, Aunt Jean is killed"—she had a difficult time saying the word—"and three weeks later, someone starts looking for something in her house."

"Because you were coming here and would, as the new owner, presumably be going through her things. You might find whatever he's trying to retrieve. So he needs to find it."

Diana had been thinking along the same lines. "He expected the house to be empty longer, maybe."

"Yes. Seems reasonable." He rubbed his chin. "Jean must have gotten involved in something that sparked her death."

"That has to be why she called me. And you," Diana added. "But did she know that whatever it was put her in danger?"

"If she realized that, I'm confident Jean was smart enough to tell Joe Cap, at least. Or someone in authority."

"Maybe she suspected something was wrong, and that's why she was trying to reach me." Diana felt renewed pang of sorrow and guilt. "I wonder if she called anyone else…and actually talked to them."

"I don't know how we'd know." Ethan frowned, and they turned onto the walkway leading to the police station. "But all this happened rather quickly—within the last month or two. Or it seems to have."

"That's true." Diana tried to think, but the familiar painful throbbing had begun at her temples. A migraine was coming on, and she was trying to think. To remember. To—

A migraine.

She grabbed Ethan's arm. "What did you say the other night? About me?"

He halted just before he pulled the door open to the police station. "Which part?" he replied with a slow smile. "About you being terribly prickly?"

She ignored a hot dart of pleasure. "When we were in the boat—you were saying something about me and—well, I hate the word, but—repressing things. It sounds so Victorian and stilted and misogynistic. Repression," she said to clarify her thoughts.

"Repression can be a male issue too," he said, still with that delicious smile curling his lips. "Repression: it's not just for women anymore."

She laughed. She couldn't help it. He just seemed to know how to tickle her humor unexpectedly. "Right. But anyway, you said something about my headaches—my migraines—being..." She bit her lip and paused.

"I believe I said something along the lines of whether it's possible your headaches could be the result of an unwillingness to allow parts of your unconscious to surface to your conscious mind. You're possibly suppressing—that's the word I used; not *repressing*—something from your consciousness."

"Yes. That." The tom-tom of pain was still there, but she was able to think clearly. "Yes, you said something just like that. But I remember you saying repressing not *suppressing*." She managed a smile. "The point is...I haven't had a migraine since that night in the canoe—and the day after was when I... well," she said, looking away. "When I believed."

"But you're getting one now?"

"Yes, but...I..." She ground her teeth with frustration. "I was trying to think of something—something in the back of my mind, and that's when it start—"

"You're back." The door to the police station opened beneath Ethan's hand, and the tall, purposeful Helga stopped just short of bowling them over. "Good timing, as I'm on my way to write up a fender bender over by the high school. Only one more day till school's out, thank God. But I have the paperwork ready for you to sign, Diana, and Cap already authorized it. Margo has it waiting for you inside."

By the time Diana finished reviewing the documents and signing them, the thread of her conversation with Ethan was gone. The headache still throbbed a little, but it hadn't deepened into agony the way her migraines usually did.

"How's your headache?" Ethan asked as he unlocked his Jeep Cherokee. He opened the door for her because even though he'd been raised by a flaming I-can-open-my-own-door-thank-you-very-much feminist, he thought it was just a polite thing to do—regardless of gender.

Plus it gave him the opportunity to get close to her for a moment.

"It's lurking. But staying in the background." She gave him a smile as she climbed in. He did his best not to be obvious as he ogled her legs, and considered himself lucky for the extra glimpse he caught of smooth thigh when her skirt rode up as she settled into the high seat.

He turned on the radio, rolled the windows down, and opened the moonroof just so he could see her short hair get blown around into tousled after-sex curls—because he was a masochist and would never actually see her with after-sex curls.

To his surprise, she didn't complain or roll up the window as Fiona, with her long wild hair, would do. Instead, Diana sat quietly, chin propped on her palm, elbow wedged against the edge of the window, seeming to be deep in thought as Kid Rock's classic Michigan anthem "All Summer Long" blasted through the speakers.

"Ethan," she said as they drove up the driveway to Jean's

house. "I want to tell you something I've never told anyone before."

"Okay." He wasn't sure why he had a sense of foreboding. Maybe it was the very somber tone of her voice, or the little vertical line that had appeared between her brows.

She was quiet for so long he thought she'd changed her mind, but if Ethan knew one thing, it was how to be patient. To let silence do its job.

Finally, as he pulled to a stop at Jean's house, next to Diana's car, she spoke. "When I'm working on a case—particularly if it's a difficult one or one that we don't seem to be in a position to win, I…do this *thing*."

She stopped, and again he waited for more.

"I sit in my office, and put on headphones to block out all the noise. I close my eyes, and I just…well, I stop thinking about everything. It's like I'm clearing my mind of the clutter," she said, glancing at him. "And after I sit there for a long time, the solution comes to me. It just kind of falls into my head. When I say solution, I mean…how to get the two opposing sides to come together, or something we missed, or some new perspective that just puts everything into place. It's like, suddenly, it's just *there*. And it always works. It's always the right solution."

Every hair on his body had lifted, prickling, but Ethan kept his mouth closed. He merely looked at her and nodded encouragingly for her to continue.

"That's why I've been given so many…well, difficult cases. Even ones that other litigators started, then messed up somehow—they'd get reassigned to me when all hope was lost. Because somehow, I could find the solution that worked for everyone—not just our firm. That's part of why I'm going to make partner this year at thirty."

She was opening and closing her hands in her lap,

watching them as she spoke. "The thing is," she continued, "I started doing it when my migraines were really bothering me. About five years ago. I would go in my office, close my eyes, put a cold cloth over my forehead, headphones on, and wait for the migraine to go away. I'd try not to think about how badly my head hurt, and so I concentrated on my breathing. I focused on that in order to block out the pain. I would count…in, one…out, two…in, three…out, four…and so on."

"A lot of people—including your aunt Jean—would call that meditation," he said quietly.

"Whatever it was, I'd just…lose the pain. And it was as if once I'd cleared the pain away, the solution could come to me." She nibbled on her lower lip the way she did when she was uncertain or uncomfortable. Then she swung her eyes—those amazing blue eyes—to look at him. "Some of the people in my office think it's like a weird thing I do. They even call it that—they'll say, 'Can't you go do that thing you do?'"

"I'm sure you jump right on that, don't you?" he said in a wry voice.

She gave a short laugh. "It makes me uncomfortable."

"It's a kind of gift, Diana."

"Well, whatever it is…the only reason I told you is because I think you might be right. About what you said about me repressing—"

"*Sup*pressing," he said, unable to hold back a smile. God, for an ice queen, she was pretty fun—in so many ways. Then, still with the smile, he said, "Wait, did you say I might be right?"

Her eyes laughed at him, but she shook her head in exasperation. "I wonder if I've been getting those migraines here because the same sort of thing is happening again. I'm…not letting the facts settle in my mind. I'm missing something."

Her eyes were wide and thoughtful, and the way she was looking up at him…

Ethan nearly leaned over to her then, nearly put his lips on hers. He wanted to taste her again, to taste those pretty lips that were no longer pruny and annoyed but soft and lush.

Instead, he reminded himself of all the reasons he couldn't and shouldn't and said, "That makes sense to me." He shrugged. "But I've got a long history of being open-minded when it comes to this sort of thing."

"Right. Well, thank you for not laughing at me."

"Diana," he said, tracing a finger over the back of her hand, "I'm not going to laugh at you. Ever."

She held his gaze for a moment, then tore hers away as she opened the door to climb out of the car. Then she stopped. "*Ethan.*"

"Wha—" He didn't finish the thought, for he saw what made her freeze. "Sonofabitch. No, stay here. Call Joe Cap. *Now.*"

He was already out of the car, moving toward the front door—which was wide open.

It had not been that way when they left, several hours ago.

ELEVEN

DIANA DIDN'T LISTEN to Ethan—at least, not completely. She didn't stay in the car, but she did call Captain Longbow's office.

"Someone broke into my house again," she told Margo, the office manager. "Please have the captain or Officer van Hest come out as soon as possible."

She was already stepping onto the porch by the time she disconnected the call. "Ethan?" She wasn't afraid that they'd interrupt the burglar—it appeared he'd left in a hurry and hadn't closed the door behind him.

"In here." His voice was grim, and came from down the hall. "Looks like we—or something—interrupted him again."

Aunt Jean's library was in a shambles this time, so clearly the intruder had been searching—and didn't care that they knew it. Papers everywhere, the desk chair overturned, drawers half opened, framed pictures tipped over, and books scattered on the floor.

But as Diana walked into the room, she smelled the distinct aroma of sandalwood. Her skin prickled, and she felt a chill in the air that suddenly started to shift and move when there was no breeze. The tip of her nose iced over.

"Aunt Jean?" she whispered without thinking—then swung her attention to Ethan, hoping he hadn't heard her.

But he'd stilled, his nose lifted slightly as if he too smelled the dead woman's perfume. And as Diana looked at him, she saw that his breath was coming out in small, white puffs.

And so was hers.

"Aunt Jean?" she said again, a little louder this time. The chill air brushed over her like light fingers through her hair. The scent grew stronger.

A movement from the corner of her eye had her spinning to see fat Arty sitting at attention in the doorway. He seemed to be looking up at something.

The hair on the back of Diana's neck prickled, standing up straight, and the chill turned unbearably cold—touching not only her nose, but her fingers as well, for when she turned, she saw that the feline's eyes were fixed on a shimmery blue sort of cloud. A watery image that couldn't seem to take shape.

But it didn't need to.

"Aunt Jean," she whispered again—this time unafraid that Ethan would hear. He touched Diana's shoulder lightly as he moved to stand behind her.

"We're going to find him," he said. "Jean, we're going to find out what happened. I promise."

The blue image swelled and shivered, and then swooped like a graceful hand across the room toward the desk and bookshelves, hovered for a moment, glowing brightly…then up and into nothing.

She was gone.

The chill left, the perfume scent disintegrated. The cat turned his back then padded away on silent feet, tail whipping and twitching in feline annoyance—whether it was with humans or ghosts was unclear.

"Well," said Ethan after a moment. He wasn't going to deny it—his heart was pounding and his mouth had gone dry. He supposed that was par for the course for a first-time experience with a ghost. "That was…interesting."

"She scared him away," Diana said quietly. "He was here, digging through her things, and she scared him away. That's why he left in a hurry, and probably why it's such a mess. She might have done so to make her point. Look—the piecrust table next to the chair is tipped over, but the Tarot card box is just sitting neatly on the chair."

"Good for you, Jean," Ethan said—and was rewarded when a book tumbled off the shelf, landing at his feet. He was relieved he didn't jump back or otherwise react; after all, he was supposed to be the one used to this sort of ghostly, supernatural activity. But it startled him nonetheless.

"Ethan," Diana said. "What do you think of this?"

She pointed to three books on the floor amid the papers, files, and picture frames that had fallen or been knocked over.

"They're on top of the mess," he said. "And why would the burglar pull those three volumes off the shelves, and leave them there? Why would he even be looking at books if he was searching for something?"

"Unless he thought it was in one of the books…but you get my point. Aunt Jean seems to have a thing for books," she said, glancing up as if expecting to see the specter of her aunt again. "I'm thinking she used them to scare him away—spontaneously flying books would do it to most people. But the last time she flung books around, they were the murder books."

"So you think she might have picked these in particular."

"Well, look at the book that fell from the shelf just now when you spoke to her," Diana said.

Ethan picked it up and laughed when he saw the title. *"The Ghost Speaks.* That's definitely Jean's sense of humor. All right, then," he said, walking back over to where Diana stood, "what do we have over here?"

They looked down at the three books.

Letters from the Leelanau.

Expedition!

Traces of History.

"Are you getting anything from this?" he said after a moment when his mind remained blank.

"Well, they're all about physical locations. Leelanau is a county up near Traverse City."

"It's also a lake, and a small town," he added. "*Expedition* is about Everest. And *Traces of History* appears to be about Colonial Williamsburg…" He shook his head. "I got nothing."

"Nothing jumps out at me either," she said, frowning down at them.

"Maybe you should do that thing you do," he said with a grin.

He loved it that her cheeks flushed prettily when he teased her. The ice queen was melting.

He really wanted to heat her up.

"Maybe I will," was all she said, punctuating it with a little sniff.

They heard a car pull up the gravel driveway.

"That must be the police." She paused, then looked at Ethan. "I think it's best if we don't tell them about what just happened. With the blue thing."

Though secretly relieved at her suggestion, he shrugged. "Your call."

While Diana was showing Joe Cap the mess inside, Ethan did a circuit of the exterior of the house. This time, the intruder had forced the metal cellar doors open, cutting the padlock with a tool—which he'd left in his haste to get away from the ghost of Jean Fickler. Though the metal cutter looked like one anyone could buy at the average hardware store, there could be fingerprints, or some other way to trace its ownership.

He looked around some more. The ground was soft from a light rain last night, but the grass was thick and didn't show any detail of the footprints around the door.

But as he came around to the front of the house where the door had been left wide open, a red glint caught his eye in the middle of the green.

Well, now... It was an inkpen. And it had definitely not been there when he mowed the lawn on Monday—*wow*. Had it only been three days ago?

It probably had just been dropped, oh, about an hour ago when the intruder bolted from the house as if the hounds of hell—or Jean Fickler—were after him. Ethan grinned darkly. Served the bastard right.

He picked it up and was even more juiced when he saw the engraving on it: *Tenth Annual Merman-Steele Golf Outing*. The date was in April—only two months ago. And the location: The Wicks Farm Golf Course.

Finally—a real clue.

When he didn't care about ambience but wanted good, solid bar food like a burger and fries or atomic-hot buffalo wings, Ethan went to The Owl's Roost. The place was a Dive—with a capital D—but the burgers were massive and the buns were soft, and it was a matter of course that a burger always wore three slices of cheese and a slab of onion a quarter-inch thick.

Only half a block from Trib's, the Roost was almost as

much of a tourist draw as the other, far more trendy and, well, *clean* place. At the Roost, decades of peanut shells had been ground into cracks in the floor from countless shoes. The place smelled like stale beer and sweat, and though smoking in bars had been outlawed years ago, there still hung that essence of cigarette residue.

It was part of the charm.

Movie posters in cheap plastic frames decorated the bar—all were from flicks in the seventies or eighties. They were hung about midway up the wall in a stripe around the whole room. Nothing got in the way of the movie poster decor—not even an air conditioning unit that had obviously been installed after the posters were hung. When the hole was cut in the wall for the unit, the installers cut right through a *St. Elmo's Fire* poster—and its frame—taking out the top right chunk of Demi Moore's face for the bottom left part of the air conditioner.

That *laissez-faire* attitude about artwork was Ethan's favorite part of the Roost—that and its extensive, ever-changing beer list written on a large chalkboard above the bar.

It was Friday night, which meant an acoustic musician would be trying to make him- or herself heard from the far corner of the place, but that was usually a losing proposition. Three large televisions were screening a Tigers game, a White Sox game, and an eighties movie that starred a young Matthew Broderick and an actress from *The Breakfast Club*.

The place was packed and there was standing-room only at the bar counter, but Ethan didn't have to search for a table. All he had to do was stroll past the huge square booth in the back corner and…wait for it…

"Ethan!" Juanita was the first one to see him, but Maxine crowed in her wake, "We have room here!"

He caught a glimpse of Baxter James, stuffed in the back

corner between Orbra and Iva, and the desperate look on his face made Ethan want to laugh. Still, this had been his plan all along, so he had no qualms about joining the Tuesday Ladies and their hostage.

"Slide over, Cherry," Juanita said, and they made room for Ethan.

"Where's Diana tonight?" Maxine demanded as soon as Ethan's ass hit the wooden bench. "We're tasting Baxter's new beer. It's not his best, but it's drinkable."

"I have no idea where Diana is," Ethan replied.

"I thought you two were—"

"Of course they aren't," Cherry interrupted Maxine. "You met Diana's fiancé the other night at the Grille, remember?"

"She wasn't wearing a *ring*," Maxine argued, her dark eyes flashing. "Are you sure they're engaged? And he's not just after her money? She's got a *lot* of it now."

Ethan nearly choked on the beer Bax had shoved in front of him and decided it would be prudent not to weigh in on that question for a number of reasons.

"Is it that bad?" Baxter asked, lifting his brows.

"The beer? No," Ethan said right away. "No, it's actually pretty good for a brown ale."

"It's an oatmeal stout."

"Oh. It's not bad for an oatmeal stout," Ethan said with a grin. Baxter rolled his eyes and mumbled something about high maintenance pains in the ass.

"Dec liked it," he muttered.

"Dec's just trying to get on your good side. Free beer," Ethan joshed back.

Maxine was still carrying on. "That boy looked like he'd be a real cold fish in bed, if you ask me. Diana could do much better than *him*."

"I can't disagree with you there, Max," Cherry purred as

her eyes narrowed speculatively, and, to Ethan's mortification, lingered on him. "You can always tell when a man's not going to meet expectations in the sack. And when he is."

"That is true. My Miguel…I could tell right away. It was in the eyes. It's *always* in the eyes." Juanita sighed and fanned herself with bloodred-tipped fingers. "*Ay-yi-yi.*"

Ethan met Baxter's gaze and read in it the same desperation he felt to be anywhere but there at the moment. *Someone change the subject, quick.*

"So where *is* Diana?" asked Iva, leaning on her elbows and fixing her bright blue eyes on him.

Everyone looked over, and Ethan suddenly felt as if he were a slab of meat being judged by a pack of very hungry wolves. "I don't know. It's not my turn to keep track of her," he said with a grin that softened any annoyance that might have filtered into his voice.

Which, maybe there was a little bit of irritation there. After all, he *didn't* know where she was on this Friday night. The problem was, he didn't have the right to be annoyed about it—but he was.

"Well, why not? Isn't her house being broken into on a regular basis? Aren't you living practically next door to her? Shouldn't you be keeping an eye on things?" Orbra said. "On her?"

After the break-in yesterday, and Longbow's examination of the house, he and Diana had amicably parted ways for the evening—even though he'd tried to convince her to sleep at his house. But she'd declined, replying that she was certain Aunt Jean had scared off the intruder once and for all.

But she hadn't mentioned anything bout her plans for tonight, and he'd gotten caught up in work around the house and jotting down notes for his book proposal. The next thing he knew, it was dinner time.

"Uh..." Ethan was saved when the waitress flitted by and he flagged her down. "I'll have a tall Guinness. *Tall*," he emphasized, ignoring Baxter's frown. "You put me in the mood for a stout," Ethan told him.

"Meaning my stout didn't fit the bill," muttered Baxter.

"Incidentally," Ethan said as soon as the waitress scooted off, "I was hoping you'd all be here tonight because I figure if anyone can help find out who's breaking in, you ladies can. That includes you, Bax," he said with a grin, and his friend casually flipped him off.

Ethan dug out the pen he'd found at Diana's house and held it out. "The culprit dropped this."

Maxine's greedy fingers snatched it from him. "The Merman-Steele Golf Outing—that was in April." She looked up at Iva, eyes clear and sharp. "That was when you met Hollis."

"It was. A whole group of them came in here the night before the golf outing, and that's how Hollis and I met. He almost skipped out on the seven o'clock tee-off the next morning, but I convinced him his group needed him. He hits from the senior tee," she said, showing a sweet dimple. "And since it was a scramble, they needed all the help they could get."

"Scrambled golf? What do you mean—"

"Oh, hush, Maxine," Juanita snapped, jostling Bruce Banner, who gave an annoyed squeak. "Who cares about what kind of golf? Scrambled, fried, *Dios mío*—whatever. Whoever has been breaking into Diana's house was at that golf outing." She petted her dog's head absently, and he calmed.

"Or worked during it," Cherry said thoughtfully. "Could be someone at the golf course."

"Or someone could have taken the pen and lost it somewhere," Orbra put in. "And the burglar picked it up."

"I know it's a little bit of a long shot, but whoever got into

Jean's house probably has some connection to Merman-Steele's golf outing. So my question is, Maxine—and all of you—have you noticed anyone in town who was here in April around that time, and has also been here recently—especially yesterday? A stranger?"

As he asked the question, Ethan felt a sudden sinking in his gut. Because he knew at least one answer. And, thankfully, before he or anyone else said it, Iva spoke up.

"Well, Hollis has been here." Her voice was very careful and her dimple had disappeared. "But I can't imagine any reason he'd want to break into Jean's house. He only met her that night. And besides...he'd never do anything like that."

"Of course not, dear," Juanita said, patting her hand. "He's such a lovely man."

"Wasn't there another man who was talking to Jean that night too?" Cherry said quickly. "They seemed to be getting along really well."

"The Abe Vigoda man," Iva said. "He had eyebrows thick and dark, almost one straight one across his forehead, like Abe Vigoda," she explained to Ethan.

"That's right. I was sitting next to them," Orbra said. "He and Jean were talking about how it was such a small world because Trace had done some work for his company in Chicago back in the...Sixties I think it was. And how they were both here in Wicks Hollow that night."

"Yes, I remember now," said Iva. "He made the connection because of Jean's last name. 'Fickler,' he said. 'Not a very common name—wonder if it's any relation to the man who handled some of our business.' That's how they figured out the connection. Tracer did commercial real estate," she said to Ethan. "That's where he and Jean made a lot of their money—real estate investments."

"Did anyone catch his name?" he asked. "And can you tell

me anything about him at all? What he looked like—besides the unibrow?"

"A yoo-na-brown?" Maxine demanded. "What the hell is that? Some sort of—"

"He was probably seventy—about Hollis's age. He teed off from the senior spot too," Iva said, speaking firmly over her friend. "Not as tall as Hollis—definitely not as good-looking. I noticed Hollis right away, of course—all that gorgeous silver hair. The Abe Vigoda guy was shorter and kind of skinny."

"He looked like Yodi—or Yogi. Who's the green guy with the big ears who talks funny?" Maxine said.

"That's Yoda," Ethan replied, then buried his smile in the cold Guinness that had just appeared in front of him. Little flecks of ice from the chilled glass slid down the sides.

Then he sobered. The man who'd knocked Diana around when she caught him sneaking in her house was taller and bigger than she was—or at least, that was how she remembered it. Of course, in the moment of shock and fear, she might have misjudged.

"Did anyone get any more information about the Abe Vigoda man?" Ethan wasn't even certain who Abe Vigoda was, but he was going to Google him as soon as he had the chance. He knew better than to pull out his smartphone in front of the Tuesday Ladies. "His name? Company he worked for? Anything?"

"It was an auto company I think," Orbra said. "Something about Auto…Technicians…"

"AutoXTech?" said Baxter.

"That could be it."

"They're in that big lawsuit with LavertPiper. I've been following the case because I'm reporting on it for the *Grand Rapids Press*." Bax's eyes narrowed. "Wait a minute. What was the name of the law firm Diana works for?"

"McMillan something," said Maxine. Her tone and eyes were back to eagle-eye sharp and contained. Almost frightening, Ethan thought, looking at her. When she was like that, Maxine reminded him of a crow: very smart, very loud and caustic, and very predatory.

She must have been a real badass back in the day when she worked as a chemical engineer. She had to have been: a black woman in the late Sixties/early Seventies, working alongside a slew of white men in a male-dominated industry. No wonder she didn't take any crap from anyone.

"Mc*Nillan*, Busher, Percy, and Stone," said Bax, who was slyly looking at his smartphone under the table. "That's Diana's law firm, and they're also the firm handling the suit."

Ethan felt a sharp tingle of interest. Hmm. Diana worked for the firm that was handling a high-profile case, and a man who worked for the company being sued had been in Wicks Hollow back in mid-April, talking to Jean Fickler. Jean hadn't been one to hold back bragging about her niece—or chatting with anyone, for that matter—so she'd surely mentioned the connection between Diana Iverson, her law firm, and the Abe Vigoda man's company AutoXTech.

And then barely a month later, Jean was murdered—there was no question in Ethan's mind that it had been murder; they were just waiting for the confirmation from the exhumation and autopsy—and a few weeks later, when Diana came to Wicks Hollow, Jean's house was broken into. Multiple times.

There was no way that was all coincidental.

But how it all fit together he wasn't certain yet.

Later that night, Ethan scrolled through all the options on his streaming services for the third time in fifteen minutes. He yawned, muttering aloud, "Can't believe there's nothing good on any of these."

The truth was, there probably was something good on one of them, but nothing seemed to catch his interest. Not even the Tigers baseball game, which was late as they were playing on the West Coast.

After their dinner at the Roost, Bax had come back to the cabin to hang out and shoot the shit, but he left around ten-thirty as he had to be in Grand Rapids early the next morning.

And now Ethan was just plain restless.

And, dammit, he knew the reason.

No matter what he did, he couldn't stop thinking about Diana. Despite having been burned by not one but two women, here he was, slipping into the sweet lure of another. And this one was a lawyer—by all accounts a major ballbuster and used to manipulating information and facts in order to do her job. God, he'd be putty in her hands if he actually fell for her and she put her mind to it.

He wasn't even certain what it was that attracted him so strongly—besides her looks. And he well knew there was more to a woman than the dressing.

Diana could be frosty, emotionless, and condescending... but he'd uncovered her softer, more relaxed side with its quirky sense of humor. And he couldn't deny she was sharp and intelligent. But most of all, when she'd looked at him with those blue eyes, so shocked and grateful that he believed her about Jean's murder and her haunting the place...he couldn't help but feel protective about her—and a whole lot of other less innocent feelings as well.

But she was still tied up with that tool Wertinger. And much as his hormones despised him for it, Ethan actually didn't *want* her to give in to the raging attraction that kept flaring between him and Diana.

Because if she did, that would make her no better than Jenny—or Wertinger himself, for that matter.

That was one thing Ethan couldn't tolerate, wouldn't be party to: infidelity.

Cady whined for the millionth time in the last half hour, smearing her nose against one of the windows. Her hackles stood on end and she growled faintly, then turned and charged toward Ethan. She whined again, bumping her damp nose under his arm, trying to lift it off the armrest of the chair in which he'd reclined.

"Oh, all right." He folded up the recliner and hauled himself upright. "You see a squirrel out there or something? Hope it's not another skunk." He opened the door for the lab to shoot out into the shadows.

Ethan stepped out too, taking a deep breath of pleasantly cool air. Then, he sniffed again. "Smells like something's burning," he said aloud. "Cady!"

The dog came rushing back to the clearing, barking sharply. Ethan could smell the acrid odor of burning wood coming in on the breeze. He frowned and stepped off the porch as his lab barked again. "What is it? You see something out there? No one would be burning leaves at this time of night," he said. "And it's pretty late for a fire…"

He looked up at the circle of black, star-studded sky through the openings of the pine trees and saw a faint mist of smoke hovering over them, dulling the brightness of those celestial bodies. The wind was coming from the southwest. He looked in that direction and, through the trees, saw a faint, oh so faint, glow.

A fire.
Diana.

TWELVE

FEAR SLAMMED ETHAN, and before he had a chance to think, he was running into the house to grab his keys. He shoved his feet into the closest pair of shoes—boots—and Cady, as if she'd been waiting for him to catch on, jumped into the jeep without waiting for an invitation, barking her head off the whole time. He followed, jamming the key into the ignition and grinding the gears as he tore out of the narrow trail and toward the triple fork in the road.

Before he even reached the clearing where Jean's house was, he saw the orange blaze shooting into the sky from the back of the structure. The gold Lexus stood in the drive and Ethan felt his heart leaping into his throat.

Jesus, God, Diana.

He tore out of the truck, leaving the keys in the ignition, and ran toward the house, bellowing her name. Cady helped by charging in circles around the blazing building, barking non-stop.

How could he have let her sleep in that house? Alone? After everything that had been going on?

He roared up to Jean's—Diana's—bedroom window, which was on the far side from the blaze. Thank God. The room was dark, and the window positioned just above his shoulders so he couldn't see much inside. He pounded furiously on the glass, shouting her name. It was then that he realized he'd left his cell phone behind—so he couldn't even call for the firefighters.

Dammit, no.

He banged on the window, used a small rock to try and shatter it, but there was no response from inside. As smoke filtered out through the small hole in the glass, Ethan tore around to the kitchen at the back of the house, where the fire seemed to be less furious. He turned on the hose and ripped off his t-shirt, then held it under the water until it was soaking, all the while shouting Diana's name amid Cady's mad barking.

Maybe the Hornbergers would hear.

Maybe she'd wake up.

Maybe she was unconscious in the middle of the smoke storm and she *couldn't* wake up.

Driven by desperate determination, he wrapped the dripping shirt around his head, with the sleeves dangling to be held over his nose. Then Ethan whaled the hose's spray head into the kitchen door window. The glass shattered and heavy black smoke billowed out, catching him in the face. Ethan reared back in surprise, but reached through the opening to fumble with the deadbolt. At last he snicked it to the side, freeing the door, and he pulled it open.

More black smoke—thick, hot, strong—burst through the new opening, and he coughed, at first paralyzed by its venom. He pulled the wet t-shirt over his mouth and nose, and bending low, staggered over the threshold.

It was a nightmare inside. A blanket of hot, heavy smoke darkened the kitchen, enveloping him instantly. Though he could see no flames in the vicinity, Ethan felt the heat searing into his bare skin. Keeping the wet shirt over his nose and mouth, he strained to see, to hear, something. But only the roar of the fire and smoke filled his ears, and he wondered suddenly where the cats were as well.

Oh, Christ, not them too.

He couldn't call out, for the smoke was too heavy, and it smothered any sound but the insistent blaze. Ethan took two steps and realized he couldn't go further—it was dark, and close, and incredibly hot. His head was spinning and his eyes and lungs burned from the heat and smoke.

With a sob of frustration, he turned. Fear lodged in his throat when he couldn't see the doorway. He couldn't see *anything*.

Then, he bumped against something that turned out to be the kitchen table, which oriented him in the proper direction. He took careful steps—his fingers brushing the hot wood of the table as a guide—until he could see the faintest outline of the doorway.

Ethan stumbled out of the house and drew great, gulping breaths of fresh night air, furious tears stinging his desert-dry eyes.

The house seemed like an inferno from here, and he despaired of any hope.

Diana.

He tried to cry out for her again, but his voice was nothing more than a croak—his throat parched and tight. His lungs seared when he breathed, and his skin was dripping sweat, but he had no time. *No time.* He'd dropped the hose on the porch, and now he paused to re-dampen his shirt and spray some cool water on his face, then bolted back to Diana's bedroom window.

As he stood outside the window, pounding on it, and looking for something to break the glass with, he heard the miraculous sound of sirens.

"Hurry!" he cried, his voice raw and desperate. Finally finding a rock big enough to break the window, he heaved it through, hoping that it would awaken Diana.

The sirens were closer, and he could feel the ground trembling from the weight of the trucks. Ethan was frantically removing splinters of glass from the window when two trucks burst into the clearing, lights and sirens flashing.

Running toward the vehicles, as if doing so would get them out of them faster, he shouted hoarsely, "She's still in there! She's sleeping in there!"

Then all at once, he heard his name. Spinning around, he saw Diana, rushing toward him on foot from the direction of the Hornbergers' house.

"*Ethan.*"

He dropped the hot, soggy shirt and yanked her into his arms. "Jesus, God, Diana, I thought you were in there!" He didn't think; he just buried his sooty face in her hair and held her tight. "Jesus, I thought you were in there."

Diana was being smothered against a sooty, sweaty, smoky, bare chest—and she didn't mind a bit. When he loosened his hold, she pulled back to look up at him as thousands of questions flew through her mind.

Even in the darkness, she could see the wildness in his eyes. But as he looked down at her, that emotion calmed and his rapid breathing slowed into a small cough. His hair was everywhere, in dark, smelly tufts and curls and waves, and soot blackened his face. His breaths rasped in and out, but he smiled, then turned away slightly to cough. There were black streaks all over his body, along with a sheen of sweat and ashes, and cuts oozing with blood and that's when she realized—

"You didn't go *in* there, did you?"

"Of *course* I went in there." His voice sounded as if he'd swallowed shattered glass. "Did you think I'd just let you go up in flames without trying to get you—and the cats—out?"

"Are you *insane*?" Without thinking, she grabbed his arms and gave him a little shake—or tried to. He was far too solid for her to do more than jolt him. "Why would you do something so—"

"Excuse me, ma'am, but you need to get out of the way," came a firm voice that bordered on annoyance.

"Right. And this man needs to be checked over for smoke inhalation damage and—everything else."

Diana dragged a protesting Ethan to a paramedic as he argued in that rough raspy voice. Only when he demanded, "The cats?" did she pause.

"They're out there somewhere," she said, gesturing toward the forest. "They were sitting on the grass when I got home. They're all right." She looked up at him. "I think...I think he let them out before he set the fire."

"You went inside a burning building like *that*?" said the paramedic, forestalling anything Ethan might have said. She lifted her eyes and frowned at his bare chest, cargo shorts, and bare feet shoved into boots.

"I didn't get very far," Ethan admitted as the paramedic used a stethoscope to listen to him breathe.

"It's a good thing you didn't," the medic said briskly. "Most people who die in fires die from smoke inhalation, not from burns—and going into a building that's burning like that without a mask or any protective covering is foolish, no matter what the reason. You're lucky you didn't lose your bearings and get lost inside there."

"Well, I wasn't going to just stand by and let her *die*," he snapped as he swiped a forearm across his blackened face. The swipe made it worse, and a crust of ashes formed in his brows and along his hairline. "I left in such a hurry I didn't have a phone and—you must have come home to find this. And called?"

"Yes. My cell didn't work, of course, so I had to run over to the house next door. Hornbergers?" Diana looked toward the house. "The house was burning when I got home, but it wasn't as ablaze as it is now. I wonder if anything can be saved," she added as a wave of grief took her by surprise.

Another loss.

And this one seemed, somehow, even more painful.

More sinister.

Ethan, Diana, and a panting Cady drove up the drive to his cabin just before dawn. The cats had declined to join them, so Diana opened the garage door at Aunt Jean's enough for them to slip inside.

All three of them were tired and sooty, but of course Ethan was the worst of the bunch, still overcome by random coughing bouts due to the smoke he'd inhaled.

Diana had tried to send him home hours ago, but the stubborn idiot had refused. He not only insisted on staying until the firefighters were finished, but he helped them where he could—managing one of the anaconda-like hoses that used the fire truck's engine to pump water from the lake.

Though she was exhausted, and the light was dim, Diana noticed how pleasant and welcoming his home was. A two-story log cabin made from squared-off cedar, its main entrance was reached via a long, screened-in porch, and topped by a broad second-floor dormer.

Once inside the log cabin, Ethan toed off his boots in a small mudroom. "Let me get out of these filthy clothes, then I'll show you—"

"I can figure things out, Ethan. Just point me to where you want me to sleep, then you go up and take care of yourself."

A little pang of disappointment surged through Diana when she realized she would have been very happy to take care of him—help wash off the soot, settle him into bed... especially as he began to unfasten his blackened shorts. Neither of them were thinking about modesty at the moment.

"All right," he rasped. "Guest room's down that hall; it has its own bath. You can find towels and—"

"Ethan. I'll be fine. Clean up, and get some rest." She was still overwhelmed by the knowledge that he'd risked his life trying to find her in the burning house—and then stayed to help fight the fire even when he was weak from smoke.

"Unless you're hungry? I'm sure I could find something in your kitchen." Diana glanced down the hall where she could see a high-ceilinged great room with a compact, cozy kitchen tucked in next to it.

His short laugh was gritty with smoke and exhaustion, then ended with a bout of coughing that made her wince. It sounded painful. "I just want sleep for now. And water. My room's up there, by the way." He gestured to the stairway as he stepped out of his shorts. He was wearing dark briefs that looked like bicycle shorts and, Diana told herself primly, they revealed no more than real bike shorts would.

But that was plenty.

"I promise I'll be a better host in the morning." He gave a

wry smile, seemingly unconcerned about his lack of clothing, then, leaving his clothes in a heap, started up the stairs.

Diana picked up his t-shirt and shorts and tossed them into the laundry tub to soak.

Then, suddenly realizing how exhausted she was, she found her way to the guest room. Diana didn't even mind when the huge black lab padded along behind her, for she hadn't had the luxury of indulging her nervousness about the dog during the last few hours.

She still couldn't believe Ethan had gone into the house to try and save her.

What a fool.

What an amazing, brave fool. She fought back a smile and a rush of affection.

He was just doing what anyone would do.

Wearily, she stripped off her smoky clothing and realized she'd have to go shopping for…well, everything…tomorrow. Dressed in a long t-shirt she'd scrounged in the bureau, she padded down the hall—which, like the rest of the house, was finished in smooth, glossy paneling—and tossed her clothing in the laundry tub to soak with Ethan's.

Then, gratefully, she crawled beneath the covers of what seemed to be a very comfortable queen-sized bed. On the floor nearby, Cady turned around and around in circles, then finally thumped herself onto the colorful braided rug near the side of the bed.

About a third of Aunt Jean's house had burned, though much of the shell of even that area remained. The rest of it, though blackened with smoke and stained with water, was still standing.

Later tomorrow—well, today—Diana might be able to walk through some of the smoldering cinders, and assess the extent of the damage. But she already knew the library had been the genesis of the blaze, and most of the upstairs and part of the bedroom Aunt Jean used was definitely gone. The kitchen seemed mostly intact as far as structure, but the smoke damage would be awful.

She closed her dry, gritty eyes and smelled nothing but smoke, saw nothing but dancing flames.

"How do you think it started?" Diana had asked when they left the ruins of the house.

The firefighter had looked at her. "It will be a little while until we know what caused the fire. You say you weren't home when it started?"

Diana nodded. "I went to Grand Rapids for the evening and when I got back, I drove up the drive and saw the house on fire."

He shook his head. "Could be anything—especially with a house this old. Faulty wiring, anything."

Diana glanced at Ethan, catching him exchanging glances with the fireman. A dull nausea roiled in her stomach, for she knew what he was thinking. The fire had not been caused by faulty wiring.

She squeezed her eyes shut tightly, as though she could block the horrible reality from her world. Could someone have been trying to kill her too? Or had they known she was gone and wanted to destroy the house—and whatever was in it?

But...whoever it was had let the cats out first. That meant something, didn't it?

Well, whatever the intruder had been looking for, it was gone now.

The chances of Diana ever finding out who or what or why were slim.

Maybe I should go back to Chicago and forget about all of this.

That thought settled in her mind as she forced herself to

try and sleep…but the last thing she remembered thinking was: *Don't you dare.*

And it wasn't her own voice she heard in her head.

It was Aunt Jean's.

Ethan peeled his eyes open to a bright wash of sunshine. From the looks of it, he'd slept till almost noon. Which wasn't surprising, since when he'd tumbled into bed the clock said five.

He'd showered briskly but thoroughly last night, but he could still smell smoke and soot coating the insides of his nostrils. *Guess I missed that part.* His eyes were dry and gritty, and there was a general ache everywhere in his body.

But worst of all, here it was—almost noon, and he was in bed *solo*, with a gorgeous, intriguing, and prickly woman just a few steps below.

Damn. What was the world coming to?

He smiled wryly to himself and scratched the hair on his chest, then was surprised by a rough cough that hurt his lungs. *Man, that was stupid*, he told himself as a flash of that terrifying moment in the dark-as-night kitchen came back. *You nearly got yourself killed.*

Thank God she was safe.

Stupid as it might have been, he would do it again. There was no way he would *not* have tried to go in for Diana. Or the cats.

The cats.

She'd said the cats were outside when she got home. *He must have let them out.*

Either that, or Aunt Jean did.

Ethan gave a little laugh that brought up another raspy

cough, hurting his lungs a little. As ghosts went, Genevieve Fickler was a trip.

And so was her niece. A nice, hot, interesting trip.

This is not the time, Murphy, and Diana's not the—

Before he could complete the thought, a bloodcurdling scream rent the air.

THIRTEEN

DIANA HAD BEEN SLEEPING SOUNDLY, curled up in one of the most comfortable beds she'd ever experienced. She'd rolled over, up against a warm body...*Ethan*, her sleep-fogged mind told her.

The thought fluttered through her in a wave of heat, and she smiled lazily in her sleep. However he'd come to be here, the memories couldn't be bad, she thought, snuggling closer... then she opened her eyes.

And screamed.

Diana stumbled out of the bed as Cady's head shot up and she looked at her with startled brown eyes.

The sound of a heavy thud upstairs, then faster, staccato thumps down random steps alerted her to the fact that Ethan had heard her.

The door to her room burst open and he flew in. "Diana? What's wrong?"

Diana gawked. He was naked, and absolutely magnificent in this natural state. For a moment, she couldn't say a word—she was caught between embarrassment, shock, and speechless admiration.

Cady hadn't moved from her place on the bed, and Ethan's gaze fell on her. Understanding dawned in his expression, then he obviously realized his state of undress. A splash of red tinted his cheeks and he ducked into the bathroom to grab a towel.

"Sorry," he said as a smile tugged at his mouth. "Did Cady startle you? I should have warned you to keep the door closed if you didn't want her in here."

"It's—it's all right," Diana managed to stammer. Although she'd averted her eyes as soon as she saw him—*all of him… every square (and linear) inch*—she could still picture his flat stomach, lean hips…and the evidence that he didn't sunbathe in the nude.

Deep breaths, Diana, deep breaths.

"I—uh—I'm sorry if I woke you," she added weakly.

"I guess we're even now, hmm?" he replied, his expression blank. When she looked at him uncertainly, he explained: "Monday? When I was mowing the lawn? I woke you up?"

"Right." He'd only been bare-chested then. Diana swallowed hard.

Ethan gestured and Cady jumped off the bed, then paused to stretch with her tail in the air.

"I'm sorry about her," he said again, tightening the towel—which, really, he was wearing so low it hardly mattered if it slipped a bit. "Other than that, did you sleep all right?"

"I slept like a rock," Diana replied.

"Glad to hear it. Well, how about some breakfast—I'll cook while you shower. You've still got some smudges on your face."

"Oh." Her cheeks warmed, but when she finally saw herself in the mirror a few minutes later, she gasped in shock and horror. She looked like a *harridan*.

Her hair was *everywhere*, literally standing on end like some sort of curly explosion. Her face was crusty with ash and soot—probably from when she was crushed against his bare, smoky, hot chest—

Stop thinking about that, Diana.

By the time she got out of the shower, the smells of something delicious were wafting under the door of the guest room. Her hair was still wet, and she was about to search for a blow dryer—but why bother? He'd already seen her looking like something from the black lagoon.

And it didn't matter what she looked like to him. Ethan thought her hair was pretty? Wait till he saw it completely out of control. He'd change his mind quickly enough.

Not that it mattered what he thought.

At all.

She opened the bedroom door to find Cady lying there across the threshold. The black lab sprang to her feet, tongue lolling in excitement, and big, white teeth showing.

"Get away," Diana suggested, beckoning with her hand.

The dog didn't move, just looked up at her with mournful brown eyes, and stood expectantly, blocking the doorway.

"Move," she tried again weakly.

Cady licked her chops, seeming to relish the size of her vicious canines, and sent a shiver of warning down Diana's spine.

"Um…nice doggie," she said, and was relieved when the dog let her tongue hang out again.

I'm not moving until you greet me in a proper manner, the lab seemed to say.

"Oh, all right." Diana gave in and patted the top of her head clumsily. The fur, a shiny black-brown color, was surprisingly soft—not coarse as she'd expected. Cady still didn't move, so Diana tried again, this time petting the dog's forehead. "Watch out," she said, and finally, heart in her throat, she pushed past the lump of fur.

To Diana's relief, nothing happened. Cady didn't bark or growl or even push back. She just followed her.

So when Diana came around the corner into the kitchen, Cady was at her heels.

"Good morning, ladies," Ethan greeted them. He was now modestly attired in a pair of twill shorts and a dark red t-shirt, and stood at the stove. His hair was dripping over his collar—so he must have done a speedy shower.

"Scrambled eggs okay with you?" he asked, brandishing a spatula and looking a little hesitant. "I don't have much else in the fridge."

"Sounds great. I'm starving," she said, sliding onto a bar stool and getting a good look at the kitchen for the first time. It was decorated with bright-colored Mexican tile in blue and yellow, and the space spilled seamlessly into a great room with its high, peaked ceiling. "You can cook."

"Well, I know how to crack a couple eggs and I'm really great at sprinkling cheese on them."

"That's good enough for me."

She'd never had a man make breakfast for her before. She'd never even had a man *cook* for her before. Jonathan's idea of cooking was calling for takeout and putting it on a plate. Once in a while, he'd even set the table.

All at once it washed over her like a bucket of cold water: the calm realization that she wouldn't care in the least if she never saw Jonathan again.

It was odd, the way her decision came—in such an unexpected way, at this moment over breakfast—and with such vehemence and clarity.

And freedom. An intense shock of freedom.

She came back to the present, to the smell of coffee (*thank God, coffee!*) and frying hotcakes, and settled back in her seat.

I'm going to break it off. Today.

She'd call Jonathan when she got back to the house—or what was left of it.

Oh, God. She squeezed her eyes shut as tears stung them. *The house.*

Aunt Jean murdered, and now her beloved house was burned half to the ground.

"Let's eat on the deck," Ethan said, breaking into her thoughts. "This way." He gestured to a small patio beyond the large, sliding glass doors that overlooked the side yard and beyond.

"We've got things to talk about," Diana said, her mind suddenly filled with thoughts and questions—and the only person she wanted to run them past, she realized, was Ethan.

He understood. He wouldn't look at her any differently if she asked those questions and posited her theories.

With this realization calming her, Diana picked a mug of coffee. She inhaled the hazelnut scent as if it were ambrosia then picked up some napkins and Ethan's coffee as well.

The deck was a stamped concrete square set off the side of the house and was just large enough to comfortably hold a three-legged fire pit and a table with four chairs.

The way the cedar cabin was situated, the lake was off to the right and could be seen more readily from the front, screened porch. But the view from this direction was just as peaceful: facing the encroaching woods, with an array of bird-feeders dangling from shepherd's hooks or tree branches in one corner of the yard. As Diana sat on one of the wrought-iron chairs, she saw a downy woodpecker land on one of the feeders with a suet bar, chasing away the chickadees. At a different feeder, a nut-thatch crept down, facefirst, to the trough feeder while a grosbeak fed on the other side.

"So," he said, looking at her as he plopped down in front

of a plate mounded with eggs and melted cheese. "I've got some thoughts."

She gave him a brief smile. "As do I."

The eggs really hit the spot—she was *starving*—and Diana almost moaned when she tasted the first forkful. Maybe she actually did, because he looked over at her suddenly, and the expression in his eyes had her flushing and glancing away.

"So, about last night," she began, and then, flustered, gave a little laugh. "I mean, about the fire."

"When you got home, the cats were outside, you said."

"Yes. The front door was open—a fact which would normally have freaked me out, but I'd already seen the flames and smelled the smoke, so that was lower on the list of concerns."

"So he set the house on fire, but let out the cats—to make sure they wouldn't die. And he obviously knew you weren't there," Ethan said. "I'm assuming that, at least, since your car must have been gone."

"My car was gone." Diana slipped another bite into her mouth to give her a moment to think before she spoke. "So, yes, it didn't appear he was trying to murder me as well."

He glanced sharply up at her, his mouth tightening; but he didn't comment. Instead, he began to focus on spearing as many pieces of pancake onto his fork as possible. "Unless it was Jean who let the cats out."

She swallowed a fortifying glug of coffee. "I was thinking the same thing. Either Jean let the cats out, or a murderer—someone who would kill a defenseless woman in her own bed—made sure to get them out of the house." She sipped her coffee. "I suppose either is possible. But I guess I'm leaning toward Aunt Jean."

He grinned at her suddenly. "Did you ever think you'd be

sitting here, calmly discussing a ghost as if it were as common as a blue jay?"

She shook her head. "Never in a million years."

So how did that make her feel?

Just as free and weightless as knowing she was breaking up permanently with Jonathan.

After breakfast, she insisted on cleaning up since he'd cooked.

"All right then. I'll go throw the ball for Cady."

When she was finished in the kitchen, Diana took a minute to walk through and admire the cabin's great room and its stately fireplace that burned real wood.

The room was furnished with a sweeping mocha-colored suede sectional and a separate, matching recliner that was positioned in front of a gigantic television screen. The floor, which was hardwood throughout the house, was protected in this room by a huge dark blue and brown-flecked rug, soft and lush beneath the feet.

A multi-colored woven blanket hung over the mantel of the broad, stone chimney—the tapestry looked like it was from Mexico or somewhere in South America. He'd said he was in Macchu Picchu; maybe he'd brought it back from there. There were random pieces of art on the walls: some, obviously from home decorating stores, and others that appeared to be originals from places like South America or Asia.

She was particularly taken by a sepia-toned photograph of a possibly Buddhist monk climbing the steps of an ancient temple, his robes tossed and blowing in the breeze.

But what really captured her attention was a photograph of Fiona and another, older woman whom Diana assumed was Claudia—the free-spirit hippie who lived in Costa Rica and made hemp baskets. She saw Ethan's eyes in his mother's face, and the shape of his chin.

Diana had no photos of her own mother in her condo.

For obvious reasons.

She joined Ethan outside and sat at the picnic table, watching as man and dog played together. She even clapped a few times when Cady caught the tennis ball neatly in her mouth, then pranced around happily. Once, the lab even brought the ball over and dropped it at her feet.

Diana couldn't disappoint her expectant look, and reached to pick it up. She recoiled when she felt its sloppy dampness, but told herself to suck it up, and managed to ignore the wetness long enough to toss it toward the lake.

It didn't go nearly as far as when Ethan threw it, but Cady chased after it gleefully.

"Uh-oh, now you have a friend," he said when the lab brought it back and dropped it at her feet again.

Diana acquiesced and threw the ball a few more times, badly, before Ethan took pity on her—and Cady—and fired the tennis ball deep into the woods.

Finally, though lulled by the idyllic, relaxed setting, she realized it was time to leave. Ethan would have to drive her back to pick up her car—which he agreed to immediately.

"I need to do some shopping," she told him, gathering up her handbag as she climbed into the jeep. Cady jumped in the back behind her, pushing her way past, and Diana was proud that she didn't even flinch. "I need some replacement clothes. And I should check in with Captain Longbow to see…well, to make a report."

She stumbled over the idea of asking Ethan to go with her, but rejected it immediately. She didn't need a man to support her, or to give her courage, and now that she'd decided to cut Jonathan loose, Diana felt even more determined to handle this on her own.

"You'll stay here tonight," Ethan said as he started the engine.

Diana gave him a startled look. "No, that's not—"

"Don't be silly. You'll stay here tonight. There's no sense in spending the money on a room here in town—unless you were planning to go back to Chicago tonight."

She hadn't been…but the realization that the option hadn't even occurred to her made Diana supremely uncomfortable. "I—"

"You'll need to stay in town for at least a few days while the investigation is going on anyway," Ethan said. "Joe Cap or the fire department might have other questions for you."

It sounded like a bullshit excuse to her, but Diana found herself unwilling to look too closely at its validity. "Well, all right. Just for a day or two. If you're certain you don't mind."

He smiled as he pulled up next to her Lexus in front of Jean's smoldering house. "No. I don't mind at all."

After he left, Diana sat on what was left of the front porch of the farmhouse and dialed Jonathan from her cell phone—which began to ring right away.

"Diana!" The relief in his voice came through the phone. "How are you?"

Her heart gave a little bump. This was the first time they'd talked since the other night, when Ethan had answered the phone. Jonathan sounded sincerely happy to hear from her. And unusually tentative.

She steeled herself into no-nonsense, emotionless mode. "I'm fine," she told him. "Fine."

"Diana, when are you coming home? I miss you. I'm sorry about the other night. I was…well, I was jealous. And I want us to work through this, and we can't work through this if you're way up there in the middle of nowhere."

"I'll be back in Chicago Sunday night," she said, gripping

the phone tighter. "I'll stop by to pick up my things around seven."

"What?" The soft, empathetic tone changed to one of shock and dismay. "What are you talking about?"

"It's over, Jonathan." Even as she said those words, Diana was aware of the unsettled feeling sinking over her, the deepening twist of nausea. *What am I doing?*

"Diana," he said, his voice sharper now. Then he drew in an audible breath and she could tell he was trying to force himself into calmness. "Okay, okay, then, if you want to take a little space, a little time to work things through, I can understand that. I can work with that," he said. "We can do that."

That little bump of nerves in her pulse grew stronger. Maybe that was the way she should approach it. Just move out for a little while, try to work things out. Not just close the door without trying again.

No. No, that wasn't what she wanted to do.

"No, Jonathan," she said, still in that calm voice she used in court—that voice which delivered only facts and well-thought-out arguments devoid of emotion. "I'm not interested in trying to work things out. It's over. I'll bring back the ring on Sunday too."

Her palms were clammy and the phone felt heavy and hot against her cheek as she heard her mother's voice deep in her head: *Now what are you going to do? How are you ever going to find someone when you work so much and are so—*

"No," she said aloud, to silence both Melanie's imagined voice and his very real, strident one. "No, Jonathan, I really do mean it."

"But…Diana. I love you," he said, his voice soft again. The desperation threaded through it made her start to question herself: *he really does care.*

But I don't. Not any more.

"Can't we at least talk about this?" he asked.

"Not right now," she said. That was the most she could give him. "Maybe someday in the future. But not now. I have to go, Jonathan—the office is calling."

Coward, she told herself over the lie—but she already knew the conversation was just going to devolve into a circular argument that would take far more effort and energy than she wanted to expend.

After all, she had more pressing things to deal with than the bruised ego of a pompous cardiologist.

"Good-bye, Jonathan." She disconnected the call as he was still talking.

And then she declined the immediate call-back from him.

Instead, she set the cell phone aside and closed her eyes, leaning against the porch railing. She waited for the fear and emptiness to climb over her, to settle there and gnaw like her mother's constant nagging.

But it didn't come.

Instead of tears pricking her eyes, or queasiness weighing inside her belly, Diana felt relaxed.

Freed.

After a long while—where she did nothing but smell the remnants of the smoldering fire and hear the rustle of breeze through the trees, along with an orchestra of bird song, she opened her eyes and looked out over the small, grassy yard. It was trampled and bore tire tracks from last night's fire-fighting. There were streaks of black on the lawn, and a few long indentations where the heavy hose had crushed the grass and flowers.

Now tears stung her eyes. Jean's lovely house was ruined. Someone wanted desperately to—

To do what? To destroy something? To find something? Why?

As Diana sat there, mulling over the abrupt turn in her life, smelling the remnants of smoke and smoldering wood in this quiet patch of land, Motto appeared from around the corner of the house.

To her surprise, the sleek cat approached and butted her head against Diana's side until she lifted a hand to pet the soft, white fur...following the receptive arch of Motto's spine all the way up, over, then along the thick, bushy tail.

"It was the right thing to do," she said. "To end things with Jonathan. Now maybe I'll be able to—"

Diana stopped when she noticed Arty. The more reticent, shyer cat was sitting off to the side, in the direction from which Motto had come. Just sitting in the grass, looking at her —almost expectantly.

But it was the object in front of the fat cat that caught her attention. That made her pulse spike and her hands go clammy. She bolted to her feet.

"*How?*" Diana breathed as she stared down at the mahogany card box. It sat undisturbed in the grass, pretty as you please, right next to the cat. "How in the hell did this get out here?"

She looked back toward the house, which was a study in chiaroscuro between the white clapboard, the gray shutters and porch, and the sooty, scorched remains of the back half.

Aunt Jean.

She saved the cats and *her cards.*

Half laughing, half crying, Diana picked up the box. Only then did she see the single card sitting there in the sunshine beneath Arty's paw.

Diana went cold. Then hot.

The meaning of the image was unmistakable: a skeleton wearing black armor, riding slowly on a dark horse. Death carried a flag with a rose depicted on it, and a man, woman, and child collapsed before him.

Death.

The Death card portends the end or cessation of something: a phase, a journey.

A relationship.

FOURTEEN

"SO SOMEHOW JEAN'S box of Tarot cards escaped not only the fire, but also the water they were spraying all over the place?" Cherry Wilder said, leaning forward with her elbows on the table. "For hours?"

They were at Trib's, a whole group of them somehow having snagged the single large booth that seated ten—and on a Saturday night during high tourist season!

The generous table was tucked near the back behind a divider made from long, narrow, wavy pieces of wood and metal that acted like an industrial style beaded curtain. Cedar, maple, bronze, copper, and brushed sheet metal shivered and danced from the ceiling, each piece suspended on a slender, elegant chain.

Ethan long suspected the proprietor had installed the mega-sized booth as a combination failsafe (to keep the Tuesday Ladies—especially Maxine and her cane—from taking over his restaurant) and personal sanctuary—a place he could join local friends when he needed a break from being celebrity chef and restaurateur for the tourists.

"And the cats," Maxine added flatly. She had a tall, dark

beer in front of her and sat at the end of the booth, likely for easy access to employ her cane. "Don't forget Jean saved the cats. Don't surprise me none, though."

"Me either," Iva said. Her eyes sparkled with delight that colored her cheeks a delicate pink. "That's the Jean Fickler I knew. You didn't really get to meet her, Hollis, dear, but she was like that. Smart, with an offbeat sense of humor, and an unflagging devotion to those cats."

"I'll never understand why people like cats so much," Juanita crooned as she looked down at Bruce Banner. From inside his mistress's bag—a relatively shallow one tonight—his beady black eyes scanned the table while his cute little nose quivered. He was likely watching for an opportunity to snag a nibble of something to eat. "Dogs are so much more friendly, aren't they, *poquito?*"

"That dog's French, ain't he? A papillon—that means butterfly, like his ears," Maxine informed Diana in a shout because she sat across the table, and not next to her. "Keep telling you, you should be speaking in French to the little beast, not Spanish." This last was directed back at Maxine's best friend and sparring partner.

"There doesn't seem to be any other explanation than Jean's involvement," Diana replied, ignoring Maxine's *non sequitur* as most of them had learned to do.

Her pragmatic tone speaking about a ghost—publicly—surprised Ethan.

How far you've come, he thought with a little burst of warmth. *How much you've unbent and opened your mind over the last couple of weeks.*

Though she wasn't sitting next to him, Ethan appreciated the fact that he could, instead, simply watch. And torture himself.

When did you become such a masochist?

But when Baxter nudged him sharply with an elbow, he jolted and looked at his friend.

"Dude. You're practically drooling, my man," he said in an undertone. "How's that moratorium working out for you now?"

Ethan gave him a steely look. "It's still in play because she isn't. And those who live in glass houses…" He looked pointedly across the restaurant, where Emily Delton was sitting with her teenaged daughter and some out-of-town friends.

Baxter shrugged. "Just trying to keep you from looking like a desperate trout."

"There is another option," said Hollis Nath. His deep, cultured voice cut through the back-and-forth between the higher-pitched ladies' arguments. "As much as you'd like to attribute it to Jean's ghost, Iva, darling, there is the possibility the arsonist removed the box himself."

Everyone at the table—Cherry, Orbra, Maxine, Juanita, Iva, Baxter, Diana, and Ethan—looked at him. Even Bruce Banner seemed arrested by the commanding voice.

"Because he was looking for something in it," Iva said, nodding. "That is possible."

"Possible," Diana replied smoothly. "But, in all likelihood, not probable. Here's why: it was sitting, closed, with all the cards in it, on the grass. It seems to me that if the arsonist removed the box to search through it, he'd either: one, take it with him and examine it later; or, two, look through it quickly then discard it just as quickly. To leave it sitting neatly on the grass, closed, with all its contents remaining inside—well, it's not likely."

Ethan hid a smile in his beer. She'd clearly had time to think through all possibilities, and her own logical, lawyer's mind assessed and discarded the ones that didn't make sense.

Yet Hollis Nath didn't seem offended by her response—as

many men of his generation might feel if given a counterpoint to his argument by a younger woman—which gave him an extra point in Ethan's book. Still, he couldn't dismiss the fact that Nath had arrived on the scene of Wicks Hollow at the same time as the Merman-Steele Golf Outing. And the intruder at Jean's house had dropped a pen from that same conference. They had to be connected. Ethan was certain the intruder was someone who'd been at the conference, and likely someone known to Hollis Nath.

He didn't want to consider the possibility that Nath himself was involved.

"Is any part of the house salvageable?" asked Cherry.

"I won't know for certain until the insurance adjustor and fire damage company assesses the situation, but I'm hopeful some of it can be saved. It would be a tragedy to have to tear it down." The sadness in Diana's voice struck Ethan as genuine, and he wondered if that meant she was considering keeping the house herself. Whatever was left of it.

"Where are you staying tonight, honey?" asked Orbra. "Do you need—"

"She's staying at Ethan's," Maxine announced, as if it were a foregone conclusion.

Everyone looked at him, then at Diana, then back again—and their collective, knowing expressions had his cheeks actually going hot.

"I wanted to be near the cats," Diana said smoothly. "Until I can find them a new home. Right now they're staying in Aunt Jean's garage."

"Do you need anything, dear?" asked Iva. "I'm supposing whatever didn't actually burn in the fire is either waterlogged or ruined by smoke. You probably lost everything."

"What about your computer?" asked Baxter in horror.

"Fortunately, I had my laptop with me," Diana replied.

"And I went shopping today for the necessities, but I'll be going back home to Chicago tomorrow. I've got—I've got some things to take care of. I'm so glad I got to see all of you before I left." She smiled.

The speculative looks went from her to Ethan again as he tried not to appear shocked by the announcement that she was leaving.

And stunned she hadn't mentioned it to him.

Not that she had any obligation to do so, but, still... tomorrow? She was leaving tomorrow? Just like that?

When had she made that decision?

Probably when her house burned down, Murphy. It was a logical reaction.

Still. The thought put him in the sourest of moods, and even Maxine and Juanita's back and forth jabbing didn't jar him from his brooding.

"Smells like rain," Diana said as she climbed out of Ethan's jeep back at his house.

It was after nine o'clock, and the sun had just set. The night air was damp and clammy, but filled with the songs of crickets, loons, and bullfrogs.

Diana heard Cady barking inside the cabin, and she instinctively ducked as a bat darted across the clearing, though it was far above her head. A single light had been left burning inside the house, and it cast a soft, golden glow from the kitchen window onto the short, stubby grass near the parking area.

"It sure is humid," he replied, sniffing the air. He let Cady out of the house, and, still barking, the black lab ran up to Diana to smell her.

She reached down to pat the dog's head, surprised by her automatic reaction, then shifted back when Cady's wet nose bumped against her bare leg. *Ew.* "Nice dog," she said, pushing Cady gently away. "Go do your thing. Go on, now."

Diana let herself into the cabin while Ethan took care of his dog, throwing the tennis ball down the incline toward the lake with a powerful arm. She'd put all of her shopping bags—with toiletries, the casual poppy-splashed sundress she'd worn to dinner, some clothing for tomorrow, and a silky nightgown—in the guest room before they left for dinner. It was too early to change into the nightgown (Diana couldn't even justify why she'd bought such an impractical thing, especially since she'd just broken up with Jonathan; the silky, midnight blue chemise had been expensive), but she definitely wanted to get out of the sundress.

Strangely keyed up, even after a dinner that required a lot of mental energy to keep up with the Tuesday Ladies and their bickering and random conversation, Diana changed into a pair of yoga pants and a tank top. By the time she padded out to the kitchen in bare feet that desperately needed a pedicure, Ethan and Cady had come back inside.

"Oh," he said, looking at her with surprise as he dumped a scoop of dog food into Cady's dish. He scanned her change of clothing, ending with her bare feet, then swooped back up. "I thought you'd already gone to bed."

"I'm not really tired," she replied, eyeing him closely. He'd become uncharacteristically quiet about halfway through dinner. If he wasn't in the mood for company, she could excuse herself and read a book (what a novel idea—pun intended) or…something.

"Did you want something to drink? Want to watch television?" He seemed strangely uncomfortable or tense. Something was off.

"Is something wrong?" she asked, watching him as if he were a witness she was cross-examining. "Are you tired or—just not want company?"

"No, no, not at all. I've got some beer in here—oh, and here's a bottle of wine." He was poking in the refrigerator, so she didn't get a good look at his face. "Fee—I mean Fiona—left it here. It's from one of the regional wineries—up near Traverse City. Did you know the vines up there are older than the ones that grow in most of France now?"

Diana did a little double take. "What?"

"Back in the 1800s, I think it was, there was a disease or infestation of the vineyards in France, and most of them died. They imported grapevines from the Grand Traverse area to replace them. True story. So," he said, smoothly withdrawing a bottle from the fridge, "even a wine snob can't argue about the quality of white wine from Michigan."

"Well," she said with a smile, "I guess I'll have to try it then. Don't let me keep you up, Ethan, if you have things to do."

"I don't. And since you're leaving tomorrow," he said as he tore off the foil on the wine bottle with a sharp movement, "we probably won't have much more of a chance to talk. About everything."

"That's true. I did want to tell you something I wasn't willing to share with the others," she replied as he slipped the corkpull's vise around the bottle head, then lowered the handle.

"Besides the fact that you were leaving tomorrow?" he said, yanking the lever back up. The cork came out with a satisfying *pop*, and he set aside the pull.

"Yes." Diana watched as he poured two glasses of wine without looking at her, without flirting with her, without any sort of the warmth and camaraderie she'd come to know and expect from him.

Something was definitely wrong, and if she'd been in the middle of a trial or hearing, she'd know just how to respond: how to treat the witness, how to get the reaction she needed. But now, she was flummoxed and, frankly, a little out of her league.

He handed her a glass and she took it, automatically bringing it to her nose to smell. Peachy, she thought—of both the wine and the situation in which she found herself.

"Let's sit down in here." Ethan gestured to the sprawling suede sectional.

The great room was lit by two large floor lamps made from solid square columns of carved wood, one on each end of the curving sofa, and recessed lights above the fireplace and along the soffit between the kitchen area and the living room. Three tall casement windows were open, facing the dark forest, and allowed a fresh, lake-scented breeze to stir the air in the room.

"So, what was it you didn't want to bring up at dinner?" Ethan asked as Cady flopped to the floor with a groan.

Diana sipped the wine. It was cold and crisp, with those peachy notes and an essence of honey. She liked it. "When I found the box of Aunt Jean's cards, it was just as I described it: the box was set away from the house, and it wasn't wet or upended or disordered at all. Just placed there pretty as you please. But Arty was sitting next to it, like he wanted me to notice him, and when I got closer I saw that—I saw his paw was resting on a card."

Ethan's reserve disintegrated abruptly, and his eyes flared with shock then fascination. "You're shitting me."

"I'm not." She smiled and went on, "Not only was the card not wet—as it would have been if it had been out all night, sitting in the wet grass and dew—it was a very relevant card. Relevant to the situation."

Aware that timing was everything, and that she had the benefit of controlling the suspense, she lifted the glass and took another sip, watching him over the rim.

"Is that so," he replied. His voice had dropped into that low rumble with which she was familiar—and found so attractive—and he contemplated her from his position at one end of the sectional. "Are you going to make me guess which card?"

She smiled and tucked her feet under her on the luxurious suede. "I think that would be entertaining. Go ahead."

"*The High Priestess.*" His eyes were dancing now as he reached over to scrub Cady on the head.

"*Pish.* That's much too obvious." She sipped again, suddenly ridiculously lighthearted and happy.

She'd broken up with Jonathan.

That whole problem, all the drama and effort related to him and their relationship—such as it was—was over. She had no ties, no obligations, no mental energy assigned to him any longer.

Ethan tilted his head, looking at her closely. "You seem in a particularly fine mood for someone whose house burned last night and whose aunt was murdered." His tone wasn't judgmental, but curious.

Maybe it was because she knew there was no longer any reason not to, but Diana found herself noticing—and enjoying—how handsome he was. Relaxed, with all that dark, thick hair that had grown out a bit from its cut, and his interested gaze. His mouth, and his tanned, capable hand that absently stroked Cady's head...

She realized he was waiting for a response, and that her pulse had kicked up a little. "Let's just say that although I'm grieving about those things—and determined to figure out what is going on—I had a conversation today that lifted a great weight from my shoulders."

"I see." The glint of levity in his eyes eased and he sobered. "Before I continue on the guessing game, Diana, I want to say something that's been on my mind for a while."

Her heart did a little skip, but when she realized his expression had become reserved and remote once again, her mood plummeted. He looked far too serious to be about to say something personal—not that he would, anyway—although he *had* admitted he found her attractive, prickly though she was.

"Go on." She knew how to keep her expression blank and her gaze expectant but not concerned. Most people had no idea how much acting and learning of lines was involved in being a trial lawyer. That, at least, was a skill she'd developed well since high school, when the merest cross word or expression would send her into tears.

"I think you should be concerned with your safety." He'd stopped petting Cady, as if he needed all of his attention focused on what he was about to say. "You've just gained an inheritance that's made you a wealthy woman—though I'm certain you aren't doing too badly at your law firm—and although it doesn't appear that you've been a target, per se—"

"Aunt Jean was murdered. So someone has already killed, and probably wouldn't hesitate to do so again," she finished for him. "I've thought of that. Then discarded the notion. Honestly, Ethan, I could be wrong about Aunt Jean being smothered—and if that's the case, then we're just dealing with a breaking and entering situation."

"You *aren't* wrong, Diana." He spoke flatly, then took a healthy swallow of wine. "Your aunt confirmed it, didn't she?"

"Well, in a matter of speaking—she mainly confirmed that she was around in a ghostly capacity."

"Diana. Even Joe Cap believes she was murdered. Even though we haven't gotten confirmation from the medical examiner yet, I trust your instincts on this. This person has killed once, and that means it's easier for him to kill again."

"But what would be the benefit of killing *me*? I—" She stopped abruptly as everything he was saying—without saying it—dumped into her head. "Someone is trying to kill me to get Aunt Jean's money."

"Or *might* at some point. In the near future. Think about this...there are all these break-ins at the house. There's a fire, where, miraculously, you happened to be away when it happened—but you just as easily might not have been. What if it's just someone setting the scene so when you *do* get killed —sorry," he said hastily, with a rueful smile. "What if it's just someone setting it up so if you do die—maybe months from now—it seems like part of the whole big picture? Or just seems like another accident."

"But why would someone want to do that? Create a bunch of accidents, then a real murder?"

His shoulders slumped a little. "I'm still working that part out. Misdirection maybe? Or maybe even setting up an alibi for one of the previous accidents?" He shrugged.

"So who would benefit from me being out of the way?" Diana said. "Or dead. That's what you're getting at." She looked at him, a strange, uncomfortable prickling in her belly. "So you want to know who would get the inheritance then. Who would inherit *my* possessions."

He didn't reply. He didn't need to.

"Well, my father is dead, and my mother is my closest relative, so according to probate, she—"

"You don't have a will?"

A will. Diana froze with the wineglass halfway to her mouth, then lowered it. Jonathan had mentioned that he'd recently changed his will to make her his heir—not long after they'd become engaged. He'd suggested she do the same—"To make things easier," he'd said.

She'd agreed at the time. Why not? This was months before Aunt Jean had died, and Diana was giddy and in love with a wonderful man. Besides, Jonathan had more assets than she did—he owned a condo on Lake Shore Drive and was a managing partner in his cardiology practice.

But she hadn't actually finalized the will naming him as her heir. It was sitting at home in a folder, waiting for her to review one last time.

"No," she replied slowly. "I don't have a signed will or trust."

His gaze probed her, but he remained silent. There was an edge to his expression now—as if he wanted to say something but was holding back.

Diana spewed out a long breath. "Jonathan and I are— were—in the process of setting up wills naming each other heir, in anticipation of our marriage. But I hadn't finished mine."

Ethan nodded, then turned his attention to Cady as if he didn't want Diana to see what was in his eyes.

But did *Jonathan* think she'd finished the will? And if so—

"Look, I know what you're tiptoeing around, Ethan," she said. "And I understand why. I watch crime shows too—occasionally. Well, rarely. But enough to know how to look for the perpetrator. *If* I had changed—or written—a will, Jonathan would be a prime suspect. But I didn't."

"There's still time," he snapped, glancing briefly at her with furious dark eyes, then whipping them back to focus on Cady. "You're not dead yet, Diana. And if he's the one who suggested changing your will—"

She said something unladylike that had him looking up at her in surprise.

"Look, there's *no way* Jonathan killed my Aunt Jean. I *know* him. I've—I've been with him. I know him. He's just not like that. And even if you don't believe me, the facts are that he *couldn't* have done it. He was in Vegas at a conference when she died—I know, because the day I found out, I flew out there to meet him. That's when I saw him with Valerie the Vicious Vixen—but that's another story." She paused to take a fortifying gulp of wine as the corner of his lips quirked at the alliterative nickname for her fiancé's lover.

"And," she continued passionately after she swallowed, "the night of the break-in—when I came home—I'd just returned from taking Jonathan to the airport."

"You didn't stop anywhere on your way home from the airport?" Ethan asked mildly. "You drove straight back?"

She glared at him. "Well, I had dinner on the way home."

He lifted a brow and she rolled her eyes.

"Then Jonathan *called* me later that night—when he got back to Chicago. After Captain Longbow left. It was around midnight."

"How do you know where he was calling from? He could have been calling from Grand Rapids, for all you know. Was he on his cell phone?"

"Of course—wait. No, I don't know—he called me on the land line. Said he couldn't get through on my cell."

"Convenient."

"Ethan, please. I know what you're trying to do—I know you don't like the man—but he's not a murderer. And he'd never hurt me. And besides—he has no motive. No reason."

"All right then," he said flatly. "I said what I had to say."

"Well, technically, *I* said most of what you wanted to say," she replied. "But I appreciate your concern, Ethan. I really do."

He gave her a noncommittal nod, then pushed himself off the sofa with jerky movements. "More wine?" he asked.

That tension was back—that sour mood—and Diana nearly declined. "Yes, thank you. It's really good." She handed him her empty glass.

He walked past her to the kitchen in bare feet and she noticed how long and narrow they were. They were nice feet, she decided. For a man. And men never needed pedicures—lucky them.

Hm. Maybe the wine had gone a little bit to her head, especially since she'd had a glass at Trib's.

"Besides," she said as he walked back into the living room with her refilled glass, and a beer for himself, "aren't we fairly certain the person who's been breaking into the house is someone who was at that conference? Someone who wanted to retrieve something Aunt Jean had?"

He spewed out a sigh and settled back in his spot. "Yes," he said. "Someone seems to want something. But whatever it was, presumably it's destroyed now because of the fire."

"So we may never know."

"Doubtful." He tipped up the dark brown bottle—which, strangely, was lacking a label—and drank. "So...back to the card that was mysteriously on the lawn this afternoon when you returned to the house. Oh, I meant to ask—where are the cards now?"

"I have them. They're with my other things in the guest room. So, are you going to guess something besides *The High Priestess*?"

He contemplated her for a moment, and the weight of his gaze brought a warm flush to her cheeks. "Something relevant to the situation, you said."

"Yes."

"Which particular situation?" he asked after another long moment as his attention lingered over her.

If he'd been a witness under cross exam, she would have described him as struggling internally with wanting to tell the truth, but being unwilling or unable to.

Either that, or perjuring himself.

"Which particular situation?" she replied teasingly, holding his eyes with hers until they connected and that sizzle zipped into her belly.

Oh, yes, the wine had tiptoed straight up to her head when she wasn't paying attention. She blinked, breaking the connection. "The fact that I had just finished a difficult conversation with Jonathan and was sitting on the steps of a burned-out house?"

She wouldn't come right out and tell him she'd ended things with Jonathan. It would feel as if she were putting a lot of pressure or obligation on him—or her. On the situation.

To do so felt too coy. Too manipulative. Just as it had been the night she asked him to answer the telephone when she knew Jonathan was calling.

Besides, she was going back to Chicago tomorrow, so what did it matter anyway? When or if she saw Ethan—or Wicks Hollow—again, it would be months.

And now that the house was mostly gone, she had no real reason to stick around.

But what about the get-away for the kids? The two girls and a boy—and the big black dog?

Whoa. Diana glared at her half-full wine glass and set it firmly on the table next to her.

That was enough of that.

"Well," Ethan mused quietly from his corner. "What about

The Lovers?" His dark eyes held hers, then eased away as he adjusted a pillow behind his back.

She scoffed. "No." Then she looked at her wine glass and considered it, but ultimately kept her hands in her lap. "One more guess."

"I don't remember that being part of the rules." His lips quirked.

"It's implied: three strikes, and all that," she replied airily.

"All right. Then I'll take Cady out."

She understood that was his way of graciously saying goodnight. Quelling a little pang of disappointment, she kept a casual smile on her face and nodded. "It's been a long twenty-four hours. One more guess, Ethan."

"How about *The Fool?*"

She lifted her brows and, smiling, shook her head. "You lose," she teased, then rose from the sofa and collected her wine glass and his empty beer bottle. A little breeze buffeted through the open windows as she padded into the kitchen, followed by Ethan and the clicking of Cady's nails on the hardwood floor.

"Thanks for your hospitality again," she told him as she carefully began to wash the wine glass in his sink. And so as to keep him from feeling awkward, she added, "Good-night. I'll see you in the morning."

He halted in the doorway to the screened porch when she started into the guest room. "Aren't you going to tell me what card it was?" He opened the door for Cady, and the chocolate-black canine bolted out into the darkness.

"Oh, right. It was *Death.*" And she closed the door to the bedroom.

Ethan had just stepped outside with Cady under a moonlit night when it sank in.

Death.

Not only a burned-out, ruined house.

But a difficult conversation with her fiancé.

The card was perfect for that particular situation.

He froze, and swore under his breath as it sank in.

Dammit, Murphy. You're an idiot.

It had been all he could do to keep himself seated at the far end of the sectional tonight, safely distant from the prim, dark-haired goddess, occupying his hands by holding a beer and petting Cady instead of reaching for Diana.

Her teasing smile, the light in her dark blue eyes, the way she grew serious and intense when she was trying to tell him he was wrong...and the enticing way she filled out that gray tank top—

Damn. You idiot.

He looked back toward the cabin, where the light in the guest room burned low and he could see the vague movement of shadow in there.

By contrast, the windows of the cabin's upper floor, where the master suite was located, were dark and uninviting.

But that, he knew, was where he'd be tonight. Upstairs, and very much alone.

"Come on, Cady. Inside."

Damn.

FIFTEEN

A LOUD CRACK of thunder woke Diana from a restless sleep. The clock next to her bed was illuminated by a great flash of lightning. It was three-thirty.

She stared at the ceiling, watching shadows come and go as lightning flickered in the distance, then closer as a boom of thunder shook the log cabin.

All at once, another crack of thunder shook the house and a gust of wind sent hard, sharp rain against the window. Suddenly Diana remembered the row of tall windows open in the living room. Had Ethan closed them?

She flipped the blanket back and hurried out of the room, the indulgence of her silky nightgown soft and sleek against her skin.

Brilliant flashes of lightning helped her find her way to the living room, and just as she was getting to the windows, she heard a clumping coming down the stairs.

It sounded like an army, but it was really just six feet: Ethan and Cady.

She was struggling to close the windows when they came

in. The wind was blowing in through them and their panes were wet. "I'll get them. That one on the left sticks."

She moved out of his way and walked over toward the screened-in porch to see what the storm looked like. She and Cady slipped into the enclosure and peered out to see trees bending and swaying with the wind, and jagged white lines of lightning spearing into the forest and onto the lake.

Since this was on a different side of the house, only a smattering of rain came in through the screen, but the cool, crisp rainstorm air filled changed the scent and temperature.

Another boom shook the house and Cady whined, pushing her damp nose into Diana's leg—which was bare under her short silky nightgown. The chill of it startled her, but this time, she bent down to pat the dog on the head instead of pushing her away.

Ethan joined them on the porch, a sleek, dark shadow. "Looks pretty nasty."

Another flash of lightning illuminated him: his hair was standing up in endearing tufts, and he hadn't bothered to put on a shirt—though he was wearing loose boxers. And the long, silvery slide of the muscles in his shoulders and upper arms was illuminated like a photograph.

"I love storms," she murmured, peering into the darkness. "Especially at night."

"Me too."

He stepped closer to her, and Diana found herself holding her breath in anticipation and nervousness as he came up behind her. Her hands were a little clammy, and her insides were a hot mess.

A very pleasant, albeit nervous, hot mess.

"Are you cold?" Ethan asked, resting his hands lightly, very lightly, on her bare upper arms. His fingers were warm against her chilled skin, which had become damp from the spray of rain. "Diana." He said her name on a quiet exhale, and she recognized that something, somehow had changed.

She felt the imprint of each of his fingers as they lightly caressed her arms, almost brushing the sides of her breasts. "It feels good. The...fresh air. And..." *You touching me.* She moistened her lips, aware of the pounding pulse in her throat.

Something had definitely changed.

Lightly, Ethan slid his hands down to her elbows and back up to her shoulders—once, twice, three times. And then he paused, cupping her elbows in two warm palms.

Another crash of thunder made Cady whine, but Ethan said nothing. He was very close behind her; she could feel the heat rolling off his bare chest, the barest touch of one of his toes against the side of her foot, and she could smell his fresh, male scent.

"It's beautiful in its power, isn't it?" Her voice was low and unintentionally husky. She wanted to lean back against him, to tip the back of her head into his solid chest. "Nature always amazes me."

His hands moved again, once more up to her shoulders, and she felt his fingers brush the ends of her short hair, skim over the sides of her neck. More shivers erupted over her skin and down her spine, and a hot, liquid heat began to gather in the lowest part of her belly. Ethan gently massaged her shoulders, his fingers brushing over the slender straps of her night chemise.

"I saw a tornado once." His voice was low and quiet in her ear as he stepped closer, slipping his arms around her from behind, crossing them over her belly—which jumped and fluttered. "It was one of the most incredible things I'd ever witnessed. I should have been in the basement, but I had to see it first...and Fifi and I made it down there just in time. My mother was furious with me for keeping my sister out there too."

"How old were you?"

He shrugged against her. "Oh, twelve maybe. Thirteen." There was a smile in his voice.

"Ah, yes, the age of invincibility." She was trying to keep her breathing slow and steady even though her heart was racing, for fear he'd realize how much his embrace affected her.

They stood there for a moment, watching the storm as it tossed the trees and splattered rain against the screendoor and closed windows. Even Cady seemed to have calmed, only giving a little whine at the loudest of thunderclaps.

"I guess I'd better head back to bed," Diana said after awhile. But she made no move to slide from his embrace.

"I'd very much like to join you." His words, unexpected, soft and heavy with desire, speared her middle and caused her to draw in her breath. "Diana," he whispered near her ear.

Before she could respond, his lips settled on her neck, in the secret spot just below her ear. Sensation exploded through her body, hot and delicious, and she caught her breath, shivering as her eyes sunk closed.

Yes.

His mouth was warm and light, and as his lips moved tenderly up the side of her neck, her knees went embarrassingly weak. Pleasure goosebumps erupted everywhere, her nipples surged and hardened, and she gave a soft sigh as he tightened his arms around her, drawing her back against him.

His mouth nibbled near her ear, kissing a vulnerable spot just behind her lobe, still gentle, coaxing, erotic. His hands slid around to cover her breasts and she heard his intake of breath as he found her ready nipples where they jutted through the silk of her nightgown. Sharp, hot pleasure jolted through her when he teased them, sliding the sensual fabric over their sensitive tips.

"I want to make love to you," he murmured unnecessarily, for she could feel every bit of the heat and desire gathered in his strong body.

He found his way beneath the skimpy straps and down into the deep vee of her neckline, cupping her breasts and using his thumbs to taunt and stroke her nipples into hard, ready points.

She could have turned to face him, to slide her hands up over those broad, naked shoulders, but he kept her firmly in place, in a gentle imprisonment of growing arousal. The silk of her nightgown was clinging to her everywhere, and although the cool rain's breeze filtered through the screens, she was warm and liquid, heavy-lidded in the eyes—but yet very much awake. Alive.

"Mm...yes," he murmured when she closed her eyes, resting her head back onto his shoulder, his mouth close to her ear. "I've been waiting for this."

One of his hands eased down over the clinging silk chemise to its hem, and the next thing she knew, his fingers were sliding up her bare thigh. Smooth and sure, his hand moved to the warm, moist center between her legs and Diana gasped softly when his clever fingers found her center. A hot, pleasurable throb reverberated through her body, swelling and pounding as his fingers went slickly to work, exploring and teasing her until she was a panting, shivering mass.

Now, both hands worked to hike up the hem of her nightgown over her bare thighs, and he lifted his face from where he'd been nuzzling her neck. Diana opened her eyes.

In the window in front of her she could see their reflections: she, with her dark head flung back, exposing a stark white throat and white thighs, he with a shadowed face, staring into the reflection. His hands pinned her against his body in some erotic game, and as she watched, their eyes met in the mottled image.

Behind her, she felt his chest move with ragged breaths and he pulled a strap off her shoulder so that one pale breast slipped out from the nightgown. Her nipple, full and tight, was dark in the center of the white skin beneath the long expanse of her throat. In that moment, instead of herself, Diana saw some exotic movie starlet, flush and lush with passion, captured in place by a pair of solid tanned arms.

The image aroused her even more, and perhaps him as well, for all at once, two probing fingers slipped deep into her wet sheath.

He groaned from deep in his chest as she gasped and pulsed around him. "You are so ready," he muttered into her ear. "Come with me now, sweetheart. Come…with me." He slid his fingers in and out and around, massaging her own tiny, swollen erection, brushing over the plump, sensitive skin around it.

Diana felt herself gathering up, the heat rushing and surging through her as his rhythm never faltered. Her toes curled into the wood floor, her fingers closed around his arm as she bit her lip, trying to keep from crying out as she drew closer and closer—and then all at once, she went over the top, her world exploding like a bright flash of lightning.

She gave a cry of release, of triumph, as the pleasure undulated through her limbs. Her knees gave out and she clung to his arms as he chuckled softly, deeply into her damp neck.

"That's what I meant," he said, pleasure and delight evident in his voice. "Ah, Diana…" He turned her suddenly and wrapped his arms around her, at last crushing her into his arms to kiss her. His hand brushed the hair from her cheek, and she could smell her own muskiness on his fingers.

Diana raised her face to meet him, to take his lips, and she felt his trembling from pent-up desire. His mouth was as sensual and his kiss as beautiful as she'd remembered, but grew hot and sleek as their bare skin connected. Now she could touch him, at last: her hand could slide up his arms, over his broad, warm shoulders, her fingers traced the curve of his collarbone; she pressed her hips into his.

"Diana?" It was a question, breathless, low, a little desperate.

"Yes…" she sighed. Suddenly, she was in his arms as he turned to carry her off the porch.

Ethan, intent and nearly blind with desire, stumbled over Cady, who'd collapsed on the floor behind him. But he was able to right himself before disaster, Diana giving a little huff of a laugh as she jolted in his arms. His veins thrummed with heat and he had one thing, only one thing, on his mind. With long strides, he carried his welcome burden up the stairs into his cool, dark bedroom.

He let her feet slide to the floor in front of the bed, and, pinning her there with his thighs, kissed her long and thoroughly as he yanked his boxers down with one hand. Then, he pulled away just long enough to whisk that soft, silky gown up and over her head.

"Ah." Ethan drew in his breath sharply at the sight of her nude body, pale in the dim light, warm under his palms.

How beautiful she was, how perfect her breasts were with their small, tight nipples, how smooth and flowing were the lines of her torso. He filled his hands with her, touching, caressing, fondling as he bent to kiss her again. Ready. So ready—but thorough. He'd be thorough.

He tumbled them onto the bed, onto the wad of blankets and mussed sheets he'd left earlier, and settled against her. Hot damp skin to hot damp skin, curves pressed up against firm muscle and coarse hair. They fit together well, and she welcomed him as he eased her legs apart.

Lifting himself away just enough to reach into the drawer of his bedside table, he pulled a condom free from its depths. With one movement, he ripped the package open, then bent to take one of those perked-up nipples into his mouth. Diana gave a sexy little tremor as he closed his lips around her, sucking and teasing her with his tongue, getting her all worked up again so that she'd be sleek and ready for him.

She was mumbling things he couldn't understand, but they sounded good: breathy and desperate, and he made short work of slipping the condom in place. And then, shifting up to kiss her full and long and hard on her parted lips, he fit himself into place and at last…ah, yes.

Home. He was home.

When he filled her, she made a soft, erotic little sound that stoked him hotter, then she grasped his shoulders and lifted to meet his thrust. At first he moved with long, slow strokes, trying to keep them easy and deep—but he'd had a two-year moratorium and it was damned near impossible to keep from sliding helter-skelter down into the hot lava of desire.

But he held himself off, back, fighting that manic slide as she writhed and shuddered and whimpered beneath him. The soft sounds of pleasure, the way her fingers dug into his shoulders, and the lovely musk of her scent on his fingers, the taste of her, the feel of her tight, liquid around him drove him mad.

Her sudden cry, low and husky, nearly undid him, and but he kept his mind for a moment longer—just long enough to make it last. To listen to her rough, addled breathing and feel her orgasm shuddering around him.

And then he stopped thinking. He rushed down that hot slide into his own pleasure and let go. And when it came, the release rolled through his body like an explosion that went on and on until his eyes rolled up into his head and his toes curled.

Sometime later—seconds, minutes, hours; Ethan had no idea—he eased down next to her, gathering her close as the thunderstorm raged beyond the windows and Cady crashed on the floor nearby.

Ethan opened his eyes to a most welcome sight: a thick tumble of ink-black hair on one of his pillows, and a lovely face, slack with sleep and, he hoped, satiation.

The blanket exposed part of Diana's smooth white shoulder, but the rest of the delights he'd explored—and enjoyed—last night were hidden beneath the jumble of covers. There were two empty condom packets on the bedside table, and he smiled to himself as he remembered the way Diana had moaned and shivered the second time—the more controlled time—that he slipped inside her as the storm raged against the cabin.

A dark blue silky thing lay in a puddle on the chair beyond, and, with another stab of lust, he recalled the way it had felt beneath his hands and against her skin.

Ethan shifted as his cock, awake and raring to go now that the moratorium had been broken, nagged him to touch that dark, shiny hair and draw that warm, curvy body up close again; to taste and caress and enjoy.

As he watched her sleep, saw the regular shift of her breathing and noticed the way she curled her hand beneath her cheek, Ethan smiled to himself. Had he ever seen the high-powered lawyer look so soft, unassuming, and innocent?

His low chuckle must have been loud enough for her to hear, for her eyelids fluttered and the next thing he knew, there they were: two dark blue irises wide open, looking at him. There was neither shock nor dismay nor—he had to admit—abject delight in her eyes as they met his.

He realized belatedly that he'd tensed a little once he knew she was awake—for there was a tiny niggle deep inside that he'd been wrong—that his interpretation of the *Death* card and her hints about it had somehow been misunderstood, and that she had not, in fact, dumped her fiancé.

That would be devastating, for now that he'd gone here, he sure as *hell* wasn't going back. Wertinger or no Wertinger.

"Ethan," she said, then immediately eased back, putting a hand in front of her mouth. It took him a second to realize she was trying to block her morning breath, and he grinned because she was so damned cute. "Good morning—what's so funny?" she demanded.

"I'm just happy to wake up next to you."

"Oh." Her eyes widened and he saw her cheeks flush pink. "That's nice."

Inside, Ethan was smiling wider and mentally shaking his head. For a powerhouse lawyer, Diana Iverson was certainly a lot more shy—and even a little nervous—in intimate situations than she was pretty much every other time he'd seen her.

Ethan didn't mind that at all, since she seemed to shed any inhibitions or uncertainties once things got going. Speaking of getting things going…He slid a hand from beneath the covers and pushed a heavy clump of hair from her face, then let his fingers trail down along her collar bone. "I always thought your hair looked like you'd just gotten up—after a wild, very satisfying bout of sex. I'm glad to know I was right."

"Ethan," she said, her eyes bolting wider and her cheeks going more red—but she didn't appear shocked as much as embarrassed, and, he thought, complimented.

"At least, I hope I'm right about the satisfying part." He

probed her with his gaze, ignoring the fact that Cady had clambered to her feet now that she knew her master was awake. Any minute now, she'd start whining to go out. "Diana."

"Oh, most definitely." To his surprise and delight, instead of blushing further, she gave him a catlike smile that sent a renewed stab of desire shooting right down to the place that mattered. "Most definitely."

He didn't give a shit about morning breath—his, hers, or Cady's (which was panting, hot and urgent, against his bare back from her hopeful stance next to the bed)—and he moved toward her, covering her lips with his as his hand slipped around to gather her close.

She appeared to lose her shyness, hooking a foot around one of his legs as she arched into him. Apparently, the sex goddess had been unleashed, because her hand went right down between them and closed over his—

All at once, Cady began to bark madly, loudly, and they both jolted. Diana pulled back, but Ethan—far more willing to ignore his first love for what was rapidly becoming his second love—dove deeper. "Lay down, Cady," he muttered, burying his face in Diana's warm, sweet neck. Ah, God, she smelled amazing. Just—

Crap.

"That's a car." Diana was pushing away more firmly now. "Someone's here."

But Ethan had already realized that, as the tone and volume of Cady's bark clearly indicated "*Visitor!*", not "*Squirrel!*" or "*I need to go out!*"

"Ignore them," he said. "They'll go away. It's probably UPS or something." God, she tasted so good: a little damp, a little musky, so smooth and soft, and the way she shivered when he sucked gently on the sensitive skin along her throat—

"On Sunday? It's not UPS." She extricated herself from him, and Ethan fell face first into the pillow.

But he righted himself in time to see her sleek white body, the enticing bounce of a pink-tipped breast, and a nice view of her sweet ass as she slipped out of the bed and dashed for the bathroom.

"Aw, damn," he muttered as he heard two car doors slam in succession. Cady had gone insane—she'd bolted from the room as soon as Ethan's foot hit the floor (a sure sign that he was actually getting up) and galloped down the stairs, barking the whole time.

Then she came racing back up the stairs, still barking her head off, as Ethan dragged on a pair of shorts. His bedroom faced the back of the house, so he couldn't see who'd driven up. And the only reason he was actually going down to investigate was so he could let Cady out. After that, he figured he could lock her in the screened porch for a while and coax Diana back to bed.

With that fortifying thought, Ethan grinned as he jogged down the stairs. Cady was so excited she knocked into him as she rushed past, one paw digging a nail into the side of his bare foot in her effort to beat him to the bottom.

Cady was still barking wildly when Ethan opened the door and stepped back to let the lab tear out. Then the cacophony went up several decibels as he heard another frenzied barking: but this one was earsplittingly high-pitched and utterly wild. As if the world was ending, and every last bit of fun was being wrung out of the creature.

And that was when the grin evaporated, because he knew that bark all too well.

And therefore, he knew who his guests were.

Damn.

"Ethan Murphy, you get that big monster away from

Bruce Banner!" shouted Maxine Took. She was brandishing her cane as she hobbled quite speedily across the rubble parking area. Her pale blue Cadillac SUV sat behind Diana's Lexus and his Jeep.

"Go! Go away!" shrieked Juanita, waving her arms ineffectively. "You leave him alone, you big brute!"

Ethan took pity on Cady, who was, despite accusations to the contrary, herself backed up against the side of the garage by the furious little papillon, who still hadn't stopped with the sonic barking. The poor lab hadn't even had the chance to properly do her business before the petite dog launched into her, and she looked utterly miserable—tail drooping, head down, ears sagging.

He scooped up the fiery Bruce Banner (aptly named) without a second thought, and, characteristically, the little beast immediately went silent. Now that he was safe, the tension fled his quivering seven-pound body, and he actually looked pleased with the situation.

The little bastard probably was.

"It's all right, Cady," Ethan said, and gestured to the area of the yard where she normally did her business. "Go do your stuff."

"Oh, thank you Ethan," cried Juanita, rushing over to take Bruce Banner from him. "I only let him out of his carrier to pee, and then that ferocious dog just ran him down over there! Are you all right, *poquito*? *Mamá* loves you, *chiquito*."

"So, what can I do for you ladies?" Ethan asked as jovially as possible. He wished now that he'd grabbed a shirt, as there was something uncomfortable about being half-dressed in front of the elderly women. At least Cherry Wilder wasn't here —she'd be the one really taking note; a thought which made his cheeks warm and had him ducking back into the screened porch where he'd left a t-shirt.

"You forgot this at Trib's last night," Maxine growled.

When his head emerged from the t-shirt, Ethan saw that she was holding Diana's sweater—a white one which had been draped over her shoulders when they first sat down at the table.

Really?

His morning was ruined because she'd forgotten her sweater?

Ethan groaned internally. Just then, the door to the cabin opened and Diana stepped out looking fresh and delicious and, oh, yes—with definite after-sex hair. At least, he was probably the only one who realized that was literally what it was, because she'd stuck a little glittery pin in it on one side to keep it out of her face. But it was definitely after-sex hair: all those blowsy, lush, billowing curls…

"Is everything all right?" Diana asked. She was holding a cup of coffee and seemed to be inhaling its essence. "Is Bruce Banner okay?" She gave poor, innocent Cady a suspicious look, then went over to greet the bright-eyed Bruce, who lapped up the attention as if it were a bloody steak.

"Now, be careful," Juanita warned when the beast growled as Diana lifted a hand to pet him. "He's a little uptight still. He had quite a fright, thanks to Cady there."

Ethan didn't even attempt to explain. He knew from experience that the best way to deal with Maxine and Co. was to agree, say as little as possible, then send them on their way.

"You left this," Maxine accused as she thrust the sweater at Diana. "Since most o' your stuff got burnt, I thought you'd be needing it. *He* wouldn't have anything you could wear with something like that." She nodded at the pale blue sundress Diana had put on. It was short, ending just above her very sexy knees, but in Ethan's mind that was the only real benefit of the loose, sleeveless thing. But the color was nice, he supposed.

"Thank you—and you're right. It's new; I'd hate to lose it. But I could have sworn I put it in my bag last night at the restaurant so that I wouldn't forget it. It must have fallen out somehow."

Diana took the sweater with a smile, but when he saw Maxine exchange smug glances with Juanita, Ethan's suspicions were confirmed.

The nosy old bat, he thought as he picked up Cady's tennis ball. She'd wanted to have an excuse to show up here this morning. Check things out. Damn…if they'd come just a few minutes later, they might have really interrupted something.

He fired the ball into the woods.

Well, he'd just have to get rid of the two ladies—

"Why, yes, I was going to head over there right away," Diana was saying. "Motto and Arty need to be fed, and I wanted to poke through some more of the ruins now that they've dried a little more. Captain Longbow said he would be coming by to take more pictures."

He did? She was? Dammit.

"We'll come with you," Maxine announced. She slid an arch look at Ethan with her sharp, crow's eyes, and he knew he'd been checkmated before he even realized he was playing the game. "I been wantin' to see the damage done to poor Jean's house. Ain't even been up to the place since she died." Somehow she made it sound like Ethan's fault.

Thus, Ethan found himself riding in the front seat of Maxine's Cadillac while Juanita and Diana drove the Lexus the mile and a half (by road) to the old clapboard house. Though he'd gallantly offered to drive Maxine, she'd have none of it—and so he was forced to close his eyes for most of the thankfully brief journey. Cady had been more than pleased to remain at the cabin—she didn't want any more encounters with Bruce Banner, and she wasn't particularly fond of Motto or Arty either.

By the time they pulled into the clearing next to Jean's house, Ethan's head was aching from hitting the ceiling of the Cadillac, for Maxine had hit every bloody pothole at full speed (which for her was a mere twenty mph, but still). He was also grateful he hadn't had time to get a cup of coffee, because it would have been spilled all over him *and* Maxine's prized Cadillac.

He took his time getting out of the car, for the sight of the burned out shell sent a renewed stab of grief through him. First Jean, and then her house. And now, Diana would have no reason to stay in Wicks Hollow—or even to visit.

His after-sex afterglow soured.

He watched from across the yard as the three females stood in front of the porch, which was still intact—along with the facade of the front of the house. Pieces of their conversation wafted over to him, and consisted of precisely what he'd expect: nostalgia, sadness, and numerous observations, commands, and opinions from Maxine offered at a high volume.

Bruce Banner picked his way around the yard on delicate feet, the hair on his oversized ears ruffled by the breeze. He sniffed and explored with abandon until he encountered Motto, the female cat with the thick tale. Then all hell broke loose.

Bruce began to bark maniacally, again, as if he were being tortured (he wasn't). However, unlike Cady, Motto had no intention of cowering in a corner. She eyed the little scrapper with clear, feline disdain, lifted her pink nose, then turned and walked off. The tip of her high, bushy tail flicked sharply, as if she were flipping him off. Ethan could relate.

"I've got to check their food," Diana said.

Ethan suspected it was an excuse to extricate herself from Maxine and Juanita, and he waffled between doing the gentlemanly thing and taking over with the two elderly ladies...or doing the purely male thing by following Diana into the garage in hopes of stealing a kiss. Or more.

He was just about to slink off after her when Maxine demanded his presence. "Ethan! Ethan, come over here right now. I need you to help me."

Well, that decided that.

"What do you need help with, Mrs. Took?" he said as he strolled closer. He gave her a sly smile, knowing what would come next.

"*Mrs. Took?* How long have I known you, young man? You know I ain't never taken on a man's name in my life—and ain't never hitched myself to one neither. What's this you're playing at?"

He took her arm and wrapped her crone fingers around his, patting them as he smiled down at her. "Now, Maxine, I just wanted to make sure you were paying attention. What did you need help with?"

She pulled her hand away and glared up at him. "Now don't you be coddling me, young man! I might be eighty years old, but I ain't in my dotage yet."

"You can help me, Ethan," Juanita said primly, looking up at him and very nearly batting her eyelashes. "Maxine and I wanted to walk through the house and see what-all's left of it."

"Well, I'd better take both of you then," Ethan said firmly. He knew better than to try and talk them out of going inside. Instead, he'd simply maneuver where they went and where they didn't go.

Maxine didn't argue, and so Ethan helped them inside. He understood that they needed to say farewell to both Jean and her house, and although there'd been a funeral, this visitation was rather like the last nail in the coffin. So to speak.

Maybe they even thought or hoped that Jean might make an appearance herself. Ethan looked around dubiously. He wouldn't put it past her.

The front entrance to the house was still intact, although Diana had left the door unlocked since the fire. But half of the hallway that led to the library and upstairs was mostly gone, and the space that had been Jean's den and library was now a pile of rubble inside three burned-out walls. All of her books were gone, and the piecrust table where she'd left her Tarot cards…and the chair that had been next to it as well. All that remained of her comfortable seat was a scorched metal spring.

No one spoke as he carefully helped the ladies pick their way toward the demolished library, where they saw an occasional charred spine of random books. Then they poked into the smoke-tinged bedroom, which had one wall burned through. They were making their way toward the kitchen, which had come through the fire with little more than smoke damage, when Ethan heard Diana calling him from outside.

Galvanized by concern, he whisked Maxine and Juanita out the kitchen door much faster than they'd come in through the front. "What is it?" he called as soon as he caught sight of Diana.

She seemed fine—excited instead of upset—so his heart settled back into a normal rhythm.

"You won't believe this," she said, hurrying over to them. She was brandishing a manila envelope. "Look what I found inside Aunt Jean's car."

"Inside Jean's car? What was it doing in there?" growled Maxine. "What is it?"

But Diana had already handed the envelope to Ethan.

He stared down at it. "It's a letter. To me. From Jean."

SIXTEEN

DIANA'S HEART WAS POUNDING, because somehow she knew this was a game-changer. "There's one for me too. They were in her car, sitting on the passenger seat in front along with some bills—sealed but unstamped."

"She was going to take them to the post office," Ethan said slowly. "She often did that—put things in her car the night before so she wouldn't forget them." He was fingering the manila envelope.

"Well, don't just stand there. Open it!" Juanita said. She was puffing slightly, as it had taken some effort to get her generous bulk across the grass at a quick speed.

"*Them*," Maxine corrected waspishly. "Diana's got one too."

"A letter from the dead." Ethan was still looking at the envelope, as if he were afraid to open it.

"A *letter* from the dead in Aunt Jean's car—which happens to be an *Expedition*," Diana said. The hair on the backs of her arms had lifted and prickled as soon as she figured it out. "Remember the books on the floor, Ethan? Letters, traces, expedition?"

He looked at her, and when their eyes connected, it was as if they were alone without two crabby, bossy old ladies watching their every move.

"Yes," he said softly, his eyes warm and brown and filled with depth of emotion: grief, warmth, and something else. Diana's heart gave a funny little thump. All of a sudden, she was *really* disappointed their morning had been interrupted. "Jean was trying to tell us."

"Tell you *what?*" Maxine's fingers were opening and closing as if she wanted to snatch the envelope from Diana. Her cane was sinking into the ground as she leaned into it. "I think it's about time you told us what the *hell* is going on here. Both of you."

"Aunt Jean—the ghostly Aunt Jean, I mean to say, gave us a message. The words were 'letters,' 'traces,' and 'expedition.' And we've just now figured out what that meant," Diana explained, dragging her thoughts from the way Ethan's thick, dark hair was tossing in the light breeze and the way his eyes crinkled at the corners as he fixed his gaze on her in that warm study. "Or mostly."

Even as she spoke, there was a sort of gentle buzz overtaking her—throughout her fingers and in her head, sort of emanating through her entire body.

It was, she thought—but would never admit it aloud—similar to the feeling she had when she did her "thing"—that thing at the office Mickey was asking her about. She glanced covertly at Ethan.

Well, maybe she would admit it to *him*.

Yes. She probably would.

A little bubbling sensation inside made her warm and wonderfully happy all of a sudden, and she cast him a warm smile. Their eyes met and his gaze went dark and hot and needy. The bottom of her belly dropped down in a hot little flip and she felt her knees go a little weak.

"Well how long did it take you to figure out what she was trying to tell you?" Maxine demanded. "Couldn't have been that hard, now could it?"

"Maybe not for a chemical engineer with a masters in math," Ethan said with a smile for the old lady. "But Diana's only a lawyer, and me—well, I'm just a college professor."

"Well, how in the green hell did she miss seeing those letters in Jean's car anyhow? It's been weeks now, ain't it?" Maxine's voice was filled with contempt, but Diana didn't take offense.

"I never looked in her car," she explained with a shrug. "It's been in the garage since I got here, and it never occurred to me to look at it. Even though I suppose I own it now. It's only because the cats have been staying in the garage that I noticed it today, when I went in to check their food."

By now, Bruce Banner had lost interest in Motto and the rest of the yard. He was bouncing around, barking, springing up and against his mistress's legs—in an effort to get her to pick him up, Diana supposed. He was a demanding little brat of a dog, but he was so darned cute.

"Traces," Ethan murmured. "What does that mean? Letters in the Expedition—we got that. But what's the reference to traces?"

He still hadn't opened the letter; neither had Diana.

What were they waiting for? She didn't know. And that buzzing sensation was growing pleasantly stronger.

"Well…Trace. Like her husband?" Juanita piped up.

They each whipped a look at her.

"Yes," Diana replied immediately. Because she *knew*. As soon as Juanita said it, she *knew*. "It has something to do with Uncle Tracer."

Her hesitation was gone, and she carefully tore open the envelope. Inside was a letter in Aunt Jean's familiar handwriting, for though her arthritis had started to get the best of her, she refused to use a computer or even typewriter.

Along with the letter were several old documents; large ones, folded into fourths. "They're schematics," she murmured as they slid out of the envelope into her hand. "Old building plans—oh my God."

"What is it?"

That spike of buzzing energy had grown so strong that her head began to pound. On the corner of one of the drawings she'd glimpsed a familiar name.

"This." She showed Ethan, revealing the corner where the name of the company, address, date, and engineering organization was listed, but keeping it folded for fear it would blow away or tear in the lake breeze.

He looked at it, then back up at her. "Explain."

"Woodstock Tool & Dye is now AutoXTech. That's the company McNillan is representing in the litigation with LavertPiper. I'm the lead attorney in that litigation."

But why was this old building schematic—from 1943!—in the envelope? How did Aunt Jean come to have it?

And why did her head feel as if it were going to explode? And the buzzing in her body feel like she'd stuck her finger in a socket?

"That can't be a coincidence," Ethan said, looking at his manila envelope.

"Ain't no coincidences," Maxine announced. "That's according to Sherlock Holmes, you know." She frowned, her lips pursing and the lines between her brows becoming more pronounced as they drew together. "Wasn't that what the Abe Vigoda guy was talking to Jean about? Turned out he knew Tracer way back, or whatnot?"

"Tracer," Ethan murmured. "He's involved somehow."

"Oh, if only Iva was here. She'd remember," Juanita said. She'd succumbed to Bruce Banner's insistence, and bent to pick him up. Now she held the little beady-eyed dog against her ample bosom, which today was cloaked in a fuchsia maxi dress.

"We don't need to bother Iva, Juanita. She's got her head all filled up with flowers and romance and all, now that Hollis man is wooing her." Maxine clucked her tongue and shook her head, her lips pursed in thought. "She *told* us Jean was talking to the Abe Vigoda man, and there was a connection about Tracer knowing him some time ago, way back."

"Why don't you hush up and let Diana read the letter," Juanita shot back. "It probably explains everything."

"Well, what are you waiting for?" Maxine demanded. Her fingers were curling and clutching more desperately now, but Diana noticed Ethan had angled himself between the papers and the old woman—surely in an effort to keep her from pouncing.

"All right. Let's go back to my house so we can spread all of these papers out," Ethan suggested. "I could use a cup of coffee, and some breakfast." He was still holding his unopened envelope.

Surprisingly, Ethan easily convinced the two elderly ladies to leave with him in Maxine's car.

Diana finished attending to Motto and Arty, the latter of whom had deigned to make an appearance now that Bruce Banner had vacated the premises, and took a few moments to scratch them behind the ears. Then she fed them each a catnip treat, made certain they had beds to sleep on in the garage, bid them a temporary goodbye (what on earth was she going to do with them anyway?), then drove back to Ethan's cabin.

If she'd hoped he'd somehow managed to convince Maxine

and Juanita they could leave this part to the two of them—herself and Ethan—she was disappointed, for both of the ladies had made themselves comfortable at the four-top dining room table.

Ethan winced a bit when the chair Juanita was sitting on creaked a little, but he was the epitome of graciousness...even when he announced to Diana, "And Maxine thought it was a good idea to call the other Tuesday Ladies to come on out too. Iva and Cherry are on their way, but Orbra's got the tea shop open. She'll be here in an hour, once she gets Bethy in to cover for her."

Oh, great.

They exchanged wry glances, then Diana had a brilliant solution.

"Why don't we go into town and sit at Orbra's? That way we can have breakfast—trust me, ladies, I know there's nothing in Ethan's fridge and I would love a cinnamon scone—and then Orbra can join us too."

And we can escape when we're ready.

Ethan seized upon the idea with such alacrity she knew he'd read her mind. "That's a great plan. Orbra's got that big table in the corner, and there'll be more room for us to spread out. Maybe Trib will stop by and help too," he added brightly.

Before Maxine or Juanita could catch up with them—and thus voice any argument—Ethan had them bundled out to the Cadillac. Diana was amazed the ease with which he did so, without appearing to actually rush them. A quick text to Cherry and Iva gave them the change of plans, and then he slid into the Lexus next to Diana.

"That," he said with a delighted grin, "was inspired."

"I had visions of breakfast, lunch, *and* dinner around that table," she replied with a laugh. "And no escape."

"And then they'd find an excuse to pull out the Scrabble

board—which Maxine knows I have, *and* she knows where it's stored." He sighed. "I made a mistake and bought the Deluxe version."

"Why was that a mistake?" Diana asked as she pulled out from the narrow, bumpy, two-track drive onto the county road that followed the north and east sides of the lake. "Dare I ask?"

"Oh, you definitely should ask—so you don't make the same mistake. Maxine only plays on a Deluxe version, because the board swivels around to face each player as it's their turn, and there's a little grid so the tiles don't move. If only I'd bought the regular game," he said with another exaggerated sigh. "I might have had a few extra Sunday afternoons to myself over the last few years...

"There was one time Maxine and Jean and Juanita were over, just visiting. I left the room for all of three minutes—just to switch my laundry—and when I came back, they had the game set up and Maxine had just played a bingo on her first move. After that, there was no stopping her—we had to finish the game."

Diana laughed, thinking about how very different Ethan Murphy was from Jonathan Wertinger. The self-important cardiologist would never spend a Sunday afternoon playing Scrabble with a gaggle of old ladies—even smart ones like Maxine and Juanita who tricked him into it.

She was still chuckling over that as, ten minutes later, she drove down Pamela Boulevard into downtown Wicks Hollow. With Ethan's guidance, she managed to find a parking place in a hidden lot that only the locals knew about. She turned off the car, tucked the keys in her bag...and the next thing she knew, Ethan was halfway into her seat, dragging her up to him as he covered her mouth with his.

She gave a soft sigh of surprise, then slid into the hot, toe-curling kiss with more ease than she might have thought, especially in semi-public. Not that she had any real thoughts at the moment.

"I've been wanting to do that all morning, dammit," he murmured against her mouth as the center console pushed into her belly and his fingers slid into her hair. "Diana. I didn't even get to tell you how amazing last night was."

She kissed him back for another mind-boggling moment, tasting and enjoying the heat of his mouth, the sleek dance of their tongues. "I thought you did," she whispered, then she took his lips again, lustily.

"Oh, God," he groaned, then moved back with great reluctance as he held her firmly in place—away from him. He looked at her with walnut brown eyes, glittering with heat. "That was one of the most difficult things I've ever done."

"Which part?" she replied in a quiet tease. "Kissing me across the console without bumping into the horn, or—"

"Not tearing your clothes off right here," he said, rubbing a temple with his fingers in obvious agitation. "By the way, check your bag before we leave the tea shop. Make sure everything's in it."

She opened her door and climbed out. "I will. I was certain I'd put my sweater in my purse last night—"

"Oh, you did. Maxine took it out. She's got some sticky fingers, our girl. Do you see what we're up against here?" he said with a pained laugh as he looked at her from across the roof of the car.

Diana's eyes widened, then she laughed ruefully. "I'm just beginning to."

It was Sunday and June in Michigan, and the weather was gorgeous. Thus, there were tourists everywhere—so thick, one could hardly walk down the street. But Ethan directed her through the back way, and they came inside Orbra's from the alley behind.

"Well that took you long enough!" Maxine's gravely voice rose above the general hubbub of the busy tea shop at brunch. "Did you get lost?" She eyed them suspiciously, and Diana found her cheeks warming—even though they couldn't have been more than five minutes behind the old ladies.

"Cute dress," Cherry said to Diana as she patted the seat next to her. "I love the blue seersucker with those pretty appliqued daisies around the neckline and hem. Almost vintage looking, but yet very modern." Then, as Diana sat, she leaned closer and whispered, "Your lipstick is smeared, and I'm pretty sure you didn't leave the house with your hair like that." She grinned as Diana frantically tried to flatten her unruly curls.

But Diana refused to let her face heat any further, despite the speculative looks from the lot of them sitting there—Cherry, Maxine, Juanita, and Iva. Nor did she look at Ethan, who'd somehow been maneuvered into a seat across the table from her.

She thought she'd discreetly fixed her lipstick, but when she looked up from doing so and found Ethan watching her, and the old ladies watching *him*, her face warmed again.

"All right," she said briskly. "I'm calling this meeting to order. We've got two packages from my aunt that were never mailed, and it's logical they're somehow related to the break-ins and her death." Her voice almost cracked on the last word, but she held firm. Had Aunt Jean really been murdered over whatever was in these envelopes?

"Maxine gave us the run-down," Cherry said. "Have you read the letter yet?"

"No. I'm going to do that now." Diana pulled the document from her manila folder, slipped on a pair of reading glasses (yes, she was one of *those* people who needed cheaters at twenty-eight), and began to read in a voice pitched loud enough for those to hear around the table, but not to carry much further into the crowded restaurant.

"'Dear Diana, I've found something that I think you need to see. I know how busy you are, and my visit to Chicago was far too long ago (even though it's been less than a year), so I thought I'd better send this to you straightaway.'"

Diana paused to take a sip of her tea; not so much because her throat was dry, but because she needed a moment to compose herself. She could hear Aunt Jean, speaking in her no-nonsense, concise fashion, as if she were dictating the letter to her right now. It hit her, once more—this time like an anvil—that she'd never see her aunt again.

That Jean's visit to see *Hamilton* in Chicago with her had been the last time they'd ever be together.

"Well, go on," demanded Maxine, thumping her cane against the floor. "Ain't got all day here, Diana."

She cleared her throat and continued, just as Orbra pulled up a chair to join them at the table.

"'It's a little complicated, but I'll make it simple. Iva has met the most lovely man—Hollis Nath, a very distinguished attorney from Grand Rapids; I do hope things work out with them—and he was first here in Wicks Hollow in late April for the big business golf outing. I met one of the other men attending with him, and through the course of our conversation, we realized Tracer had done some work for this other man's company way back when he was just getting into commercial real estate. (I won't tell you how far back; that would put too obvious a stamp on my age—although it was before my time. But might I remind you that Tracer was fifteen years older than me.)'"

Diana choked back a giggle—as if she didn't know how old Jean had been—and then went on. "'Maxine got to calling the man Abe, after an old actor named Abe Vigoda (look him up, because I'm sure you wouldn't know him, considering *your* age and your lack of time to watch TV). The interesting thing is that this man—whose name is really Martin Kelliski—is one of the higher-ups (I didn't get his title, some bigwig) at AutoXTech.

"'I remember you telling me in our last conversation that there was going to be a big court case with AutoXTech and another company, and that you were going to be involved—or your law firm was—and it got me to thinking. Martin Kelliski remembered Trace from when the company was called Woodstock Tool & Die, and that name definitely rang a bell for me for obvious reasons. I thought I'd look through Tracer's old papers—that man kept everything; and you know I haven't gotten around to clearing it all out yet. Maybe I'll just leave that for you to do after I die.'"

Diana stopped abruptly, the back of her throat burning. *Dammit.*

"It was a joke, honey," Cherry said, patting her hand. "You know how Jean was—irreverent and pragmatic at the same time. That's why she makes such a great ghost."

Diana nodded, but avoided looking at Ethan. She just didn't think she could handle it if there was any bit of judgment or accusation in his eyes—especially given the way she was feeling about him.

Oh, God, this was not a good time to be thinking about *those* feelings.

She cleared her throat, took another drink of whatever tea someone had poured for her (it wasn't half bad), and turned the page. "'So I thought if I had any old paperwork, it might be useful for the court case. I remember you telling me about how you have to go through discovery and get every bit of documentation you can find about anything related to the case or the parties involved—well, anyway. It was something to do.

"'Well, I think I found something that might be important! Some old drawings from Woodstock Tool & Die's original plant on Lake Michigan—and I looked it up online and there it was. It's the property involved in this lawsuit. So I thought you must need it.

"'Because, Diana, if you look at the page with the underground drawings, you'll see something very strange. And very bad.'"

"What is it?" Juanita was crowding forward, her breasts spilling onto the table in front of her, edging against her crumb-filled plate. Bruce Banner squeaked from somewhere in the vicinity of her lap, and she adjusted accordingly. "What did she find?"

Diana stopped reading out loud; she skimmed the rest of the letter and as the situation became clear, felt anger and understanding sweep over her. She put the letter down—the rest of it was private anyway and she would not read it in front of them. Especially Ethan.

"I'll explain," she said in her most lawyerly voice, and began to dig out the folded up building schematics she'd tucked in her purse. "It'll be easier that way," she replied, moving the letter out of reach of Maxine's crabby hands.

She laid out the sheaf of drawings on the table and immediately saw what Aunt Jean had observed—that wonderful, amazing, brilliant old smarty-pants. Trust Genevieve Fickler, devoted tree-hugger and lifetime member of The Sierra Club, to notice.

"This is a drawing of the original Woodstock manufacturing plant, which was built in the early 20th century—probably before World War I, or maybe right after. You can see here: it's right on the big lake. Now, look here." She flipped through the paperwork to the page that showed the underground level of the factory, and stabbed a finger at it.

"Do you see this? This pipe right here, buried deep inside the lowest level of the factory?" She looked up at everyone, realized they were all eating and she was really hungry (last night had been very active, after all), and snagged a cinnamon scone for herself.

"That pipe..." Maxine's voice had changed from accusatory and demanding as she hauled to her feet to pore over the drawing. "It leads to the *water*." She looked up, her dark eyes gleaming with comprehension. "Those *bastards*. They were dumping factory waste—*right into Lake Michigan*."

Diana nodded, biting into the scone as the others around the table leaned in to look.

"But how could they get away with that? It's so blatant!" Iva said; then she answered her own question. "Right. This was way back, wasn't it? Before environmental restrictions were in place."

"That's right." The scone tasted heavenly, and it was all Diana could do to keep from moaning over it. Instead, she took another generous bite.

"But what does it mean? And why is someone willing to *kill* over this? It was a long time ago. It wasn't illegal then," Juanita said.

Diana gulped down a splash of tea, then explained. "It's only conjecture, but it makes sense. It makes complete sense. See, LavertPiper is suing AutoXTech because the land they bought—which is the site of this old Woodstock factory—has more environmental cleanup than they'd been expecting or led to believe in all of their research and due diligence. They believe AXT should help pay for the extra cost, along with sharing any penalties they might get from the EPA.

"AXT, on the other hand, owns a lot of different pieces of land—old factories many of them—and they're countersuing LavertPiper so they can make an example out of them: don't try to come back and sue us after you've bought the property. AXT doesn't want to run into this situation with any future sales.

"*But*, what this old schematic shows is that when AXT was Woodstock Tool & Die, they were clearly dumping waste into Lake Michigan. This shows they're liable, and could even incur penalties now." Diana rested her hands on the table. "The problem is, I've never seen this drawing before. And I've seen *everything* they have at AXT related to this property. Which means—"

"Which means *someone* wants to make sure this document isn't found," Ethan said.

"And that someone must have known this document exists. Or suspected it did." Diana looked around the table at her audience, each of whom was expressing their agreement by nodding.

"It was the Abe Vigoda guy," crowed Maxine. "He looks older than God—he was probably involved back then."

"And you wanted to set him up with Jean? A man older than God? And he wasn't that old. No older than you or me. *Ay-yi-yi*!" Juanita threw up her hands. "Even so, he wasn't more than a baby in the 30s."

"Well, he probably knows about it anyway. And *I* wasn't setting up Jean with him," Maxine retorted. "*You* were."

"I wouldn't do that. His eyebrows were terrifying," Juanita argued. "It was like they had a life of their own. I'd never do that to Jean!"

"It makes sense," Ethan said, lifting his voice over the squabbling ladies. "Maybe this Abe Vigoda-like person destroyed—or knows they were destroyed—the other copies of the schematic. And maybe he just put two and two together that the original paperwork would have been with the commercial agent who sold the property the last time it was transferred—which was probably in the '60s?" he asked Diana.

She nodded. "Right on the money, Ethan. My Uncle Tracer was obviously involved in the sale, and that would have been roughly the timing of the transaction. Anyway, I think this is enough information to get the police involved—let Captain Longbow know."

Cherry had been tapping purposefully on her computer tablet, and now she spoke up. "I did a quick Google, and here's a picture of Martin Kelliski—the Abe Vigoda lookalike. It says he's on the board of directors for AutoXTech, and is retired from the company. My God, why *doesn't* he do something about those eyebrows?

"Anyway, I haven't noticed Kelliski around Wicks Hollow at all, since that first time at Trib's—but I do remember him from then. Have you seen him, Max? Or anyone else? Because if he's the one who did all this…one of us probably noticed him in town, and if we can attest to it, that will help the case."

Diana took the tablet, then shook her head. "No. This can't be the man who broke in. From the pic, you can tell he's not very tall, and he's kind of slight and skinny. Remember, he ran into me when I surprised him at Aunt Jean's house that night. It's definitely not this guy. Plus, he doesn't look strong enough to have smothered her, even if she was in bed and sleeping." Her lips curled with disgust. "And those eyebrows—or, should I say, that *one* eyebrow. It *does* look like it's alive, Juanita." She looked up at Maxine with narrow eyes. "I can't believe you would have tried to set up my Aunt Jean with him!"

"Let me see that!" Maxine grabbed the tablet with wild fingers as Cherry tensed nervously. "It was even worse in real life," she admitted as she looked at the picture of Martin Kelliski.

Then, with a few violent tappity-taps, she began to manipulate the tablet as it bumped against the table. She stopped suddenly. "Wait. This one. *This one!* Right here."

"What?" Ethan asked, leaning over her shoulder. "That man? Standing next to Kelliski? What about him?"

Maxine looked up at Diana. "He's the one. This guy, right here." She stabbed a finger at the picture. "I've seen him at least two times here in Wicks Hollow. I bet I know which days, too."

Diana took the tablet. In the photo was Martin Keller, and the caption identified the other man as Lawrence Amerson. "I know him," she said, tapping lightly. "I've met him…somewhere. Some meeting." She looked at Maxine. "You're sure?"

"Maxie never forgets a face," Juanita said staunchly. "If she says she saw him here, she did. If she says he's the one, he is." She patted her friend's dark, gnarled hand with her lighter, fucshia-tipped one. "Makes it hard to go about your business in town with Maxine around, but it's true."

"That's damn right it is," agreed the old bat. "Can't hide nothing from me."

"Well," Ethan said, sitting back down. "I'm thinking it's time to call in Joe Cap. Tell him what we know, and wrap this thing up. He can get with the authorities in Chicago and go from there."

Even Maxine couldn't find a reason to disagree, and so Ethan and Diana decided to make their escape from the Tuesday Ladies and stop in at the police station.

As they left Orbra's Tea House, Diana felt her cell phone vibrate deep in her bag, which was pressed up against her side. She pulled it out to check and saw that she'd missed a call from Jonathan.

Three calls.

And four texts.

Her ebullient mood plummeted, and she tucked her phone back away.

"Don't tell me that's your office," said Ethan, glancing curiously at her. "On a Sunday."

"No." She didn't need to say more; didn't need to give any explanation. Ethan wasn't even asking. But her mouth, uncharacteristically, kept moving. "It's Jonathan. He's been trying to reach me all morning."

"Ah." Ethan sounded unbothered, but a definite pall descended, like a tense curtain, between them.

And before Diana could figure out how to respond and what to say, they were walking up the steps to the police station. She straightened her shoulders.

She had other matters to attend to now. Ethan and Jonathan could wait.

SEVENTEEN

DIANA DIDN'T INTEND to return Jonathan's call, but once they finished giving the whole rundown to Captain Longbow and they stepped back out into the gorgeous summer afternoon, her phone buzzed again.

"You might as well answer it," Ethan said, though she wondered how he'd even heard it as it was buried in her bag. His voice was studiously even-tempered, but she sensed an undercurrent of something that, probably, she would need to uncover.

Diana sighed, then capitulated and dug out the phone. "Jonathan," she said by way of greeting.

"I've been trying to reach you all day," he said in something shockingly close to a whine.

"Is something wrong?" she asked dutifully, then was angry with herself for falling into the trap.

"*Yes,* there's something wrong. Didn't you hear?" He sighed, then went on. "Are you on your way back? Is that why I couldn't reach you—were you driving through the boonies?"

"No," she replied, handing Ethan the fob to the Lexus as

they approached the hidden parking lot. "I'm still in Wicks Hollow."

"Diana, it's after three o'clock! I thought you'd be back by now. It's a five-hour drive, isn't it?"

"I'm not. I—uh," she glanced over at Ethan, who had a very set look on his face as he pushed the ignition button and settled into the driver's seat. "I'm not going to be back in Chicago tonight after all." She hoped she wasn't overstepping or making assumptions.

But…based on the kiss in this very car only a few hours ago—no, she didn't think so.

Yet, Ethan's expression remained blank and set as he maneuvered the car out of the lot.

"You're not?" Jonathan sounded stunned. "When *are* you going to be back? I thought you were coming to get your things tonight. Did you change your mind? Look, Diana, something's happened, and I…I really need you. To talk to you."

She had her phone against the ear closest to her side of the car, so she was pretty certain Ethan couldn't hear the other side of the conversation, despite the taut volume of Jonathan's voice. "What happened?"

"I thought you would have heard. It's been all over the news—but you're not even in Chicago, are you?" His voice became a little petulant, then he continued in a calmer tone. "Ginny Farren. The office manager at the practice. She was—she died last night. She was…it was an overdose they think. I'm just—it's awful."

"Oh no," Diana said with genuine shock and sorrow. Since beginning her relationship with Jonathan, she'd gotten to know Ginny quite well, and appreciated the young woman's efficiency and cheer. "I would never have suspected she had a drug problem."

"That's why it's so terrible. No one suspected—and now, suddenly, she's gone." His voice, which had risen into that tight coil, settled once more into something calm but coaxing. "Diana. I really need to see you. This is…really hard on me. Couldn't you…when will you be back—you know, to pick up your stuff? Tomorrow?"

She resisted the urge to look at Ethan, did a quick calculation, and hoped she wasn't making a huge mistake—and large assumption. "Probably Tuesday. I'll let you know when I'm on my way over—it'll probably be in the evening."

"*Tuesday*…I don't know if I can—all right. Please. Just call me when you're on your way—or if anything changes and you decide to come back sooner. I'll…I just need to talk about this thing with Ginny. I just can't wrap my mind around it. She's gone…and so suddenly. And…what are we going to do at the office? She handled *everything*."

Diana felt a sudden rush of relief that *this isn't my problem. He isn't my problem*.

Not anymore.

And it was because of that, because she really, truly didn't give one more rat's ass about Jonathan and his bloody practice any longer, that she didn't snarkily ask him why he wasn't calling Valerie the Vivacious Vixen to cry over—and ask how to handle the practice.

When she finally disengaged herself from the call, after Jonathan ranted for another few minutes, she realized Ethan was driving them along the sweet, smooth curve of the county road that led north and slightly east from the town, up and along the western side of Wicks Lake.

The green, rolling hills that cupped both the town and its namesake lake were blanketed by pink, yellow, and orange wildflowers, scrubby bushes, and lush, leafy trees. In some places, the trees made dark, inviting tunnels around and over the road, bringing a welcome shade from the sun. To the left and west, between the trees, she could see hints of the blue sparkle of Lake Michigan and felt a renewed plunge of sadness that Woodstock Tool & Die had been dumping into that mighty and gorgeous vessel for decades.

"Sorry about that," she said when the silence felt heavy and foggy in the vehicle. "Thanks for driving."

"No problem."

"I...uh..." She started to lick her lips nervously, then mentally told herself to straighten up and grow a pair.

What the hell was wrong with her? If he wasn't interested in having her stay, that was no big deal. It had only been one night.

"Obviously you heard the conversation, and you've probably got some questions."

"A few."

She rolled her eyes discreetly, but went on. "I wasn't making the assumption I'd be welcome to stay at your house for another day or two, but it's too late to drive back to Chicago tonight."

"I see."

"And I have to find someone to watch the cats."

"Doc Horner or I can do that, Diana."

"Right. Well, I can always grab a room at one of the B&Bs in town if it's not convenient—"

"It's High Season. They're booked to the rafters."

"Right. Well, I'm sure I can find a place—"

"Diana." His voice was cool, and there was a white line near the corner of his mouth. Her heart did a little, ugly thunk.

Maybe she *had* misread the situation. After all, she didn't have that much experience with men—especially sexy, semi-famous ones like Dr. Ethan Murphy. Sure, he'd probably been more than happy to take advantage of the situation—

"I made an assumption last night," he said, still driving, still handling the car expertly as they swooped gracefully around curves and skimmed down the incline of a gentle hill. Wicks Lake sparkled its own vivid blue on the other side of the road, peeking between pines, oaks, and birch.

"The assumption that I was leaving today?" she asked nonchalantly.

"*No.*" His hands shifted their grip on the steering wheel. "Look, based on what you told me about the Death card, and about the conversation you said you had with Wertinger, I came to the conclusion that things were over between the two of you. Otherwise, I would never have…well, things wouldn't have happened the way they did. Last night. So if I was wrong, you need to tell me. You'll stay at my house, but the sleeping arrangements will be…different."

"I see." Her voice was calm, but inside her belly was doing grateful, relieved flutters. Thank God she hadn't misread things. "That's commendable of you, Ethan. Thank you."

He muttered something under his breath as they turned onto the narrow dirt road that led to their respective houses. When she saw the way his fingers tightened on the steering wheel, she realized she had to stop reveling in her internal relief and clarify the situation.

"It's over between us. Jonathan and me," she added quickly, just to be clear. "I ended things with him yesterday—you were right. He wasn't happy, but I was clear. I have no regrets or second thoughts, either. Believe me. And today, well…he was expecting me to come by tonight to pick up my things. I'd told him I was driving home today."

"Something you didn't happen to mention to me," Ethan said in a low voice that wasn't quite devoid of emotion. She caught a hint of stiffness in there, perhaps, and felt a renewed pang of guilt.

"I didn't mean to *not* tell you...it just didn't occur to me that it would matter. Until this morning, I mean," she added quickly when his mouth tightened again as they jounced along the potholed track. "And then things sort of spiraled out of control with Maxine and Juanita coming and the letters...And then, well—I didn't want to make any assumptions myself. About...anything."

He glanced at her, then returned his eyes to the narrow road. "It was because of what happened last night that you caught me by surprise when you announced you were leaving today."

"I can see how that would be. I'm sorry—that was rude, as you've been so hospitable—"

"Christ, Diana, it's not about me being a damned innkeeper." He braked a little more sharply than necessary, jolting them to a halt in the parking area at his cabin. "And I'm not being fucking hospitable. I'm being—"

She'd never know what possessed her to do it, but later Diana realized it had been the perfect thing: to reach over, grab him by the shirt, and yank him across the front seat to kiss him.

Oh, yes. Definitely the right thing.

His body, vibrating with tension, stilled for a moment, then eased into calm and softened into slick sensuality. He curled his hand around the back of her head and met her kiss with his own, drawing her as close as possible in their awkward position.

From inside the cabin, Cady was barking like a maniac, alerted by the arrival of the vehicle. Ethan smiled against her lips, gave her one last luscious nibble at the corner of her mouth, then pulled back and studied her with warm, chocolate eyes.

"Let me take care of her, and then we can finish this… conversation…inside."

"Does that mean there's room at the inn after all?" she teased, sliding her hand down his warm, stubbled cheek and jaw.

"Most definitely."

Ethan stretched lazily.

Sun rolled in through the wide, sliding doorway that overlooked the back yard from his generous master suite. A warm, delicious, lake-scented breeze wafted through the screen door. The birds were singing their version of the "Hallelujah Chorus" as they fed at the collection of feeders below, and his well-sated hormones were humming their rendition as well.

It was Monday morning. Late morning. Nearly noon, if he was going to be honest, and why not?

There wasn't a better reason for sleeping in and lounging about than spending it with a lover. Especially after a most delightful span of nearly twenty hours since they'd cleared up all the lingering misapprehensions and communications that had threatened to keep them apart.

He'd let Cady out a little past dawn and came back to a warm bed with a fascinating woman sleeping in it. Then he felt Diana slide from the bed some time ago, and when she came back, she brought her laptop and two mugs of coffee. He'd sipped politely (even though he wasn't quite ready for caffeine), then dozed some more while she tapped on her keyboard, scrolled through her email, and did whatever it was that got her up—really up; not just to let the dog out—at the ungodly (and unnecessary) hour.

He loved summer.

He loved Wicks Hollow.

He loved his work, his dog, his cabin in the woods.

He loved Diana Iverson.

Ethan's eyes popped wide open as his heart stopped for, literally, thirty seconds. He almost had to thump his chest to get it going again.

Nope. Not possible. No way.

How long had he known her? How long had it been since they'd stopped being suspicious adversaries?

Impossible.

But a little voice bothered him deep inside: *You know what you want. You always have, Ethan. It's never been a matter of weighing and analyzing and deciding for you. When you find the right thing, you just* know.

That wasn't his own conscience or inner guide speaking to him. No, that was Jean Fickler. She'd said those sorts of things not only to him in person, but also in the letter she'd written —and never sent.

The one he opened last night when he had a private moment.

How could she have known? How could she have known I'd fall for her niece?

"What is it?" Diana had removed her reading glasses (she had no idea how wildly sexy she looked with the so *not*-lawyerly sparkling blue cheaters she wore...along with after-sex curls and nothing else) to look over at him.

He just smiled at her and pushed away the nagging little voice. "Have I mentioned I have a fetish about naked women wearing geeky glasses?"

"I don't believe you have." She pushed said glasses back up her nose, eyes sparkling with interest. "Tell me more."

"Why don't you put that laptop aside so I can," he said with a smile.

Oh, yes, a Monday morning, lolling about in bed for hours with a sexy, smart, prickly (sometimes) woman was about as good as it got.

The only thing that would make his life perfect at that moment would be if there was someone else to let Cady out.

But all good things must come to an end, so some time later, Ethan finally rolled from the bed and took his first love outside to toss the tennis ball.

Because she'd been rather neglected over the last twenty-four hours, he spent extra time exercising her—and even took her down to the lake for a swim. The water was perfect: not too cold, and just the right amount of refreshing for an early summer afternoon. A few boats were out—he saw Trib driving by with a handsome man he didn't recognize on a sleek pontoon that zipped quietly through the water, and a few fishing boats. There was a canoe and two kayaks as well. Some kids were swimming from one of the public rafts near each end of the lake. And Cady was panting happily as they paddled about in the water.

Life was good.

By the time Ethan came back from exercising Cady—by taking a swim, from the looks of their dripping bodies—Diana had showered, dressed, finished a call with Mickey (who hadn't heard about the unhappy death of Ginny the office manager and demanded all the details), and was just plating a simple lunch with what she'd scrounged from Ethan's meager pantry and fridge.

To her relief, he left the wet, stinky dog in the screened porch to dry off. She was becoming used to the big, dangerous-looking canine, but that didn't mean she liked having her underfoot. Diana was never certain what might set off a dog like Cady and turn her angry or aggressive. Not that the black lab had done anything other than bark at newcomers (or squirrels)…but you never knew. She had scarily big teeth.

"Thank you," said Ethan, looking at the plates with something like dismay. "I didn't mean for you to have to cook for me."

She lifted a brow. "As long as you don't mind that I was digging around in your pantry and fridge, I don't mind at all. Plus, I was hungry."

"You probably didn't find much," he added—and she realized that embarrassment over the lack of options (and maybe the fact that his fridge wasn't exactly spotless) was part of the reason for his dismay. "But you can dig around in my pantry, fridge…or anywhere else you want…any time." He gave her a sly smile and she laughed. "At your own risk."

"Well, I did find some moldy green stuff that might once have been green beans."

He smiled wryly. "Oops. I think Fiona brought me those a few weeks ago. She says I need to eat more vegetables."

Diana, who'd noticed a terrible lack thereof—moldy or otherwise—didn't comment other than to lift her eyebrow. "After we eat, I need to go check on the cats. And I should do some work too."

"I'll run to the grocery store," he said brightly. "Since you'll be here for dinner tonight…?"

"If you want me to be," she replied with a smile.

"More than anything—well, except world peace. Or a

World Series win for the Tigers. And even then, it would be a toss-up."

They were just finishing the very skimpy lunch (tuna salad with crackers, some apple slices, and a few small tomatoes that were verging on wrinkled) when Diana's cell phone rang.

"Sorry," she said. "I need to be available for the office—and this is a Chicago number."

He shrugged. "Hey, it's Monday. You're supposed to be working." He frowned. "I guess I should be working on something too. My agent is waiting for a new book proposal."

But it wasn't anyone from her office. Instead, it was a detective from the Chicago PD.

EIGHTEEN

ETHAN'S EARS perked up when he realized the caller wasn't Wertinger *or* Diana's office, and from the expression on her face, he thought the news—whatever it was—was more good than bad.

He cleared the table and washed up while she took notes and murmured things to herself, allowing the person on the other end (it sounded like a woman) to do most of the talking. Then he went to towel off Cady so she could come inside and eat.

He couldn't help but notice how Diana edged away whenever his beloved lab came near her, and the wariness that had her looking over every time Cady barked. Almost as if she expected the lab to launch into some sort of snarling, Cujo-like mass at any given moment. Even when Cady was calm, Diana hardly acknowledged her, and Ethan had to admit it broke his heart a little.

Cady was a lover of a dog, and Diana was *his* lover, and he wanted his two girls to get along. But clearly, Diana did not appreciate the canine species.

"Well, we'll just have to change her mind about that, won't

we, girl?" he said, giving her sleek fur a pat as he finished drying her.

When they came back in the kitchen, Diana was off the phone. She looked up and there was a glint of relief in her eyes.

"Good news?" he said as he filled Cady's food dish.

"Yes. They've got Lawrence Amerson in custody and are going to charge him. Apparently, he gave up quite a bit during the interrogation when Detective Brewer brought him in. Between Maxine seeing him in town—apparently the detective got a call from her, and she was very specific about seeing him at the gas station on the same day Aunt Jean's house was broken into. That along with the fact that he was at the golf outing here in April, as well as some telling activity on his credit card—they're feeling pretty confident he's the perpetrator."

He came up behind her and began to gently massage her slender shoulders. Damn, they were tight—considering how hard he'd worked to help relieve her stress over the last day. Guess he'd have to work at it a little more. He smirked to himself. "So he's in custody in Chicago, and you're here."

Safe.

"I can't believe he killed Aunt Jean," she said, staring into space. "Over a piece of paper."

"It all comes back to money," he said. "The paper would destroy AXT in the lawsuit, and that would cost a lot of people a lot of money."

She nodded. "The question they're still trying to determine is whether Lawrence did all this on his own, or whether someone else—like Martin Kelliski—was involved."

He sat down next to her as a thought struck him. He considered his next words carefully...but, oh man, he had to ask. "You—and your firm—are representing AXT in the lawsuit, correct? But showing that schematic—well, it'll cost them in the suit. If there are no other copies, and no one else knows about it, why would you even—"

"Disclose it?" Her voice was cool and her expression became marble-like. "Precisely. Why would I submit a document that I know would lose the case for my client—or at least cost them in a number of ways?"

"Right."

She looked at him steadily. "Because it's the right thing to do. It's the *ethical* thing to do. I could get slapped by my firm —I might even lose my chance to make partner—and our client could dump us to the tune of a loss of millions of dollars a year...but at least I'd be able to look at myself in the mirror every day."

He felt his insides uncoil. There was no doubt she was speaking the unvarnished truth. "Do you always do the right thing?"

"I try."

Ethan smiled, then leaned forward, sliding his hand along her smooth, warm cheek. "So do I." She smiled against his mouth as he kissed her tenderly. "You're a hell of a woman, Diana Iverson."

"I try."

Diana pulled up to Aunt Jean's injured lake house and parked her Lexus in front of the detached garage.

"Here kitties!" she called brightly, then stood there waiting to see if they'd make an appearance from inside the smoke-blackened house, the cracked-door garage, or from somewhere in the depths of the woods.

Though she couldn't see it, she glanced in the direction of

Ethan's cabin—less than a mile to the south through the woods—and smiled. It was all she could do to keep from humming to herself, and spinning around in a little dance.

He was really *wonderful*. And witty and interesting and thoughtful and, as Mickey would say, "mad in his sexiness."

Since yesterday, when they'd come back to his cabin after the "meeting" in town with the Tuesday Ladies, they'd just moved along in sync: enjoying each others' company, spending time doing their own work separately, enjoying the weather, and of course making love.

He was pretty damned good at that, she had to say. A little flutter of heat reminded her of the way he looked at her when he was moving inside her—like he really *saw* her. And thought she was beautiful.

The only imperfection in the whole arrangement was Cady and her wet, inquisitive nose—and those big teeth. But Diana could get used to her, if things kept going and got serious...

"What am I thinking?" she said aloud, walking over to the porch. *What does all this mean?*

Slow down, Diana. Slow the hell down.

As she sat, Motto made her appearance. Her dainty pink nose poked from around the corner of the porch and the rest of her followed as she sauntered over for some attention.

It was, Diana decided as she scratched Motto under the chin, nice to have a moment to herself to *think*. Ethan had gone into town a while ago to run some errands and get groceries, and she'd come over here to see to the cats. And to have some space to *think* about all of this. It felt as if her life had been turned upside down again...but in a good way this time.

They'd both agreed that tonight, their last night together (for now anyway), would be spent eating a late dinner on the upper deck of his cabin while watching the sunset—just a few feet away from his big, comfy, well-used bed.

Ethan wasn't *delighted* that she was leaving to go back to Chicago—though of course he understood the necessity—but he'd made it clear he'd miss her. And that he wanted to keep seeing her.

Could they continue this relationship with him in Wicks Hollow and her in the dog-eat-dog, eighty-plus hour a week legal world of Chicago? Of course, he'd be back on campus at U of C in a couple months, and in the meantime, she could *theoretically* come up here on the weekends—

Diana looked over as a movement in the woods caught her attention.

When the movement became a figure, then a person and she recognized him, she gasped aloud and bolted to her feet so quickly Motto jumped back and hissed.

"Jonathan! What on *earth* are you doing here?"

He walked out of the woods—what had he been doing in there? Why was he even *here?*—gaping at the house.

"What happened? When did this happen?" He was staring at the burned out shell of the farmhouse. "Diana, good God, what happened?"

"About a week ago," she said, still utterly flummoxed by his presence. She hadn't realized she'd never told him the house had burned. "What are *you* doing here? Where's your car?"

He gestured vaguely into the distance, still staring at the remains of the house. "Well, that explains why you weren't answering the phone here. And that does change things... still," he said, reaching into his pocket, "I can work with it. I'm flexible."

When he withdrew his hand, he was holding a gun.

NINETEEN

"WHAT—WHAT ARE YOU DOING?" Diana could hardly form the words; the situation was so completely surreal.

How could he be here? With a gun? Aiming it at her?

Why?

What was going *on*?

To her surprise, he sat down next to her on the porch, still holding the revolver—and keeping it pointed in her direction. He unslung a small pack that he'd been carrying over his shoulder and leaned against the porch column so he could watch Diana.

And keep the gun trained in her direction.

"You shouldn't have broken things off," he told her in his smooth doctor's voice. "I needed you to marry me so I could set things right. I *planned* it. I planned it *all*. And then you fucked things up." His voice went harsh and tight, and fear skittered down her spine.

Though her heart was pounding wildly, and her palms had gone sweaty, Diana managed to rein in her scattered, shattered thoughts. She was a lawyer; she'd learned how to work—to think, to interrogate, to analyze, to switch gears—under pressure.

Not *this* kind of pressure, but still...

"Set what things right?" She kept her eyes on the gun even as he began to dig around in the pack with his free hand.

"I need the money, Diana. I owe some unpleasant people a lot of money." He pulled out a bottle of wine and a glass. "A little change of plans, but this will work out just fine," he murmured to himself.

"How can you—but Jonathan, you're one of the top cardiologists in the Midwest. You've got plenty of money and investments—"

"I don't have *enough*," he snapped and, settling the bottle between his legs, he twisted off the metal cap. She noticed it had previously been opened—the seal was broken—and a little frisson of nervousness worked its way up her spine.

He'd put something in that wine. She was sure of it.

"Why do you owe people money?"

"Gambling, my darling. I've gotten myself in quite a bit of a mess. Too many conventions in Vegas and Atlantic City—and there was the one in Monte Carlo last year too." He shrugged, then, keeping the gun steady, he poured a generous amount of red wine into the glass. "You're going to drink this, Diana."

She bit back the obvious negative response and obediently took the glass, her mind racing to try and find a way out of this situation. Motto had disappeared after her initial shocked hiss, and shy Arty was nowhere to be seen either.

So much for hoping the cats might step in and scratch the hell out of his eyes. And where was Aunt Jean when she needed her? The thought was so absurd, she almost giggled.

Nerves. Good grief, she had to keep her nerves under control: calm and cool as steel.

"What should I toast?" she asked, pretending to contemplate the wine. "Aren't you joining me?"

"No." He looked at her sharply and gestured with the gun. "Drink it, Diana. I'd rather not shoot you, but I will. And your demise will be a lot more painful than what I have in mind if I have to use the gun."

"So you're going to kill me. I don't understand why. At least give me that." She lifted the glass and took a sip even as she tried to figure out a way to dump some or all of it.

"Because I need money—your money. You're a very wealthy woman now, Diana. Thanks to me—"

She gasped, and purposely spilled some of the wine. "You? You killed Aunt Jean? You *smothered* my aunt?"

"I needed the money. I told you. When I first met you, I thought you were attractive—in an uptight, ice queen sort of way—but when I learned you had an aunt in Wicks Hollow, I became more curious. It doesn't take a rocket scientist to realize the property here on this lake is worth a tidy sum. So I checked her out. And then I did some more research and found out about her investments and so on—and then you became even *more* attractive to me." His smile was edging into leer territory, and Diana swallowed back a plug of nausea that surged into her throat.

"You killed her? But how? You were in Vegas when she died."

"I made a detour on my way there—on Wednesday of that week. Don't forget, you didn't get the call about the death until Friday. That was a boon I hadn't expected, actually.

"You see, on that Wednesday, I'd made arrangements to have lunch with your aunt—without telling you or anyone, of course, under the guise of getting her permission to ask you to marry me. I convinced her to keep it a secret from you as well. She invited me here, which worked out perfectly for me—no one would notice me in town. Small towns are notorious for busybodies and old biddies who can't keep their noses out of other peoples' business." His face darkened suddenly, and he lifted the gun. "Drink it, Diana. You stop drinking, I stop talking. When I stop talking, I start shooting."

She lifted the glass again, intending to take only another small sip—but he moved the barrel of the gun under the glass and lifted it so she had to take several gulps. Some of the wine ran down the sides of her mouth, but she swallowed more than she wanted.

He leaned over to refill the glass, keeping the revolver directed at her.

"So that's why you didn't want to sleep here when you came to visit me," she said thoughtfully. "Couldn't stand to sleep in the same room—the same *bed*—in which you'd murdered her." She ended with a little sneer in her voice, even though she knew it wasn't smart to antagonize him.

What a damned coward he was.

"I came back that night—the same day we had lunch, so she wouldn't have time to blab to anyone. I'd unplugged her phone while I was there in case she had any idea of calling you or anyone, and I watched and waited to make sure she wasn't going to leave." He paused, giving the refilled glass a pointed look, and she lifted it to take another drink. "I had a bad moment when she walked out to her garage carrying some mail, but she didn't leave. So then I just waited until it got dark, sneaked in, and did what I had to do. Drink."

She took another gulp, and the wine sloshed horribly in her stomach. She wondered what he'd do if she vomited. Maybe she should force herself to do so.

But then he might shoot her.

"You won't get my money, Jonathan, so this is all in vain. There's no reason to do this."

"Oh yes I will. Because even though we aren't married, you still changed your will to leave everything to me—conveniently, it was before your aunt even died. No one will question it. So I'll reap the financial benefit without having to go through with the actual ceremony." He laughed a little—and it was an ugly sound she'd never heard from him.

A leap of hope had settled in her chest. "Jonathan, I never signed those papers. The will I had drafted. I never made the change."

His eyes glinted with delight. "Oh yes you did. And so did I. And we even had our wills notarized—at the same time. There won't be any question whatsoever about your intent."

"Notarized? But that's impossible."

"Not when your office manager keeps her notary seal and notebook in her desk drawer—where anyone can get to it."

"Ginny. How did you get her to—oh my God, Jonathan, did you kill her too? Did you give her the overdose?"

He shrugged. "Loose ends. Can't have them. She didn't even realize what was going on until it was too late. I came by her apartment to drop off some things for the practice. She invited me in of course, and we started with a bottle of wine something like this one." His smile was cold and flat. "She always had a thing for me, and when she learned you and I were having problems…well, Ginny was a willing ear."

"A bottle of wine like this one? Is there poison in here?" Her insides surged violently. "Drugs?"

"No, for Christ's sake. Ambien. Sleeping pills. Three of them ought to do it—mixed with the wine, it'll make you very…pliable. Then I think you should go for a swim." His smile was cold and determined. "It'll be very sad when they pull you out and find your empty wine bottle sitting on the dock, with the remnants of sleeping pills in it."

"Jonathan, you don't have to do this. Two murders? That's

not the kind of person you are." She gestured with the glass and realized how unsteady and overcompensating her movements were. Damn. Everything was slowing down. Her thoughts, her actions... "You know, they'll probably cut you a deal."

He laughed uproariously. "Diana, darling, you know better than that. Both deaths—and then you as well—were premeditated. All will be clear counts of murder one. There's no deal on something like that. In for a penny, in for a pound. Now," he said, standing abruptly, "finish that wine or I'll put a bullet in your face."

TWENTY

WHEN ETHAN PULLED into the parking area at his cabin, he was mildly disappointed not to see Diana's Lexus there. That would give him time to put the groceries away and maybe even open the excellent white wine—from Leelanau County—that he'd snagged at the store...right from under Maxine Took's nosey nose.

But when he got out of his Jeep to let Cady out from the screened-in porch and caught sight of a flash of black and white in the yard, he paused.

"Arty? Is that you?"

Jean's cats never ventured this far from her house—maybe he'd seen a skunk. Though the day was just considering sliding into dusk and skunks were nocturnal, that didn't mean he hadn't seen one.

But if he had, it might be rabid...so best not to let Cady out right away. At least until he figured out what he'd seen.

Meanwhile, inside, his lab was going ballistic.

"Calm down, Cady," he said, looking around the corner of the house to see if there was any sign of skunk, cat, or anything else that might set his dog tearing off into the yard or forest. "I know you smell something. Let me bring in the groceries first, and then I'll see if it's okay to let you out. We don't need you getting sprayed tonight of all nights."

He smiled to himself at the thought of tonight—which would be bittersweet, but, he was determined, would also be quite enjoyable.

Cady was so agitated, it was a real battle to fight past her with four bags of groceries slung from his hands, and a bottle of thirty-dollar wine under an arm as he slid through the cracked doorway without letting the lab slip past him.

"Calm down," he said. "I haven't been gone that long, and —what the *hell?*"

He paused just inside the interior door from the screened-in porch. He stood in the hallway that led to the kitchen and allowed the grocery bags to slide to the floor.

Jean's mahogany box was in the center of the hall, upended. The black silk was in a wad on the floor, and cards were strewn in a grand sweep along the hardwood floor.

"How the hell did that happen," he said to himself, even as the hair stood up on the back of his neck and he felt very *chilly*.

The last time he'd seen the box, it was in the guest room with the rest of Diana's things. She would never have done such a thing, even before she began to open her mind to allowing the cards to inspire and guide her. There was no way Cady could have done it; she was confined in the porch area, and besides, she'd never bother with something like that unless it smelled like steak.

He knelt to pick them up, hardly noticing that Cady was still whining and barking and galloping back and forth between the interior and exterior doors of the porch.

"Just a minute, Cady!" he said sharply. "I know you smell something—just—hold on."

He was picking up the cards when he noticed that all of them were facedown except three. And those three were lined up together—not neatly, but in a sketchy row—as if someone had laid them out while in a hurry.

The Tower.
The Devil.
Death.

Ethan slowly picked up the cards. All of them were depictions of ugly, dark, violent images. *The Tower* was on fire, with people falling from the windows, fire blazing…He didn't like this. Not at all.

Not—

He spun around at the sound of a crash and a tearing noise, just in time to see Cady blast through the screen door to the outside.

"Cady!" he shouted, bolting after her.

Something was wrong, something was—

He nearly tripped over his own feet when he got outside and found Cady standing there, panting wildly, staring at *Motto and Arty*. Quietly. With no barking, no whining, no cowering…

And the two cats were sitting there, two pairs of eyes fixed on him, tails twitching like angry whiplashes as they looked from Cady to Ethan and back again.

What in the hell *is going on here?*

He felt like he was in the *Twilight Zone* or a *Black Mirror* episode.

His dog whined desperately, suddenly, looking from him to the cats, to somewhere in the distance—

Toward Jean's house.

Good God, how stupid could he *be?*

"Go, Cady!" he said, suddenly terrified. He didn't know

why, but it was clear Jean knew, the cats knew, and so did his dog.

The black lab bolted into the forest barking wildly, and the two cats streaked after her. Ethan hesitated for a split second—to grab his keys and drive or to just *run?*—just as he heard the sound of crunching tires on the drive.

Cursing with frustration, then wild with hope, he looked over, hoping to see Diana's Lexus. Instead, it was a pale blue Cadillac that jounced around the curve.

"Jean's house!" he shouted, pointing wildly as he started toward the woods in that same direction. "*Call Joe Cap!*"

If he was wrong, he'd apologize to Joe for the false alarm.

But he knew he wasn't, and he tore into the woods without waiting to see whether Maxine had heard him.

Thank God he was wearing good shoes instead of sandals, he thought as he tore through the forest. The ground was uneven and sprinkled with random patches of grass, wintergreen, trillium, moss, and lots of sticks, low-growing bushes, and spindly saplings. He leapt over a fallen birch, ducked under a leaning maple, pushed through bushes that scratched his face and tore at his hair.

Diana. Diana.

Please get to her, Cady. Whatever it is, get to her!

He could hear his dog, still barking wildly—and then the sound of a feral yowl that was probably one of the cats.

But it was the sound of a gunshot that fairly stopped his heart.

TWENTY-ONE

DIANA THOUGHT she heard a dog barking, but her brain was so foggy, she wasn't certain. She'd finished her doctored wine, drunkenly sloshing as much of it out of the glass as she could without making it obvious.

The world was spinning and she really wanted to throw up, especially when Jonathan loomed over her as she sagged against the porch column and grabbed her by the arm.

A spike of terror shot through her, piercing the fog—was he dragging her down to throw her in the lake now?—and she kicked out feebly.

But she missed him by a mile and the next thing she knew, he had her by the back of the skull, his fingers yanking on her hair as he dragged her head back and forced the bottle of wine against her mouth. The hard glass crushed and bruised her lips, and clunked against her teeth as he forced it into her mouth.

"Drink, goddammit," he said, pouring it into her so roughly she couldn't breathe and began struggling as she choked.

Her vision wavered, and she tried to cough and fight free,

but the wine burned everywhere, and her head was murky, and she couldn't twist her face away—

And then suddenly, she was falling. Her head hit something behind her and there was definitely barking now—real barking—and some animalistic yowl, followed by an ugly snarl that seemed to fill her ears. Loud, violent noises she couldn't identify.

Then the shriek of a man—shocked and pained—and more snarling, then the crack of a gunshot.

Clutching the porch column to pull herself upright, Diana tried to wipe her face as she coughed and gagged and at last managed to drag in a real breath—but more drops of moisture came in with it and she began coughing uncontrollably once more, all the while trying to focus on what was going on around her and pull to her feet at the same time.

There was more barking and snarling, and something that sounded like another yowl, and another human sound of agony—but it all merged together and she wasn't certain what was real and what was in her fogged head.

One thing was certain: Jonathan was no longer holding her, and that meant—

"Diana!"

The sound of her name, shouted frantically, cut through the oatmeal of her brain, and she tried to look in the direction of the noise…but the world tipped, tilted, swam, and everything seemed to be moving in very slow motion.

Nevertheless, she gave herself a good, hard shake and focused as hard as she could just as hard arms came around her.

She fought them at first as the wine and drugs roiled violently in her belly, until she recognized Ethan's voice in her ear, "It's me, Diana. It's me. You're safe. You're—"

She looked up at him, focused enough to meet his eyes

and see that it *was* him, was the man she loved, then pulled away desperately. He let her go this time, and she turned, staggering to her feet, and vomited up all of the churning liquid in her belly.

Somewhere in the top layer of her awareness, she heard a cry of disgust, then something like cheers.

And then another voice she recognized again: "Serves the damned bastard all right, it does."

Was that Maxine Took? No. Surely not. She was very mixed up…

Diana lifted her face, wiped her mouth, and now that her stomach was empty, the world seemed to steady a little…just enough for her to see the old, dark woman leaning on her cane —which was pressed into the soft, panting belly of Jonathan Wertinger, sprawled on the ground below the porch.

His clothes were torn and he was covered in blood, and Diana's fresh red-wine vomit had splashed all over his face and chest.

"Couldn't'a done better myself," said Maxine, and jabbed him once more with the cane. "Don't even think about moving, you bastard."

"I—can't…breathe…" groaned Jonathan.

"Too damned bad," Maxine shot back, and there was a definite whoosh of breath and a high groan from Jonathan, as if she'd leaned on her cane once more.

Strong arms came around her again, and this time Diana didn't fight them. She leaned back against the comforting strength, the familiar feel and scent of Ethan. The world still spun, and she needed him to hold her upright, but she was safe.

"Diana, oh thank God," he said over and over in her ear.

She heard the sound of a siren coming closer—or maybe it was just something else screaming in her ears…She tilted a little and her knees buckled. Ethan tightened his arms more, holding her upright.

"It's Joe Cap," he said. "And the EMTs. They're coming. They're going to check you out and make sure you're all right. Oh, God, Diana, when I heard that shot, I thought…"

Then all at once, a bolt of realization shot through her and she tried in vain to straighten up in his arms.

"Cay…dee," she managed to force her lips to move. "Oh…God, Cady…" She tried to look around, but all she could see was gray light and vague shadows. "Shot…?"

"She's all right. She's fine," Ethan said.

"Where is she?" Diana forced the words out. "Need to…"

She was lowered to the ground, and as she listed to one side, she felt the soft, warm fur of a panting dog next to her. She smiled, and with great and awkward effort moved her hand to rest on the most beautiful dog in the world.

And then she passed out.

EPILOGUE

"I NEVER GOT to ask what happened to your face," Diana said, reaching to touch Ethan's marked-up skin.

They—she and Ethan, along with Maxine, Iva, Juanita, Orbra and Cherry—were sitting in his living room. Cady was on the floor within easy reach of her hand so Diana could stroke the lab's head whenever she thought about how Cady had saved her life.

Which was a nearly constant thought. So the dog was getting a *lot* of petting.

It was the next day, Tuesday, and Diana had—against her vociferous arguments—been kept overnight at the county hospital to make certain she had no ill effects from Jonathan's cocktail. Thanks to the fact that she'd puked up most of the drugs and alcohol, she'd slept off the remnants in only a few hours and was feeling clear-headed and relatively perky today, all things considered.

"Running through the forest," Ethan replied. "Ran into a few bushes and trees."

"And tell me again how you came to be there, Maxine?"

Diana asked as she cuddled closer to Ethan in the corner of the sectional.

"Yes, tell us the whole story. Some of us have businesses to run and can't go gallivanting off whenever the mood strikes us," groused Orbra.

"Businesses to run...or studly distinguished lawyers to bang," Cherry added with a sly look at Iva.

The other woman's cheeks pinked and she looked, Diana thought, just as satisfied as she herself did. Good sex with the right man—a caring, respecting one—did that to a gal.

"I ran into Ethan at the grocery store—he bought the last bottle of my favorite wine from up to Traverse City," Maxine said, giving him a steely glare. "Whatever happened to respecting your elders, young man?"

"I respect you, Maxie," he replied with a grin. "That's why I wanted to buy that last bottle—so you could keep your head clear and help catch a murderer."

She snarled at him, but continued her story. After all, she had the spotlight and didn't have to fight for it. "When Ethan was loading up his groceries after he paid, I saw he dropped a package of chicken there by the cart. It wouldn't do for it to go bad, so Juanita and I brought it over here."

"The same way you noticed I left my sweater at Trib's Saturday night?" Diana asked sweetly.

"The exact same way," Maxine replied, meeting her gaze with a dark, glinting, knowing one of her own.

Diana smiled. They understood each other perfectly.

"And it's a damned good thing I did," Maxine went on, fingers gripping the cane. "Because *I* was the one called in the cops while I was driving over to Jean's house—"

"*That's* a ride I'll never forget," Juanita interjected. "*Ay-yi-yi!* I think I'm scarred for life. There's a reason you're not supposed to text and drive at the same time—"

"I wasn't texting, you old fool," Maxine shot back.

"Well, you were dialing your phone and driving, and it was worse than when I—"

"Well, I got there safe, didn't I? And got the cops there? *And* helped catch a murderer."

"A *multi*-murderer," Juanita said with a nod and a complacent smile. "We both did."

"I don't really know what happened," Diana confessed. "I was kind of out of it."

"I was on my way running through the woods when I heard Cady barking and then it sounded like a cat yowl—"

"Looked like Motto laid some good tracks on that murdering bastard's face before he knocked her away," Maxine said. "Good for her!"

"And then I heard a shot as I was still running through the woods," Ethan continued, "and that just about stopped me dead right there."

"It missed Cady," Juanita said. "We saw it. Good girl." She reached over to pet the happily panting lab, ignoring the low growl from Bruce Banner, who was tucked in her lap. "Good thing I left little Brucie in the car, huh, *chiquito*?"

"We saw it all happen," Maxine said. "Cady attacked that bastard, and the cats joined in. One of them bit him on the back of the leg—it was Arty. He tried to shoot them—he was a terrible shot. Diana, you were collapsed on the ground and we thought you were *dead*—but he missed and then Cady went for him again and he musta dropped the gun."

"I was just coming out of the woods at that moment," Ethan explained, "and I got over there just as Maxine whacked him across the head with her cane. He fell like a stone."

"I tripped," she said in a prim voice that fooled no one.

"Exactly," Juanita said with a grin. "It was impossible for

you to avoid him. And that's how I told Joe Cap it happened too."

"And then, I don't know, somehow I had my cane in his belly, and he was moving around so much I couldn't lift it up high enough to get it away—strength in my arms ain't what it used to be," Maxine said piteously.

"He was moving around an awful lot," Juanita agreed. "And you got real tired, didn't you Maxine? I saw you had to lean real heavily on your cane, or you would've fallen over." She nodded, looking around the group with a smile. "And that's how I explained it to Joe Cap."

"And then Diana horked all over him," Maxine crowed. "That was the best part of it all." She laughed, and it was a deep, rolling sound that reminded Diana of the ocean roaring through a narrow channel.

"And then Bruce Banner and Cady tried to clean him up," Juanita said, patting her dog. "Didn't you boy? Tried to lick that bastard clean."

Cherry made a disgusted face, but she was laughing anyway. "And you—fortunately—were the one who retrieved the gun, Ethan?"

"Yes. I—"

"He grabbed it right from under my nose," Maxine grumbled. "Second time that day he beat me out on something! I was just reaching for it, and he damn near pushed me out of the way so he could grab it first."

"Oh," said Iva, her eyes lit with laughter she didn't dare release, "it was probably just as well, as you were busy keeping Jonathan restrained, weren't you, Maxie?"

"Coulda done a better job if I had the gun," she muttered.

Diana exchanged looks with Ethan and they both managed to keep from chuckling out loud.

"So now what?" asked Orbra, always the pragmatist. "Are

you staying or are you going, Diana? And what's going on with the two of you? And how about those cats? And what about Jonathan?"

"Well, he's going to be charged with two counts of murder one, and also attempted murder," Diana said. "But as it turns out, he wasn't the one breaking in and he didn't set the fire—he was truly shocked when he showed up at Aunt Jean's and found it burned. He'd assumed he'd find me staying there and as it turned out, it was really just *his* luck that I happened to be there when he arrived."

"I'm sure he would have found another way to get to you," Ethan said in a hard voice. "And it might have been back in Chicago—when there was no Maxine to save you," he added.

"Well, it wasn't, and I'm safe, and all is well. Lawrence Amerson confessed to the fire—when they began to accuse him of murder, he realized things were serious, and he began to talk.

"As for me," Diana continued, looking around at them, "I'm not going to sell the house. I'm going to fix it up and use it as a weekend getaway from Chicago." She looked at Ethan. "Probably."

"Or you can stay here," he said with a soft smile.

"Or I can stay here."

"And what about Motto and Arty?" asked Cherry. "The two of them seem…pretty content."

They all looked over at the cats, who lounged on two separate, very large cushions on the floor in front of the fireplace.

"They and Cady seem to have called a truce, since they had their moment of glory in taking down a murderer," Ethan said.

"And saving my life," Diana added, reaching to scratch the lab's head again. "We think they're going to get along just fine here at the cabin."

"And what about the two of *you*?" demanded Maxine.

Diana found herself—and Ethan—the object of five pairs of glinting, expectant eyes.

"You know Jean always talked about getting the two of you together. *I* told her it was a crock, never happen, but I guess I *could* be wrong. Once." Maxine nearly smiled.

"Well," Ethan said with his own smile, "I guess we'll have to see what Jean and her Tarot cards have to say about that." He nudged Diana gently. "Don't we?" He grinned down at her and gave a subtle wink.

"I think that's a good idea." She reached over to pick up the mahogany box, which now had a place of honor in Ethan's living room instead of on the piecrust table at Aunt Jean's.

She opened up the box, took the cards from their black silk wrappings, and shuffled gently. She wasn't an expert, but she knew how to keep a certain card on the bottom…

So when she chose a card, it was the one from the bottom.

She laid it out on the table in front of the Tuesday Ladies.

The Lovers.

Don't let announcements and news get stuck in your spam folder! Sign up for SMS/Text messages and help keep your inbox uncluttered.

Not sure how? Here's a cheat sheet diagram:

MORE WICKS HOLLOW GHOSTLY ROMANTIC MYSTERIES!

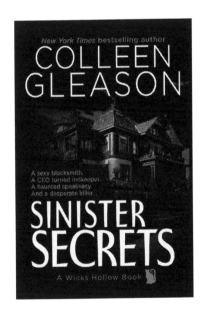

A sexy blacksmith.
A CEO turned innkeeper.
A haunted speakeasy.
And a very desperate killer…

Leslie Nakano needs to make a major life change—getting away from the dog-eat-dog corporate world, as well as getting past a personal loss—so she buys a large turn-of-the-century mansion in Wicks Hollow, with plans to renovate it and turn it into an inn.

She doesn't care about the rumors that it's haunted—she just wants a new life.

But she sure wouldn't mind finding the missing gems that belonged to Red Eye Sal, a bootlegger who lived in the house during Prohibition.

Blacksmith Declan Zyler, who has more work than he can handle, working on historical restorations, has suddenly acquired a fifteen-year-old daughter he never knew he had. This turns his life upside-down when he decides to take on the role of single father.

When Leslie hires Declan to restore the iron staircase in her inn, neither of them realize they are disturbing a spirit from days gone by…and until they determine how to put that ghost to rest, neither Leslie nor Declan will be able to move on with their lives.

NOW AVAILABLE!

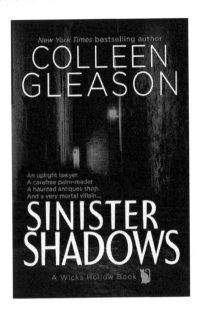

An uptight lawyer.
A carefree palm-reader.
A haunted antiques shop.
And a very mortal villain…

When Fiona Murphy inherits a small antiques shop from an old man she met only once, she's filled with surprise, confusion and delight—and a little bit of terror at having a new responsibility in a life she prefers to be free and easy.

But as she takes over ownership of the quaint shop, odd things begin to happen. Lights come on and off by themselves, even when they are unplugged…and there is a chilly breeze accompanied by the scent of roses even when the windows are closed.

H. Gideon Nath, III, is the stiff and oh-so-proper attorney

who helps settle Fiona's inheritance. Despite her flightiness and fascination with all things New Age (which he considers bunk), he finds himself unwillingly attracted to her.

After she finds an unpleasant surprise in one of the shop's closets, scares off an intruder in the store, and uses her skill at palmistry to read Gideon's future—of which she seems to be a part—Fiona begins to realize that her free and easy life is about to change…whether she wants it to or not.

COMING MARCH 13, 2018!
Pre-order now.

A NOTE FROM THE AUTHOR

Intrigued by the little spitfire Bruce Banner, Juanita Acerita's papillon? I'd like to introduce you to the inspiration for little Brucie—my own darling papillon named Ranger.

ABOUT THE AUTHOR

Colleen Gleason is an award-winning, New York Times and USA Today best-selling author. She's written more than forty novels in a variety of genres—truly, something for everyone!

She loves to hear from readers, so feel free to find her online and say hi!

Get SMS/Text alerts for any
New Releases or **Promotions!**

Text: **COLLEEN** to **38470**

(You will only receive a single message when Colleen has a new release or title on sale. *We promise.*)

If you would like SMS/Text alerts for any **Events** or book signings Colleen is attending,

Text: **MEET** to **38470**

Subscribe to Colleen's non-spam newsletter for other updates, news, sneak peeks, and special offers!
http://cgbks.com/news

Connect with Colleen online:
www.colleengleason.com
books@colleengleason.com

ALSO BY COLLEEN GLEASON

The Gardella Vampire Hunters
Victoria

The Rest Falls Away

Rises the Night

The Bleeding Dusk

When Twilight Burns

As Shadows Fade

Macey/Max Denton

Roaring Midnight

Raging Dawn

Roaring Shadows

Raging Winter

Roaring Dawn

The Draculia Vampire Trilogy

The Vampire Voss: Dark Rogue

The Vampire Dimitri: Dark Saint

The Vampire Narcise: Dark Vixen

Wicks Hollow Series

Ghost Story Romance & Mystery

coming February 2018

Sinister Summer

Sinister Secrets

Sinister Shadows

Sinister Sanctuary (Summer 2018)

Stoker & Holmes Books

(for ages 12-adult)

The Clockwork Scarab

The Spiritglass Charade

The Chess Queen Enigma

The Carnelian Crow

The Lincoln's White House Mystery Series

(writing as C. M. Gleason)

Murder in the Lincoln White House

Murder in the Oval Library (Sept 2018)

The Marina Alexander Adventure Novels

(writing as C. M. Gleason)

Siberian Treasure

Amazon Roulette
Sanskrit Cipher

Writing as Alex Mandon
The Belle-Époque Mystery series
Murder on the Champs-Élysées

Made in the USA
Middletown, DE
11 August 2022